HALO

R.C. STEPHENS

COVER ARTIST: SARAH HANSEN @ OKAY CREATIONS

FORMATTED BY POLGARUS STUDIO

To my children. Mommy loves you infinite google!

"Not all those who wander are lost"- J.R.R. Tolkien

PROLOGUE

Rogers Park, Chicago
Christmas morning 2002
Thomas

I lie in bed waiting for Halo to wake up. I know Christmas was a big deal around her house when she was growing up. Even though her parents are gone I still want her to feel the magic of the holiday. When I was a kid Christmas was another shitty day in my life. Nothing to celebrate. Another mark on the calendar moving me closer to the time I could leave my father and my dirty past behind.

Halo begins to stir in bed, shifting toward me with her eyes shut. A sweet smile plays on her pink, lush lips and my chest bursts with love for this woman.

"Hey." Her morning voice is raspy and thick. She opens her eyes. I couldn't love this woman more even if I tried. She's my everything.

"Hey yourself." I grin as my eyes roam over her rosy nipples. The memory of making love last night gets me all hard again. I would take her right now if I didn't have something planned. I let out a grunt.

She stretches out her arms and her body moves into a delicious curve. I lean down and close my mouth over her nipple. Damn, she tastes good.

I groan. "Baby, you can't be teasing me now. It's Christmas morning and I got stuff waiting for you under the tree downstairs."

"Stuff?" Excitement grows in her eyes. "Like presents?" She instantly pops up to her knees, bouncing on the bed. She's too cute. It's taking everything in me not to claim her right now. I want to give her Christmas.

Seeing her smile means everything. Not too long ago she was drowning in darkness. The healthy gleam in her eyes tells me she's feeling good now. It will make my news a little easier to deliver.

"Yes, baby, the stuff is presents." Before I can say anything else she pops out of bed and grabs her T-shirt off the floor. I must have thrown it there last night during our lustful attempt to actually make it to the bed as opposed to having sex on the floor again.

There's nothing wrong with floor sex but it can get hard on the back and Halo's knees. Halo throws on the shirt and darts down the hallway. I hear the small patter of her footsteps as she makes her way down the stairs. I slip on my boxer shorts and follow her. I placed a number of presents under the tree and she won't know which to open first.

I swiftly walk down the stairs to the living room where our Christmas tree is shining bright. I look out the window to see a small dusting of snow falling from the sky. Halo seats herself on the floor in front of the presents. This is my second year with a Christmas tree and her second year without her parents—bittersweet.

"Which one do I open first?" she asks like a little girl rubbing her palms together. It makes me laugh. I mean we are young. I'm twenty and she's nineteen. We were both forced to grow up too quickly. I guess it's memorable times like this that we cherish.

"If I knew presents made you this excited I would try to get more." I chuckle.

"It's not just the presents, Thomas. It's Christmas. Do you feel that? It's magical." She stares out into space with a peaceful look on her face.

"Sure baby, I'm feeling it." I look down to the chub in my shorts from this morning's perusal of her body.

"Thomas," she chides, punching my shoulder.

I chuckle again. "I'm just joking, this day is special for me too." She's too cute. I lean in, pressing a soft kiss on her lips. I pull away and lean toward the first box I want her to open. "This one." I pass her a little red box wrapped in pink ribbon. She opens it in a hurry. It's a thong from Victoria's Secret. It's not meaningful, but I couldn't help picture how hot she would look in it.

"Thank you." She leans forward and places a kiss on my lips. Then she rises to her feet and walks over to the closet by the front door. She retrieves a box from the closet and comes back to the tree.

"This is for you," she says, extending the box with one hand. I pull her toward me, guiding her to sit in my lap. Then I open my gift. It's a dog tag. Engraved. "I will always love you. You are the light in my darkness." My chest grows tight.

I enlisted in the navy and went through SEAL boot camp, passing with flying colors. Then I was shipped out to Coronado, California a year ago for more training.

Becoming a SEAL was a dream I had all my life. Originally I wanted to be a SEAL to get away from my father. Then I met Halo. She was only fifteen and perfect. She made me want to be a SEAL for an entirely different reason—I wanted to prove myself worthy of her.

I haven't told her yet, but I'm deploying. I was putting it off until I knew the depression was better. I also know that she could feel me itching to leave. My friends from boot camp had already been assigned to teams that had left for Afghanistan. Being a newlywed meant I could put it off for a while. Now I was deploying. I worried she would take it hard. That's another reason I wanted to make

Christmas extra special for us.

"Halo, it's perfect, baby." I lean over and give her a kiss. "You are the light in my darkness. I know you know I need to leave. I wanted to talk to you about it, but..."

Her finger presses to my mouth. "I know...I know you need to go. I've known for a while. I guess I was selfish trying to keep you here all this time."

"There isn't a selfish bone in your body. You were having a hard time and it was completely understandable. You're stronger now. You're going to be okay. You're busy with school and you have Jenny. You will be fine without me, Halo. I don't think you realize how strong you really are." I pause for a minute because I want her to open her next gift. "Here, open this." I pass her a little silver box; this one has a little gold bow on top. She turns on my lap so she is sitting with her legs wrapped around my waist. She opens the box and her jaw drops.

"Thomas, it's perfect," she gasps taking it out of the box. It's a silver locket.

"Here, let me." I take it out of her hand and show her the engraving on the back.

You're my Halo, my ray of light.
I will always find my way back to you

She laughs.

"We clearly think alike." She nods, proud of herself. It's true her name is quite original. We've used "halo" as a term of endearment many times. It's a reminder that when a person is drowning in darkness, another person can show them the light.

"It's perfect, Thomas."

"It opens up. You can put two pictures inside," I explain, showing it to her.

"I will have to get some pictures made."

I place the necklace around her neck and her palm closes over the locket, holding it close to her heart. I place the tags around my neck.

"Baby, I ship out tomorrow. I've known for a couple of weeks, but I didn't want you walking around sulking for my last days at home. I thought it's better we had a quick goodbye." I speak the words softly, but inside I'm cringing, hoping she isn't mad.

"Thomas…" Tears roll down her cheeks. "I know this has been coming. I know you need to go. It's okay. I've told myself it's okay since we had our first date four years ago. I've been preparing myself mentally for this. You will be great and you will do good in this world." She leans forward and places a wet kiss on my mouth. I can feel her tears on my face. I love her so damn much it hurts.

"Baby, I love you. I'll probably be gone for a while. I'll try to stay in touch as much as I can but I've been told that I may be off radar for long periods of time…" I pause because my next words aren't easy. I take a deep breath. There really is no easy way to say this... She's young and beautiful and we fell in love and married young. If something were to happen to me she needs to know that she needs to move on.

"Don't say it, Thomas." Her tears continue to fall and she nods. "You're it for me, baby." She says it adamantly and I believe her. I was her only boyfriend and her first everything.

"Halo, listen to me." My thumb grazes her cheek, wiping away her tears. "I'm a SEAL now. We go on high-risk missions. I need to know that if something happens to me that you won't check out. You need to find yourself a new husband and make a life. You are nineteen years old and the most beautiful thing I have ever seen walk this earth. I know I'm asking for a lot here, but I need to hear you promise me you will. Now that being said, I promise you that I will do my damnedest to come home to you. I will find you in the dark; you can trust that. Just in case, please say the words." I beg her as if it's my least breath. I know she would always keep her promises to me and this one is important. My own tears spill.

I'm a realist. Living a difficult life makes you into one. There are no ifs about it. I wipe gently at her tears and look at her with pleading eyes, chipping at her stubborn walls until they are fully broken.

"I promise." She nods then claims my lips hungrily. The thought of her being with another man makes me crazy possessive. I know deep down I need to do everything I can to stay alive, but the reality of being a SEAL doesn't always allow for that. The heat between us ignites and within seconds I yank down my boxer shorts and have my cock buried between her legs as she rocks on top of me. I need to own every inch of her because that conversation about her moving on has just done crazy things to my insides. As I bury myself inside her, I cleanse my mind. There is nothing else—just me and her. The way it should always be.

CHAPTER ONE

Five years later
January 15, 2008
Rogers Park, Chicago
Halo

It's happening… This. Is. Real.

Shit! I lean over the side of my bed and brace myself. *Slow breaths, Halo. You can do this. Everything will be okay.* I take a slow breath, but the pain is too intense.

I'm losing it. What should I do? It's too soon. This baby wasn't meant to come for another three weeks. Jenny and Dave aren't back from Florida yet. Who the hell should I call?

Fuck! Here comes another one. Holy hell, it feels like my insides are being squeezed to death. This can't be good. My contractions are five minutes apart. Little beads of sweat trickle down my forehead and my heart accelerates.

I never anticipated being alone for something like this. For this I was supposed to have a partner by my side.

Thomas had stuck by my side. He'd put his own dreams on hold. I knew with everything in me that he would always be by my side.

The contraction subsides. I rise from the bed, huffing out slow breaths as I wobble over to the window facing the backyard. I place my hand on the cool glass, which feels nice on my heated skin. The sky is a midnight blue and the stars are sparse. I watch the clouds slowly moving and concentrate on breathing slowly through my nose and exhaling out of my mouth.

I'm on the verge of panic. Being alone means I don't have the luxury of melting down. "*Even darkness must pass,*" I whisper the wise words of Tolkien, keeping my eyes glued on the large backyard covered in at least two feet of snow, anything to distract my mind from the fear that threatens to swallow me whole. Thomas and I had shared a love of books. We quoted Tolkien's words all the time.

I look back to the clock on the night table. It's three a.m. Even though Thomas has been gone for just over seven months, I still sleep on my side of the bed. It's messed up, but when someone like Thomas makes a promise to come back to you no matter what, you believe it, you breathe it and it enters your soul. People like Thomas are loyal. They don't make promises and then break them. They sure as fuck don't walk out on their pregnant wives. When he left on previous deployments I always missed him when he was gone and waited for his return. This time was different. I waited for him to make contact. It never came. Then the divorce papers were delivered and I understood…

Fuck! Fuck! Fuck! I usually don't swear, but I can't stop cussing. This pain is maddening. I'm going to lose it in a minute. Maybe it's good Thomas isn't here for this because all I can think about right now is gripping his balls and twisting so he can understand my pain.

Flakes of snow begin to fall from the sky. Usually I love watching the snow fall. It relaxes me on a good day. Right now it's only adding to my anxiety. I'm worried about driving myself to the hospital with the snowy roads. My car is more of a death trap than a vehicle. I turn away from the window and walk over to the closet. I grab an orange beach bag off the floor and I begin to fill it with pajamas and a change of clothes. I thought I had more time to prepare.

My best friend Jenny was overdue for all three of her children. I thought going beyond the baby's due date was the norm. I was hoping Thomas would sense my broken heart and walk through our front door when I needed him most.

I tried reaching him through all the routine channels. I even called some of the wives of his fellow SEALs on his team. I figured they would be sympathetic to my situation and they definitely were. They asked their husbands about Thomas. Avery, the wife of one of Thomas's fellow SEALs, said that Thomas had seemed pretty messed up but that he was definitely on active duty. I then asked her to send the message for him to call home since she was in contact with her husband. That call never came. A couple months later I learned his team had gone dark and they were expected to stay that way for a while.

I step into the bathroom and with shaky hands throw my toothbrush and some toothpaste in the bag too. I planned to take off school a week early and buy diapers, get sleepers and fix the truck. With being a teacher I didn't want to leave the classroom while in the middle of a unit. I wanted to wrap things up. With the baby coming three weeks early my plans have been quashed and I am now unprepared. Unfortunately for me none of my plans ever seem to work out.

Ow! Shit! Here comes another one. The bag slips out of my fingers and my hands go to my swollen belly to brace for the impending contraction. My face scrunches up. I can't do those damn slow breaths I was taught to do, because these damn contractions are owning my ass.

I think that was four minutes. I hunch forward as the contraction rips its way through me. I close my eyes and pray. I pray that Thomas will walk through the door this second, or that Jenny will for some unforeseen reason end her vacation in Florida early.

"Charlie what should I do?" I ask, looking into the brown eyes of my Golden Retriever. She stares back at me and I can tell she understands what's happening. I'm sure she'd try to help if she could speak. I don't know how I would have gotten through these last months without her. She has cuddled me and let me cry on her more times than I care to remember.

"What do you say, Charlie? Ambulance or a taxi?" Charlie tilts her head to the side and lets out a cute little moan followed by a louder bark. "Taxi it is then." I pat her head. An ambulance will make me even more anxious than I already am. I'm about to lose my shit in another minute.

I walk over to the phone on the nightstand and call the cab company. A man with an East Indian accent picks up and tells me he could have the cab here in five minutes. I bet that's even faster than the ambulance. My heart is racing a mile a minute and my hands are clammy. I hang up the phone and try to focus. I'm not sure I will make it through this on my own. I always had it in my head that somehow he would come home for this. I really believed that when he left it wasn't final. I was his Halo. He promised me that I was his fucking Halo...

I quickly throw on a pair of sweat pants and a sweatshirt. My hair is tied up in a messy bun at the top of my head. I pick up the beach bag and throw in a hairbrush. I know I'm running out of time before another contraction hits and I need to make it down the stairs... Nothing in my life goes as planned why should giving birth be any different?

As I reach the bottom of the stairs another contraction hits. I topple over, trying to breathe like I was taught in my prenatal classes. Charlie is rubbing her body along my leg. My only thought is that the prenatal teacher was batshit crazy. There is no way I can breathe through this pain. It's probably more like I will stop breathing. I'm dying…

No. I will keep my shit together because I need to be strong. This baby inside me is going to need a strong mother. I've been trying to convince myself of this for the past seven months but I feel like I am fooling myself. I met Thomas when I was fifteen. Since then, he's been my whole world. Now that he isn't here, I'm a broken mess, scared of raising this baby on my own.

The contraction finally passes. Feeling spent and thirsty, I waddle to the kitchen for a glass of water. I gulp down one glass, then another. While I'm at the sink, I fill Charlie's water dish. I take care of her food too, reminding myself to let the neighbor know that she'll need to look in on her.

I head for the door, knowing the cab will be here soon. I pass the living room and I spot a photo of Thomas and me on the mantel. I walk over to it, feeling hot fury burning in my chest.

"Damn you, Thomas Wells," I hiss at his picture. "You promised me you were the sticking-around type and this doesn't fucking constitute sticking around…" I pick up the frame and lay it face down. I've put most of our pictures in a box in the attic. Right after he left, I was in so much pain, felt so alone. Staring at his photographs made it hurt more.

This was the only picture I left around the house. It was taken after we got married. We both look so young and hopeful. The prick knew how to get me pregnant, he just couldn't manage to hang around. My gaze shifts to my water polo trophies on the shelf by the fireplace. Even looking at the trophies right now makes me angry and I feel like chucking them across the room. My parents thought a team sport would be good for me when we moved out here. It's how I met Thomas. Anger stings its way up my throat. I realize how resentful I am. I know I need to get myself together because I can't show the baby that I resent its father. I know better than that.

I make my way to the door and put on my boots and winter coat. Charlie takes a seat beside me, looking up at me with soppy brown eyes. "Don't worry, girl. I'll be just fine. I'll be back with a baby in hand." I pat her on the head. Two minutes later a bright light shines into the house followed by a loud car horn. The cab.

I leave the house and lock the door with my little beach bag and purse on my shoulder. As I approach the cab, the cabbie looks at me a little wide-eyed. It's now three-thirty in the morning and a very pregnant woman is climbing into his cab.

"Where to ma'am?" he asks as if he already knows—he just wants me to choose a hospital.

"St. Joseph's Hospital…" Another contraction strikes and I hold on to my belly screaming. My head falls back when he accelerates abruptly.

"Holy shit! Ma'am, I'm driving. Just don't have that baby in my cab." I can't even answer him. This contraction is even stronger. I just hope I make it to the hospital on time. Having a baby in the back of a cab with no drugs is simply not happening.

The driver is driving like a maniac down the slippery roads. I hope he doesn't kill us trying to get there. The contraction subsides. Phew! I use my breathing time to shoot my neighbor Maggie a quick text asking if she can stop by and take care of Charlie. The cab stops abruptly and I jerk forward, feeling a strong need to pee. He pulls up to the front of St. Joseph's and I reach for my purse to pay him.

He looks like he's sweating. "It's okay ma'am. Don't pay me, just go…please just go," he practically begs me.

I'm too panicked to pay him much attention. I take my purse and bag and leave his cab. If these contractions are regular, another one should hit in about a minute. As I walk toward the hospital entrance, warm liquid slowly trickles down both my legs. Shit! I've either just peed myself or my water broke. I really have no clue. All I know is that I am uncomfortable and wet. The air is brisk and cool as I make my way through the sliding doors of the hospital and up to the information desk.

"Labor and delivery, please," I ask with a hint of a smile since it's the best I can manage under the circumstances.

"Sure ma'am, that's the tenth floor. Should I call for assistance?" the young African American man behind the desk asks with a kind smile.

"Huh. Aghhh!" I topple forward as I brace myself for another contraction. "I need an epidural," I scream. This is getting intense. The man leaves his desk and comes around to my side. He jogs over to the entrance and grabs me a wheelchair, huffing a bit.

"Have a seat, ma'am. I'll get you to the tenth floor." I take a seat, trying to breathe through this pain. It's too damn much. My insides are crushing me. Finally, I sense some relief when the squeezing sensation eases into a dull pain.

The physical pain turns into sadness as I'm rolled down the hallway. My father moved our family away from California when he got a job in this hospital. I was so angry at my parents for taking me away from my friends and my life in LA. I was happy there.

My father was a doctor and my mother a university professor. They had me later in life because they had trouble conceiving. When they finally had me, I became their life. When I was born, my mom took one look at me and was convinced I had a halo around me and hence my original name. After trying to have a baby for over a decade, she doted on me every moment of her time.

It wasn't necessarily a bad thing until they became worried about my friends and their influence on me. To "save me" we moved halfway across the country. I remember coming to the hospital to visit my father. Getting wheeled down these familiar halls causes those painful memories to rip a hole through my heart.

"Agh," I cry out again as the man wheels me toward the nurse's desk. We finally come to a stop. "Thank you, sir," I bite out through the pain.

"Good luck." He waves, looking at me sympathetically. He should be sympathetic. I'm about to split in *fucking* two!

"How far apart are your contractions?" A nurse with brown, short hair and wearing glasses low on her nose peers over her desk at me.

"My contractions are four minutes apart and I have a warm liquid oozing its way down my legs," I snarl. I think my voice must sound like Darth Vader.

"Are we waiting for a partner?" she asks. Jenny was supposed to be my birthing partner. She's soaking up the sun right now. I look down to the band on my finger. Why am I still wearing it? Gah! I should have taken off the ring, especially now that we divorced, but I felt like if I took off the ring I would lose all hope that he would come back to me. It's ridiculous and pathetic. Now I feel like whipping the wedding ring at the damn wall.

"I'm on my own," I reply, feeling the words sting my throat. I let out a breath, my body weak and tired from the contractions.

"Okay, well, I need you to fill out the insurance paper work first. I will have one of the nurses come by and get you," she answers with a frown. She passes me a clipboard with a shit-ton of papers. I'm really happy I have good insurance from work. Being a teacher and working for the city means I have at least that. I can afford to have this baby. Even though I know it's going to be hard with being a single mom. I don't want to return to work immediately. Ideally I want time with my baby. I begin to fill out the redundant questions when my belly begins to clench again. I squeeze the pen in my hand so hard the plastic snaps and ink spurts over my hand.

"Oh dear," the nurse behind the desk mutters as she watches me. My head is thrown back, and I must look bright red because I'm not breathing through this pain. "Do you have an insurance card? I'll finish this up for you." She walks around the desk with a cloth in her hand and wipes the splattered ink off my hand. She cleans it but it doesn't come off.

"Ye...es... It's in my wallet in my purse," I murmur. She takes my purse and she must find what she needs because a few moments later she says, "All done. Let's get a doctor to look at you."

She wheels me through two large, white doors. We pass many delivery rooms and as my ears register the sounds of voices—some male, some female—coming from the rooms, I can't help but think of Thomas. I desperately wish he were here to witness the birth of our child.

"Please lie on the bed. We'll hook you up to the monitors and have one of the residents come in to see how far along you are." A pleasant young nurse with blond hair smiles.

I ask about getting something for my pain as she helps me out of my clothes and into a gown. After I'm settled on the bed, she reassures me that they can get something for me as soon as they assess my condition.

It's a relief when—after they hook me up to the monitors—I hear my baby's heartbeat. That little heartbeat warms my own heart and I exhale a long breath. There is light at the end of this tunnel.

I hope I can do okay by my baby. I think about my own parents—they made their mistakes but they still did the best they could. I feel so far away from the teenager who was once given everything that it's hard to reconcile who I am now with who I was just a few years ago.

I barely register meeting the doctor and when the anesthesiologist comes to administer the epidural, I just try to hold on through the pain. They assign me a delivery nurse—her name is Judy and I love her smile—and she's so kind I want to weep.

"How are you doing, Halo?" Judy asks and I practically want to hug her. I don't remember the last time someone asked me how I was doing.

I don't have too many close friends except for Jenny and Dave. They don't judge, they only support me. I have a larger group of friends and coworkers who I eat lunch with on school days, but those friends were more for the good times, not the bad. There was no way I was going to cry them a river.

Thomas and I were given the option of living close to a military base so that I would have the support of the other military wives. I had always considered that option and then panic would begin to rise in me. The house in Rogers Park was all I had left of my parents. I felt like if I moved away I would lose the connection I felt there. As it was, I had felt guilty about fighting with them. I felt that if they somehow knew I stayed in the house they would be happy. And somewhere along the way Chicago became home. Thomas and I had built special memories here. I didn't want to leave those behind either.

"Well, Judy, I could be better. I'm kind of freaking out wondering how this baby is going to come out of me," I admit, raising my left brow.

Judy throws her head back, laughing. "You don't need to worry. Your body was built for this. Why don't you try to sleep? It can take a few hours for things to progress since the epidural slows things down. You need your strength for pushing later on. I will be sitting here watching your machines." Her voice is soft and reassuring.

"Thanks, Judy." I smile. There is something about her demeanor that relaxes me. I feel I can trust her. I close my eyes and drift off.

***

January 6, 1999
National Water Polo Competition
Halo

"Don't be so nervous." Mom smiles, looking into the backseat of the car. I am staring out the window of Dad's SUV and biting my nails. It's snowing outside. I hate that it's snowing. I want to see sunshine and palm trees not a grey sky and slushy streets.

"And stop biting your nails. Your team is going to do just fine. You guys are the best. Just do the best you can and we are always proud of you. You're number one to me anyway." Mom gives me a silly grin.

"That's right, kiddo, stop taking this so seriously." My father gazes at me in the rearview mirror. "We thought it would be a good way for you to make friends. I don't want you stressing over this." His thick, silver eyebrows are scrunched together.

"It's fine, Dad. So I am a little competitive. Competition is a healthy part of life." I grin.

I am nervous as hell even though I'm desperately trying to hide it from my parents. As their only daughter, I'm expected to be independent, confident and to take everything with grace. That's not really me. I'm shy. I haven't been able to make even one genuine friendship since we moved. I'm confident about my schoolwork. I don't pay much attention to my physical appearance because I've been taught that it's what's on the inside of a person that counts. Hence my lack of makeup and my simple clothing. I'm an average girl, auburn hair, brown eyes. Nothing special and I'm okay with that.

I like to win. I have a competitive streak that gets my blood pumping. Today's competition is on the national level. Teams from all over the country will be competing and, yes, I want to win.

When we arrived in Chicago I didn't make friends quickly. My parents—who had been concerned about drug use in the schools I'd gone to in LA—thought I should take part in a sport. Sports demand teamwork and friendship and my folks were sure athletics would keep me out of trouble. I was a strong swimmer and so my mother enrolled me in water polo. It turned out I had strong ankles and a wicked eggbeater kick that allowed me to excel in the sport. I went from recreational water polo straight into the competitive league and today I would participate in the finals.

As we enter the building for the competition, I see a sign indicating that the boys are competing today as well.

"Bye, Mom! Bye, Dad!" I wave as I saunter toward the locker room.

"Bye, honey," they both call simultaneously. I sometimes wonder if they're secretly Siamese twins, they are so much alike.

"Hey." One of my teammates—Amanda—smiles at me as I walk through the doors.

"Hey," I reply.

"The guys are here too. We can scope out some hotties," she says with a giggle. She was already in her bathing suit. I place my bag in a locker and begin to change. Scoping out boys is the last thing on my mind right now. I'm fifteen and a half years old and I've never had a boyfriend. I had guy friends in LA, but I was never interested in anyone enough to take things to the next level. Chicago is the same story. No one catches my eye.

"Yay hotties," I cheer back to Amanda, hoping not to sound too sarcastic. I don't want to offend her by not sharing in her enthusiasm.

We both walk out to the pool deck together. There are benches lined up along the walls for the teams. I looked up to the bleachers and my parents smile down at me, waving proudly. I guess that's how it is being an only child. Your parents only have you to focus on. I inhale a long breath and let it out, feeling a little exasperated.

My team begins warm ups and I stretch with them. Next to us is a team of boys. My gaze slowly drifts over to them. They're stretching too. Maybe I am checking for hotties. When we finish our stretches, all the girls take a seat on the bench.

"So which one do you like, Halo?" Amanda asks, taking a seat beside me and tilting her chin to the boys' team.

"Hmm." I tap my fingers on my chin playfully.

My gaze makes an abrupt stop on a guy who is hunched over. He's bigger and more muscular than the rest of his team. He looks like he must seriously work out. I can tell that he's caught me ogling when our eyes meet briefly. He stands and I pull my gaze away quickly. My face turns beet red. I look off to the pool, hoping to save myself from his returning stare.

Looking away doesn't solve the problem. I feel his gaze on me now. I can see a devilish grin on his face out of the corner of my eye. I take slow breaths, wishing my cheeks won't turn pink, but my pale complexion betrays me.

Amanda leans over so her lips brush my ear. "It seems like you've caught someone's attention." She smirks and nods her head over to the guy. Great! Now it's obvious we're talking about him. This can't get any more embarrassing. I'm definitely not schooled in flirting or anything that has to do with boys other than friendship. I may be a hopeless romantic at heart but it's not something I would ever admit. I do have a few romance novels that I indulge in between my Tolkien reads.

"Amanda, don't gesture." I smack her thigh. "Now he'll know we were talking about him," I snap in her ear. That's when I feel a dark shadow looming over us. I take a large gulp as I turn my head to see the shadow's cause. The guy—the hottie—is standing in front of us. Jesus!

I flinch and the pink nuisance crawls up my neck toward my cheeks again as my heart picks up speed. I suddenly felt dizzy and out of breath and I cackle thinking I remind myself of a heroine from one of the romance novels I enjoy reading. I was crushing on this boy. A definite first for me.

"Hey, I'm Thomas Wells." He extends his hand to me. His voice is smooth but deep. Holy hell, my heart is beating a mile a minute.

Get a hold of yourself, Halo.

I extend my hand shakily. "Hi Halo," I reply with a voice that's barely audible. Amanda nudges me in the shoulder and confidently extends her own hand.

"Amanda, nice to meet you, Thomas Wells," she says with a flirtatious smile. I want nothing more than to whack her upside the head.

"So are you girls competing today?" he asks, his dark blue eyes glued on me. There's something about his eyes as they dance mischievously, taking me in. Holy hell, he is beautiful.

"Uh...yes...are you?" I ask with a shaky voice.

Get a grip, Halo. You sound like a scared child.

I've always had lots of guy friends. I never get nervous like this. I can't stop my eyes from checking him out, either. His muscular arms and six-pack abs are drool-worthy. I lift my eyes back to eye level and notice his sexy grin. My cheeks flush some more. A part of me wants to run away and find composure.

"Yeah, I'm hoping we are going to get first place today." He flashes a perfect smile and white teeth. I'm happy that his attention is on me and not Amanda. I nod my head when he replies and I give him a shy smile. I don't want to be acting so idiotic. I want to be funny or sexy; none of that is happening for me.

"So, Halo, is this your first competition? I don't remember seeing you around."

"I've been to a few competitions," I reply, "but this is my first national. I was born in LA. We just moved out here six months ago. And you?"

"Ah, a California girl..." He grins as if there's an inside joke I've missed. "I was born in Florida. My family moved out here when I was two. We live in Rogers Park." Holy crap, his smile is sexy. My insides are shaking and I don't like this loss of control.

"Oh! I'm in Rogers Park too," I respond with an attempt at nonchalance, but I feel as if I fail miserably when my voice rises an octave. I know Rogers Park is a relatively big neighborhood but he can't live too far away. The thought excites me.

"Well, Halo, I will need to see you around Rogers Park then," he says with yet another flirtatious grin. Butterflies dance in my chest. Jesus! Pathetic. He flirts well. He turns and goes back to his team and my heart continues to flutter. I am no longer focused on the competition when delectable Thomas is flexing his muscles on the bench beside my team.

The competition gets under way and we win the first round. When Thomas gets in the water, I feel gooey-eyed watching him. His team is super good and he is definitely the star. My stomach flips in the most delicious way watching him.

Amanda nudges me again. "Thomas has the hots for you. You should totally hook up with him." I'm not sure what she means by hooking up exactly, but I definitely want to be seeing him again.

When Thomas leaves the water after his team basically creams their competition, he walks directly over to me, sopping wet. My hormones are kicking in big time and I feel like my insides are doing somersaults.

"Nice job." I smile nervously.

"Thanks," he replies, running a hand over his buzzed brown hair. "I love swimming and I love the competition. How about you? How did you get into it?"

"Ah well, I used to do swim competitions back home and when we moved out here my parents thought I should do a team sport and water polo just made sense since I'm not very athletic otherwise." I try to think of some way to continue our conversation and ask, "How about you? Are you expecting some university scholarship or something? I saw how good you are."

He chuckles and looks down to the ground. When he looks up, I notice again how gorgeous his eyes are—a dark blue I've never seen before.

"Not exactly," he says. "I am not going to college. I compete because I want to apply to be a Navy SEAL. It's my ticket out of Rogers Park," he explains.

"You don't like Rogers Park?" I asked with a hint of curiosity. According to my parents it's the best place on earth. I beg to differ.

"We aren't from the same area of Rogers Park I'm guessing, but no I don't like it. I live with my father and I can't wait to leave. I've been training since the day I turned fifteen. There's a SEAL training camp in Great Lakes, Illinois and that's where I'm headed. Then I'll be property of the navy and allow them to take me wherever that may be as long as it's away from here."

I can't help but sulk.

"Yeah, I wouldn't mind going back to LA," I mutter.

"How old are you anyway?"

"I'm fifteen. And you?"

"I just turned seventeen," he replies, biting his lower lip again. I wonder if it's a nervous habit. "Are you going to give me your number?" he asks. He obviously didn't have self-esteem issues. I look over to my side and I see Amanda practically drooling as she watches us.

"Ah!" He takes a step back as if he's tripped and holds his hand up to his chest. "I'm wounded. You seriously need to think about it?

Well, that's a first." He shakes his head.

Oh geez! He must have lots of girlfriends. Leave it up to me to be lusting after a player.

"Well, if that's a first then you don't need to worry," I snap at him, not liking his arrogance. "You must have them waiting in line for you."

He looks almost bewildered and remains painfully quiet. It makes me feel like I have the upper hand and I like it for once. Maybe I've been drooling too much and he senses it. Not happening.

"There's a line, but it's your number I want," he replies with a cocky grin.

"Thomas, I am not that kind of girl," I answer harshly.

"Halo, I know you aren't and that's why I want your number." His tone is filled with challenge.

"Fine," I snap again. I'm not even sure why I'm irritated. I should probably feel special. I look around, wondering where I can find him a piece of paper. Amanda stands and walks over to the assistant coach. She rips a piece of paper from his clipboard and takes his pen. After she hands them to me, I write my number down and pass it to Thomas.

"I'll be calling, Halo. You can be sure of that." He grins, holding the paper and waving it at me like he just won the lotto. Then he walks away without a goodbye.

We come in first that day for the girls' competition and Thomas's team also comes in first for the boys. I grin for the rest of the ride back home and when I lay in bed that night thinking of Thomas's smile and his blue eyes, I feel delicious butterflies floating happily in my chest and stomach.

I just can't get the self-assured Thomas Wells out of my mind. He said he was from the other side of Rogers Park. Did he mean the lower-income side? That stuff doesn't matter to me anyway. I know my father hopes I'll become a doctor like him one day, but I'm still undecided.

Three days pass and I don't hear from Thomas. I sulk, figuring he's just another stupid player.

When he finally calls on the fourth day, I'm not sure if I want to talk to him. "Hello," I say quietly into the phone.

"Halo, it's Thomas. Would you like to hang out tonight?"

"Tonight? Uh..."

"Is it short notice?"

"No, uh... It's just..." The sound of his deep voice has me dying to see him again. But I have a science test to study for... "Yeah tonight is great," I say, quickly choosing him over studying. His chuckle makes me feel like I've made a great choice.

"Okay," he says. "Give me your address. I will pick you up in twenty minutes."

I give him my address, put down my phone and panic. Is this a date? Like a real date? I glance at my closet. Should I change out of my jeans? Put on makeup? I decide not to worry about what I look like. I have enough to worry about—like what Thomas and I might do when we "hang out." I was new at this.

Twenty minutes later the doorbell rings and I plummet down the stairs, hoping to open the door before my mother does. I don't make it, though. My mom opens the door and there he is—Thomas Wells with clothes on. He's wearing a ripped pair of blue jeans and a black leather jacket. His brown buzz cut has sprinkles of snow in it. He smiles widely when he sees me.

"Mom... uh... this is Thomas Wells. We are going out for a bit." It's not much of an explanation, but I hope my mother won't embarrass me by asking a bunch of questions.

Thomas extends his hand and my mom shakes it hesitantly while glaring at me. Thomas Wells looks like the epitome of a bad boy and

I don't care at all. In fact I kind of like it. I notice he's holding a motorcycle helmet in his other hand. *Uh-oh…*

"Halo, a motorcycle in this weather is like a death trap," Mom says in her loudest "no way" voice.

"Oh, don't worry Mrs…" Thomas pauses. I'd never told him my last name.

"Pearson," my mother inserts. I avoid her eyes and quickly put on my coat and boots.

"Mrs. Pearson, I'm very careful and I drive slowly." He tries to sound reassuring, but the picture he makes is working against him. The helmet, the leather jacket, the hot-as-hell grin. I know my parents won't be down with the idea of me leaving with him at all.

"I'm sorry, Halo. I don't think so," my mother says apologetically.

An uncharacteristic surge of defiance comes over me. There is no way in hell I'm not going to go out with Thomas. He makes me feel good. I like him. I'm tired of my parents trying to control my life. I hadn't had a choice about moving to Chicago. Tonight it was going to be *my* choice to hang out with my new friend.

"I'll see you later, Mom. I'll be fine. I won't be home too late." I give her a peck on the cheek. She wasn't expecting straight-out defiance from me, because she stands there in stunned silence as I take Thomas by the hand and lead him to the door.

When we're outside, I close the door with a solid thud. He looks down at me with an amused grin.

"Come on," I urge. "We need to keep moving before she comes out here and drags my ass back inside."

Thomas's eyes sparkle. "Okay, okay. Put this on." He passes me the helmet. I put it on and we climb on his bike.

"Wow a motorcycle…this is my first time," I admit feeling my nerves build. I want to spend time with Thomas but I'm not an idiot. I know my mom is right about motorcycles being dangerous in the snow.

"Sorry, I can't afford a car. I work as a mechanic's helper part time. He's a nice guy. He helped me build this bike from old scraps so I can get around. I know it sucks in the winter. I wasn't kidding. I'll take it slow."

"That's impressive, Thomas. I can't believe you built this from scratch." I grin a little too much. I try to tone it down a bit. Being with Thomas is exciting. Being with Thomas on his bike is even more exciting. My life is boring and this is definitely out of my norm. True to his word, he drives slowly and carefully through the neighborhood and onto a street with lots of markets and shops. He pulls up to a coffee shop and we go inside.

We find a table and I sit, keeping my coat zipped and my hands shoved in my pockets. "You're freezing," he says, almost like he's chiding himself. "What can I get you to drink?" He rubs his hands together. His skin looks red and chapped and as cold as mine.

"I'll have an Earl Grey tea with milk," I reply with a slight blush. I'm on my first date with the hottest guy I've ever laid eyes on. He gets the drinks and we settle in, talking for hours as if we're old friends. He tells me how his mother left him when he was two and how he lives with his abusive alcoholic father. His openness causes me to open up too. We've only just met, but there's something so comfortable about the way he watches me from across the table, like he's intrigued by me and he cares what I say.

After talking to him for about three hours I know more about him than I know about my teammates—girls I've spent twenty hours a week with for the last six months.

"Is your father why you want to leave so badly?" I ask him.

"Yeah, pretty much. I live in a shithole. I need to get out of this place."

"Why don't you use your skills at water polo to get a scholarship? You could probably go to a university for free." My parents have always taught me that education is number one.

His eyebrows come together and the lines around his mouth crease deeply. "Halo, we don't come from the same place. My father has always told me I'm dirt. He blames me for my mother taking off. There is no way I'm going to college. I'm going to be a SEAL. That's what I want. I'll show them I'm not a nobody." He jerks his chin sharply. He won't argue about this point.

I looked down at his strong hands. They're gripping his mug tightly. "Thomas, I have a feeling that your father doesn't know ass-shit." There's surprising vehemence in my tone. I want to stomp across town and kick his father's behind.

Thomas's face contorts at my words, almost like he doesn't believe me.

"Seriously, Thomas," I say. "Your father sounds messed up. From what I've seen since meeting you, you're a pretty awesome guy." I sound so sure I surprise even myself. It's taken me just a few hours to realize there were no walls where Thomas Wells and I are concerned.

For such a badass looking boy on the outside he sure sent me for a loop. He leans across the table and my heart skips a beat as he places a soft kiss on my lips. My eyes close and my breath quickens. I perform an internal happy dance, thinking it's the best first kiss a girl could ask for.

A stupid grin erupts on my face. But then Thomas says, "I'm sorry for kissing you."

I'm confused. I'm sure those kinds of kisses shouldn't be followed by an apology.

"Don't be sorry," I tell him. I want him to do it again.

"I don't want you to think I was using you or something." He pulls his gaze away from me. "I like you," he says shyly. I get the feeling he's not shy with girls very often. Probably never.

"Thomas Wells, is this a first for you?" I ask with an almost mocking tone.

"Yes, it is, Halo Pearson." He grins widely, his out-sized self-esteem returning.

"I'm guessing you've had lots of girlfriends," I say, narrowing my eyes.

"I have, Halo. I'm not going to lie. But you really are the first one I've liked."

I blush again and he gives me another light kiss. I feel my body gently float up to the clouds.

"So what do you do for fun?" Thomas asks, looking at me intently.

I look down at my empty mug, feeling embarrassed. "I read books."

When I glance up at him, his eyes are wide. "Me too."

"Really?" I ask, surprised. I haven't pegged him as a bookworm type.

"Yeah, I work out a lot. I need to be in shape for when I sign up to be a SEAL. I heard boot camp is brutal. When I'm not training, I read. We don't have cable. I get books from the library."

"Wow. So let me guess, Thomas. You compare yourself to Ralph from—"

"Halo, I think I just fell in love with you," he says, cutting off my sentence.

"Huh? How do you know what I wanted to say?"

"You said 'Ralph'. You've read Golding's *Lord of the Flies.*" It's a statement, not a question.

I nod. "Is Ralph your inspiration? The boy who represents order and civilization," I continue with my analysis and comparison of the protagonist, Ralph. "He watches how the other boys give in to bloodlust and savagery and yet he doesn't succumb. You are a calculating guy, Thomas. You are doing everything you can to make a better life for yourself, and joining the navy means that you also want to fight the bad guys and save society."

Thomas leans back in his chair and gives me a panty-dropping grin. "Halo Pearson, everything about this night has been unexpected. Your observations are close, but what you forgot is that when Ralph kills the boar he experiences the thrill of bloodlust and violence. There is evil within Ralph too as within all humans. He then finds himself in despair, but it's his desperation that enables him to cast down the Lord of the Flies."

I'm in awe when he continues, "Don't frown, pretty girl. It's not a completely tragic ending. There is good. If you see me as Ralph, then my father is Jack, the antagonist that represents savagery. I don't intend to let the savages win." He winks.

I smile widely. "I'm glad. I think you're pretty amazing."

Something that seems dark and painful passes over his features for a brief second. He smiles but it looks forced. I'm not sure what just happened.

He looks at his wristwatch. "Whoa, it's really late. I should get you home. It's a school night. I don't need your parents hating me. I have to take you out again."

When Thomas drops me back home, he helps me off his motorcycle and removes my helmet. He walks me to the door. Before I go inside, he takes me in his arms and drops his head toward mine. Our lips collide, but when the kiss begins he's slow and gentle, running his tongue along mine. Hot, red fire shoots between my thighs.

I want more. I place my hands on the back of his neck, drawing him closer. The kiss grows even hungrier as our tongues collide and I learn his taste. He's sweet from the cocoa but there are layers there that I can't wait to get to know. I'm drawn to him, need more of him.

He pulls away, placing his hands on my shoulders as he stares down at me with dazed eyes. He's panting like I am.

"Uh, yeah. Okay… Wow." He exhales a long breath and runs both hands over his buzz cut. "You have a great night, Halo Pearson. I will need to see you again soon."

He walks down the steps of my front porch and climbs on his bike. Again, there's no goodbye.

No goodbye…

January 15, 2008
Rogers Park, Chicago
Halo

My eyes open. Nurse Judy is standing beside my bed with a slight smile. "You must have been having quite a dream," she says, patting my shoulder. "You and the baby are both doing good. Your contractions are closer now. We must be getting close. I'll find the doctor and have him come check you," she says before leaving the room.

I'm halfway between dreamland and being awake. I've dreamt about my past with Thomas so many times. The good times and the bad. As I think back to those times I remember the chip on his shoulder. He was the boy from the wrong side of town. Not only did his father put him down, my parents didn't accept him either.

Right now I try to concentrate on the good. I need to relax for my baby. The day I met Thomas was one of the best days of my life. Getting married was a great day. And today will be amazing because I will be meeting my son.

There's a weird beeping noise on my monitor and my heart begins to beat rapidly. The doctor arrives and checks the monitors. His brow furrows and he places a hand on mine. "Halo, the baby's heart rate is dropping. We need to get you in for an emergency C-section."

"Will my baby be okay?" I ask as my eyes fill with tears. I feel droplets of sweat break out along my forehead. I feel like I can't breathe.

"Relax, Halo," Nurse Judy says as she takes the doctor's place at my side. "Breathe. You need to stay calm. It will be better for you and the baby."

"Relax?"

"Yes," she says calmly.

I see colors flying past my eyes. There are lots of doctors around me or maybe nurses. Everyone's wearing blue scrubs. My heart thumps quickly and I can hear each beat ringing loud in my ears. I'm sweating and the room feels stifling.

A bright light shines in my face. It looks like a halo. It reminds me of my parents. My father was an obstetrician and would always run to the hospital at night to deliver babies. I wish he were here now to help my little one. The doctors talk amongst themselves. I'm too panicked to understand what they're saying.

"Halo, they will be doing the procedure now," Nurse Judy explains slowly.

This is all happening too fast. I'm supposed to push this baby out and now everyone is frantic around me. I won't have anything to live for if this baby dies.

There's a strong pressure in my abdomen. I close my eyes and open them again. I'm not sure how much time passes.

"And here he is…" Dr. Kramer is grinning, lifting my small baby in his arms before passing him off to a nurse. I hear the tiny cries and my own tears begin to flow.

"He looks great," the doctor says and I take a long breath. I've just lived through the scariest moment of my life. "The nurse will bring him over to you in a moment."

"Thank you," I reply. My throat feels dry and my voice is low and raspy.

Dr. Kramer leaves my side and a resident explains what's happening. They'll need to keep me and the baby in the hospital for a few days because of the C-section. I nod. I don't care about anything except seeing him.

"Look at your handsome little fellow," Nurse Judy says as she brings my baby up to my face so I can get a better view. I can't sit up to hold him, but just looking at him wrapped up in the little blue blanket makes my heart swell. He's perfect. I sigh a contented sigh.

"Do you have a name for this handsome fellow?" she asks.

"Mmm. I thought of calling him Brandon Pearson after my father."

Nurse Judy winks. "That's lovely. Brandon is a strong name for a strong boy.

CHAPTER TWO

January 18, 2008
Halo

Jenny saunters into the hospital room looking flushed and holding her palms over her cheeks. "Halo! Oh my God! Show me that little boy of yours!"

She bounces toward the bed where I'm holding Brandon, her blonde bob swinging, her blue eyes dancing. Jenny has been my best friend since college. We've become more like sisters than friends. She's stuck by me through thick and thin. She's been my rock since Thomas and I started having trouble.

She was scheduled to be my birthing partner, but that didn't work out when little Brandon decided to make an early entrance. Despite Brandon's dramatic entrance to the world, he's been the perfect baby. He's been feeding well and not crying too much.

I pass Brandon over to Jenny and her floodgates open. "Oh my, Halo. He is just so precious. He looks exactly like...." She bites her lip. I know what she wants to say.

"Like me. I know. Thank you." I grin and nod. She gives me a knowing look. I carried that boy for eight months and one week. I did everything myself. There was no way I was going to give Thomas

Wells any credit for anything—not after he left us high and dry.

"He's so precious, Halo," she repeats, staring down at him in awe. She takes a seat in the chair by my bed. "Maybe you two should come stay with us for a while. You know. Until your C-section heals and you get back up on your feet." She looks at me expectantly, obviously assuming I will take her up on her offer. But I simply can't impose on her like that.

"Thanks, Jenny. I appreciate the offer so much, but you have three little kids of your own. You don't need me and a crying baby hanging around." I take a deep breath, knowing she isn't going to fold easily.

"Halo Pearson, don't give me that crap. You are coming to stay with us and it's final. C-sections take time to heal. You have little Brandon here to think about. Stay with us until the stitches come out." She pulls her attention away from me and gazes at Brandon gooey-eyed.

He really is a sight to see. I kind of forgive my mother right now for calling me Halo. I really do feel like there is a ray of light around that boy.

"How long will you be holed up in this place?" Jenny asks, looking around the room with distaste.

"Another few days at least. He swallowed meconium, he's jaundiced, he was born a little early and I have to stay because of the C-section. The nurse has been taking him under bright lights a few times a day. It's a little hard on me because I hate being away from him, so I make myself walk over to the nursery to watch him in those incubator things. My stomach kills me when I walk." I abruptly realize I shouldn't have said that. It will only confirm her argument that I should move in with her.

Jenny frowns. "Halo, I'm happy that you're trying to get up and move around. I'm just scared you will overdo it when you go home.

Babies can be draining at the beginning. You have to take care of yourself. I understand the separation anxiety, though. I remember when the nurse wanted to take Tyler to the nursery so I could rest when he was born. She began to wheel him out until I flipped out and began screaming for her to give me my baby back."

Her expression is dramatic and I begin to laugh, picturing the scene. I forget how much it hurts to laugh and I bite my lip.

Jenny's shoulders suddenly slump and her lips turn down. "I feel terrible that I missed the delivery." Her eyes begin to tear and I hate that she feels bad.

"Don't feel bad. Brandon surprised me too. He was three weeks early. There was no way you could have known." I tilt my head and watch her cooing at Brandon. She's been so good to me. I don't know how I would have made it through these last eight months without her.

Jenny smiles sadly. "You must have been so scared. Just thinking about it makes me shiver. I swear if I ever get my hands on that Thomas I will ring his neck." As the last words leave her mouth, I realize that I have to let go of the resentment and so does she.

"Jenny," I say. "We have to stop bad-mouthing Thomas. I know we've had our share of cussing him out these last few months, but it needs to stop, for Brandon's sake. He will grow up and he will want to know who his father is. I only plan on telling him the good. He needs to be reassured that he was created in love. That his father leaving had nothing to do with him. I mean, Thomas was so messed up over his own mother abandoning him. It defined his whole life and I don't want that for my son. I want Brandon to grow up feeling confident and loved." I trail off as tears flow down my cheeks.

This is the part of raising him on my own that scares me the most. Doing right by my boy. Raising him to be a strong, confident man. Convincing him that his father leaving had nothing to do with him.

Having lived with Thomas for so long, I knew the hardship I was facing.

"Oh, honey, he will know. We will all make sure of it. I'm sorry. No bad-mouthing Thomas." A stray tear rolls down her cheek. "You hear that, Brandon? Your father was actually a superhero. He left to fight all the bad guys in the world. He wears a special uniform and he ensures all our safety."

Her words make me happy. Brandon will one day feel proud, but deep down I feel let down.

Jenny sees me wiping my eyes and says, "It's the hormones, Halo. I was a mess after Tyler. It's called baby blues. I didn't get it so much with Olivia and Sam though. Your friends will help you pull through. Speaking of friends—have you heard from anyone lately?"

"I don't know. Maybe. I haven't checked my cell phone."

Jenny, reading me like a book as usual, shakes her head. "You can't hide from them forever, Halo. They all care about you."

I want to agree with her. Problem is, I still feel ashamed. The abandoned woman… The rational part of me knows better, but the feeling in the pit of my stomach won't subside no matter how many pep talks I give myself. "I know," I say. "I'm just not ready to face everyone yet. I still feel…"

"Say it. It's okay," Jenny urges me.

"Abandoned, alone… I'm embarrassed." I shake my head.

Jenny frowns. "You have nothing to be embarrassed about. Thomas was messed up over the Iraq deployment. There are stories about soldiers everywhere. Our friends understand, Halo. You need to give them some credit. It will be good for Brandon too. He'll have friends to be around. Kiley is only one month older than him and Melissa is home. You guys can hang and do coffee or something. You need to return to the land of the living."

"I know… I plan on doing right by this boy, Jenny. I want him to socialize and have a normal childhood. I want him to have a father…" At this, Jenny furrows her brow. "Don't look at me like that," I say. "Thomas may have been the greatest love of my life, but I know I will need to go out and date and build myself a new life for Brandon's sake. He deserves a family. Thomas divorced me. Now I'll find another man and I'll find a way to love him." I raise my chin and straighten my spine.

Jenny shrugs. "Hey sister, all the power to you. I can ask Dave to set you up."

I smile. "I don't mean I'll find a man now. I literally just gave birth. I mean, look at me." I look down at my still-swollen belly and gently press my fingers over the space where there will soon be a big scar. "Brandon was worth every mark."

"Don't talk to me about marks," Jenny says. "I've had three children and I wear my stripes proudly. You should too. Any man who has a problem with that isn't worthwhile anyway."

"Agreed." I smile. Jenny places Brandon back in my arms.

"I wish I could stay longer, but I have to get the kids. Olivia starts swimming lessons tonight," she says apologetically.

"Don't sound sorry. You take care of your family. Brandon and me are doing fine," I say with an assertive tone. It's not hard to say the words. We are fine. He has brought happiness to my life.

"I guess." She leans in and gives my forehead a kiss. Lingering, she gives Brandon a kiss too. "Hmm… he smells soooo good. Bye, Brandon, see you soon." She caresses his little cheek.

"I love touching his little hands and his little face." I look down happily at my boy.

She leaves and I'm still smiling at Brandon a few moments later when a nurse walks through the door. She's new and I don't like her as much as the other nurses. Probably because she's blonde and young and makes me feel like a mess every time I look at her.

"Ms. Pearson, has Brandon fed?" she asks.

"Yes, he just ate about twenty minutes ago."

"Okay! I'll take him to the nursery now—we'll likely be gone a couple hours."

"Actually I was hoping to follow you there and watch."

"Are you sure?" she asks, obviously surprised. "It really would be best for you to use this time to sleep. You need to get as much sleep as you can so you have strength to take care of him."

"Okay," I relent.

She swaddles Brandon in a blue blanket and places him in his little baby bed on wheels and takes him out of the room. I think of Jenny telling me how she suddenly had a fit of panic when the nurse took her son the first time. I want to yell out too, but I don't have Jenny's assertiveness.

On a rational level I know he's safe in the hospital, but still… I feel antsy when he's not next to me.

I put my head down on the pillow and close my eyes, but a few minutes later I'm still wide awake. I want to toss and turn but I can't move with the stitches.

Screw this. I throw the blanket off and slowly place my feet on the floor. I manage to stand and I find another gown to put over my bare behind.

I carefully make my way out of the room, holding my swollen stomach. It's painful. I use the handrails on the wall as I leave my room and walk down the hallway toward the nursery.

I realize my behavior is on the erratic side, but I want my baby. He's all I have.

I make my way past the elevators, still clutching the handrail. I feel a little dizzy. The elevator dings and I'm distracted by the sound. My hand slips off the rail and I lose my balance. I hit the floor, my shoulder taking the brunt of my fall. I feel the impact deeply in my stomach and the raw edges of my incision.

I look up to see a wheelchair coming toward me. I don't know if the aide pushing the chair sees me and I groan, overcome with panic.

"Miss, don't worry. I will call for help," the aide yells. He presses a button on a pager and the loud sound of static echoes through the hallway.

This is so embarrassing and stupid of me. Tears spill from my eyes as I hold my stomach. My fear increases when warm liquid runs along my fingers.

"I think I ripped open my stitches," I mutter through the cutting pain.

"Help is coming, Miss," the aide assures me. He glances at the man in the wheelchair. "Sorry sir. We will just wait for help." He glares at the pager and says something under his breath. "I'll be right back."

"That's okay," the man in the wheelchair responds with a deep husky voice. "You do whatever you need to get this woman help."

Half his face is covered in white gauze and he's pretty banged up on the parts that aren't covered. He looks like he's been to hell and back. "I'll stay here with you until someone comes to help." The side of his mouth I can see turns up. "It's not like I can go anywhere anyway," he says pointing to his casts. "I'm Ryder, by the way. Geez, where are my manners?" He leans forward and holds out his good hand to shake mine.

I look at him with wide eyes. I'm in fear of bleeding out on this floor and he's making introductions? What's wrong with him?

"Ryder… Ryder…" I feel woozy. Then everything goes blank.

***

"Hi there, Halo." Nurse Judy hovers over me, giving me a chiding grin. "You gave us quite a scare falling like that and passing out. You've been checked out and you're okay, but I think you've probably learned your lesson about walking on your own?"

"I have."

"You better take care of yourself so you can take care of that handsome baby boy," she says, putting her hands on her hips.

"I'm sorry… how is my little guy doing?" I look around the room, feeling a little panicked that I don't know where he is.

"He's fine. He's in the nursery."

"I would like to see my boy." I'm feeling groggy but I desperately want to see Brandon.

"I'll go get a chair—you stay put. You'll need to take it extra easy now that you've been stitched back up."

She leaves to find the chair and I have a sudden flashback of meeting a man in the hallway.

Judy returns and helps me into the chair. "Okay, let's go, Halo, easy and slow now."

"Thanks. You are so good to us." I smile up at her.

"I was once in your position—a single mom. I know what it's like. You need all the help you can get. Don't go acting all proud like you can do everything yourself because the only one who will suffer is that little boy." She rolls me down the hall and we finally pull up to the nursery's clear glass window. I see Brandon fast asleep and peaceful in the little incubator machine. Judy leaves me, and I place my hand on the glass and let out a slow breath.

I want to reach out and touch him. *Oh, Brandon, I hope I do right by you. I feel like I have so much to learn. I wish I could give you a daddy because you deserve a daddy.*

"Which one's yours?" a voice from behind interrupts my intense thoughts.

"The one in the incubator," I respond without looking away from my baby. I should turn my head and not be rude, but my baby is all that matters to me now.

"He looks like a tough little guy," the deep voice continues. I feel like I'm being rude so I pull my gaze from Brandon and look over to the stranger.

"Aren't you..."

"Yeah, I watched you take that fall. How're you doing? Probably better than me." He laughs. He looks back to the hospital attendant who is standing behind his wheelchair. "Sir, can you give me a few minutes here before we head back to the room?"

"Sure, man, I'll be back in ten," the hospital attendee replies.

"I'm okay. I just gave birth. He's my first. I'm still learning." I don't know why I'm explaining anything to this complete stranger. I should maybe be scared, but he looks like he is too broken to cause any harm.

"Well, I wish I could offer advice... I guess I don't have children." He stares into the nursery.

"You guess?" I ask with confusion. You would think a person would know if they had kids or not.

"Yeah, I've got amnesia. I was fighting in Afghanistan and my team was ambushed by a roadside bomb. Apparently our vehicle exploded and everyone died except for me." I watch him and wait for some sort of reaction but he doesn't have one.

I can't help but think about Thomas as I look at this man's scarred face. I assume that Thomas is still on active duty. If something happened to him, I guess I would be informed. Unless he removed me as his next of kin. I don't know what plans he made after the divorce.

My sorrow—about this man and about Thomas—must show on my face, because he says, "Don't be so upset. I can't remember shit. I just know that I feel like I was hit by a ton of bricks. More than half my body is either broken or incinerated."

"I'm so sorry," I respond and tears begin to roll down my face uncontrollably. "I don't know what's gotten into me." I swipe at my tears. I'm usually not so emotional. When Thomas would tell me stories about Afghanistan I put up a tough front so he would feel comfortable talking to me about it.

"I don't mean to be upsetting you," he says. "I've been in and out of hospitals for four months now. I woke up in a hospital in Germany back in September. Then I was transported to a base in Washington DC before they sent me here for some specialized surgeries. I don't have any family. I will be transferred to the VA hospital soon. I can't imagine having to live in a hospital, but it is what it is." His eyes are unfocused—as if he's trying to call on memories he's not sure are there. "I don't know if it's a usual thing for me to be talking to a stranger about my problems. I just don't know." He shakes his head slightly. *Poor guy!*

"I'm sorry… It's Ryder. Right?"

"Yeah. Ryder St. John," he replies with a sure nod. "And you are?"

"I'm Halo." I smile, but I don't extend my hand. He's still a stranger in a hospital.

"Halo. That's an interesting name."

"Yeah, I get that a lot." I give him a quirky grin. Story of my life, people commenting on my name. "It must be tough. I'm sorry you have to go through so much." It's awful that he feels so alone, that there are so few options for soldiers injured during active duty. I've heard about so many sad cases—about men who returned to their families facing huge roadblocks in a new life.

"Well, I have a final surgery on this leg of mine. Then more skin grafts on my face, then…a long road ahead of me. Physical therapy…" He pauses with a pained look on his face. The hospital attendee returns.

"I better be getting you back to your room, sir." He steps behind Ryder's wheelchair and looks down at him.

"Yeah, sure thanks," he replies with a gruff voice. "Well, it was nice talking to you again, Halo. I'm glad to see you are okay after that fall." The right side of his mouth turns up slightly.

"Bye, Ryder. You take care." I smile at him as the aide wheels the chair away.

He looks so lost and alone. I kind of relate. I turn my head toward the nursery. They're taking Brandon out of the incubator. I ask the nurse with a hand motion if she is bringing him to me and she nods. I watch as they exit the nursery. The nurse places him in my arms again and my heart swells with love as I look down at him.

Oh, Brandon! I don't want to fail you as a parent. I want to give you everything I can.

The reality is that I have to put him into daycare in only two months. It's the amount of time I am given for paid maternity leave. I get six weeks of paid leave then I'm using two weeks of sick days. I would love to stay home longer with him, but I need to plan ahead. I have to save for a rainy day.

If Thomas were here he would tell me I worry too much, and to take things one day at a time. But he isn't here and I have decisions I need to make. Do I take Jenny up on her offer to move in with her? It seems overwhelming. I hate to impose.

It's hard not to feel helpless as the nurse wheels me back to my room. She places Brandon in the small bassinet and helps me into bed. She tells me I should expect a longer hospital stay because of my ripped stitches. After she leaves I notice the bed on the other side of the double room is now occupied. The new mother is asleep and her baby is fussing loudly. The world feels like it's closing in on me. I can't wait to leave.

CHAPTER THREE

May 17, 2000
Halo

Thomas said he would come pick me up later, but I decide to surprise him. I have my driver's license even though I don't do much driving since I don't own a car. My parents usually insist on taking me places.

I quickly slip on a pair of blue jeans and a coral-colored T-shirt. The weather is warming up but the evenings are cool, so I grab my jean jacket on the way out.

My father has a conference in New York City this weekend. I was more than excited when Mom said she would join him. They've never left me alone before. I grab the car keys and lock up the house.

Walking down the driveway to my Father's black Cadillac Escalade, I'm feeling a little antsy. Or maybe just excited. The SUV is big and I hope I don't put any dents in it. I pull out of the driveway, finding it hard to maneuver down the narrow street.

I know Thomas's address, but I've never been to his house. We've been together for sixteen months and I'd like a visual of the place he goes to when we aren't together. I'm more than curious about where the boy I've fallen in love with spends his time. As I pass Sheridan and head over to East Rogers Park, I notice the buildings look older and a little grungier.

I finally pull up to an apartment building that matches the address I saw on Thomas's license. Parking the Escalade takes all my nerves. I seem to be the chief entertainment for a group of boys with red and black bandanas on their heads hanging out on the sidewalk.

Maybe this wasn't such a good idea. I'm in the parking spot now, though, and I tell myself to be brave and persevere. I grab my little backpack with my cell phone inside and head out of the car toward the front door of the building. As I walk, the boys begin to cheer and whistle. My heart plummets further. Maybe this isn't a good idea. Thomas may come here every night, but Thomas is big, tall and very strong. I look like a skinny wimp next to him. Ignoring them, I slip quickly into the building's entrance.

I look around, my hands clutching my backpack tightly. The door I just came through opens behind me, and I swivel quickly, holding my breath. It's a short older woman clutching onto her purse like me. She smiles at me and uses her key to open the entryway's inner door. She turns to hold the door for me and I follow her in. I guess I don't look like much of a threat. The older lady goes to open her mailbox and I wait for the elevator.

The elevator is old, and the stench of smelly socks permeates the small, enclosed space. The elevator jerks to a stop and I step off. The hallway smells like cooking food *and* smelly socks.

I'm not sure which environment is worse. I stroll down the hallway along the old rubbed-out burgundy carpets while I keep my eyes on the numbers on the doors, looking for number 806. I knock lightly on the door. The Beastie Boys are blaring in the background and the raspy voice of an older man sounds loudly through what must be very thin wood.

Thomas hollers, "I'll get it it's probably one of your whores anyway." My jaw drops. I want to turn and run away. The door flies open. Thomas's blue eyes go round when he takes me in. "Ah, Halo, what are you doing here? I thought we said I would come get you," he says, running his hand through his dark brown hair. His eyes look unfocused.

"I thought I would surprise you. I'm now thinking this is a bad idea," I respond as my heart sinks in my chest. I bite my lip, unsure what to do next.

An old raspy voice hollers, "Well send her in." My blood turns cold...

"It's not for you," Thomas turns his head and yells back. Then he looks at me and rolls his eyes while smiling nervously. He's clearly trying to cover for his father's revolting words.

"What do you mean, asshole? No one would come here for a piece of shit like you." His father sounds irritated as his voice grows louder and becomes clearer. I sense he's headed this way. This is bad!

I feel a light breeze as the apartment door behind me whips open and I startle.

"Thomas what's going on out here?" A middle-aged woman with blond hair stands in the doorway, her hands on her hips.

"Sorry, Miss Randall." Thomas lowers his head. The woman's tough stance slackens as she takes in the scene and her eyes turn soft.

"Thomas, you go get this nice girl home and fast," she orders with a calm voice while looking at Thomas sympathetically. A young man walks up to the door in her apartment. He has Down Syndrome. He looks like he must be our age with dark blond hair and brown eyes. His brows are drawn together as he looks to his mother for answers.

"Is everything okay, Mama?" he asks.

"Yes, you go back in and finish your work," she says patiently to the boy. Then she turns her attention back to Thomas. "Thomas just needs to take his friend home," she explains and he shrugs, turning away from the door.

A man who looks about twenty years older than Thomas

approaches the front door. He's the same height as Thomas, only he has bad posture and brown eyes. He must be drunk by the way he's swaying.

"What did you say, you dumbfuck?" He whacks Thomas across the head with a heavy hand. I wince. The man turns his attention to me. A lazy smile spreads slowly across his lips as he leans on the doorframe. He smells like he hasn't showered in a while. I take a step back.

"Thomas," Miss Randall cuts in. "Now."

Thomas looks frozen in his spot.

"Well, well, well, what do we have here? A young little whore. Do you want to get up in my bits?" he asks and I take another step back, cringing. Thomas's face contorts and it's as if he snaps out of whatever was distracting him a moment ago. My chest constricts as I begin to get a clearer picture of the type of life he leads.

"Halo, please go. I'm sorry. I'd walk you to your car, but—" He looks at his father and then at me. "Wait. How did you get here?" he asks quietly with confusion in his tone.

"My father's car," I reply anxiously. This was a mistake. I need to get out of here.

"Thomas, take the girl yourself and make sure she gets to her car okay," Miss Randall orders with a motherly tone. Thomas's gaze bounces from Miss Randall to me and then to his father. His eyes look distant and confused.

"I'm going," Thomas says, looking at his father. It's a statement not a question. I'm guessing he's never defied his father before.

"Going? Going where the fuck do you think you're going? She's a stupid whore. You don't go following after stupid whores." He punches the door without flinching. "Go fuck yourself, Miss Randall. You probably need a good fuck, anyway." He waves a hand toward the poor sweet woman.

“Would you shut up?” Thomas snaps.

Miss Randall retreats into her apartment.

His father’s eyes roll and he straightens his shoulders. “You stupid fuck,” he mutters.

Thomas steps out of the apartment quickly, forgetting to put on a pair of shoes. He takes me by the arm, guiding me back toward the elevator. My pulse is frantic.

“I need to get you back to your car. I need you to lock your doors once you’re in there. Drive home and forget about me,” he says as if he’s giving me the weather report in Canada.

“What?” I ask, completely stunned. He isn’t being rough but he needs me gone. I understand he’s trying to protect me, but… The elevator descends while his jaw is ticking nervously and he presses the elevator buttons as if he’s trying to make it go faster. We arrive on the main level and he takes my hand, pulling me forward.

“Thomas, I…”

“Halo, please. I don’t need your sympathy.” He continues to guide me by the arm like I’m an errant child, pulling me toward my car.

“Thomas, you’re barefoot,” I say looking at his feet. I don’t know what else to say. We get to the car. I notice some key scratches along the side. My father is going to kill me.

Thomas opens the door for me and I step inside. Leaning into the door, he says, “I’m sorry, Halo. I never meant for you to see this part of my life. I don’t know who I was kidding by dating you.” He shakes his head. “I was clearly kidding myself. Go home and wipe your mind clean where I’m concerned.” His eyes look like they’re welling with tears that may never be shed.

“Thomas, don’t be ridiculous. I don’t care about your father. You’re clearly different. Don’t let that man define you.” I say the words assertively but it doesn’t matter. He bows his head and begins to shake it from side to side. I wonder if he's heard me at all or if he's intentionally blocking out my words.

"Halo, please go," he pleads and it's almost a whisper. He won't even look me in the eye. He pulls away, hits the power locks, closes the door. I watch in the rear-view mirror as he runs back inside with his head still bowed.

CHAPTER FOUR

January 21, 2008
Halo

I'm making slow progress. Nurse Judy comes by often to help me get out of bed, because if I don't start moving around, I'll be in trouble when I go home alone. The doctor says my new stitches are healing nicely. Brandon's breathing is clear and his jaundice is all better too, which means we may be leaving the hospital soon.

I've had enough of this place. My roommate just got released to go home with her husband and baby. I have to admit how incredibly jealous I feel that they got to go home as a family.

I find myself staring at the door to my room, hoping that Thomas will surprise us.

I had done the same thing at home—waiting endless lonely nights hoping that Thomas would walk through the door at the moment I needed him most. He always told me I was his saving grace. I need him to be mine now.

"Brandon, how about we go visit a friend?" I coo at him even though he's fast asleep. I watch his little exhales and inhales. He's so sweet. I press the call button for the nurse's station. It's five p.m. and Nurse Judy is on duty. I don't know how I would have made it through all this without her.

"Yes, dear," her sweet voice comes through the speaker.

"I'm sorry to bother you, but I thought Brandon and I could go visit Ryder. He mentioned he's having a surgery today. I don't think he has any relatives..." I wonder if Nurse Judy will think I'm crazy. But Ryder is a wounded soldier who deserves honor and respect and I would like to at least offer him some comfort if he's in pain.

Apparently Judy doesn't think my request is a bad idea and soon she's wheeling me down the hall. It's too far to walk in my state. I hold Brandon in my arms as we make our way to the wing of the hospital where Ryder is staying. I hope he doesn't think I'm a stalker.

She wheels me into his room and gives me a knowing wink. "Just buzz me when you want a ride back," she says. I think she thinks I like Ryder, but it's not like that at all.

He's lying in bed. His face is fully bandaged now. The white gauze is wrapped around his head, covering most of his face. There is an opening for his eyes, which are blue and bloodshot. There is an opening for his nose and mouth. Poor guy. I wonder how he will look when the bandages are off. The cast is off his leg and he's now wearing a brace. His stare is blank.

He turns his head slightly to acknowledge us. "Hello," he says with a tired, raspy voice.

"Hi! Hope it's okay we came to check on you. You know...after your surgery."

"Thank you. I feel like I should be the one checking on you after your nasty fall." His voice is gruff. He must still be woozy from surgery.

"I'm okay."

"You should be more careful. You have a baby to take care of."

"You're right. It was stupid of me. This is all new to me, being a mother. I wanted to see Brandon so badly I wasn't thinking."

"It means you're a good mother. That's nice."

"So how did it go? You don't have the cast anymore," I say, looking down at his leg.

"Getting rid of the cast is a relief. At least now I can scratch my itches. I'll have the brace on for a good month. I'm told it went well. My skin should heal. I may have a few slight scars along my cheeks. During my last surgery my nose was reset and my cheekbones were restructured." He chuckles softly. "I really don't remember what I'm supposed to look like, so the change in my appearance won't make a difference. Now my left knee has some screws in it and I'll probably have a slight limp the rest of my life," he explains matter-of-factly. "Guess I fared well considering men died in the ambush. I wish I could remember them. Their names… something, my mind is blank. Makes me feel like shit. I'm sorry… I'm probably talking about myself a little too much here. You have a little baby. You don't need to hear my problems."

"Actually I'm happy to listen. I really don't mind. I'm glad your surgeries went well."

"How about you, Halo? Where is the boy's father?"

His question makes me feel like I've been slapped, but I know I need to start getting used to answering it. "His father is a SEAL," I tell him.

"And where is he?" Ryder asks. With his face all bandaged up it's hard for me to gage what he's thinking.

"He's on active duty. I don't know where he is. We aren't married anymore," I admit. It's always hard to say those words out loud. The reality of them hurts.

"Oh! Must be tough," he mutters. "I mean, being on your own." He lifts his hand to his face. "Shit! This itching is going to drive me nuts."

"Oh no! You're itchy under the gauze?" I ask, feeling sorry for him.

"Yeah. I was told not to touch my face at all, but these damn bandages are itchy."

"How much longer do you have to be in here?" I ask, trying to take his mind off his present state.

"I leave tomorrow. I'll have to go to the VA Hospital."

"So you think you'll have to stay there for a while?" I ask. I know I'm prying. This man is a stranger. He doesn't have a family. He doesn't know who he is. I feel bad for him. I know what it's like to have no one to rely on.

There's a light knock on the door and I turn my head.

"Uh, Halo… Hi." Jenny appears in the doorway. I know she's wondering what Brandon and I are doing in this wing of the hospital visiting a complete stranger.

"Hey, Jenny, come in," I say, motioning to her. "This is Ryder."

She walks into the room hesitantly, giving me a sideways look.

"Hi, Jenny. Nice to meet you," Ryder responds with a low, deep voice.

She nods at Ryder and then looks at me. "So I just spoke to your nurse—she told me where you were. There's a good chance you guys will be released tomorrow. I can drop by after work and take you home. Dave installed the base for the infant car seat in my car, and we're all ready to have you stay with us."

I feel kind of embarrassed discussing this in front of a stranger, but Jenny doesn't leave me a lot of choice. "I was thinking Brandon and I would go home," I tell her. "I've had extra time in the hospital. I've been walking around a bit. I can set things up for us on the main floor so I don't have to do the stairs too often at the beginning. I think we'll manage." I smile hesitantly because I know Jenny isn't going to take this well.

"Let's go back to your room, please," she snaps. Yup, I was right.

"Jenny, I love you. And I appreciate everything…" I pause and my gaze focuses on Ryder's bandaged face. Suddenly an idea hits me. "I think I have a solution," I announce as a light bulbs continue to turn on in my head.

"What?" Jenny asks, crossing her arms over her chest, her eyes wide.

Ryder seems just as interested as he turns his head to look at me.

Maybe I feel a connection to him because of Thomas. Maybe it's because I know we're both alone and needy. Or it could be I'm thinking of the bigger picture—the concept of honoring those who have stood for our freedom and the idea of setting a good example for my son. I've met a lot of SEALS in my life. Friends of Thomas's. They've all been honourable, determined and trustworthy. There is also the fact that I feel like I've been granted a miracle. Brandon's delivery shook me to the core. When his heart beat slowed it was the scariest moment in my life. God has blessed me and now he has placed this broken man in my path. Maybe it is my job to offer him a hand. Yes, he could stay at a military facility, but that seems like a cold and lonely place to be, a last resort.

"Well," I say. "I have the garage apartment set up." I focus on Ryder's bandaged face. "Ryder, would you be interested in renting the space from me? It isn't very large, but it's enough space for one person. I could use the rent money and I'm guessing you don't have a place when you're released from the hospital..."

Jenny's jaw goes slack and Ryder slowly nods his head. "That sounds good," he responds.

Wow! That was a quick response. He must have been dreading staying at a military facility. I was right.

"Halo, I'm sorry," Jenny says, her blue eyes snapping fire at me. "But this is fucking crazy. You don't know this guy from Adam. He could be a serial killer for all you know. He may be a wounded soldier, but he is still a stranger. This is plain stupid." She throws her hands up in the air. Then she moves closer and looks down at Brandon, "I'm sorry for the bad words little guy," she coos.

"Jenny, how could you say that?" I ask, feeling thoroughly insulted.

She winces. "I'm sorry. I don't mean to come across as harsh. I'm just worried."

Yes, I know she's right to worry. Because I don't know anything about Ryder St. John. I'm just going on instinct—he seems so alone and lost. That was me when my parent's died and Thomas saved me. And that is me now facing the biggest challenge of my life, parenthood.

"I don't *think* I'm a serial killer," Ryder says, mild humor in his voice. "But you can speak to my doctors. I can show you my release papers from the navy. I am being compensated so I can pay rent." His gaze shifts to the baby in my arms. "I wouldn't even mind giving you a hand with the little guy. I don't know if I have any experience with children, though. I just can't do much moving for about a week 'cause of the grafts."

I nod my head at Jenny. "Satisfied?" I ask.

"Satisfied? Satisfied? Halo, I am seriously worried that you are even considering this. You have a little baby to take care of and this man is a stranger. People—no, actually not people—*new mothers* don't allow strange men near their infant sons. I'm worried about you, Halo." Her short blonde hair is tied back in a small ponytail and she's wearing a white puffy winter jacket and a pair of tight blue jeans. Her face is flushed and she places her hands on her waist, squaring her eyes at me.

"I don't think he's dangerous." I shrug, wondering if I've finally lost my sanity.

She pulls her phone out of the back pocket of her jeans.

"What are you doing?" I ask, furrowing my brows.

"I'm calling Dave. I want him to come meet Ryder and see what he thinks," she says, glaring at her phone.

I look over to Ryder and mouth, "Sorry."

He nods. His response is totally laidback. There doesn't seem to be anything dangerous about him.

Jenny begins to rant on the phone. I'm completely embarrassed that she's showing no filter where Ryder is concerned. He doesn't seem to care either way. She gets off the phone and places it back in her pocket.

"Dave will be here in the morning. He will talk to the doctors who know Ryder here as long as Ryder consents. If everything pans out, fine." She purses her lips. Then she walks over to me and gives me a hug and places a small kiss on Brandon's forehead. "Bye for now," she says and then she turns on her heel and leaves the room.

I know her intentions are good, but it's hard to imagine moving in with her and adding to her already chaotic household. I have never been one to impose and I don't know if I can handle her busy household.

Ryder is quiet for a few moments. "Are you sure about this?" he asks finally. "You don't have to do this. I will figure out where I am going."

"Yes, Ryder. I am sure about it. Do you know what role you played in the military?" I know Jenny is right in that I should find out some basic information about him.

"They tell me I was a SEAL," he answers solemnly.

"Oh." My chest constricts and it's suddenly hard to breathe. "Where were you when you got hurt?"

"In Afghanistan."

"Which team were you with?" I ask. My heart is hammering so hard I can barely breathe.

"Team Six." he answers with that same calm, cool voice. He

doesn't realize how his information is affecting me.

"Have you heard about how your team members are doing lately?" I know Ryder's memory was affected by his accident. But there's a chance he might have heard some recent news about his fellow SEALs. I long for information about Thomas. At the same time, I don't know what I would do if heard something had happened to him…

"No. Nothing specific."

"Okay," I answer calmly. I need to remember that the reason I haven't heard from him is not because he was hurt. He's chosen not to stay in contact.

Accept it for what it is, Halo, and move on.

I try to think of good things to ask Ryder. But it's hard to ask a guy with memory loss about his life. "So," I say. "Have the doctors and therapists you've been working with been able to give you much information about *you*—about your past and the things you're unable to remember?"

"Not much. I didn't read my file in depth. The surgeries and therapy have taken up most of my time and energy. The doctors told me to focus on getting better physically first."

That makes sense. He's been through a lot.

"And you would want to rent the space? I need four hundred dollars a month." I need to be upfront about money. The extra income will ease my worries a bit. Especially since I will be putting Brandon into the care of a caregiver who will give him one- on-one attention. It costs an arm and a leg.

"Yeah, seems like a good solution for a guy who doesn't know who he is or what he wants. I have a psychogenic amnesia, it means I've repressed my memory because of severe stress. The doctor's think it's a bad case of PTSD from the explosion. I was awake and disoriented when I was found. My memory was supposed to return by now. The doctors aren't sure if or when my memory will come back. In the meantime, it would be a relief not to be surrounded by guys who served—I can't exactly swap stories about my time, you know?"

"I can understand that." Once again I'm impressed by the kindness in his eyes and his quiet resolve about his situation. "I hope you'll find some answers soon. I recently went through something difficult of my own and I know how hard it is to heal when something goes wrong."

He smiles warmly. "You don't know how much your words mean to me right now. Feels great to talk to someone other than a doctor or nurse or therapist about this kind of thing."

I smile back. "I'm glad I can help in any way." I respected Thomas's dedication to his mission and it's easy to respect Ryder—a guy who has so obviously given up so much—for his dedication too. I look down at Brandon. He's beginning to fuss. "I better get going. This little guy needs to eat. I'll be in touch tomorrow about making arrangements for the apartment."

"Sure, sounds like a plan." Ryder answers. For a moment he looks like a lost boy. I use Ryder's call button to ask the nursing station to call the post-partum ward. Nurse Judy arrives a few minutes later to bring me back to my room, it's strangely hard to leave.

CHAPTER FIVE

Past
August 18th 2000
Halo

"Thanks, Mom. Thanks, Dad. The cake was unreal." I give each of my parents a peck on the cheek. When I take our plates to the sink, I can feel them glaring at me. I'm expecting this reaction. They don't want me to leave.

"I thought you would stay home and hang out with us," my mom says with a soft voice. "It's your seventeenth birthday."

I feel bad, but the reason why I'm leaving is because they wouldn't invite Thomas to share in the celebration. Besides, it seems like a normal thing for a seventeen-year-old to go out with her boyfriend on her birthday.

If my parents only knew how respectful Thomas really was they wouldn't be behaving this way. I know most of their issues with him have to do with their idea that he's lower class—and that makes me see red. Also, it makes me extremely reluctant to take any of their advice.

He wants to take me to the lake so I quickly head up to my room to change.

I like what I see in the mirror—the white sundress looks good with my auburn hair. I roll on some cherry-red lip gloss and spritz some vanilla mist on my neck. I put on sandals and head down the stairs, hoping not to meet the scrutinizing glare of my parents again. To avoid another argument, I decide to wait on the front porch.

As minutes tick by, nerves flutter in my chest. He's usually punctual. I worry that he was really insulted over not being asked to dinner. He shrugged it off like he shrugs off most things, but I could tell he was hurt by my parents' rejection. It hurts me too that they can't respect the fact that I love him.

Finally I hear the roar of his bike coming down the street. Usually he gets off the bike to come greet me or say hello to my parents. Tonight he pulls into the drive but doesn't budge. I walk over to him, feeling tension crackling in the air. My heart skips a beat when I see his eye is black and the edge of his nose is rimmed with blood.

"Hey, baby," he says with a wide smile as if he doesn't look like hell.

I climb on the back of the bike and grasp Thomas around the waist. "What happened?" I ask, brushing my lip against his ear.

"It's nothing." He shrugs and revs the engine.

"That's not nothing, Thomas."

"Let's just get to the lake and talk there. I feel like your mother is watching us through the window." He's probably right.

He heads toward the lake and when we get to Sheridan we go north. We drive for ten, fifteen minutes, heading up through the suburbs. I'm wondering where we're headed when he answers my unasked question "I'm taking you someplace different tonight," he calls out above the wind brushing his face. "We need a private venue for what I have planned."

I can feel the tension radiating from his body as we wind through roads leading past big houses—amazing mansions that look over the lake and have private beaches. We turn down a narrow road and a beach comes into view. We park in a secluded spot close to a path that leads to the water. The place is dark but I feel safe with Thomas. He retrieves a blanket from his saddlebag and we head for a grassy area that's shielded from the breeze and totally out of sight from any pathways or houses. I've never been on this part of the lake before and it's beautiful—like we're worlds away from any other people or the city.

After we get settled, I place my hand on his arm. "Will you please tell me what happened to you?"

"You don't want to know," he answers with a clipped tone. His jaw is rigid and every muscle on his outstretched legs is taut. I've never seen him like this before.

"What's gotten into you?" I ask softly.

When he looks at me there's pain in his dark blue eyes. "It was just a bad night. But now I'm with you and I want to celebrate." His smile seems forced.

"Thomas, I can see you're upset." The lake is calm. It's a warm, beautiful night and it makes me sad Thomas can't enjoy it with me. I flex my fingers against his arm, silently urging him to talk to me. The sky is clear, the stars sprinkle the midnight blue sky, radiating light into the dark world. Tonight should be special for Thomas and me.

"I did something, Halo." He hangs his head low. His knees are pulled up to his chest and his arms are clenched around his knees. He looks like he's protecting himself from something. Anxiety makes my heart race. This is bad. I can feel it in my bones.

"Tell me, Thomas. You can always tell me. That's what makes us *us*. We talk, we share." My voice cracks. I can't stand to see him in pain.

"You aren't going to want to hear this," he warns.

"Just tell me. I'll listen whether I like it or not."

"You're going to leave. I don't want you to leave."

"I'm not leaving. Have a little faith." I want to reassure him. I know he has issues about being left.

"Oh, Halo. 'Faithless is he that says farewell when the road darkens'." He gazes into my eyes and takes my hands.

"Tolkien." I grin.

"My bookworm." He kisses my forehead, his lips lingering. "You won't like to hear this, Halo..." He pauses to take a breath. "But I went with a crew and helped them lift a delivery truck."

"What does that mean in English, Thomas?"

The question earns me a huff and a laugh.

He drops my hands. "It means I helped a bunch of guys steal stuff off a truck. Then I took my cut." He stares at me as if he's waiting for me to get up and run. At the same time I notice the muscle in his jaw is ticking and his knee has begun to bounce.

He's such a dichotomy. There's the good Thomas who is trying to remain civilized despite the hardships he lives with every day. And there's the bad Thomas who succumbs to the dark reality he is faced with. I know most humans battle the good and the bad in their lives. I just hope in Thomas's case that the good will prevail. I have faith that it will.

"Why?" is the only word I can form.

"Why, Halo? Because I don't have money. I hang around people that scrape to get by. I am bad blood. My father is an alcoholic who beats me and my mother couldn't get away from me fast enough. Your parents were right not to have me over to their house tonight. Bad blood shouldn't be mixing with the likes of you and your family." The words are knife-edged. I can feel them pierce my heart. I knew he was upset that he was excluded from my family's birthday celebration, but I never expected him to do something so rash.

I put my arms around him. "My mother has her own issues. I'm pretty sure it has nothing to do with you. My parents are being ridiculous and unfair. I feel responsible that you went out tonight to prove them right. You may have stolen tonight, but you can always give it back. You can always make this right. You are not bad blood; you are not a thief. I love you with all my heart and if you have faith in me, faith in us, then you would understand how much you mean to me. I know my words are meaningless to you. I know you have to believe those good things about yourself, but they are all true." I cry into his neck. He releases the grip he has on his knees and wraps me in his strong arms. I fall into his lap and he presses his forehead to mine. "You are not faithless, so don't say farewell."

"You're so perfect, Halo. I don't get what you see when you look at me." He says this like it's a prayer.

"I see a guy who loves with all his heart. I love our talks, your honesty. I love the way you love me and do things to make me happy. My body sings with life when you're near, Thomas. I've never felt anything like this before."

"I know..." He squeezes his eyes shut, gritting his teeth. "I know." In his words I feel his feelings for me. His pain. My parents are jerks for making him feel worse.

"Please don't pull away. Stop hanging around those thieves. If you continue to steal, you'll ruin your chances with the navy. You've been working so hard. You can't mess that up now."

"I may have already messed things up. Cops showed up tonight. I ran away in time but I'm not sure if they got a good look at me. If they did, I'm screwed." He runs his hand roughly over his mouth.

"I'll cover for you this time, but please promise me no more nonsense. No more talk about bad blood. I love you. I can't hear it," I insist even though my stomach is in knots. I'm worried he'll be arrested.

As I sit in his lap, he brushes his lips softly against mine. "I bought you something," he says, leaning back and pulling a box out of his front jean pocket. "And no I didn't steal it. I used clean money I made at the mechanic shop." He opens the box. Inside is a gold chain with a heart charm attached to it.

I gasp and my hands come up to cover my mouth. "Thomas, it's beautiful."

He takes the chain out of the box and places it around my neck. I lift my hair out of the way so he can see what he's doing. He clips it on and gives my neck a soft kiss that sends shivers down my spine. I look down at the heart locket, feeling giddy.

"Thank you." I place a soft kiss on his lips.

He leans forward to kiss my neck and begins spreading slow, soft kisses up toward my earlobe. The kisses intensify and I feel his tongue spreading heat across my nape. I roll my head, reveling in the sensation and a little moan escapes my lips.

"Oh, Halo. I know what you want, baby. I just don't know why you want it to be me."

I know exactly what he's talking about—I'd asked him to sleep with me tonight.

"Thomas, I only want you. I've only ever wanted you. No one can get me this stirred up. Only you." I brush my thumb along his jaw.

"Keep talking, baby. I like to hear how stirred up I get you." He slowly lowers me onto my back. We had fooled around quite a bit, trying pretty much everything except for actual sex. There's no way he's backing down from me now.

"I love you, Thomas. I want you to make love to me."

His guttural growl goes straight between my thighs, instantly soaking me. "Halo, I love you so dammed much. I've dreamed of hearing you saying those words to me. I hated this place until you came into my life. But I'm dying now because I don't want to leave you. The navy was supposed to be my escape, but I don't want to make love to you and then leave you behind. You're my ray of light. You are my only reason for living. I'm going to have to go soon, baby, but know I will always do everything I can to make my way back to you." His blue eyes make me promises his words would never be able to express.

"I know. I understand why the navy has been your dream. I get why you have to do this for you. Know that I'll be here waiting for you." As I say the last words, Thomas dips his head and presses his lips to mine, sucking my lower lip. He brushes his tongue along the opening of my mouth and our tongues meet and dance, erotically caressing each other. He presses his groin between my thighs and I can feel my inner thighs pulsating with need.

"Thomas, please," I beg.

"You are so sweet, Halo. You taste like a forbidden fruit but..."

"Don't do this to me please, I need you..." I beg.

"I know, baby... I know, I just..."

"Thomas, you are all I need. Please believe me." I want to finally penetrate the wall he has built around himself. The wall that makes him feel unworthy, the wall that obscures his judgment.

He lets out a loud growl. "I may not deserve you, but I am making you mine. I am going to brand you so that even if you figure out the truth it will only be me you think of."

He lifts my sundress over my head. I'm glad we came to this secluded place and not our regular spot on the lakefront. With urgency he unclips my bra and I arch my back, pressing my already taut nipples against his warm body. His mouth closes over my nipple. A strangled moan escapes my lips as I grip the back of his hair, tugging and pushing him closer to me. With his other hand, he tantalizes my other nipple.

I am all sensation and lust. In one swift movement, I remove his black T-shirt and throw it behind us into the grass. I run my hands over his pectorals and down his rock-solid abdomen. His body is firm and hot under my touch. My fingertips skim the front of his jeans and I feel his long, hard girth through the denim. I'd rubbed him with my hand before, and I'd even used my mouth on him, so I know how large and thick he is. Despite my nerves, I need him inside me so bad.

"You are my saving grace, Halo," he whispers as he kisses his way down my abdomen.

I don't have any sexy lingerie, so when he makes his way to my panties and shoves his nose between my legs, inhaling and growling, I almost lose it. He has this special way of making me feel sexy. His hands are big and rough-skinned from work. I love the way his roughness meshes with my soft skin. He presses his palm against my inner thighs and slides a finger inside me while he lowers my panties with his other hand. "You are so pure and perfect. Thank you for this gift." I let out a loud moan as his finger explores me. Thomas's expression is heated and his cheeks look flushed.

He withdraws his finger and the loss of his touch is agony. He slips his finger into his mouth, tasting me. "So sweet."

He lowers himself, dipping his head between my thighs. His tongue slowly licks my clit. I'm seeing rainbows, beautiful rainbows. My body is bowing to his hot tongue as it runs up and down my folds. He moves with such grace I know I will be coming apart at the seams in moments.

"Thomas, please." I'm overcome with lust. This night, this place is perfectly romantic. The water sparkles from the moonlight. The sky is clear and the air is fresh. There isn't a soul in sight which is good. The trees are close together and I don't know who in their right mind would venture in here at night. Thomas assured me I was safe and I feel safe with him. My orgasm is so close that any coherence leaves my thoughts.

"Scream, baby. I want to hear you scream my name."

"Oh, Thomas! Oh, oh, oh." I moan loudly as the strongest orgasm I've ever had rips through me. I feel like I'm having an out-of-body experience. My body tingles from the tips of my fingers to the tips of my toes. I'm elated. When I finally come back down to earth, Thomas is wearing a big grin, clearly proud of himself.

He slowly moves up my body and places a soft kiss on my lips. At first I'm taken aback at the taste of my arousal on his mouth.

"You see how sweet you are, Halo? You have no idea what you do to me."

I lower my hand to undo his jeans. I shove down his pants and boxers, caressing his ass along the way.

"Are you sure about this?" he asks as his nose glides across my neck.

"Yes. And now, Thomas Wells. You better make love to me."

He chuckles. "Aren't you insatiable, little miss Halo Pearson?"

"Only for you, Thomas." I sigh and that's all he needs for permission to reach over to his jeans and pull out a condom.

"I'm guessing you're not on birth control," he says shyly.

"No." I shake my head.

He rolls the condom over his cock, then reaches between my legs to circle my clit with his thumb. "I'm just going to make sure you're wet all over. It will make it easier for me to enter you."

My body responds to him instantly. I can't get enough of him or the idea that in a moment he'll be inside me.

"I love you and I want you to know how much you mean to me. I'm not a virgin, but I've never felt this way before. The girls in my past meant nothing. With you, I want this to last forever. I don't think I can ever let you go." His voice almost sounds sad.

"I don't want you to let me go," I tell him. "I can't see my life without you in it."

"I don't want to make you promises I can't keep. I don't know about marriages and happily ever after. I don't know what they look like or what I am supposed to do to get there."

"I think you're wrong about that. You may have had shitty parents but you always do nice things for me. I know my parents have been giving me a hard time lately but they've always been good to me and they've always loved each other. I know what happily ever after looks like and I want it with you." I press a kiss to his lips. His eyes close and our kiss continues. Thomas is in pain and so I'm in pain too.

"Let me love you," I say against his lips "Let me love you like you love me."

"You don't know how badly I want that, Halo." In this moment I understand that Thomas Wells has never been loved in his life. His mother left him and his father is cruel. Yet I can feel Thomas's love for me radiating off him in the most intense way. My heart is melting and reforming around his. In this moment we were melded together and in this moment I know our love will last an eternity.

"This is me and you, Thomas. Me and you forever."

"Yes, baby. Me and you forever," he confirms as the head of his cock meets my folds. I'm not scared. I know there may be some pain, but this is more than sex. It's me and Thomas joining ourselves forever and always. He uses his cock to rub my clit gently and my breath quickens.

"Please," I breathe out.

He slowly enters me and I feel myself stretching as he fills me. He goes slowly at first. "I love you, baby," he whispers, placing a soft kiss on my lips. At first he watches me closely, ensuring I'm okay. Then I feel my hips moving in rhythm to his thrusts and his eyes close and his face flushes. "You feel so good, so tight," he groans at the back of his throat. "I don't think I can hold on."

"Don't hold on. Let go, baby. This is me and you." And he lets go, picking up his rhythm. It's bittersweet pain and sensual lust mixed into love. He's grunting and I love how he's coming undone despite the fact I'm fighting through the pain.

"Are you okay?" he asks, likely sensing my discomfort. "We can stop," he offers.

"No. Don't even think it. I was expecting it to hurt the first time."

He moves slowly, controlling his movements.

"Please," I say. "I want you to let go. The pain isn't so bad. A few more times and I know I'll be enjoying this."

"I'll definitely make sure you enjoy this the next time. I can't hold on, though. Being inside you. You're so tight. So warm...." His words trail off and I feel him stiffen inside me. He's hot as hell when he comes undone.

I don't come, but I feel content. I just found the other half of myself. We're a whole now. I know these moments are rare and real for him.

He pulls out of me slowly so the condom won't slip off. He rolls to my side, panting. I place my head on his chest and listen to the beat of his heart, his chest rising and falling with each breath. He is completely a part of me now. As much as the thought scares me that he will soon leave, it also warms me to know he's promised to always come back.

I know I'm setting myself up for heartache—I don't have a choice. I didn't choose to love Thomas. It just is what it is. He owns my whole heart. I may be too young to understand what love is. But I know my own feelings. And Thomas Wells owns every part of me.

***

About two weeks later
September 2, 2000

"Halo, where are you going?" my mother asks as she comes down the stairs. She looks beautiful with her auburn hair blown pin-straight. She's wearing a short-sleeve, cream blouse and a black skirt. She looks fit and great for her age.

It's my parents' anniversary tonight. My father is supposed to be back from the hospital soon to take her for a nice dinner to celebrate thirty years of marriage.

"Thomas is picking me up," I tell her. "You look beautiful, Mom." I smile and give her a kiss on the cheek. "Happy anniversary."

"Thanks, Halo. I wanted to talk to you for a minute," she says with a hint of an apology. I roll my eyes. Of course this will be about Thomas.

"Honey, I was speaking to Mary Lou this week. She asked me if I knew that Thomas was arrested last week. I told her I had no idea and then she said, 'Oh well I know Halo hangs around that Wells boy all the time and I was wondering if you knew what happened'." As she repeats Mary Lou's words, her voice morphs from pleasant to angry.

"He wasn't arrested. He was brought in for questioning." My defenses are going up fast. "He had nothing to do with it. His friends got arrested and the police thought he was involved but he wasn't involved. He was with me at the time of the robbery." I hope my exasperation doesn't show in my voice. I lied for Thomas. I knew it was wrong and illegal, but he would have never gotten involved to begin with if my parents hadn't made him feel like he wasn't good enough.

"So now you are providing that boy with alibis? Is this the type of daughter I've raised?" She tilts her head as she looks down on me. I hate that look.

"Mom, I didn't provide him with anything. It was true. We were by the lake that evening." It was the best night of my life. Of course I remembered it.

Do I feel guilty about lying to my mom? I did. There were no ifs, ands or buts about it. I also felt that she was the one who had put my back to the wall when she didn't include Thomas in the family celebration of my birthday. The lie was therefore justified.

"What is that supposed to mean? Did you sleep with that boy, Halo? Because boys like him are only interested in one thing and once you give it to them they are gone." Her voice has gone shaky. There was definitely someone from her past who had hurt her. Too bad she had to compare this no-name to Thomas. "Besides," she says, "he obviously hangs around kids who are trouble."

A part of her statement was true. I knew some of the people Thomas knew were bad news. What my mom didn't understand was how far Thomas had come considering his circumstances.

"Mom, Thomas is not like that. He is wonderful and amazing and I wish you would give him a chance. I love him and I don't plan on breaking up with him. Thomas is smart. He wants to enlist in the navy..." I pause because it doesn't seem like she's even listening to me.

She looks worried and exasperated. Her gaze meets mine. "You've slept with him," she says with a wounded voice. It's not a question.

I sigh, hating how she has turned something beautiful in my eyes to something ugly in hers. "Yes," I answer. I am seventeen years old. I shouldn't have to explain this to my mother or feel bad about loving somebody. Suddenly my annoyance turns to anger. I will not give her the power of making my relationship with Thomas something bad or dirty.

"This is all bullshit, honestly," I tell her. "You brought me here from LA. Thomas Wells is the first thing here for me that's felt right and good. And yes I love him. I shouldn't have to feel bad about that," I holler while my mother looks back at me with wide brown eyes. It's as if she's looking at a stranger.

"You listen here…" She points a finger at my face. "I warned you, Halo. Your father and I will never accept him and he will only end up breaking your heart." I wince at the sound of her shrill voice.

I hear Thomas's motorcycle pull up to the house. I turn to the door and look back at my mother. "I'm leaving. If you can't accept Thomas then you don't accept me." I put on my new black leather boots and slam the door behind me, feeling enraged as I stomp toward the motorcycle. Thomas pulls off his helmet. He stares at me warily before he passes me the helmet.

His brows are furrowed as he asks, "What's going on? You look pissed."

"Let's go," I answer. I've never spoken to my mom like that before and I feel shaky.

I try to clear my mind as we drive to the lake. Even though it's early evening, the air is hot and humid. We park near Rogers Beach and as we walk down the sidewalk, I regret that I didn't put on a bathing suit under my shorts and top. The lake looks calm and refreshing and I'm tempted to jump in.

"It's a pretty hot day do you want to find a place in the shade?" Thomas asks. He takes his saddlebag and places it on his shoulder.

"Yeah, that's perfect. I'm not wearing a bathing suit anyway," I answer with a monotone voice.

He throws his arm over my shoulder. "Talk to me, Halo. What happened?"

"I don't think you want to hear it." We find a spot to sit in the grassy part of the park beneath some trees. Thomas takes off his black T-shirt and, although the view of his broad chest and muscular abs is nice, it reminds of me of other things I don't want to think about.

He's been training hard lately and I know he'll be leaving for boot camp soon.

"I had another fight with my mom. She heard about the arrest. I told her you weren't involved, but I don't know if she'll ever accept you."

The muscle along his jaw pulses. "Halo, your mom is right. You are smart and beautiful you could do a lot better than me."

"Cut it out, Thomas. You know I only want you."

He shakes his head. "You don't understand. What I'm saying is that even though I know you can do better, I love you and I'm not letting you go. I'm gonna make something of myself and then you'll be honored to take my name." He says this while looking me square in the eye. His blue eyes are so deep. The honesty in them makes my stomach flutter.

I brush my hand along his jaw, wanting to ease his tension "Why, Thomas, if I didn't know better I would think that was a proposal." I blink my eyes and bat my eyelashes at him, teasing him.

He doesn't smile, though. He seems dead serious when he says, "I kept telling myself not to sleep with you because you deserved better. But you gave yourself willingly. With love. You're mine now and I will never let you go. I'm going to prove your parents wrong. I have a plan. I'm going to be a success with the SEALs. I'm thinking I should talk to your parents about our future. I'm not giving you up so I need to convince them I am not a bad guy and that my intentions toward you are pure."

"I love that idea. But it's their anniversary tonight. My mom was upset over the way I left. I think it would be better to wait until they're a little more chill."

"Okay." He rubs at the back of his neck. I put my arms around him, drawing him down so I can kiss his lips.

"I don't know how I will get by every day without seeing you. I miss you when we separate at night," I admit, pulling my gaze from him. He slides his thumb across my chin. I caress the back of his head and his neck.

"I hate being away from you too, baby, but I have to do this. You know how important it is for me, for us. I'll always come back to you. You're my halo and I will be able to find you even in the dark." He grins and covers my mouth with his. His lips are warm and I love the taste of him. Touching him sets my entire body on fire. We've managed to have sex a few times since my birthday. I've snuck him into my bedroom when my parents have been out and it only gets better. He groans into my mouth.

"I can't get you naked here so we better stop," he says as he runs his hand along my behind and slides his finger into my shorts." He groans again. "You completely undo me, Halo. I don't know what it is about you but from the moment I saw you it was like gravity pulling me toward you. I know I'm selfish for wanting you because you make me feel so good..." I put my finger to his lips to hush him.

"You're amazing, Thomas Wells, and I'm the lucky one," I reply placing a soft kiss on his lips. His brows draw together and his forehead creases despite the fact that he's kissing me. It's hard for him to believe my words. It breaks my heart because he's such a good and loving person that's working hard for a better life. He doesn't deserve to feel this way. In attempt to pull him out of his own darkness as his eyes close and he leans forward to kiss me I pull away and stand up quietly. He falls into the air and opens his eyes. I stand quickly and kick off my boots. "Last one in is the king of the world!" I yell as I head straight for the beach and the water. I know I probably won't make it into the water before him. But it's hot and I need to cool down.

"You aren't wearing a bathing suit," he hollers, but I'm already kicking up sand on my way to the cool lake water. The water hits my hot body with a shock and I gasp with joy.

I look back to the grass. Thomas is shaking his head while kicking off his biker boots. Then he comes running to me. I watch as every muscle and sinew in his body flexes beautifully. He's beautiful *and* kind. I love him so much.

He stomps through the water and dives into me. He clasps me in his arms and rubs his nose along my nose.

"You're something else," he says, shaking his head.

"And you are king of the world," I holler.

"Shh, you crazy girl." He captures my lips in a hot kiss. His tongue feels warm against mine and I wrap my legs around his waist. He pulls his head back and looks down at my breasts.

"Holy fucking hell," he hisses. My yellow tank top is sticking to my chest, giving him a nice view of my perky nipples.

I look into his dark blue eyes breathless, "I wish there was some where we could go to be alone. I bet my parents have left for their dinner by now. We should go to my house." I offer with a raspy voice.

He kisses me again and the heat between us grows stronger. "I will prove your parents wrong, I promise you," he whispers against my lips.

"You don't need to prove them wrong, because you prove me right every day."

"How did I ever find you?" he asks, nuzzling me. "I'm going to marry you someday, Halo. You have my word. I will go off to become a SEAL and I will marry you." He captures my lips in another hot kiss.

***

In my bedroom Thomas takes his time undressing me.

As his lips brush my ear, I feel tingles run down my body. His rough hands glide over my breasts and I arch into his touch—it sends my body spiraling into flames. He's always soft and gentle with me despite his strength. His lips graze my nipple and then he covers it with his mouth, sucking, but not too hard. I moan in response and this urges him downward as he spreads kisses down my belly. I know where he's headed.

Right now my world is Thomas. There is no one and nothing else when we're making love. As he licks me between my thighs, I buck off the bed, calling out his name.

He sends me into a soaring orgasm as his strong tongue assaults me in the best way possible. Rainbows spring into my vision. My breathing is erratic and I moan at the top of my lungs.

"I love how crazy you get," Thomas says, leaning over me. "You're the sexiest girl ever." He grins.

"I get crazy for you," I huff as I come down from my high. I smooth my hands over his broad shoulders and push. He knows what I want and he flops onto his back. I don't wait. I bend over him and take his cock in my mouth, letting the head hit the back of my throat.

"Jesus, Halo, easy or I'm going to come before I get a chance to be inside you." I love how his voice goes gruff and low. It does things to me, makes me crazy in love. As I continue sucking, I run my tongue along the shaft and all around. Thomas's fingers are in my hair, tugging. It drives me wild when he does that.

I move lower, tonguing and licking his sac. He throws his head back and groans. I love undoing him, taking away his hard-won control. I take his cock back into my mouth, sucking him hard and fast. I feel him lengthening and strengthening and I know his release is near. Finally, he groans loudly and hot cum spurts into my mouth. I suck it all down until there's nothing left.

I slowly climb back up his ripped abdomen to his broad chest and lay my chin on him. He looks like he's on top of the world. I know he doesn't feel like this often because of the way he grew up. Right now he's looking pretty damned pleased and very adequate and I liked having that impact.

"What?" he asks, looking down at me.

"You're hot," I say with an amused grin.

"Not as hot as you." He gets up and pins me to the bed, hovering above me. With his free hand he reaches over to his jeans on the floor and pulls out a condom. He slides it on. "I love being inside you," he whispers as he rocks his hips in and out of me. "I love how wet you are," he continues. His voice is like a drug I can't get enough of. It sets me on fire. It does things to my body I can't quite understand. I began to build again. His sexual stamina is ravenous and meets my own need perfectly. He picks up pace, rolling his hips and rubbing me in all the right places. He's strong and controlled with his movements. We move our hips in rhythm and my insides begin to clench and tremble. We finally come together in a sweaty heap of scattered limbs.

"I love you so much," he says, pulling me down against his side to snuggle as our chests heave up and down from the exertion and adrenaline.

"I love you too," I say, reaching up to place a soft kiss on his lips.

We doze for a while, content.

The doorbell rings. For a moment, I'm pretty sure I just imagined the sound. But it rings again and I sit up, looking at Thomas, wondering who it could be. My parents would use their key.

We quickly wiggle out of bed and throw on our clothes. I'm well aware that I'm a rumpled mess and whoever it is will know what we've been up to. I go downstairs on wobbly legs, even though I know I have Thomas right behind me to protect me.

I open the door and I know right away that nothing can protect me from the grim expression of the policeman standing on the porch.

He introduces himself but I barely register anything beyond the fact he's a Chicago police officer. "Are you related to the Pearsons?" he asks.

"Yes. They're my parents." My heart is beating so crazily in my chest I can't breathe. I've seen scenes like this in movies. My knees give out and Thomas catches me.

"Can I come in?" the officer asks gently. "It might be good for you to sit down."

I shake my head violently. "Just tell me," I beg.

"I'm sorry." His voice is solemn. "There was a car accident. A drunk driver. Your parents were killed on contact."

The rest of that night is fuzzy. Thomas holds me for hours as I grip him for dear life. He comes with me to identify their bodies.

"*Even darkness must pass*," he repeats numerous times in my ear, quoting our favorite author. "I'm here for you. I won't leave you."

I want to believe him. The words give me hope, but the darkness envelops me.

CHAPTER SIX

September 2, 2001
Halo

I was set to attend the University of Chicago to work on my psychology degree and eventually get into education. Given the circumstances, the University accepted my request for deferral until January. Thomas felt it would be better for me to start school sooner rather than later. A post-secondary education was not on his own agenda, but he knew how much it meant to me. Despite my dark and spacey mood he kept me focused on that goal.

He surprised me when he enrolled in paramedic training. He spent six months in training to become an Emergency Medical Technician. He went to the bank for a student loan which surprised me even more. It shouldn't have, I know. I witnessed his ambition when he trained to prepare for boot camp.

"Baby, come downstairs. I made you breakfast," he whispers lovingly close to my ear.

I can't move, let alone think of eating. It's exactly one year since my parents were killed.

"Please get out of bed," he pleads. I sense his worry. I know he won't like my answer. He's been caring for me since the day my parents died. The next morning he went home, packed all his belongings when he knew his father would be at work and never turned back.

My life still feels like a bad dream. I crave normalcy. I keep hearing mom's voice and my dad placing his keys on the front door mantel at the end of each day. My mind is playing tricks on me. My heart is aching badly. Worst of all, guilt consumes me.

"Baby, please get out of bed. Or at least drink something." Thomas places the tray on the night table and takes a seat on the bed beside me, caressing my hair. So loving and dedicated.

"Thomas, you don't have to take the day off today," I chide him. He has already given up so much for me. I hate feeling so down and useless. I can't help myself either.

"You know I can't work today, baby. I wish I could do something to help you gain some closure. They're watching over you from up above. They wouldn't want to see you sad." It's an argument he's made many times over the past year. He's my life coach, guiding me step by step down a path I'm unable to follow. I know he's putting his dream of becoming a SEAL on the back burner for me.

"Halo, I can't see you like this," he rasps, looking helpless. I hate that I make him feel like this. I hate everything about my situation. I can't break the cycle either.

"I'm sorry, baby. I don't mean to be like this…" I begin to apologize as tears began to fall again, so many tears. I wish I could control them.

"How about I help you up and you take a shower? I will put some music on for you. Maybe it will relax you." I nod and he lifts me in his strong arms. He puts me down in the bathroom and turns the water on in the shower, helping me inside. I wait for the warm water to rejuvenate my aching body. Nothing happens. Thomas waits patiently in the bathroom, never leaving me.

September 11th, 2001

We wake up to disaster. The planes hitting the Twin Towers. It looks like a movie. It can't be real, but it's real, a nightmare. Our world is changing for the worst. Thomas sits glued to the television. Reporters reveal more and more information slowly but surely about the attacks. Days pass slowly…more information comes to light. My chest aches for all those who lost their lives. Death has taken up residence in my life and won't leave….

His jaw ticks as he watches the news describing the war in Afghanistan. Troops are being deployed. Talks of terror and what it means to our new world. I know he's itching to go. As I watch the casualties and the cruelty of the September 11th attacks, I remain quiet. I've become selfish after losing my parents. I can't handle losing him too. He knows it. He's all I have and I'm broken.

I want to be okay. I know I need to find strength somehow. I know he wants to enlist and leave. I know I have to be okay with it. It was the first thing he confessed to me on our first date. I want to be enough for him. I know by now I'm not saving the darkness inside him. He needs to enlist. He needs to save the world to feel good. In order to do that he has to leave me.

CHAPTER SEVEN

January 22, 2008
Ryder

I've been in and out of hospitals for four months now. I feel like a fucking wrecking ball tore through my head. From the looks of my body I gather I was in good shape before the attack. Shit. My reality is that I have lived with pain, hospital rooms, needles, pills, surgeries for longer than I care to remember. I hate the sterile smell of a hospital. I know that. I hate that my body feels so broken. Most of all I hate that I'm so fucking alone.

The only visitors I've had have been Halo and that cute baby of hers. Must have been fate that day she fell in the hall. Because she became a friend. Someone to talk to. It's so important to have someone to talk to.

As I think about the information I have been given about myself I feel totally disconnected. The man I read about and hear about from the people the navy assigned to help me doesn't seem like me. It's like I've read a story about a man I don't know and I'm trying to convince myself I am him. None of it feels right. It's maddening.

I don't even have a family member I can go to for advice or help. Someone to tell me what I was like. What I like. What type of man

I was. I must have been a real asshole because I have no one. I may not know much but I know there is something very wrong with that. They think they can help me get my memory back. The doctor said I'm suffering from a bad case of post-traumatic stress disorder and that I've managed to block the old me out completely. I figure if my situation is that bad maybe the old me isn't worth remembering.

I'll continue to get wound therapy and physical therapy and now I am so relieved to know I'll have someplace "normal" to come home to while I continue my treatment.

I hope I'm making the right decision by taking the apartment Halo offered. Anything seems better than a hospital, more treatment centers. I like talking to her. It comes easy. I don't know why she would take interest in me. I think she pities me. I have a feeling that should be problematic, but I like her. She's pretty. She's kind and I like the way her face lights up when we talk. I even like the way she looks at her baby.

None of it makes sense to me. I am going on pure impulse. Maybe that's the wrong thing to do. Her friend clearly has issues with me taking the apartment. I know it's selfish of me, but the way I look at it I don't have a choice. I just want to feel free. Breathe air… I don't know.

I guess the next thing is to take this small bag of belongings and go to her hospital room. She said to meet there. I guess I'll see where the wind takes me.

CHAPTER EIGHT

January 22, 2008
Halo

There's a knock on the door. "Halo, it's Dave. Are you decent?"

I have my bags packed and I'm wearing a jogging suit. I am *so* ready to leave this place. I call out, "Yeah, we're ready."

He enters the room with a bright smile. Dave is a good, stable guy. He works full time for an insurance company as an adjuster. He's a good father to his three little children. He is also very handsome, standing well over six feet tall with dirty-blond hair and hazel eyes. He and Jenny make a beautiful couple. They aren't wealthy, but they get by with what they have and they're happy. I think Thomas always looked up to him as a man because of the way he took care of his family.

"Let's see this little man," Dave says, picking up Brandon and grinning at him. "You are one handsome fellow, aren't you? You look exactly like—"

"Hey," I holler, cutting him off. "I know he looks like me, dammit."

Looking at Brandon is a constant reminder of Thomas and I know other people who knew Thomas will make note of the same thing. But I have to ignore it. I completely adore Brandon just like I adored his father. No matter what Thomas has done I can't control how I feel. As mad and angry as I am, I still love him.

"Ah, Halo." He lowers his voice and moves closer. "Jenny was mentioning you offered to rent the garage to some stranger here at the hospital." His tone says he doesn't believe it. "Do you really think that's a good idea?"

"I already explained this to Jenny," I tell him. "He was in the military and he was injured. He has money to pay rent. I need money since I have to take care of Brandon on my own. It makes perfect sense." I shrug, lifting the diaper bag onto my shoulder.

"Jenny is worried. And if Jenny is worried, it means I will never hear the end of this." He chuckles but then his face turns serious. "Seriously, it does send off alarm bells. You don't know this guy or what he's capable of…"

Dave trails off because Ryder is now standing in the doorway wearing jeans and a worn-out-looking shirt. I notice how tall he is for the first time. He's built too. The navy does create big, strong soldiers. I know that.

Ryder takes a few hesitant steps toward Dave. He must have heard our conversation. "Hey, I'm Ryder. Uh, you don't need to worry… I mean, I can understand why you are worried. You don't know me from Adam and I don't know myself too well, either. I can barely walk on my left leg and I'm covered with these…" He gestures to his bandages. "But they come off in a week. For now I'm a mummy." He chuckles to himself. It's throaty. My heart clenches because he seems so lost. "If I were going to kill her, she'd definitely have a head start." He laughs again. I laugh too. Dave's eyes go wide.

"Dave, he's joking," I chide, shaking my head. Dave isn't amused one bit.

"I think I'm a nice guy, man," Ryder says. "I seem to get along with Halo." He nods as if he likes his answer. Dave doesn't look convinced.

Dave looks at me, draws his brows together, then looks at Ryder. "Yeah, sure man. I guess." He shakes his head. "Do you mind introducing me to your doctors? I need basic information, man. We need to know that you are an actual soldier and not some lunatic making up a story," he explains to Ryder.

Ryder nods. "I don't mind. I told them you were coming."

Dave looks at me and shrugs. "Sorry, Halo. I promised Jenny I would."

"Yeah sure," I say with a small smile. Inside I'm thinking it isn't such a bad idea.

Ryder follows Dave out of the room. I take the time to feed Brandon one last time before leaving. Breastfeeding can be a challenge—it's hard to know how much food he's actually getting and my nipples are sore all the time. It doesn't deter me, though. I love being able to feed my son like this. I like the bonding time.

About fifteen minutes later Dave returns with Ryder and two patient transporters with wheelchairs, one for me and one for Ryder.

"He checks out, Halo." Dave nods to me and I feel my cheeks flush when Ryder looks my way, shrugging his shoulders. "He was a model soldier. Injured on active duty. He's suffering from PTSD." Dave nods to me and I know he's thinking of Thomas and silently asking me if I want to deal with that again with a complete stranger. I shrug and he eyes me warily then he lets it go and I am glad. I like that I can do something good for Ryder. I hold Brandon in my arms as I'm wheeled to the hospital entrance.

"I'll go get the car," Dave says, placing the infant carrier beside me and looking back to me and Ryder. "You're a good person, Halo," Dave calls out before he leaves.

"Thanks," I call back.

Ryder and I sit on a bench in the entryway waiting for Dave. It's awkwardly silent. I'm not sure what to say after he's convinced us he won't try to kill me and Dave went to verify it was true with his doctor.

"How's the leg?" I ask, trying to break the silence.

"Shitty. I guess physical therapy should make it better with time. Doctors said I'll always have a slight limp."

"I'm sorry," I answer, not knowing what else to say.

"That's life, I guess. It would help if I could remember how it happened."

Dave pulls up in his SUV and comes running around the front to help Brandon and me. The patient transporter watches as Dave places Brandon in the car seat. Ryder sits in the passenger seat.

"Thanks, Dave."

"Please stop thanking me." He smiles. As the SUV pulls out into traffic, the car is silent and it's a little uncomfortable, but maybe it's me. I sit in the backseat with Brandon while Ryder sits up front.

Dave glances at me in the rear-view mirror. "So we stopped by your place last night and set up the crib. The bassinet is on the main level. Jenny thought it would be more convenient there. We also put the playpen on the main floor and there's a baby bath in your bathroom. Jenny said she'll make a pit stop at your house after work today before picking up the kids… Oh yeah, she also stocked your fridge." Dave chuckles. "I hope I delivered the message in its entirety. She made me memorize it this morning."

I smile back at him knowingly. "Thanks so much, Dave. You guys have already given me so much. I don't know how I can ever repay you. Jenny is busy—she doesn't have to stop by. I'll manage on my own." I'm so grateful that I have such a special friend.

"If you need any help, you can just holler for me." Ryder turns his head and looks at me. Dave flashes me a warning glance in the mirror.

"Thanks, Ryder. You might be even more challenged than I am with the baby care, though." I appreciate his offer. But I'm not sure what an ex-SEAL would know about a newborn child.

"Yeah, okay, sure. I figured you were new at this too. You seem good at it. I get you're an independent woman." He smiles at me. Is he just goading me? Is he flirting?

I don't respond. Dave is glaring at me in the rear-view mirror again. Should I be nervous about Ryder St. John? I don't know.

His appearance intrigues me. I don't know what's waiting under those bandages but just looking at his body I can tell he's definitely sexy in a rugged kind of way. I know I shouldn't be thinking about him in that way at all, though.

I guess it should be a kind of relief that I can even acknowledge I might find a guy attractive. I know I will eventually start dating again, but it's hard to imagine. Divorce papers sure made things with Thomas final, but still, it's hard to think about loving someone else. And now I have Brandon to think about. I pull my gaze from the window to watch Brandon sleeping content in his car seat. I love watching him. His tiny lips, his little button nose.

We arrive at the house and Dave helps us inside. He kicks off his boots and so I guess he's staying. He watches Ryder carefully as we head through the main hall of the house toward a door leading to a garage apartment. Thomas and Dave transformed our garage and Dave's garage into an apartment a number of years ago so the men would have space to hang out and drink beer on the occasional weekend. Our apartment had been barely used since Thomas was on deployment. Now it was going to be used for rental income.

I show Ryder the features of the apartment. The floors, bathroom and kitchen all look new and modern, but the furniture is super old. Then again everything in the house is old. Everything belonged to my parents. Thomas and I continued to live in the house after my parents died but we never changed anything. I felt like their belongings were my last connection to them.

The house was beautiful, but some things have aged and definitely require some updating. If Thomas and I had stayed together I would have wanted him to fix things up for Brandon's arrival.

"I hope you like the place," I say, fidgeting a bit as I stand in the middle of the apartment looking at Ryder. Dave is quiet, standing beside me and holding Brandon in his seat.

Ryder shrugs. "I don't really know what I like. It has a bed, a couch, a TV and a kitchen. I'm assuming I should be good here. It's weird how I know certain things and not others." He shakes his head. Again my heart aches for him. He must feel so alone.

"Okay then," Dave says. "How about you and Brandon head in the house to get settled." I can tell he's still worried, but I've made the decision to rent to Ryder at least for a little while. And I'll have to stick with my decision.

Leaving Ryder to continue exploring the apartment, I slowly walk back through the door and into the house. Dave still looks wary, so I reassure him again as he hands Brandon to me. "Don't worry," I say. "We'll be fine. Thank you for picking us up."

"No problem. Ring if you need anything." He leaves out the front door and the house is suddenly quiet. I smile down at Brandon as I take off my coat and boots. He's here. He's finally home. I definitely pictured this day differently in my mind. I had hoped Thomas would be here, of course. A lone tear falls down my cheek. Brandon is slowly waking up and he moves his arms under the blankets. I extract him from the blankets and the carrier and carry him over to the living room.

Jenny really did think of everything. The playpen is set up with a changing table stacked on top of it. The pockets are stuffed with diapers and wipes and other essentials. I change Brandon's diaper quickly. It comes easily because I was around after all three of Jenny's deliveries and after. When I'm done changing Brandon, there is a light knock on the front door. I look through the peephole. It's my neighbor Maggie.

When I open the door, Maggie is practically bouncing and Charlie barks, wagging her tail.

"Charlie," I call out, patting her head. "I missed you, girl."

"Let me see this baby of yours, Halo." Maggie says, extending her arms. "I still can't believe you took a cab to the hospital while you were in labor. You should have called me, girl. That ain't cool." I hand her Brandon and she smiles down at him. "What a handsome fella. You look exactly like your—"

"Maggie, he looks like me," I interrupt. We walk into the living room and take a seat on the couch. Charlie sniffs at the new items in the room calmly and then plops down on the floor by my feet. I'm lucky she's so well behaved and friendly. My instincts tell me she won't have any trouble adjusting to life with Brandon.

Maggie draws her brows together and looks at me like I've lost it. "Yeah, Halo, of course he totally looks like you." Maggie and her family have been living next door for the last five years. They've been great neighbors and I've enjoyed getting to know her two boys.

There's another light knock on the door. Ryder's voice calls out a low, "Hello?"

"Come in," I call. The door opens a bit and my belly hurts as I stand. "Hi, Ryder." I motion for him to come inside. He limps into the house and I wonder what Maggie will think of him being my tenant. Will she be the next friend to think I've lost it? Or will she see it for what it is—me helping out a wounded lost soldier.

"Hey," Ryder says. "I was going go to the supermarket. Wanted to see if you needed anything. Diapers or baby supplies or something?" His mouth tugs up on one corner. Out of the corner of my eye I notice Maggie ogling. I'm not sure what she's thinking. Ryder looks like a muscular mummy. I inwardly chuckle even though I do feel bad for him.

"That's nice of you to offer, Ryder. It seems as though Jenny has thought of everything." I gesture toward the well-stocked changing area and smile.

"Jenny is a good friend." He nods.

"Yes." I notice Ryder is looking at Maggie. "Oh," I say, "where are my manners? Ryder, this is my neighbor Maggie. She and her husband Joshua live next door with their two boys. Maggie, this is Ryder. He's renting my garage apartment."

Ryder takes another step into the house. "Nice to meet you ma'am," he says politely.

Maggie is still holding on to Brandon so she doesn't have a free hand. Her jaw drops a little and she looks between Ryder and me. "Nice to meet you, Ryder," she says with a wide grin. I think it's a good sign she's not alarmed by the news.

"Well, I better be going." I can tell by the low tone of his voice how unsure he feels. *Poor guy!*

"You can't walk, Ryder. Your leg…the bandages… It's not that close." It's the end of January in Chicago. The streets are slushy. It's cold outside.

"I'm alright," he responds with a nod. "I was going to take a cab."

I nod. "That sounds like a good idea." I wish I could see his whole face. He's so quiet and I'd love to be able to read his facial expressions. His head is slightly lowered and his shoulders hunched.

"Maybe when you're feeling better you can borrow my hus—my, um, ex-husband's truck. I never use it and it would be fine if you needed it to get around." I'm not sure if his injuries or his bandages might hinder his ability to drive.

"That's a kind offer." He winces and I begin to wonder if he needs more help than I can offer. "I'd better get outside to meet the cab."

"It was nice meeting you, Maggie." He smiles.

"Nice to meet you too," she says.

He nods to me. "Halo." He leaves and closes the door.

"Halo, what is going on?" Maggie squeaks.

"He's got amnesia. He's a wounded soldier," I say.

"Holy shit, Halo! Where did you find him?"

"Would you be quiet?" I wave at her. "He probably heard you." I grin to show her I'm not mad, just embarrassed.

"Come on, Halo. That man is smoking hot. You see that, don't you?" She scrunches her brows together. "And this broken soldier thing he has going on…mmm…girlfriend." She shakes her shoulders.

I roll my eyes at her playfully. "Honestly, Maggie, he's just a guy I met at the hospital. He's a wounded vet. He's been medically discharged. He has no family…"

"Yes, Halo, I know you like to pick up the strays." She gives me a knowing look and stares down at Charlie. Thomas had found Charlie in a storm three years back. It had been spring, and on a cool, windy night Thomas had found her limping down the street. Thomas brought her into the house and we'd discovered a small stick that had been lodged in her paw. We'd put up signs, but no one ever claimed her. I'd been so grateful for her after Thomas had left. I swear she sympathized with every word and tear.

"It's not like that, Maggie."

"No! So what's it like?"

"I uh…." My shoulders deflate. "I don't know. He was easy to talk to and he didn't have anywhere to go. I need the money from the rent. It just makes sense." I settle against the back of the couch.

"Okay, if you say so." She looks down at Brandon. "He's sleeping. I'll put him in the playpen. You should try to get some rest." She has a sympathetic look in her eyes. I hate that my friends and neighbors see me as the abandoned woman. I just hate it. I wonder if it will ever end. I know a fresh start would probably be good for Brandon and me, but all my memories of my parents and Thomas are here.

This is the place where Thomas and I were building a life. I can't give it up, not yet at least. *You're my halo. I will always find my way back to you.* Those words… His voice is still so clear in my mind. The truth is, I'm scared if we move he won't find his way back to us.

"Do you think I'm crazy renting Ryder the space?" I ask Maggie.

"You're a kind woman, Halo. You're a dedicated teacher and a great friend. I'm not surprised you are trying to help Ryder. If you're asking me if he looks dangerous? I don't think so. He does look lost. It's nice that you are helping him out."

I sigh. "He didn't have anyone come to visit him the whole time he was in the hospital. Four months, Maggie, and not one visitor."

"That is sad," Maggie confirms.

"I know. Right?"

"Yeah." She gives my shoulder a squeeze. "Just keep your eyes open and be aware. If something seems off let me know right away. We'll be right over. I'm serious."

"Thanks, Maggie. And thanks for taking care of Charlie."

"Sure thing. My boys adore her. Now they're bugging Joshua and me for a dog. I don't know. We'll see." She gives me a gentle hug then she turns to leave.

"Bye, Maggie."

"Take care, Halo. If you need something or have any questions please call, no more proud bullshit," she says as she makes her way out the door.

With Brandon fast asleep I stroll into the kitchen and open the fridge to see what Jenny has stocked. About twenty minutes later I have food ready and sitting on the stove. Brandon begins to stir, making that cute newborn baby cry. I make my way over to him.

This is totally fine. I can handle this on my own. I pick up Brandon slowly and sit back on the couch to breastfeed him. He latches on and I sit and watch him feed. My stomach is sore, my nipples are sore. I was probably on my feet for too long preparing the food. I'll take some Tylenol once he's finished eating.

I suddenly feel super sleepy from all the exertion of coming home. The thought of sitting for another meal alone depresses me. Brandon eats and falls back asleep. I slowly place him back in the bassinet attached to the playpen. The house is eerily quiet. I walk into the kitchen to fill Charlie's bowl with food and water.

"How are you doing, Charlie? I'm sorry I had to leave you on such short notice. Did you see Brandon? He's absolutely perfect isn't he?" As I talk to Charlie, she tilts her head to the side looking at me. I pat her on the head and find myself looking over at the door leading to the garage. Ryder is probably home by now. I wonder if he managed the grocery store okay. And I realize he's probably eating alone too.

Would he want to join me? I ignore the warning voices of Dave and Jenny in my head and slowly get up and walk to the door that connects the garage to the house. I knock lightly and wait.

"Just a sec," I hear Ryder holler.

He opens the door a moment later wearing the same blue jeans as earlier, but he's shirtless. Holy hell, he has an eight pack. His chest is smooth. He has a tattoo on his shoulder. It's a Navy Trident. I know it well. My heart stammers as I look at him.

Thomas never got any tattoos. He wasn't very hairy, but he had some chest hair that led to a happy trail... My eyes drift lower. Ryder is smooth there too. I suppress the urge to run my hand over his skin, soothe his scars...

The navy really produces some incredible male bodies.

Don't think that, Halo. You just miss your husband, your love. I close my mouth abruptly, realizing it's hanging open. *Get a grip Halo.*

I realize he has a shirt in his hand. He puts it on quickly, ending my show. He stands there with an expectant look, probably wondering why I'm standing in his doorway.

"I made some chicken stir-fry and rice. I was wondering if you wanted to join me for dinner. I thought maybe you weren't completely settled in and that you were probably hungry." I finally stop babbling long enough to hear his answer.

"Thanks, Halo. That would be great." He gestures at the door. "Ladies first."

We walk back into the house together and down the hallway past the living room. "How's the little guy doing?" Ryder asks tipping his chin toward a sleeping Brandon.

"He's great. He does regular baby stuff like eating and sleeping. Nothing eventful has happened yet." He walks over to the playpen and gazes down at Brandon with warm blue eyes. He smiles and looks around the room. His gaze lingers on the mantel over the fireplace.

I still have my trophies there. I don't know why—I should move them and redecorate. I haven't done much with this house since my parents died. I clearly have issues with hanging on to the past.

"What are the trophies for?" Ryder asks, walking over to take a look. He lifts one and reads what's written on the plaque. "Water Polo Competition, Halo Pearson first place." He glances over at me. "Impressive. Do you still play?"

I laugh. "No, haven't played for years." A familiar ache rises in my chest.

I walk into the kitchen to get an extra setting for dinner. He follows me.

"Wow! Looks great. I'm not sure the last time I had a home-cooked meal." Ryder rubs his hands together and takes a seat across from me at the table. My heart clenches as I realize he's sitting in Thomas's seat.

I will never eat across from Thomas again. My son will never look into Thomas's blue eyes and see where his came from. I swipe at my eyes quickly, hoping Ryder won't notice my tears. I read about hormones in my pregnancy book and I've heard about them from Jenny and the nurses at the hospital. I know things can get pretty wonky after delivery. This must be what they were talking about.

I pass Ryder the stir-fry and then place some rice on my plate. Then we do a switch. "Are you okay, Halo?" he asks with that low, deep voice. I put my fork down because I feel too upset to eat and suddenly I begin to sob.

"I'm so sorry. This is so embarrassing." I rub at my eyes, willing myself to get my shit together.

"Hey! You don't need to apologize. I know we don't really know each other, but I think I may be a good listener. Do you want to tell me what's on your mind?" He sets down his fork too.

"I'm sorry. You must be hungry. You should eat," I urge. My voice cracks and I can't seem to stop my damn tears. "You didn't realize this, but you decided to come home with a post-partum crazy woman." I smile through my tears.

My face must look red and blotchy. This is so not like me, breaking down like this in front of a stranger. Charlie walks into the kitchen and rubs her head against my leg. I pat her head and she plops down beside me. I'm convinced that this dog is somehow very in tune to my every emotion.

"She's beautiful. What kind of dog is she?" Ryder asks, looking down at Charlie.

"She's a Golden Retriever. She's very clever." I wipe my nose with a napkin.

"How old is she?" Ryder asks. I get the feeling he's trying to distract me from whatever's making me sad. He doesn't realize that answering the question will just trigger more sadness.

"I don't know. She was a stray and my husband—I mean ex-husband—found her. She was hurt, cold and alone in a storm. We brought her in and she's been by my side ever since," I explain and more tears begin to fall.

"She's loyal," he states, looking down at Charlie.

"Yes."

"It's him isn't it? Talking about him makes you sad," Ryder says, and it's not a question.

"I guess it still does. It's silly, I know. It's been almost eight months. I should have my shit together by now."

"It's not silly. You just had a baby and you're by yourself. I may not remember anything about myself, but I know that is not how the world works. I get that a baby should have a mother and father. Do you uh...know where he is?"

"No. You should really eat. You must be very hungry." I pick up my fork and begin to eat. Ryder does too.

"Did the military inform you of anything?" he continues to pry. I should be bothered but something tells me he is asking more for himself.

"No, last I heard he deployed and he's on active duty." I take a bite of rice and chicken. I can do this. I can talk about Thomas. I can eat while talking about Thomas. I won't break down while talking about Thomas.

"I see. I didn't mean to pry. I just wondered if my ex would have been notified of my injury. I hope I didn't upset you." He shovels food into his mouth. "This is so good, Halo. Feels like heaven to eat a meal prepared by a good cook like you. Must be forever since I've had one."

I want to ask about the ex he mentioned, but I know I shouldn't. I realize I'm unsure about the military's policy about notifying exes regarding injury or death. I want to ask him about that too. Would it hurt his feelings? Open up emotional wounds for both of us?

Too many questions run through my mind and, feeling warm and anxious, I reach for the cool glass of water in front of me. I realize that he paid me a compliment and I didn't respond.

"Thanks, Ryder," I tell him solemnly. We finish eating and Ryder stands.

"You prepared dinner, so let me at least clean up." I watch gratefully as he clears the table and wraps up the leftover food. He quietly washes the dishes at the sink. I'm kind of thankful he's helping because I'm feeling uncomfortable pressure at the point of my incision. I lean back and wince a bit. Ryder notices.

"You're in pain. Is there something I can do?"

"Umm…" I need help getting Brandon up the stairs but he has limited movement with his brace. I'm not sure how stable he would be anyway. Problem is that my stomach feels like it's splitting in two.

"What is it?"

"I'm worried about getting Brandon upstairs. I don't know why the thought is causing me to panic." I admit. I feel foolish. What would I have done if I were here alone? Probably sleep on the couch. I'm suddenly very glad Ryder is here. His presence is reassuring. Especially if, god forbid, something were to happen. I don't like the unexpected. I don't like to think about the unexpected. My parents' death, Thomas leaving—those were things that shaped my life. Now I feel like I have no control over my destiny.

"I can help you get him up the stairs," he offers.

"Thanks, but it's hard for you too. I saw you flinch when you took a seat at the table."

His cheeks flush and he looks down to the floor before he looks me in the eye. "Halo, they took skin off my behind and put it on my face. It's hard for me to sit because it stings. I'm taking antibiotics to prevent infection. My leg feels a lot better since the last surgery. I don't sleep with the brace. I wear it so I don't overexert during the day. Truth is, I feel a little stir crazy. My mind is telling me I should go for a jog. Only my body is in no condition." He laughs. "I think I can carry him up the stairs—I'll take it slow. I'm guessing I'm in less pain than you. It will make me feel better not to feel so useless right now." His gaze pulls away from me and I can see the loneliness seeping its way to his heart.

"Okay," I reply with a faint voice.

"Thank you," he says, staring deep into my eyes. His gaze is holding a million emotions. I think he is thanking me for trusting him and for not treating him like an invalid. I'm not sure.

We both make our way over to little Brandon sleeping in the playpen. I lift Brandon in my arms and give him a peck on the forehead. Then I pass him to Ryder. Even the small movements are painful now. I'm thinking I will do one last feeding and then take some Tylenol.

I follow Ryder up the stairs at a turtle's pace, which is fine by me. The stairs are hard on me even without Brandon in my arms. Ryder takes a step with his good leg and the leg in the brace follows suit slowly. I inwardly chuckle. We are both a real mess.

Ryder pulls me out of my reverie when he says, "I won't let anything happen to him. I understand that he's precious. That part of my brain seems to be working."

He reaches the top step and I follow a moment later. His words are endearing and I feel something like happiness warm my insides. It's been a while since I've felt this way.

I don't want to analyze my feelings, though. I tell myself that it's just the good karma that comes from helping a wounded soldier. That's all this is. I'm still trying to convince myself as I say goodnight to my unexpected knight.

CHAPTER NINE

Ryder

I climb the stairs slowly while looking down at the little baby sleeping in my arms. My leg is fucking killing me, but holding him makes me feel content. I wonder if I'll ever have the chance to be a father.

Right now it's hard to imagine how I would find a woman to be with or love me when I don't even know myself. I'm not even sure when I had sex last. I know I haven't lost any of the urges. I've certainly been appreciating Halo's beauty. I may not know what type of woman I liked in the past, but I sure liked her long auburn hair and those big round brown eyes. More than anything I liked that she was willing to talk to me.

After our conversation at dinner, I can't help but wonder about her ex. And mine. It's one of the issues I've been struggling with. The psychiatrist I've been working with hasn't been a lot of help. I mean, how can he answer the basic questions I'm dying to know? Like why I broke up with my wife. And why the hell I'm so damned alone in this world.

Halo tells me which door to enter and I gently place the little guy in his crib. Halo's movements are slow and controlled. I can see she's in pain. I look around the room and see white walls and a simple light wood crib in the center. It's plain and not very babyish.

"Thanks, Ryder," Halo whispers, patting my shoulder.

"Sure thing, he really is adorable," I reply and her face brightens. "Well, I better be going," I say as we leave the little guy's room. "I can show myself out. You don't need to do the stairs again. I can tell you're hurting."

"Thanks, Ryder," she responds and then she lets out a yawn, stretching out her arms. My gaze lingers on her for a moment too long. I turn my head. I don't want her to think I'm a creeper. I just find her beautiful.

I stop mid-step and turn to her. "You know, I think I can help you fix this place up. If you want me to?" I glance at the room's white walls again. "I can paint the little guy's room and make it look more like a nursery." The offer is instinctive—I'm not exactly sure where the urge to help with a project like this comes from.

"I don't want to trouble you," she says as her mouth turns up. I like her smile.

"It would be no trouble. I've been in a hospital bed too long now, and I really don't have anything to do while I'm finishing up therapy and my treatments. I know I'll need to find a job eventually, but for now I wouldn't mind working on your house if you will let me."

"I don't have much money to pay you," she says, biting her lower lip.

"I don't want money, I just need something to do. You'd actually be helping me out since I'm supposed to be moving around more now." I don't want her to think I'm some charity case, but I need time to figure things out.

"That would be great, Ryder. Thank you." She yawns again.

"Okay, go get some sleep. You need to take care of the little guy," I say as I turn to head down the stairs. It's slow going because of my leg and when I make it down, I walk over to the front door and ensure that it's secure. I make my way into the garage apartment, closing and locking the door behind me.

The apartment is pretty simple and the furnishings are old, but I would take this place over the hospital any day. I take off my jeans and climb into bed wearing my boxers. I really need to get to a store and buy some clothes. Maybe an extra blanket because the heat isn't all that great out here. It's almost February and we still have a while to go before spring.

I close my eyes and lie in the bed thinking of Halo. I wonder what kind of idiot would walk out on an amazing woman like that. I close my eyes, hoping that maybe tonight I will remember… a dream or some fragment of my past will turn up in my memory. I shut my eyes and I feel myself drifting off.

It's burning hot outside. I'm wearing lots of gear and BDUs. I have an AK-47 in my hands as I walk down an abandoned street. A long, rundown building makes up most of the street. It's divided into many little houses. I have a team of men following me. I'm the leader. I kick open the first door and point my gun in all directions while scanning the area for terrorists.

"Clear," I holler and motion for my men to follow me. The air is dusty and it's burning hot. We make our way through the house searching, scanning. It's clear. We make it into a backroom, and a shot goes off. It hits the wall next to a marine and *takes a chunk off the stone. The marine jumps out of the way. I step in front, aiming my gun. There are more shots and all of us start to shoot. It's so fucking loud I feel like I will go deaf. I wonder if one of those shots will land in my chest and be the end of me this time. "Would it fucking matter?" I hear myself say.*

I wake up from the nightmare and find myself seated on the bed panting and covered in sweat. What the hell was that? It felt so fucking real. The sound of gunshots. The fear. The unknown. Would a terrorist sneak up behind me? End me? What the hell? That happened. Shit that fucking happened. It must be real.

I wonder if my memory is returning. The thought of getting my memory back starts to scare the living shit out of me. I must have seen a lot and been through a lot. Those men who were following me. They must have been on my team. I don't have an appointment with the psychiatrist scheduled until next week, but I'm thinking I should see him sooner.

I can't fall back asleep again. My heart is racing a mile a minute. I'm trying to dig my brain for more information. The doctors explained that I can't force it, but in my dream I said it wouldn't matter if my life ended. Why did I feel that way?

***

I open my eyes feeling heavy and tired. I look over to the stove in the kitchen area. The clock says eleven o'clock. I spent half the night staring at the ceiling. I must have fallen back asleep close to morning. I throw the blanket off me and shiver. This place is cold, dammit. I walk over to the small washroom to relieve myself, remembering the dream from last night. I rub at my eyes but the bandage interferes. Fuck! I brush my teeth and stare at myself for a long time in the mirror. The color of my eyes is all I see. Something should jog my memory, but I don't see anything familiar in my reflection.

I walk out of the bathroom and hit the floor. I begin a set of stomach crunches but my ass burns so I switch it up to push-ups. My body protests. I try to get up but I can't bend the one knee and I'm stuck on the floor. It only pisses me off further. I slowly straighten myself out and take deep breaths. Motherfucker! I hate feeling so broken. I'm all sweaty now so as soon as I can manage to stand, I hop in the shower. The bandages make it difficult but I do the best I can. I keep my mind on the next minute, the next hour. I'll see how Halo is doing. I'll ask her what color she'd like to paint Brandon's room.

After I shower I put on the same outfit I wore yesterday. These are the only clothes I have, and it's damn embarrassing. Shopping is another thing I should put on my agenda today. The team of officers and counselors who've been helping me transition told me my wages are being deposited into bank account for me and so I'll need to figure out my finances at some point too.

I take a few deep breaths, trying to pull myself together. This "normal" life shit is going to take some getting used to. I knock on Halo's door and wait. It takes a while for her to answer. She finally opens the door with a bright smile, holding Brandon swaddled up in a blue blanket. I smile widely at both of them.

"Good morning."

"Hello to you too, Ryder. But it's already afternoon." She giggles. "I've been up every three hours feeding this little guy." She's still smiling, but I can tell by the bags under her eyes that she's tired. She's wearing white sweatpants and a loose pink T-shirt. Her auburn hair is tied up and messy looking, but to me she's beautiful.

I run a hand over my hair nervously. "Sorry. Good afternoon, ma'am." I'm not sure why I say that—it just comes out.

"You did not just ma'am me, Ryder. I am not some old lady." She pushes her lower lip out and I can feel my dick going hard. *Shit.*

"No. I'm sorry, Halo. You are definitely not an old lady." My gaze involuntarily travels over her body. She may have just had a baby and her belly may be a little swollen but she's a beautiful woman. "I, uh, didn't sleep well last night. I had a nightmare that kept me awake half the night. I'm sorry. I'm not on my game today." As I apologize I wonder once again if I should be revealing any of this to a woman I hardly know, or if I should be keeping it for my counselor. "Um… If you don't mind, I'll take you up on that offer to borrow your truck. I need to go over to the VA Hospital in North Chicago. Then I'd like to get some paint for Brandon's room and um..." I look down at myself and feel my face flush. Damn. Would the old me have been so flustered by a woman?

Halo nods, her brown eyes patient and kind. I appreciate the fact that she isn't looking at me like I am a mental case.

"Yeah, of course, take the truck. Honestly, it's a piece of crap and I hope it doesn't break down on you. I have some errands to run too. But Brandon is still too small to take out in this weather... Tomorrow we'll have to go out for our first appointment with his pediatrician, but I'm going to ask Jenny to give us a ride." Her lips curl into a perfect smile.

"I can take you guys," I offer without stopping to think.

"Really?" Her brows scrunch together.

"Uh, yeah. I remember you mentioning how busy Jenny is with her family and stuff. And I don't have much to do." I grin and shrug my shoulders. I feel so unsure about everything.

"Thanks, Ryder." She smiles widely again. Her dog walks up to me and rubs her body along my leg. I pat her on the head and she looks up to me, tilting her head.

"Nice dog," I murmur. Halo is looking down at her dog with a curious expression.

"What is it?" I ask.

"Nothing." She shrugs but it doesn't seem like nothing. "Ryder, don't take this the wrong way but do you need some clothes?" She winces as she asks the question. I know she isn't trying to embarrass me, but I'm flustered.

"I do. Apparently my personal belongings were on the sparse side. And, like I said, I haven't had to time to shop yet."

"I see." She looks me up and down. "I'm not sure, but you may be able to fit into my ex-husband's things. If you want to come upstairs, I can show you what there is," she offers.

"Are you sure it's okay? I mean, you don't mind?" I stutter a bit.

"Honestly, I was planning on donating it all. At least this way I know it's going to good use."

I shrug. "Great."

She walks toward the stairs with Brandon in her arms. "Do you need help?" I offer, referring to the stairs.

"Thanks. I feel a little better this morning. The pain seems to be worse at night. Probably from over-exerting all day." Still, she takes the stairs slowly. I follow her lead up and into a fairly large room with a big bed and rustic wood furniture. She walks into a closet and walks back out. "Can you hold him a minute?"

I take the little guy in my arms and cradle him to me closely.

"There's tons of stuff. I'm assuming you need some jeans and shirts?"

"That would be great," I say.

A moment later she walks out with a pile of jeans, a bunch of black, white and grey T-shirts and a black hoodie.

She drops it all on the bed.

"Thanks, that's great."

"You can use my bathroom if you want to try stuff on and see if anything fits."

I grab a pair of jeans and a white T-shirt from the top of the pile and head into the bathroom. I quickly get out of the dirty clothes and, as I slide the jeans over my legs and ass, they feel a little snug. The T-shirt is a little snug too. Especially around my chest. Her husband was clearly smaller than me. But the clothes will work for now and are better than nothing, for sure. I walk out of the bathroom carrying my dirty clothes.

"Do you have a laundry machine I can use?" I ask. I am commando right now but I figure it's information that's better kept to myself.

"Yeah, it's in the basement. I can show you how the machines work later." Her head tilts as she looks me up and down. "Not a terrible fit. A little snug but close enough." She grins.

"Thanks, Halo. It's great. It will hold me over until I make it to buy some clothes."

"Do you need to eat something?" she asks. I don't want to inconvenience her but my stomach is growling. I should probably just make myself a peanut butter sandwich with the groceries I bought yesterday, but for some reason I don't want to go back to the apartment. I'd rather spend time with her.

"I'll pick up something along the way," I say, smiling appreciatively. "You've already done too much for me."

"Don't be silly. You're helping us out too. The least I can do is make you a sandwich," she replies. We carefully make our way down the stairs and I notice the way she so carefully holds Brandon.

"Uh, can you hold him for a sec?" she asks again after we get to the kitchen.

I nod and she places him gently in my arms. I look down at him and let out a contented sigh. Halo laughs at me and turns away.

"So I have bagels. With cream cheese or peanut butter?" She opens the door to the fridge and glances at me over her shoulder.

"Uh, peanut butter is good," I reply. It was exactly what I could have made out in the garage.

"Do you like jam?" she asks.

"Yeah, strawberry if you have it."

I watch her move around the kitchen, grabbing ingredients and popping the bagel in the toaster. The baby begins to stir a little in my arms making me nervous.

"Relax," Halo says, looking over at me. "He probably needs to eat."

I nod.

When the bagel is ready, she puts the plate on the table and I carefully place Brandon back in her arms.

"You eat. I'll just go to the living room to feed him." She leaves and I'm a little bummed. I was hoping she could stay and talk some more. I wolf down the bagel and it hits the spot. Even though I feel like I could go for another, I stand, put the plate in the sink and head to the living room.

"Hey, Halo? Would you tell me where I can find the keys to the truck?" As I enter the room I realize half her breast is in the baby's mouth. She flinches and I cover my eyes with my hand. "I'm sorry," I say. "When you said feed the baby, I assumed it would be with a bottle."

Halo giggles. "I'm breastfeeding because it's good for this little guy. The keys are on the kitchen counter."

I go back go back to the kitchen and find the keys. Again, I will my man parts to calm down. It's seems fucking wrong to be thinking of Halo as hot at this moment. The woman just had a baby and her husband abandoned her. The thought makes my blood boil.

"Do you need anything?" I holler as I pass the living room and head for the front door.

"We're good for now. Thanks, Ryder. Maybe tomorrow we can pick up some groceries after the doctor's appointment."

"Yeah sure. I'm leaving now." I walk outside and I'm thankful when the cold air hits my hot face.

CHAPTER TEN

Ryder

I drive north in Halo's ex's truck. It's weird that I know how to drive it so easily. The thing is a beast but it seems like second nature to steer through the narrow streets. As soon as I hit the VA, I'm going to check in with my therapist. I feel like I'm fucking lost. I'm like some kind of incompetent child right now—everything's a challenge. Clothes, food, money, transportation. It's pissing the shit out of me. I turn up the radio, hoping to distract my thoughts. The dance music sounds cheesy, so I flip through the radio channels until I hear what sounds like a country song. I tap my thumb on the steering wheel as my head moves to the beat of the music. Not bad. I check my rear-view and side mirrors, remembering the directions to the VA that the folks at the other hospital gave me before I was discharged.

About fifteen minutes later I pull into the hospital parking lot and lock up the truck. It's old, it rattles like hell and I don't like the thought of Halo driving it. But that's a project for later.

Inside the big building, I limp my way to the section where I'm supposed to check in. I give the secretary my name and take a seat in the crowded waiting room. I'm thinking I don't look as bad as some of the guys here, even though I'm still in mummy mode. Yeah, I have burns on my face, I had some facial restructuring and I'll always have this damn limp, but some of these guys are missing limbs.

As I wait—bouncing my good leg nervously—I can't help but wonder about the story behind every injury of every person in the room. I can't help but wonder about my own fucking story.

A nurse finally calls my name and I head in to meet the doctor.

CHAPTER ELEVEN

Halo

There's a knock on the door and I peek out of the window to see Jenny shivering in the cold. I quickly waddle over to the playpen to place Brandon inside so he doesn't get a breeze from the open door. I waddle back to open the door.

"Hey, hon." Jenny steps inside and gives me a peck on the cheek. "It's my lunch time and I've been worried about you," she says, slipping off her boots before following me inside.

"Thanks, Jenny. Brandon and I are doing well." I smile. "Can I make you a coffee or tea?" I ask as we slowly make our way to the kitchen. The C-section has definitely slowed me down and walking is still a big pain in my ass.

"Coffee would be great," she says, rubbing her hands together. I walk over and hit the kettle and prepare two mugs. I'm not drinking coffee since it isn't the best with breastfeeding so I take out a bag of chamomile tea.

"So how is motherhood?" Jenny asks.

"It's good. Brandon is a good baby. The feedings in the middle of the night are kind of hard, but I guess with breastfeeding it makes it easier. I don't have to fuss with disinfecting bottles." I take a seat beside her at the kitchen table. She turns her head and looks around.

"I didn't notice the truck on the driveway when I pulled up," she says, scrunching her brows.

"Oh, Ryder borrowed it to run some errands," I respond.

Jenny shakes her head. "So now you are loaning him your car… Is there anything else I should know about?" she asks suspiciously.

"No! What do you mean?"

"Oh, I don't know…" She trails off. "Does he come in here for visits?"

"Hmm, we had dinner together last night and he's going to paint Brandon's room."

"I knew it," she snaps.

My eyes turn wide. "Huh?"

"You've got the hots for him," she says with an excited yet accusatory tone.

I glare at her as if she's grown two heads. "Seriously, it's not like that." I get up to make the coffee and tea. My stomach is turning a bit in a bad way that she could even say those words. How can I have the hots for another man? It doesn't sit well with me. This is only me helping him out. And, yes, if I gain a friend that's okay too. I've learned with losing my family that friends can be just as important.

"So what's it like?" Jenny asks, placing her chin on her hand.

"I don't know. He's a nice guy. He doesn't really know anything about himself. He's clearly been through a lot mentally and physically with his last deployment."

"So is this you being the accommodating military wife to a complete stranger?" she asks, causing my jaw to go slack.

"No," I hiss, feigning innocence.

"I'm sorry, Halo. I don't mean to offend you. It's just not like you to let a complete stranger into your home and around your child. He's even driving your car for fuck's sake," she says, raising her voice a little.

"Would you keep it down with the ef-word? Brandon is in the other room."

She flinches. "Sorry. It's just Dave and I are worried about you." Her features soften.

"I appreciate it, Jenny, I do. But I'm a grown woman. I think I have my senses about me. I don't see something wrong with helping Ryder get back on his feet. Him being here is good for him and it's good for me. In the sense that, yeah, it does get lonely having meals by myself and it's nice that he's offered to help fix up the house, but that's it. There is nothing romantic going on."

"Okay, fair enough." She lifts her mug and takes a sip.

I set down my tea and sit back in my chair. I'm not sure if I should tell her my thoughts—I'd like her opinion, but based on what she's just said, I'm not sure if she'll understand. "He did mention an ex. I'm not delusional where he is concerned. I know this is temporary. The reality is that I am still holding out that Thomas will eventually get his shit together and come meet his son. Has Dave heard anything?"

"No, hon, he hasn't." Jenny shrugs her shoulders sorrowfully and her lip turns down. "I'm sorry, Halo. I'm just worried about you," she says, extending her hand and closing it over mine.

"I know and I appreciate it, but let's be honest. I just went through ten hours of labor only to be cut open by a knife. I can barely walk, my nipples are freakin' killing me from breastfeeding and I can't take a shit without panicking about how much it will hurt. I'm not exactly in a state to be drooling over some hot guy." I laugh.

"Shit, Halo, I know giving birth isn't easy, but you're right. Ryder is damn hot. At least you have some eye candy around here." She waggles her brows.

It's actually funny that she thinks he's hot because most of his face is bandaged. Something tells me it's going to be a good-looking face but we could both be wrong and he may actually look like he's been taken out by a wrecking ball. Either way, it doesn't matter. He seems like a good person who has been through a lot, and there is nothing wrong with helping out when people have been knocked down in life. I know that because I have been knocked down.

"I do wish I could see his face under those bandages," I admit to her. "I'm curious what lies underneath them."

"I'll tell you what's underneath those bandages—a whole lot of male hotness."

I burst out laughing and smack her in the shoulder. She falls back in her chair in a fit of giggles, holding on to her stomach. "Dammit, I can't laugh." Her face scrunches like she's in pain.

"Huh? Why not?"

"Those damn exercise videos of mine. I've been doing these really intense ones and my muscles are screaming right now." She shakes her head with a slight grin.

"Well, you look hot, mama," I tell her.

"Thanks. I better be going. I'll see you tomorrow for that doctor's appointment," she says as she drinks down the remainder of her coffee and walks over to the sink.

"Actually, Ryder is going to take us. I didn't want you to miss out on work." I wince a bit because it does kind of look bad.

Jenny gives me a knowing look. "Uh-huh!" She nods and I follow her to the front door. She puts her jacket and boots back on and leans in to give me a hug. "I will call you later."

"Thanks for stopping by," I say as she leaves.

After I shut the door behind her, I take a long breath. Her words resonate. I know she's right. This isn't like me to let a stranger into my life this way. She's also right that Ryder is hot, but I'm waiting for Thomas. I signed those divorce papers because I realized I couldn't save him. It didn't mean I stopped loving him. I still held out hope where

Thomas was concerned. I was serious when I told her my head isn't in a romantic place right now. I'm sure Ryder knows that too. I mean, look at me with this swollen belly and the black bags under my eyes. I'm definitely not at my finest right now. I walk over to the playpen to take a peek at Brandon. He's fast asleep. I lie down on the couch, within hand's reach of the bassinet, and close my eyes for a bit. The sleepless nights are definitely catching up to me.

***

June 6, 2006
Halo

I stalk into the master bedroom, feeling pumped up on anger and hormones.

"Thomas, would you get your damn ass out of bed? It's already five o'clock and I was hoping we could have dinner together." I drag the sheets off him and then walk over to the window to open the curtains. He's been awake all night and now he's sleeping through the day. I swear I feel like he's doing this just to avoid me.

"Halo, dammit, I'm tired. Just let me sleep." He covers his head with a pillow to block out the light.

Usually I do as he asks—I've been letting him sleep every day for the past two months. Since he got back from Iraq he hasn't been the same. Something happened on this deployment that he doesn't want to talk about. After his first deployment in Afghanistan, he was off kilter for a few weeks. But although he was spacey and tired, he was still here with me. We were still us. We were still living our lives.

Something happened this time and I wish I knew what it was. I want to help him. He just won't let me in. I fear something is really wrong with him.

"Thomas Wells, I've spent all day making us a romantic dinner, you could at least have the courtesy to listen to me." I smack him in the back.

I've been feeling like shit these last few weeks. At first I didn't understand what was wrong. I thought I was having some sort of sympathy pain for Thomas. My doctor informed me differently. I'm pregnant.

I was both ecstatic and shocked. I mean, he's only been home for two months and we've only had sex twice the entire time. I'm twenty-three years old, almost twenty-four, and I've been waiting to have this man's baby for the past three years, but he was never ready. He never wanted children because of his shitty upbringing. He was scared of repeating his own parents' mistakes.

This last deployment was a long one, eighteen months. I remember what he'd said to me before he left, "You're my Halo, my ray of light. I will always find my way back to you."

It was our thing. I wore his locket around my neck with the same words held close to my heart every time he walked out the door. My heart always left with him and I hoped he would keep that promise.

This time he's come home, but something is off. It's as if he's kept his promise about bringing his body back to me, but his mind and soul are in the desert halfway around the world.

I stand there watching him and finally he drags his limp body from the bed. Of course he's completely naked, giving me a nice view of his sculpted behind. He trudges over to the bathroom and I leave the bedroom. I make my way down the stairs, taking large breaths that make me feel lightheaded.

Thomas had reservations about being a good husband when we got married and yet he's been the best husband. It will be the same with the baby. As much as I didn't plan this pregnancy, I'm happy about it. I'm not getting any younger and a part of me always worried that my window of opportunity would pass me by and I would never have the chance to become a parent. This child is a surprise but a blessing nonetheless.

I give my belly a gentle rub. "We can do this, little one. I know he'll be thrown off at first, but he doesn't mean it. I know he'll come around. He'll have to come around."

"Babe, were you just talking to yourself?" Thomas passes me in the downstairs hallway with an amused grin on his face. He places a light kiss on my cheek and rubs his hands together. "Do you need my help with dinner?" he asks with a sleepy grin.

Good. His mood is chipper. This will all be okay. "Sure," I say. "You can get the drinks."

I've set the old dining table for a romantic dinner complete with long, white candlesticks. It's only five o'clock, but it's become dark and cloudy.

Thomas follows me into the kitchen. I pull the roast out of the oven and he compliments my cooking, as usual, and gives me a hug. I'm grateful for the attention, but I'm anxious about getting dinner on the table. I plan to tell him my news while we're eating.

"Do you want red or white wine?" he asks.

Damn. I can't answer that. "I'll have red," I reply. I can always fake it.

As we settle down to eat, I watch him carefully, gaging his mood. Each time he comes home I seem to worry about him more. He's traveled the world on training sessions and deployments both short and long. Now he's a mess and it breaks my heart. I'm excited about the baby, and I just want my Thomas back.

"This is delicious, babe." Thomas smiles at me from across the table as he takes a bite of the roast. I'm too nervous to eat. I haven't felt like eating meat at all, but I know it's Thomas's favorite meal and he wasn't eating properly over in Iraq. I wanted to spoil him now that he's home.

"Can I pour you some wine?" he offers. I nod so he fills my wine glass halfway. He pours himself a full glass. A wave of frustration rolls over me because I know he has been drinking too much since he came home. I worry how that will affect the baby and me.

He lifts his wine glass to make a toast. "This is to you, Halo. You're my light. I know I've been in a pissy mood since my return, but I'm working on it. I love you, baby. I love you so much."

"I love you too, Thomas." I smile at him. After we clink our glasses together, I pretend to drink.

He rises from the table and comes over to me, placing his palm at the back of my neck and leaning over me. I lift my chin and grant him access to my mouth. It's been a while since we've connected like this and I've missed it deeply. His hands move to my waist, lifting me up against his body. I wrap my legs around him, loving how he can hold me so easily.

He carries me to the empty half of the long table and sets me down gently. He bends over me for another kiss and I'm loving the attention. This is us. This is the man I married. His improved mood couldn't have come at a better time. I can taste the wine on his tongue as the kiss deepens. He pulls his head back, giving me a loving smile.

"I need inside you," he says, his tone husky and wanting.

I unfasten his jeans as he runs his palm over the center of my chest and down my abdomen to cup my sex.

"Get undressed," he orders, and I love the command in his tone.

I sit and remove my shirt and bra, watching his gaze, loving how it heats up. I'm so needy. I want him to touch me now.

"Thomas," I call out, my voice breathy.

"My Halo," he replies, and in one swift movement he removes my leggings and underwear. His lips connect with my abdomen as he spreads soft kisses around my belly. My need skyrockets.

"Thomas, please," I beg. I'm so worked up I can barely form a coherent thought. He slides his finger inside me and my hips buck, needing the friction.

"So wet," he replies. His blue eyes sizzle into a burning inferno and he pumps his finger in and out. In and out. Then he circles my clit with his thumb. I moan his name.

I feel my orgasm waiting to explode and he replaces his finger with his thick shaft. My chin turns up and my head falls back. He pumps into me hard and fast, his face flushed with a look of pure ecstasy. I love making him come undone.

"Halo," he grunts.

"Aghh!" I cry out as I move my hips into him, pressing my clit along his shaft. Thomas is relentless and rough.

It wasn't always like this between us. The lovemaking used to be softer, more gentle. Since the deployments that's changed. He's changed. He needs more and I want to give him what he needs. The truth is I'm enjoying this side of him. I can feel the table shaking beneath me, but I don't care. I need this like I need air right now. Our connection, my husband. I need my husband.

We finally come together. I scream out Thomas's name and he grunts mine. When we finally come down, we cling to each other, breathing raggedly. He buries his head in my neck and whispers, "I love you so much. So much." Then he pulls away.

"I love you too, baby. You've been so distant lately." I try to hide the pain it causes to say those words. He helps me off the table. We get dressed and I realize how much more relaxed I feel. And how much more relaxed Thomas looks.

"I know. I'm sorry. I..." His grin is lazy and edged with sadness. We settle back in our chairs. The food is still warm and I watch Thomas dig in.

"What is it?" I ask, hoping he'll continue what he was saying. The candles flicker. There's a flash of light outside the windows—the storm is about to break.

"Ah, nothing. It's Sunday tomorrow. Let's go to the lake or do something fun."

I can tell how hard he's trying. But I know he's putting on a show for me instead of letting me in. I hate that he feels like he needs to pretend.

"Sure, that would be great." I force a smile as I pick at my potatoes. I can hear the rain coming down hard. I coach myself to just tell him my news. He's in the best mood he's been in since he's returned and he's paying attention to me. But my stomach is churning and I'm worried about keeping these potatoes down.

"What is it, Halo? Just spit it out… I can tell you have something on your mind. I'm sorry I haven't been a good listener lately but I'm trying to do better."

I notice that his hands are little bit shaky when he runs them through his hair. I know he's trying, but I also know he might not be able to handle whatever's bothering him on his own. "Babe, I can see it's hard for you, have you mentioned any of this to the therapist?" My question is hesitant. I know he doesn't like that he's been forced to seek professional help due to his medical leave.

He smashes his fist onto the table, and I jump. "Dammit, Halo." His eyes are angry.

I flinch and push my chair back. I don't know who this man is sitting across from me, but he is not my Thomas. I don't know how I'm supposed to tell him about the baby now. But it would probably be worse if he finds out when my belly starts to grow.

His head falls to his hands and he's muttering to himself. I think he may have lost it completely and I wish I could speak to his therapist to find out if he really understands what's going on in Thomas's head.

I walk over to him and wrap my arms around his large shoulders. He turns to me and buries his face in my stomach. He rubs his cheek against my belly, gripping my shirt like he's holding on for dear life. My heart twists in my chest. He became a SEAL not only to protect our country, but to prove something to himself. To prove he was worthy of my love. It kills me that he's paying such a terrible price.

"Baby, I'm here. Talk to me," I plead as I hold on to him and run my hands gently through his hair.

He pulls his head back and his blue eyes are red around the rims. He looks like a lost little boy. I wish I could get through to him. "It's okay, Thomas. You're home now."

"I can still hear it in my head, Halo—the gun shots, the explosions. I left my friends there to come home to you and it's eating away at me. I need to go back but I don't want to leave you either. I don't know what the fuck is happening or what I should do."

The mere mention of him leaving again causes my own heart rate to stammer. He can't leave, not now. I can't be alone for this. Suddenly there's a loud clap of thunder followed by a strong bolt of lightning and I jump. Thomas jumps too. He's been doing that a lot from loud noises since he came home two months ago. It's part of the reason he was given a medical leave. I rub his back, trying to console him. I know this isn't the time but I take a deep breath and pull together every ounce of courage I have.

"Babe, I need to tell you something..." I hold his face in my hands. I gaze down at the features I love so much, and I know everything will be okay. It has to be.

"What is it, Halo? You made us this special dinner. You probably have some great news and I'm just fucking everything up."

"You haven't messed anything up," I say softly. "I'm happy you're talking to me. I want you to always feel like you can tell me what's going on in that head of yours." My voice is shaky but I feel proud to say the words. "Thomas, we're having a baby."

He's been looking lovingly into my eyes, but the minute I finish my statement, his jaw drops and his blue eyes widen. He pulls away from me, shaking his head. Now he's rubbing his scalp over and over again, his movements shaky and uncontrolled.

Shit. This isn't good.

"Thomas, relax," I say. "This is us. This is a baby we created together. Everything is going to be okay. You went off to fight the war and now you're home. You're my hero. You'll be this baby's hero too."

He remains silent and jerks his chair back. He stands up and paces the room as he mutters to himself. I can't understand what he says. A loud clap of thunder reverberates through the house and he flinches. My heart breaks every time he does that.

He looks at me accusingly. "You know how I felt about having a baby. How could you do this to me?"

Now it's my turn to drop my jaw. "I didn't do this to you. I did this *with* you," I answer, feeling wounded.

"I thought you were on birth control," he spits out.

"I was, Thomas. I don't know how I got pregnant. I just did."

"This is fucking bullshit." He's still pacing. One of the dining chairs gets in his way. He picks it up and hurls it. It smashes against the wall, splintering into pieces. I jump back, frightened, surprised, confused.

"I'm not doing this with you, Halo." He's breathing hard and his voice is raspy.

"What the hell is that supposed to mean?" I ask him, tears clogging my throat. "We've been married for almost four years. You know I want a family more than anything. I kept waiting and waiting for you while you fought all the bad guys and proved that you were worthy of me. That was all you, Thomas. I never felt that way. I always only wanted and accepted you. I'm not getting any younger and I'm happy this happened. I think it's a blessing..." My voice trails off as tears fall down my cheeks.

"I was never good enough for you! I never deserved you, Halo.

And the baby would deserve so much more than what I could give it as a father." He stares at my stomach like there's an evil threat inside it. I wrap my arms protectively across my waist. "I've got to… To go. I can't deal with this."

I don't know how to respond. He's obviously losing it and I'm scared. I knew he was going to take the news hard. I know he needs time to adjust to the idea. But that doesn't make it any easier when I see him head toward the door and throw on a jacket. He shoves his feet into shoes, as if he can't get away from me fast enough.

A second later he's out the door. My blood turns cold. He's never done anything like this before. Deep down I'm scared he's leaving for good.

I go to the front window and pull back to the curtains to watch him. It's pouring outside and he's getting drenched. The sky lights up again and he falls into the grass with his hands over his head. I don't know if I need to call an ambulance or what I should do. I throw on my raincoat and rain boots and follow him outside into the storm. The wind is blowing hard and I hang on to my hood as I walk toward him, bracing myself against the strong gusts.

I get down on my knees beside him. The wet grass penetrates my pants. "Thomas, it's okay. It's just the thunder." From a distance I hear Charlie barking. She must think we've lost it.

"Huh…what?" He lifts his head like he's confused but happy to see me at the same time.

"It's okay. The noise and the flashing—it's just the storm." I point to the sky.

He slowly stands up. "I'm sorry, Halo. I need to go." He pulls the keys to his truck out of his pocket.

"Thomas, please," I cry out. He's all I have. Fear is gripping me by the throat as one of my worst fears play out. Being left alone. I've had nightmares for years about being left alone after my parents died.

He doesn't turn back. The truck starts with a roar and he whips out of the driveway, tires squealing as he speeds away from our home.

This can't be real. I drop my head and I see his dog tags wet and glistening in the grass. I know he wears his tags from the navy all the time because he's required to, but he always wore the ones I'd given him too because he felt like I was close to him when he did. He's worn them since the day I gave them to him. He said they brought him good luck.

The thought makes my stomach sink. I pick them up out of the grass and hold them to my heart. I can't help but read this as some kind of message. I stand out in the rain for I'm not sure how long. Almost long enough to have ridden out the storm.

I'm awake all night, hoping he'll come home. He never does.

Finally, I sleep. My cell phone buzzes at three-thirty in the afternoon. Jenny's name is on the screen. Deep down in the pit of my stomach I know...

Thomas isn't coming home like he always promised me he would. Iraq did something to him and apparently the halo I've kept burning for him has gone out.

My cell rings and rings, and I finally pick up. "Yeah."

"Do you want me to come over?" Jenny asks sympathetically. Shit. She knows.

"Is he there?" I asked in a sleep-clogged voice.

"Yeah honey, he was here. He slept in the garage. Dave has been trying to talk with him all night. He wants to go off medical leave and get reinstated for active duty. He wants to ship out."

Her words are like a knife stabbing through my heart and my tears go into free fall. I wasn't expecting this. I wasn't expecting this at all.

CHAPTER TWELVE

Thomas
June 6, 2006

It feels so good to finally be asleep. Since I came home from Iraq two months ago I haven't been able to shut my eyes without hearing gun shots, without seeing blood, without hearing the last screams of my best friend Chris as I watched him get shot during a street battle in Ramadi, Iraq.

Pacing the house at night makes me crazy. I know I'm disturbing Halo who is a light sleeper. I couldn't take it anymore and went to the military doctor. He prescribed sleeping pills. I've never been one for drugs, but I had no choice. The sounds in my mind were sucking me into a dark, dark place. I wasn't sure if taking a leave was the right thing to do but since I've been unraveling I know it's been a good decision. The only part I hated was meeting with the military psychiatrist and having to reveal how torn up I was. Having to admit that Chris's death destroyed me wasn't easy. I hate to admit weakness. And I guess that in itself is a weakness.

Halo is so worried and I want to reassure her, but I can't. Not this time. My last deployment was so much worse than the rest. Chris had been my best bud since boot camp. He was running away from a shitty life in New York and we clicked instantly, helping each other through the brutality of boot camp and then BUD/s training in Coronado. It was the first time I had left Chicago, my first time being so far away from Halo.

I want to stop thinking about all of it, put an end to the endless cycle of grief in my head. Halo and I discussed having babies over the years. I figured eventually I would have the courage to say yes to her. I loved saying yes to her. I loved making her smile. Right now I couldn't make her smile. My head was stuck in Iraq. I see Chris's face when he laughed, that cocky bastard. My stomach dips. I unfortunately can still hear his screams when he was shot. I still feel his blood running over my body as I carried him back to the outpost. Those memories haunt me. It's why I took sleeping pills. I hate to admit that I'm in pieces because it's not who I am, but I'm a fucking head case. I take the pills and wash it down with any hard liquor I can get my hands on. I know what that shit does. How cruel it makes people. I can't stop myself if I wanted to. My life feels so damn dark. It's the only way to get some peace and quiet and allow my body to calm down for a short while.

My head is all over the map as my wife pleads with me that everything will be okay. The problem is I can't look into perfect brown eyes that are so pure and tell her that this world is tainted. That I am tainted. As the rain pours down on us I feel myself slipping further and further from reality. My head is muffled to the point that her words aren't clear. There's a thunderous clap. I hit the ground, wondering where my gun and artillery are. As the cool liquid runs over my body it feels like blood. I'm jolted back in time. I'm carrying Chris on my back trying to get back to base. The wetness… He's bleeding so bad it soaks through my clothes. My breathing is short and labored. I'm walking down the streets of Ramadi, Iraq when I hear Halo's reassuring voice. I lift my head, realizing I am on our front lawn. The wet grass is all over my hands, soaking my knees. It isn't blood.

I shake my head, trying to focus on Halo. I'm too worked up. She's trying to console me, but I can't be consoled. I can't bring her into my darkness. I won't.

Before I know it I'm in the truck, aware that I should not be driving in my state but I'm too fucked up to care. After driving for a few moments I pull over to the side of the road and bang my head on the steering wheel repeatedly. I can feel a bruise forming on my forehead. I'm fucking losing my mind. I stare out the window to the dark sky, to the slits of rain falling hard on my windshield. Why? Why fucking now? I scream up to the sky.

How can I raise a baby or take care of a baby when I am so messed up? I can't repeat my parents' mistakes. I take a deep breath and put the car back into drive. I should go to Dave's and park the truck before I get arrested for a DUI.

I'm thinking of Chris again as I steer through the pouring rain. And I'm thinking about the baby—Halo's baby, my baby—as I drive aimlessly for hours. Or, hell, what do I know? Maybe I've only been driving for a few minutes.

When I pull into Dave's driveway, my head jerks forward as I slam the truck into park before it's completely stopped. As I walk up to the front door the front light comes on. I see a shadow in the window. The rain has slowed down and so has the damn thunder. *Fuck, look at me.* I want to chuckle to myself. *I'm scared of the fucking thunder.* Before I reach the door, Dave opens it up slowly.

"Hey, man," he says, eyeing me warily. He's wearing a pair of plaid pajamas, and it strikes me how damn *normal* they look. I envy Dave that he has his shit together. He has a nine-to-five job, he comes home at the end of the day to his wife and children and he wears plaid pajamas. That fucking rocks.

"Hey," I mutter.

"Thomas, are you drunk?" he asks, quietly taking a step outside. He looks pissed.

"Maybe," I respond, feeling my body sway a bit.

"Get in the garage, Thomas. What the fuck is going on with you? You drove drunk?" There's disgust in his tone now.

"I'm fucked up, Dave. Halo is pregnant and I am fucked up." Before I have a chance to elaborate, my phone rings. Tuck's name lights up the screen. I'm actually pleased to see he's calling. We've both been back on home soil for two months, and he's the only other person who can understand what I'm going through right now.

"What's up, man?" I ask, answering the call.

"Not fucking much," he responds. "I hate being home. I've been taken off medical leave. I'm shipping out next week."

My eyes squeeze shut. There is no fucking way he is going anywhere without me.

"Tuck, I don't know man… Things are messed up for me," I begin to explain and I know he would listen, but he wouldn't get it. He's never had what I have with Halo. But even as I say the words, I know I have to get away from here. Right now fighting a bunch of psychotic terrorists is the only thing that will save me. I need to go back. I have to finish this war off. If not for myself, then for Chris.

"Yo, Thomas. You with me man?" Tuck asks.

"I'm here, man. I'm with you." I've got some work to do before I can return to active duty. I need to get approval, I need to clean up. "There's no way in fucking hell you're doing this without me," I tell him. I lost Chris. I can't handle losing anyone else. I can't stand by and not fight this war.

"Lakehurst, New Jersey. Eight days from now," he says gruffly.

"I…I might come hang with you before then, okay?" I already know he'll say yes. It's just who he is.

"Of course, man. You know you always have a place by me, but Thomas, are you drunk?"

"I'll see you tomorrow, brother. I got to go." I hang up the phone when I see Dave staring at me with his jaw dropped and his eyebrows furrowed. His garage is set up like an apartment—I helped him renovate it after I got back from Afghanistan the first time. Now I'm grateful that he has a place for me to crash tonight because there's no way I could walk into his house now with Jenny's scrutinizing eyes on me. She would probably take a butcher knife to my neck if she knew what was happening. Instead I spend an hour trying to rationalize my actions to Dave. He's not buying it.

"You're leaving? Halo is pregnant? What are you on, Thomas? Are you on drugs or something? Because I don't need that shit around my wife and kids." He waves a finger at me in a threatening way. I want to laugh because he may be as tall as me, but I outweigh him by a good fifty pounds. But nothing about this is funny.

"Dave, don't fucking judge. You have no idea what I've been through…"

"I may not have an idea what you've been through, but you must be crazy if you're going to put yourself through it again and leave a pregnant wife behind. That's not manning up. That's being a fucking coward," he hisses.

"You're right, Dave. I'm a fucking coward, but my brothers are shipping out. There is no way I'll let them fight this war without me. My team is still out there. I got leave but it wasn't a permanent leave. Halo knew that. I can't be with her, Dave. I've been sucked into this war too deep. I've seen bad things, I've done bad things. I lost my fucking best friend." As I continue my rant I realize that Dave hasn't said anything to me for a few good minutes. I see the disappointment in his eyes. He's quiet and I'm too messed up to care what he thinks.

"Thomas, you need to sleep this off. I don't know if you're drunk or high, but you are talking out of your ass. Go crash on the bed and we'll talk in the morning." He's so calm, I'm not sure he's getting it.

As soon as he leaves, I fall onto the bed and pass out.

When I wake up at the crack of dawn I'm sober, with a splitting headache. I know Dave—and probably Halo—probably expect me to come to my senses about all this, but I don't feel any differently. And I know I won't change my mind tomorrow or even next month.

I shower and then use a disposable blade I find under the sink to shave my face and head. I call a cab on my cell and make arrangements to travel to Tuck's place. I leave the keys for the truck on the small kitchen counter with a note asking Dave to get them back to Halo.

Weirdly, I think about my father. I want to find him, scream at him for wrecking my fucking life. But as I head down the quiet, sleepy street, I rethink blaming my dad. I know this shit is on me.

CHAPTER THIRTEEN

Ryder

When I tell the doctor about my dream last night, he thinks it's a good thing. He said not to pressure myself, but I may start having more dreams and, slowly, slowly, I may start to learn more about the man I was. He urged me not to get my hopes up, though, because there's still the slight chance it won't happen.

The best part of my visit is getting an ID with a medical discharge. It makes a trip to the bank and the DMV possible. The bureaucracy crap is a drag, but when it's done I actually get excited about the idea of buying paint and supplies for painting Brandon's room. I can picture Halo's smile when it's finished…

I pull into a shopping center I'd noticed on my drive to the VA. I stop at an Old Navy and buy some essentials. I was happy to see my bank account was relatively healthy. I'm not rich or anything, but I have enough to get by. So my next stop is an electronics store for a new phone. I'm much happier about shopping in the Home Depot. In the paint department I stare at the samples and paint chips. I'm attracted to primary colors and I figure that makes sense since Brandon is a baby. I go a little crazy and take the sales guy's advice—two colors in different shades and a border with a baseball theme.

I feel a sense of hope—or maybe it's just a feeling of usefulness—as I load the paint and supplies into the truck. Then I head back to Halo, hoping I don't get lost along the way.

CHAPTER FOURTEEN

Halo

It gets kind of lonely sitting in this big house all day. With Brandon sleeping it's so quiet I can hear the old plumbing rattling in the walls. At least I convince myself that's what the noise is—hopefully it's not some mouse who's taken up residence in my walls.

Brandon is a good baby. He sleeps for most of the day and when he isn't sleeping he's eating. I'm tired and achy so the chance for rest is welcome. I've tried watching some soap operas but I just can't get into it. I even picked up my journal to write a bit. It was soothing for the first half hour but then it made me feel antsy again.

Writing about my feelings after Thomas left was a good way for me to vent my emotions. I've never been an incredibly open person. I've always kept issues to myself. I never wanted to burden my friends with my sometimes morbid thoughts, but morbidity can take over when you lose your family to a drunk driver. My thoughts remind me of Thomas. The way he stood by my side after my parents' death. He was on my case about finishing my last year of high school and ensured I applied to college. When my depression worsened he put off enlisting and took classes in order to become a paramedic. Thomas Wells spent six months in classroom training for me. I want to laugh and cry at the memory. He sacrificed his dreams for me.

My cell phone rings and I see Jenny's name pop up on the caller ID. She was just here earlier and I'm surprised to hear from her again so soon. "Hey Jen."

"Halo, I forgot to mention earlier. The girlfriends want to meet Brandon. Would you prefer to have everyone over individually? Or can we invite everyone in one shot? I can help you prepare everything. You won't have to do a thing…it's just everyone is a little worried about you and they want to meet the little guy. We could do an evening thing, that way they will all get babysitters and leave the littles at home. What do you think?"

I know she means well but I am in no mood to entertain and I still feel like shit. "I don't know, Jen. I still feel pretty raw."

"I know, babe. I was thinking we could put it off for a couple weeks. It's just that everyone needs notice to coordinate and get babysitters and all that."

"Yeah, okay. I guess I eventually will have to socialize."

Jenny snorts into the phone. "You think? You haven't seen anyone since Thomas left. I know you've been through a tough time but I think it would be good for you to start talking to our friends again, become more social, you know. Brandon is small now but give him a few months and he'll enjoy the interaction of other babies and kids. It will be good for him."

"I know, Jen. Believe me, I know. It's just hard right now. I love my baby dearly with all my heart, but right now he's only sleeping, eating and pooing." I chuckle sadly into the phone.

"That's how it works. You'll get used to it. Soon he will be smiling and doing other things, and let's just say that you should get ready for that little guy to melt your heart."

"I know. He already does. I guess I'm just in a funk," I respond. There's a knock on the door and I say, "There's someone at the door so I gotta run. Yeah, let's do it. Book something."

"Okay, hon. You take care." Her tone is worried and frankly I'm worried too. I read about post-partum depression in my pregnancy books and it seems like I may be suffering.

I get up and go to the door. Charlie's sitting there, wagging her tail. I see Ryder through the peephole. He's carrying a big box and his arms look strained. I hold onto Charlie's collar and open the door.

"Hey, uh... I bought paint. I realize I probably should have asked you what color you wanted to paint the little guy's room. The man in the store said blue is most popular for boys but at the last minute I decided to get green too." The box is filled to the top with gallon-size pails of paint. There's a big bag on the porch filled with what looks like rollers and brushes.

"Wow. Ryder, that was very kind of you. Blue is great, and so is green. Here let me help you." I tell Charlie to go lie down and then reach for the bag.

"Oh no you don't," Ryder says, stopping me. "You go sit and rest. If this is a good time, I can come in and show you the colors. I bought a special paint that doesn't emit fumes so it won't affect the little guy. Go back to where it's warm." The cool air has whisked its way into the front hall and I shiver. I'm only wearing a nursing bra and a white T-shirt with grey sweatpants. I notice Ryder's gaze drops to my chest before he quickly looks away. His quick glance makes me feel self-conscious. When he turns around I look down to my chest to see my perky milk-filled nipples poking through the fabric of my shirt. Damn nursing bra doesn't have padding.

I cross my hands over my chest as Ryder brings the paint into the house. "Did you want to choose now? I wouldn't mind getting started now. I don't really have anything to do." He shrugs and I feel bad for him because he always has this lost look.

Ryder steps further into the house and once again I notice how big he is. It's not just a size thing—it also has to do with his presence in general. He begins to explain the different shades and shows me the border he bought. I gaze at his hands again. The skin is rough looking, scarred from the burns he suffered. My heart clenches again—I can't help but think about our soldiers putting their lives on the line to keep us safe.

"I love it. You made amazing choices." I can just picture how it will look in Brandon's room. Ryder's kindness has really thrown me for a loop. For a guy who doesn't remember anything about himself, he sure is a kind soul.

"I'm glad you like," he says, his mouth turning up at the corners. I wish those bandages would come off already. "Is it okay if I head upstairs, then?" he asks, looking at the staircase.

"Sure," I say. "Thank you."

He slowly starts up the stairs with the box of paint. I watch him, thinking that it really was a smart idea to offer him the garage.

I head into the kitchen and begin to prepare dinner. I hate preparing meals for one, but now that I'm breastfeeding I feel like it's important for me to eat the right foods for Brandon's sake. Tonight I've planned on a roasted chicken with potatoes.

As I peel the potatoes, I hear Ryder whistling from upstairs. The tune is familiar but I can't place it. My mood lifts a bit now that the house isn't so quiet. By the time I've got the chicken ready to put in the oven, I hear Brandon stirring in living room.

I waddle in to pick him up, his body curling naturally into mine, his head settling against my chest. I look at his tiny features and I can't help but smile.

I take a seat in my usual corner on the couch and breastfeed him.

"Hey, Brandon," I whisper to him, "your room is going to look so nice. Our friend Ryder is up there preparing your room to be painted right now. He even got you a little baseball border. I think you are going to enjoy playing baseball one day. My dad taught me how to hit a ball and how to throw a curve ball. I'm going to teach you those things too." I smile, looking down at him, watching his jaw moving slowly up and down as he eats. My grim mood lifts. How can I be sad, when I have this gift in my arms?

My eyes grow heavy and I fight the urge to close my eyes. The sleepless nights are taking their toll, but Brandon is still eating. I'm paranoid about falling asleep with him in my arms. My head feels like a heavy rock as I struggle to stay awake. I notice Brandon's little mouth movements have slowed. I get up slowly, hoping to put him back in the bassinet and grab a nap. I am suddenly drunk-tired and I need a few minutes to replenish. Luckily, he goes down easy.

I head back over to the couch and rest my head against the pillow and close my eyes.

***

I startle and my eyes open abruptly. I heard a loud noise. A thump from upstairs. A moment later I hear Ryder holler as if he's hurt. I quickly check on Brandon—he's still content in the land of sleep.

"Ryder," I call softly as I slowly make my way up the stairs. My incision is aching and I hate that I can't go any faster. I make it up to Brandon's room and find Ryder on the floor holding his knee.

"Oh my! Are you okay?" I rush toward him with concern.

"You didn't need to go up those stairs. I'm fine." There's irritation in his tone.

"What happened?" I ask.

"I'm fine. It's no big deal. I couldn't reach the top of the wall so I took the little step ladder from the closet. I took off my leg brace then forgot I shouldn't bend my knee as I climbed the ladder. Lost my balance." His cheeks flush. "Some SEAL I must have made," he mutters under his breath.

I don't want to make him feel any worse than he already does so I look at the progress he's made. He's only started the edging, but it's a beautiful color. I can't wait to see it finished.

"Maybe you're pushing yourself too soon," I say, placing a hand on his shoulder. "How about you take a break and come down and have dinner with me?" I'd hoped to brighten his mood, but now that I've made the suggestion my cheeks become hot and rosy. I mean, why would dinner with me improve his mood? I feel stupid now.

"I don't want to impose. You've given me a place to stay and now you're feeding me?" He smiles wryly.

"First off, your rent money is much needed. I get maternity leave, but once the eight weeks is over, I am placing Brandon in private care, which is very expensive. Two weeks of that time is from my sick days. I don't want to use more sick days because I may need to use them to be with Brandon if he gets sick. I'm a teacher. The kids at school are constantly picking up viruses..." I ramble on. This is clearly TMI.

"You know I could pay you more rent," Ryder suggests. "And I should. Especially since you've been feeding me too."

"Don't be ridiculous. I'm not taking more money than we agreed to. And now you're painting my son's room for me. Do you know how much that would cost if I had to hire a painter?" Ryder tilts his head as if he's considering my argument. "So what do you say about dinner?"

"I'd love to have dinner," he says. He struggles to his feet and towers over me, smiling.

My cheeks flush and my stomach drops. He makes me feel things I don't want to be feeling. I'm obviously out of practice with making friends with men.

I pull my eyes away from him and walk to the door. "Perfect. It should be ready soon. Come down whenever you're ready." I leave the room and let out a slow breath.

Before heading to the kitchen, I check on Brandon. He's still asleep and it's likely he'll be down for at least another hour.

I'm taking the chicken out of the oven when Ryder enters the room. "Mmm that smells really good," he says with that low gruff voice.

"Thanks. It was one of my husband's favorite recipes." As soon as the words are out, I bite my lip. I hate that I'm still living in the past. I also realize that I have an incredibly hot and kind man who is standing in my kitchen waiting to eat with me. If this was another time and I was a different person I may have been all over Ryder St. John.

I quickly set the table and Ryder helps me carry over the food. When we sit, I tell him to help himself. He puts a modest serving on his plate and waits for me to serve myself. Apparently manners aren't one of the things he's forgotten.

"So tell me about yourself," he says, taking a bite of chicken. His eyes suddenly close and he makes a groan at the back of his throat. "Jesus, woman. You can cook. This is seriously delicious."

I laugh and take a bite too. Then I watch him eat for a minute, mesmerized by the way he's enjoying the food. I'm guessing he must have been on a long deployment where he only ate ready-to-eat meals that Thomas always described as a bunch of nastiness mixed together.

"So?" He looks at me expectantly, waiting to hear my response to his question.

"I'm an elementary school teacher. I teach sixth grade. Jenny is my best friend. You already met her…" I trail off because I'm not sure what else to say without mentioning Thomas.

"And?" he asks with a forkful of chicken halfway to his mouth.

"I don't know. Ask me questions. What exactly do you want to know?"

"Do you have any hobbies?" he asks.

"I like to read in my spare time. Sometimes I write a little too, but it's just for me. I like to swim—you saw the trophies from my water polo days. I swim laps over at the community center, and kept it up throughout my pregnancy. I thought if I was in good physical shape it would make delivery easier. I never expected to have a C-section—it's certainly made life a little difficult now with the recovery."

"Yeah, I can relate to unexpected stuff in life making for difficult recoveries. I'm looking forward to being active again someday. I'm guessing I'm likely a good swimmer if I made it through SEAL training." He continues to eat quietly and then he smiles. "You forgot to mention cooking as a hobby. You're good enough that you must practice a lot."

I thank him and I can tell by his expression that he's got a lot on his mind. I stay quiet, hoping to encourage him to talk.

"It's hard," he says. "You know…not remembering. I don't know what to expect from myself or if what I'm doing is even okay. I could be living on a base, or surrounding myself with other guys who are in treatment. But my instincts tell me I'd be better living on my own."

"You seem to be doing well," I agree. He's managed to go out and get things done.

"Thanks. I don't know about well, though. I fell off that step stool like a fool. I hate that I feel so shaky. And I hate that I feel like I'm in limbo. Men in my unit died, and I keep thinking that I probably should have died too. I feel bad for not remembering them or honoring them. From what I've learned, SEALs have a strict code of honor. I never went to my teammates' funerals. I don't even know who or where my friends are. There's no honor in that, is there?" His blue eyes gaze at me and I can't ignore their intensity.

"I'm sorry," I say. "It must be so hard for you—I wish there was some way I could help. Did the counselors at the hospital have any advice today? Have you had any glimpses into your past at all?"

He nods. "I had a dream last night. The counselors think I'll likely have more. It's something I both wish for and dread. The dream was pretty horrific."

He bows his head. I want to stand up and give him a hug—he probably hasn't had any human contact in a long time and he looks like he's drowning in a sea of pain. It's interesting that I've never felt the typical barriers between me and Ryder—the walls I usually put up when I meet someone new or interact with strangers. From the moment I met him at the hospital I've sensed that he was kind and non-judgemental.

I slowly get up from my chair and walk over to him. When I place my arms across his broad back, he lifts his head, startled, and suddenly stands. I'm a little taken aback and when he looks down at me I feel oddly uncomfortable. But then he gently hugs me in return and my discomfort disappears. He is like a gentle giant and I don't feel scared at all. In fact his embrace is welcome. It's been so long since I've felt a warm body and strong arms around me. We linger like this for a moment.

Ryder pulls his head back and he drops his arms. "Dinner was delicious. I'm sorry if I darkened the mood." His mouth turns down slightly.

"Don't be silly. I enjoy the company. This house has been pretty quiet and dull for a while. I'm happy to have Brandon now and he's definitely brightened my world, but it's nice to spend time with an adult too." I give his shoulder a squeeze. I look down at the table. "I should clean up before Brandon—"

Right on cue, I hear Brandon's sweet noises from the other room. I laugh.

"You go to him." Ryder tilts his chin toward the living room. "I'll clean up."

"Are you sure?" I ask. I like having him here but I don't want to take advantage.

"Yes. Please. Go."

In the living room Brandon is stretching his arms out and his little body curls. He's so delicious. I smile down at him. "Hey there, buddy. Are you hungry? Thanks for giving your mom some time to eat." We settle on the couch and Brandon gets right to it. I hear Ryder clamoring with the dishes in the background so I know there's no danger of boob flashing at the moment.

After a few moments his voice calls from the kitchen, "Hey, I'm all done in here. Do you need more time in there?"

His voice with its husky, deep timbre reminds me so much of Thomas. A sudden wave of worry washes over me. Am I missing Thomas so much—so entrenched in my past with him—that I've latched on to Ryder in a way that's completely outside of reality? I've been through so much that it's hard to understand my wants and needs right now.

"He'll be done in a few more minutes," I call out.

"No worries. Take your time. I'll hang out in here for a while."

"Thanks," I say.

"Hey," he says again. And I smile over the fact we're carrying on a conversation between the two rooms. "I know it's getting kinda late, but do you want to watch a movie?"

I look at the grandfather clock and see that it's only eight o'clock. I think about what I normally do in the evenings—how I usually get into bed and stare at the ceiling. And think of Thomas. Watching a movie with Ryder sounds a lot more appealing. It would be okay to hang out with him some more. He's a *friend.*

"Sure," I reply. Brandon has finished eating so I say, "We're all done in here. You can come in any time."

He strides into the room. "I'm going to take a quick shower and change clothes. I don't want to sit on your nice couch with paint-spattered clothes. I'll be back in a few?"

"Yeah, sure. I'll give Brandon a bath."

"Okay. Uh, do you want me to carry him up the stairs for you?"

"Thanks, Ryder. I'd appreciate that. How is your knee feeling?"

"No worries," he answers, walking over to me. "Do you want to put that blanket on me or something…so his face doesn't touch this crusty shirt?"

Oh wow! Was he really just considerate enough to ask that? My stomach flips. I know I can't be swooning right now.

"Thanks," I say again. I stand and place the little burp blanket on Ryder's shoulder. I hand him Brandon and he cradles him in his thick arms. Brandon's face rests against the blanket on his chest, and, of course, all kinds of foolish thoughts swirl in my head. Like how good they both look like that, and how it seems as though Ryder would make a great father. And how much I long for Brandon to have a dad someday.

I force my thoughts to shut down and I follow Ryder up the stairs. He tells me, "I put Brandon's crib in your room. The man at the store said it was low-fume paint, but I figure he's so tiny it would be better for him in there."

"Thanks, Ryder," I say and he walks over to my room and places Brandon slowly in his crib. Then his gaze lingers on me for a moment.

"So I'll see you soon," he says.

I'm almost breathless when I reply, "Just come in when you're ready. If I'm not down yet you can look for a movie on the TV. What kind of movies do you like?" I feel like I'm babbling. I'm nervous and I need to chill the heck out.

Ryder shrugs and looks at me blankly. "I don't know."

Shit! "I'm sorry. I'll come help you choose when we're ready." I shouldn't have asked that.

"Sure. See you soon," he says, turning and limping out of my room. I hear the stairs creek as he slowly makes his way down each step. I leave Brandon in his crib and turn on his little mobile that plays a soft Mozart tune. As I prepare his bath, I try to relax. I can do this. I can watch a movie with a man who isn't Thomas. Ryder is a friend. Ryder is a friend.

***

Half hour later Brandon is bathed and wearing a clean blue sleeper. I've showered too and I've thrown on a pair of black yoga pants and a grey shirt.

Ryder is only a friend. I repeat the mantra. This is not a date. There is no point in trying to look pretty so I wear something totally basic to drill home the point. My wet hair is in a messy bun and completely unattractive.

I carry Brandon down the stairs and find Ryder sitting on the couch and holding the remote control.

"I hope this is okay," he says.

"Of course it is." I smile at him and take a seat on the opposite end of the couch. He's wearing what looks like a new shirt and jeans and I realize he must have bought them today.

"So what should we watch?" I ask and he passes me the remote control.

"You decide," he says, smiling.

"Sure." The TV is one of the only new things in this house. It's a smart TV and we have Netflix. It was the one thing Thomas and I decided to splurge on. As I flick through the movies I ask Ryder, "What are you in the mood for? Action, drama, romance…" I look into his blue eyes.

"Honestly, I don't care," he replies.

"This one looks good," I say, pausing my scrolling on a comedy starring Ben Stiller. "Jenny saw it in the theaters and said it was hysterically funny." I don't know why I feel nervous about something as basic as choosing a movie.

"Whatever you like," he says. "I guess *The Heartbreak Kid* it is." He sinks down into the couch. He folds his hands over his abdomen and I begin to download the movie. Brandon has fallen asleep in my arms and I put him in the bassinet. The movie begins and I try to get comfortable on the couch.

"When are the bandages coming off?" I whisper to Ryder as the introductions start. I like the scent of his soap. I like the smell of *him*.

Stop it Halo! I chide myself again.

"Tomorrow," he whispers back, facing the television.

My stomach does somersaults. I'm both excited and anxious to see his face. It's been strange talking to the bandages. The scent of him wafts over me again. Sweet Jesus!

It's not like I want to do anything sexual anyway. My body is still healing from the trauma of a C-section and two rounds of stitches. I shake my head, hoping he hasn't noticed me making any strange faces while this dialogue continues in my mind.

You're angry at Thomas. This is what this is. You know you would never touch another man, my inner self argues, and I know she's right.

I get out of my head and focus on the movie. Ben Stiller is hilarious and I find myself giggling a lot. Ryder laughs too. It's definitely a funny movie, but there are some awkward sexual scenes that make me feel a little uncomfortable. An hour into the movie I yawn. This is now a late night for me. When I stretch out my arms, I notice Ryder pulls his gaze momentarily from the television to look at me. I settle into the cushions and try to concentrate on the screen.

Without realizing it I must have fallen asleep. When I awake, the movie is just about to finish. I'm also lying in the crook of Ryder's arm. It feels nice. The yummy man smell wafts up my nose again.

"I'm sorry." I look up at him and apologize.

"Please don't. This feels nice." I don't move or say anything else. He's right. It feels nice.

He suddenly begins to caress my hand. It's a rhythmic motion—almost like he's making love to this one small part of my body. It feels good, but I'm not sure if I should pull away.

His chin tilts and, as he looks down at our hands, I see his eyes go wide. He shoots up to a standing position. "Jesus! I'm sorry… That was inappropriate of me. I'm not sure why I did that." He runs his fingers through his hair. "Would you like me to go?" he asks.

"No, Ryder, it's fine. Let's just finish watching the movie." I'm not sure what's happening. Did he not realize what he was doing? Maybe he was zoned out. Or maybe he was just doing what his "old" self would have done? I wonder.

The movie continues and Ryder keeps to his side of the couch, his hands perched carefully on his torso. A part of me wishes I was back in his embrace.

The movie ends and I don't know if it's hormones or emotions or the fact I don't know how or what to feel about the man sitting next to me, but suddenly I feel tears tracking down my face. Which is ridiculous because it was a funny ending. And because it's what I do every time I get emotional, I think of Thomas. I wonder where he is, if he'll ever come back, if he'll ever meet his son—

"You're upset," Ryder interrupts my misery.

"It's my hormones," I blame, shaking my head.

"Come here," he says, placing his arms gently around me. "It's your husband isn't it? The movie made you think of him." It's a statement, not a question.

"Yes," I sigh sadly.

"Why did he leave? I mean if you don't mind me asking," he murmurs. He always seems unsure, like he's wondering if he's asking or doing the right thing. I attribute it to the amnesia.

I can't look him in the eye when I begin to speak, but I know he's listening intently. "He came back from a deployment really messed up. He spent most days in bed. I found out I was pregnant and he didn't take the news well. He had a hard time growing up. His upbringing was always a chip on his shoulder. It didn't matter what I did to try to make him feel better—his past haunted him. He was scared of being a shitty father like his own dad. I think he was so messed up from Iraq that everything just threw him for a loop and he left. Jenny and Dave told me he was going to deploy again. I don't even know how the navy allowed him back on active duty because he was such a mess. The only explanation I can make is that it was more important for him to return to his friends and comrades overseas than to be with me."

I wipe away my tears and continue, "Being a soldier was first to him. I should have prepared myself, because the first day I met him he told me his plan was to be a SEAL. It was his dream. When he returned the first time it took a few weeks to readjust to civilian life but he did. He was my hero fighting terrorists in Afghanistan. When troops were called into Iraq he left again. All my friends were having babies. I was jealous and scared that my chance to have children would pass. Unfortunately, when we did finally conceive he didn't view it as a good thing. I knew he dedicated his life to being a SEAL. I also thought he was dedicated to me too. He was messed up when he left, but I hoped he would come to his senses and return home. I haven't heard from him since the night I told him about Brandon. Then the divorce papers came and I didn't contest them. Soldiers don't need to be on home soil to file for divorce. The divorce was finalized and that was the end of our relationship."

"Shit, Halo. That sounds rough. I'm sorry you had to go through that. It makes me wonder why I got divorced at such a young age. I haven't looked through my file yet. I've only seen my basic information and I was divorced under marital status." His thick voice drifts off.

"So you don't know anything about your ex?" I finally look up and ask him.

I hate myself for asking the question. I'm not asking for his sake. I'm suddenly asking for my own. I like having him around and I wonder if his ex-wife will walk into our lives and somehow stake a claim on him. I wouldn't blame her if she did. If I knew where Thomas was right now I would probably do the same. Geez! It also makes me wonder if Thomas has found the company of other women or a specific woman. The thought makes my stomach roil.

"No, I haven't looked into it. I feel like it's unfair to search for someone until I get my own answers." His reply causes my heart to sink. I don't know what I was thinking. This man is only here to rent space from me. Clearly I didn't expect him to be a permanent fixture around here. I really am loopy from all these hormones.

"Let me help you get Brandon upstairs," he says, smiling down at me.

"Thanks, Ryder." I smile back warmly and retrieve Brandon from the bassinet. I pass him into Ryder's able arms.

"He really is a handsome fellow," he says looking down at Brandon with warm eyes. Then he turns toward the stairs and I follow close by, enjoying the masculine scent of his body wash. Although he moves stiffly, I sense doing this for me makes him feel good.

In my bedroom Ryder places Brandon gently into his crib. This almost feels routine. He turns to look at me in the dark room. Moonlight shines in through the window, giving a slight glare off his bandages. "Thank you for tonight. I had fun." His mouth curls at the corners. His eyes train on my lips and my heart flutters.

"Yeah, it was fun," I reply, trying not to give away how flustered I feel. He leans forward and my heart plummets. I've never been with anyone else besides my husband. He continues to lean forward and my breath catches as he makes contact with my cheek and then quickly pulls back.

"You have a good night," he says, stepping away. "I can lock up for you downstairs." After he leaves, my hand goes up to touch my cheek in the spot where his lips just connected. I sit on the bed and will myself to breathe. I can't even describe what I'm feeling. A part of me feels guilty for the brief kiss because this is the room Thomas and I once shared. A part of me feels turned on and a part of me really likes Ryder. I slowly climb into bed and stare at the ceiling. I think about Ryder's words from earlier—how he won't go looking for his wife because he doesn't know who he is. What if something bad happened to Thomas and that's what kept him away from us? Realistically I know that's not the case. I was in touch with some of the other wives on the team. Thomas is on active duty. He left me and I need to accept the finality of what that means.

CHAPTER FIFTEEN

Ryder

I head back downstairs and make sure the doors are locked before I head back out to the garage apartment. I don't know why I reached out to kiss her like that. I wish I could kick my own ass now for doing it. I wonder if it will make things awkward between us now.

Dammit. I couldn't help myself. She's so pretty and that smile of hers lit up the dark room and before I could even register my feelings, my lips connected with her soft skin. I knew to be gentle. I understand she's fragile. I was there when she fell in the hospital and saw the blood run through her gown. I was worried for her but I tried to distract her. I figured panicking at the sight of the blood would have been no help.

The garage is cold and I take off my jeans and put on a hoodie. I didn't buy any pajamas. I'm not sure if I am a pajama kind of guy. I get into bed and the old mattress creeks. I pull the covers up to my chin and stare up at the plastered ceiling. This place is frigid. I don't want to bother Halo, but I am thinking that maybe I can take a look at the heating myself.

Tomorrow I'll finish the little guy's room and then I'll ask Halo if she'll let me paint the rest of her house. Hell, looking at the floorboards on the main floor, I was thinking that they could use a good sanding and some new varnish. I am not sure how I know these things or if I was handy before. I figure it's a good way to keep my mind busy while spending time with Halo and that cute baby of hers.

I close my eyes and feel myself drifting.

The air is stagnant and musty. I'm in my fatigues with a gun in my hands and ammunition strapped across my body. There's another SEAL walking in front of me holding a long gun. There's another SEAL behind me holding a smaller gun. We're walking along a dirt road. The sun is blaring above us. I can feel sweat trickle down the back of my knees. We're scoping the area. There are insurgents here. We have to be careful that one of them doesn't pull a fast one on us. We have to set ourselves up so we have the backs of the marine unit coming *in. We enter an old vacated building.*

"Top floor," the man behind me shouts. I don't turn back as we enter the building and make our way up three flights of stairs. This uniform is fucking heavy but not as heavy as the artillery I'm carrying. The SEAL begins to set up and I assist behind him, prepping all our ammunition.

"Are we ready?" I ask, looking at the man ahead of me.

"All good," he responds.

He sets himself up. He's the sniper. I'm just here to assist and provide cover. We use our binoculars and spot the insurgents hiding in a building across from us. Motherfuckers have a sniper set up. Well, fuck them.

"Insurgents, across," I announce to the SEAL, who takes the binoculars.

"Motherfuckers have three small kids with them," he bites out.

Fuck. Why do they have to go dragging their kids into this war? They don't fucking value life like we do that's for fucking sure. He shoots and hits the insurgent beside the sniper. Now we've been spotted by the sniper for sure. A long run of shots are fired, and it's fucking hard on the ears. I wonder if one of those bullets will end up inside me. I fucking hope not.

I lie flat on the ground, waiting for the gunfire to cease. When the sniper has an open shot he closes in on the insurgent sniper and shoots. He's fucking awesome—I'll give him that. A bunch of insurgents begin shooting wildly. I pick up my rifle and get three clean hits.

Another SEAL calls out with a large smile, "That's how you get em' motherfuckers!" In the moment he loses focus, a shot is fired and blood splatters.

"Fuck no…" I crash into him and pull him down to the ground to keep him away from any more shots. Our sniper still has his M107 in position. "Fuck! He's bleeding out," I call out, feeling like my insides are being torn apart. Tears well in my eyes. I call for assistance on the walkie but it's going to be fucking hard getting a jeep in here with all the insurgents hiding in their damn holes. "I'm getting him out of here, watch my back," I say to the sniper and I don't know if I'm yelling or not because my ears are still ringing.

"I got you," he answers, holding onto his rifle while packing the ammo. I flip Rover on my shoulder. He's been shot in the left shoulder but who knows how close the fucking bullet is to his heart. We've been a team since fucking boot camp. There are six of us but only three of us were sent on this particular mission. I can't believe he lost his focus. I always told myself that I can't lose focus, not even for one second. That one second can cost you your life.

"Fuck, Rover. You hold on man. We're with you," I tell him as I make my way down three flights of stairs with an extra 200 pounds on my shoulders. He begins to mutter and I'm glad he isn't dead. My lungs are pinching for air. I need to get him back to base. He needs help fast. The sniper follows closely behind, aiming his gun. This is our second deployment together. These men are my brothers. If I had to, I would give my fucking life for either one of them.

As we walk down the deserted street, I know I'm in more danger now of getting shot with Rover on my back. We walk for about five minutes and then more shots are fired. I feel the impact but not the shot.

"Motherfuckers," the sniper shouts and begins shooting every fucking insurgent he sees. I keep walking and don't turn my head. I try to stay focused on getting back to camp. Besides, he has the best fucking aim on our team. When the area quiets down, I hear his voice again, but it's muffled. With the sun beating down on me, I feel like melting.

"He's fucking gone," he mutters and swipes tears from his eyes.

"What the fuck! Don't say that," I say angrily.

"He has two fucking bullet holes in his back," he says, his voice filled with sorrow. "Don't fucking stop walking. We need to get back to base. We need more men with us. You stop now and we are all fucking dead."

I continue to walk, my muscles screaming. Holding onto Rover in this heat is fucking debilitating. Sweat is running down my face and I crave water, but I know I can't stop and it's important we get his body back to base. I concentrate on putting one foot in front of the other. It's all I can do. This war is fucked up. We finally get back to base and Rover's body is prepped to be shipped home. His wife is going to flip the fuck out. I can't stop thinking of my own wife back home. I want to get back to her. This fucking war is far from over. I can't leave my friends behind and lead a happy life. I've been sucked into this hellhole, deep.

My eyes flip open. My body is covered in a thin sheen of sweat. I sit up, holding onto my head. I feel like I'm fucking losing it. Memories of the dream are on constant replay in my head. I remember saying I have to get back to my own wife. I wonder where she is and what happened to us. It felt like I loved her deeply in the dream and I was hanging on for her. A part of me wants to grab Halo's car keys and head over to the hospital for answers, but it's the middle of the night. I have to know if those men existed. Is there a Rover? Am I losing it?

I close my eyes and ease back onto the pillows. My heart is thudding loudly in my ears and I can still hear the shrill sound of gunfire.

***

Through the fog of sleep I can hear knocking. Whoever it is can wait because sleep feels good.

Knock. Knock. Knock.

I want to holler out and swear, but then I get my wits about me and realize where I am. *Shit!* I'm in Halo's garage. That must be Halo knocking on the door. I quickly get out of bed. I'm only wearing boxers so I slide on the jeans I left on the floor last night. I must have whipped off the shirt and hoodie I put on after I woke up from that nightmare.

"Hey," I say, opening the door.

Halo tilts her head to the side. "Are you okay?"

I feel like shit, so I am assuming I look like shit. "Yeah, I guess…" My bandages are itching like hell and I want to rip them off and scratch. I can't wait to get them off later.

"Oh! It's noon and Brandon has his pediatrician appointment today at one. You mentioned you would take us and…." She trails off, biting her lip. Her forehead is creased. "Are you sure you're okay? Because I can just ask Jenny to pick us up. I mean, she offered anyway." She looks a little flustered. I don't want her thinking I'm irresponsible.

"No. I'm…uh, okay. I just—I don't know."

"What happened? Did you remember something?" She takes a step inside the apartment. I move away from the door, locate my shirt on the end of the bed and put it on.

"I'm not sure. I had a dream and it felt real. The soldier in my dream had a name. They were people I cared about. A SEAL was killed…. my friend…his wife…" Anxiety builds in my chest.

"You really don't have to take us. It's obvious you're having a bad day…"

She is so understanding. I assume it's from years of being married to a SEAL.

I place my hand on her arm gently to stop her from turning away. She looks up at me with her beautiful round brown eyes. Her lashes are long and full. She's so pretty. "I want to take you two. Can you give me ten minutes to shower and get ready and I'll knock?"

She smiles sadly at me. I don't like that she feels sorry for me. "Okay sure, thanks. I'll hit the Keurig and make you some coffee."

"Thanks. Coffee is perfect." I grin.

She leaves and I exhale a long breath. When I go to the VA later to take care of the bandages, I'm going to try to get in to see my therapist. I need help processing this dream.

I take a quick shower, throw on some clothes and find the heavy winter coat I bought. I knock and she meets me at the door with a travel mug of coffee. I thank her and watch her carefully, checking for signs of awkwardness after that kiss I gave her last night. I know it was just a brief peck on the cheek. But the reality is I wanted more. I don't know where her head is at, especially now that I know how her husband left her.

"We're ready to go," she says and I notice she's already in her coat. Brandon is in his infant carrier on the floor beside her.

"I hope I didn't keep you waiting too long," I say. I try on a smile, but it isn't happening for me. I feel heavy today, like I'm carrying the weight of the world on my shoulders.

"No worries. We still have lots of time," she says, leaning down to pick up the carrier. She's already got a diaper bag slung over her shoulder. I'm no genius when it comes to baby things or giving birth, but that carrier with the weight of the baby inside must be heavy for her.

"Why don't you take the coffee and I'll get him?" I suggest.

She nods and takes the mug. I pick up the carrier. As I lean close, my arm brushes hers and I can't help notice how her breathing falters slightly. I don't know if this is wishful thinking, but I'm happy to see some reaction out of her where I'm concerned.

The little guy looks up to me with his dark blue eyes. "Hey, Brandon. How are you today, buddy?" I smile down at him. The smile comes naturally and I no longer feel like I'm trying to hide my somber mood. I lean in to put the little guy in the back seat of the truck and Halo hands me the keys.

We climb into the front seat and, as the truck starts up with a rattle, I ask, "Is this truck safe enough? It seems like there are a few mechanical problems."

"The doctor isn't too far, but, yeah, I'm pretty sure it needs a mechanic. I meant to take care of a bunch of things before I gave birth, but little Brandon here took me by surprise." She's shivering and so I turn up the heat. "At least there's heat." She smiles as her lips chatter.

"I can take a look at the engine when we get back," I offer.

"Do you know about cars, Ryder?" she asks turning her head toward me.

As usual, I don't know how to answer. I'm not sure if my offer came from wanting to do something good for her, or because I actually know something about engine repair.

"I think I can take a look. It can't do any harm." I shrug. Good enough answer, I reassure myself.

"Thanks," she says, and looks back to check on Brandon. She gives me the directions to the doctor's office and we arrive ten minutes later. We get out of the truck and I help her with the infant carrier and the diaper bag.

When we get inside, we pause in the clinic's entryway. "Is it okay if I borrow the truck later? I'm getting the bandages off and I also want to see if I can get in to see my therapist."

"Uh yeah, sure, what's going on? Is it the dream you had?" Her warm brown eyes are kind and caring and my heart swells.

"Yeah, it's the dream. There were people in it I cared about. Someone died. I need to know if it was something I imagined or if my memory is coming back."

She gives my back a gentle rub. I like the soothing contact, but it also makes me feel like she sees me as incompetent and I don't like that at all. I'm guessing my former self liked to take charge. She glances at the door leading to the pediatrician's office. "Thanks so much for helping us out, Ryder. My stomach is still sore and I really would've had trouble with that car seat on my own."

"It's really no problem," I answer. I take a step toward the door, thinking I'll head out to the truck and give them privacy for the appointment.

"Why don't you wait for us here inside?" she suggests, tipping her head toward the office.

I nod and follow her into the clinic's waiting room. It's much more lively and comfortable than the waiting rooms I'm used to and when she's called back to see the doctor with Brandon, I settle back in the seat and try to relax. I'm nervous about what my own doctor will be able to help me with later. And I'm glad for the distraction that Halo and Brandon provide.

The visit doesn't take very long and Halo is pleased with the doctor's report on Brandon. We're all quiet on the way home. I make sure they're both settled in the house and ask, "So is it okay if I head over?"

"Yeah, go. It'll be good for you to talk with your doctors if possible."

"Thanks. See you two soon." I smile at her and walk out the door. Something about her makes me feel lighter.

At the hospital I'm told my regular therapist is unavailable but that if it's an emergency they can get me in to see someone else. Fine with me. I can't stop thinking of my dream. How it felt to be over there.

I'm nervous as hell when they call my name and guide me back to a therapist's office. He introduces himself—his name is Bob Daniels, he's a therapist and he served in Viet Nam—and, after I'm seated in a comfortable chair, he takes a few minutes to review my information on his computer.

"Okay. What brings you in today?" he asks, looking at me over his glasses.

I explain my dream then ask, "I need to know, does that man exist or did he die?" My heart is beating fast and my palms begin to sweat. I wipe them on my jeans, feeling like I can't get the answer fast enough.

Bob nods and taps his chin. "Interesting. Let's see what I can find." He taps at the computer some more, frowning as he reads the screen.

"Please," I say. "I just want to know if Rover existed at all or if my mind is playing tricks on me. My dream was so intense."

"I can tell you that you did serve with Rover. He was killed in combat. So that might indeed indicate your dream contained elements of reality. And it might also indicate that some of your memories are coming back." His eyes are kind and his voice is concerned. "But you need to continue with your therapy. It's important not to push yourself. Take things slow."

My stomach churns. The dream was real. The pain I felt over his death was real. I feel like I'm going to be sick. "I don't know the name of the other man who was with us. He was a sniper."

"You're awfully anxious right now. Try to relax." Bob removes his glasses and eyes me warily. "I didn't suffer from amnesia after I was injured in Nam, but I had bad dreams. Woke me up at night. Cold sweats, unable to sleep."

I can completely relate. "Yes," I murmur. "It's so hard."

"I know, son. It's hard. This road you're on is a hard road. Give yourself time to heal. Be patient," he says and it seems like he really understands.

When I don't respond he asks, "What are you feeling?"

"What am I feeling?" I repeat. "I'm feeling like I can't breathe. I'm feeling like I just lost my best friend." The low timbre of my voice rises and I want to scream and shout at the top of my lungs. "Why can't I remember anything else?" I look at Bob helplessly.

"I don't know, son. It's likely that it's your body's defense mechanism. This is your mind's way of protecting you from the pain you experienced. The amnesia seems to be a direct result of your trauma. I think you'll slowly begin to remember things." He stands and I realize that, with his frizzy hair and intelligent eyes, he looks a little like Albert Einstein. "Look I know you've been through a lot. I know what it's like to lose your close friends to war, but running away from those memories and running away from yourself won't solve the problem. You need to face the truth, you need to find yourself and you need to make yourself a life. It's not an easy road but it can be done," he says, patting me on the shoulder. "I've lost and I've loved and I'm still here helping shitheads like you." He grins. "You'll be meeting Dr. Wembley for regular appointments. I'm here for those in between moments when you panic and need a place to run to." He gives me another pat on the shoulder.

"Well, thanks then, Bob." I extend my hand to shake his. He shakes my hand in return. I'm still trying to register my panic and his words.

"You take care," he says, turning back to his desk. He takes a seat and begins to write notes.

"Bye then," I call out as I walk through the door.

I need to find a life. I need to make myself a life. I need to remember my own life. I repeat the doc's words in my head not sure what happens next. *Be patient,* I repeat as I head on over to the wound clinic. I might not be able to make huge progress with mental therapy but at least today I know I'll do one thing productive—see the end result of the skin grafts. Who knew? It could be that seeing my face today will jog more memories.

When I arrive at the clinic, they're able to see me right away. As I sit on a table in an exam room, a nurse slowly unwraps the bandages. I breathe deeply as air hits my skin. It feels good. She gently washes my face with a cloth and gives me instructions for care. Then she passes me a mirror. I stare at my reflection for a long while. My skin isn't completely smooth and there are a couple jagged scars, but I think maybe it's a handsome face staring back at me.

"You should be pleased with the results," the nurse says, pulling me out of my thoughts.

"Ah, yeah. Thanks."

I zone out on the way back to Rogers Park. When I get inside the garage apartment, I take off my jacket and unload. Then I take a few deep breaths. I'm not sure why it's important for me to show Halo my face but it is important. We get along well and I like her and I sense she may like me too, but it's important for her to know what I actually look like.

I knock on her door and she answers. Her jaw drops and she places her palms on her cheeks. "Wow." She looks almost confused, maybe disappointed, but then the emotion passes and she smiles.

"Say something else," I say, feeling very self-conscious. "I need more than 'wow'. I'm not sure what 'wow' really means."

"You look great. I mean…I didn't fully see your face before, but, um, I think they did a great job." She lifts her hand and caresses my cheek. "The skin is smooth."

I've grown a bit of a beard. I'm not sure I like it but I can't shave for a few more days just in case I cut myself. I love that she's touching me. It feels so damn good. I know she's missing her husband and I have so many questions left unanswered in my own life, but a part of me wants to live in the moment. A part of me wants to feel good now. Is it so much to ask? I just spent four months of hell in a hospital. Can't I enjoy life? Enjoy Halo just a little bit before reality sinks in. Before I need to leave, maybe go find my ex-wife...

"Thank you, I think."

"Really, you look great. You're a handsome man." She smiles and her cheeks flush.

Bingo! That's what I needed to hear. I relax now. She finds me handsome. *Now the real work begins* is my first thought, but I want to punch myself out for thinking it. Seeing her pine over her ex-husband should be enough to deter me away from her but it isn't. I more than like her. I'm more than attracted to her. Maybe the old me would have done the respectable thing and walked away. The me of today can't. I may not remember the explosion, but my body has sure felt the impact. Life is short and I want to at least enjoy some of it. Even if it means taking something that isn't mine.

CHAPTER SIXTEEN

February 20, 2008
Halo

Time is flying by quickly. It's been three weeks since Brandon and I came home from the hospital. I'm definitely feeling more like myself. I can move around easier and my cute son has filled out and grown quite a bit. Ryder has been renovating the house these last couple weeks.

He's become a good friend. He shows up in the morning, works on the house and I make him lunch. Usually PB&J sandwiches because they're convenient and I like them too. When he's done working on the house in the early evening, we all get cleaned up, have dinner and meet on the couch to watch a movie.

He's been getting little snippets of memories in his dreams. Remembering is painful for him. I was glad he was able to open up to me about how he was feeling. It made me think of Thomas and the way he shut down on me, especially after his deployment in Iraq. It also confirmed in my mind that—whatever Thomas was suffering from—it wasn't me who could have saved him. He would need to find his own peace and I only prayed he would.

Ryder has been open with me about his feelings and thoughts.

The moments he does open up mean something special to both of us. I can tell by the way he looks at me with reverence. I may not have been able to save Thomas, but I feel like I make Ryder's life a little easier, even a little happier. He's been my saving grace in this mess. He takes away the loneliness I've been feeling in the pit of my stomach since Thomas left. I've been working hard on myself not to feel guilty about the good feelings that Ryder evokes in me. He leaves every night with a small kiss on my cheek. It isn't much, but our connection has become meaningful. He even spends time holding Brandon. He talks to him with a sweet baby voice, which just about melts me every time.

Jenny and Dave have come by a few times with the kids. They were excited to meet Brandon. I was happy to hear Jenny tell them he was a cousin since we don't have any family. Jenny and Dave have also become a lot more laidback where Ryder is concerned which is a relief. Dave and Ryder even seem to be developing a friendship.

Having so much time on my hands, I have been reading *Lord of the Flies* again. Sometimes out loud to Brandon. It was Thomas's favorite book after *Lord of the Rings*. As I hold Brandon in my arms and read the familiar words that Thomas used to recite to me, my heart clenches. There were so many different facets to Thomas Wells, I'm just sorry Brandon won't have a chance to know him. I'm sure Thomas would have liked discussing those books with his son one day.

Today Ryder hasn't done any work on the house. All the renovations are done. Dave found a handyman who worked by the hour to help Ryder, since the floors were a messy job and we wanted to get the painting done sooner rather than later. To avoid the fumes and the mess, I packed up Brandon's things and we stayed at Jenny's for the week while Ryder and the handyman were sanding, varnishing and painting. It was nice to spend time with Jenny, Dave and the kids. Jenny invited Ryder over for dinner every night too. I am glad, though, that it is all behind me. It's good to be back home. I'm enjoying the peace and quiet. Jenny really does run a busy household. Ryder's been busy cleaning up which is a ginormous help since I have Brandon to tend to. He's awake more hours in the day now. I want to cherish every moment I can with him before I have to return to work three weeks down the road.

Tonight we are hosting the gang and Ryder is staying to hang out which should be interesting. I mean, it's not like Ryder and I are an item but he's still my guest, he's still living in my home and he isn't Thomas. My friends only knew Thomas and me. I haven't really socialized since back when we were a couple.

Jenny stayed home from work today to prepare all kinds of appetizers and now Ryder is busy in the kitchen doing whatever Jenny asks him to. The two of them are intent on not receiving my help, which is fine by me because Brandon has been up repeatedly the last few nights. I'm exhausted. When we took him for another check-up yesterday, the doctor said it could be a growth spurt.

Ryder shoos me away from the kitchen so I take Brandon and head upstairs for an early bath and shower in preparation for our "welcoming the baby" party.

The truth is I've been living in sweat suits since the day we came home from the hospital and it would be nice to curl my hair and put on a dress for a change. Maybe feel more like a woman than a milking cow. I don't mean that in a bad way either.

Brandon sits nicely cooing in his bouncer while I take my time washing my hair. I step out of the shower and wrap a towel around my body. I spend some time drying my hair too, blowing it out and curling it on the ends. I've definitely been in better spirits lately. I grab the bouncer with Brandon still seated and carry it into my bedroom.

"So what should your mom wear tonight?" I ask, looking down at him. He just sits there looking like the handsome fella he is.

I step into the closet and brush my fingers over a line of dresses I haven't worn for a very long time. My eyes land on a red dress I use to wear occasionally when Thomas would take me out to dinner. He really liked it. If I were being honest with myself—which I don't want to be—I would admit that I want to look pretty for Ryder. The thought makes my cheeks flush, but I can't help the way I feel. He's been such a help fixing up the house and he won't take a penny from me. He's great with Brandon, which is seriously huge in my book. He's easy on the eyes, that's for sure. His rugged scars only make him that much more sexy and the connection we have through talking is so deep.

I slip on a pair of black lace panties and put on a black nursing bra. There is no way I'm squeezing my breasts into one of my old bras tonight. I'm not thinking actively sexy thoughts—honestly, the thought of having sex and the idea of anyone coming near my incision scares me to death—but I wouldn't mind *feeling* sexy for a change. I'm happy with the mama fashion, but I miss feeling like a woman too.

When I put on the red dress, I'm relieved it actually fits. The criss-cross bodice should give me fast access for breastfeeding emergencies and the stretchy fabric hugs my new curves graciously. Red lipstick and black pumps finish the look. I gaze in the mirror and catch a glimpse of the old me. I like what I see.

I'm dressing Brandon when I hear the doorbell ring. Ryder hollers that he'll get it. We've agreed to keep Charlie up here on the second floor behind a gate. I can hear her whining quietly.

For the next few minutes I hear the front door open and close while Dave and Ryder bring in all the food that Jenny prepared. I dress Brandon in a cute pair of khaki pants and a light blue button-down shirt. He looks like a little man. He's even got Thomas's husky frame. As much as the thought of Thomas once hurt me, lately it hasn't been so bad.

Me and my little guy head down the stairs and into the kitchen.

"Hey, hon. Don't you look beautiful," Jenny says, embracing me. "And you're just a handsome little guy, aren't you?" She caresses Brandon's cheek with the back of her hand. She leans in closer and whispers, "Is this get-up for the stud?"

"Jenny," I chide her, but I can't help the tinge of pink that erupts on my cheeks. She waves me off. Ryder comes through the front door with Dave, carrying more trays. Dave walks by me first and says hello to Brandon and me. Ryder does a double take and stops.

"Halo, uh, wow. You look great." He smiles, looking at my body appreciatively. "You too, little guy." Ryder inserts one of his big fingers into Brandon's little fist. I notice Jenny and Dave staring at each other with knowing expressions. I want to tell them that it isn't what they're thinking, but I'm not sure it would be the truth. Something has been happening. I just don't know what exactly.

Jenny begins to set up all the platters on the dining room table and I comment, "Geez, Jenny, you made enough food here to feed an army. Thank you so much for this." I smile at her. "You're too good to us."

"It works both ways, Halo. You know you've done your share of helping me." I guess she's right. I helped her after all her births and—when she miscarried and fell into a depression—I would bring over meals and feed her kids while she recovered.

The doorbell rings and when Ryder opens the door, I see Maggie and Josh. "Well, hello there, Ryder," Maggie says, passing him a bottle of wine and giving him the one-up.

"Hi, Maggie." Ryder smiles and gives her a kiss on her cheek. She giggles like a school girl and her husband rolls his eyes at Ryder and then introduces himself by extending his hand for a shake.

Over the course of the next several minutes the rest of the guests arrive—they're mostly my friends from college, couples who used to hang out with me and Thomas. Everyone fusses over Brandon and exclaims over how good I look. It's gratifying but a little exhausting and I'm glad I have such good friends in Jenny, Dave and Ryder to help me navigate the small crowd.

We head into the dining room to sample the food and I hear Chad—who used to be a good friend of Thomas's—discussing sports with Ryder. Ryder seems to be holding his own and I'm both pleased and worried for him. I know he's been remembering a lot more—he tells me his dreams are still coming on strong. But the more he remembers, the more concerned I get about the fact that he'll leave some day. He'll need to figure out what went wrong with his marriage, find family members and friends. I worry about what he'll discover, both for the impact it might have on him and, selfishly, for how it will affect me and Brandon.

"Ryder, you've done one heck of a job on these floors," my old friend Derrick says as he picks up a nacho and dips it into the spinach dip.

"Thanks, man. I've enjoyed doing it and, yeah, they turned out all right." Ryder looks down at the floors in an appreciative way. He did more than an all-right job. He brought out the authentic character of the wood and gave it a squeaky new shine. They look amazing.

"Yeah, Derrick." Derrick's wife Sam jabs him in the side. "The floors look amazing. Why don't you fix ours up?" She's half joking and half serious.

"You're sending us all to the shit house." Derrick chuckles as he looks at Ryder.

"Sorry, man, but look at it this way—I haven't been working, so

I had time to do the renovations. Would you want your husbands fixing the house or paying the bills?" He looks at my girlfriends and then pops a party sandwich in his mouth.

"Okay, Ryder. Point taken." Melissa's and Sam's responses are almost identical.

"You were in the military weren't you, Ryder?" Maggie asks.

"Yeah." He nods. Suddenly I feel a little worried. I don't know if it's the military wife in me, but I fear that someone will ask him the wrong question and set off some of his PTSD triggers.

"I was in the military too, man," Joshua says.

"Oh yeah?" Ryder looks his way with an interested expression.

"One deployment to Afghanistan and that was it for me. Maggie said you went out three times. I commend you, brother." He shakes Ryder's hand.

Suddenly Brandon turns fussy in Sam's arms. He's been passed around since we came downstairs. I'm guessing he's hungry.

"I think that's my call, Sam," I say, walking over and taking Brandon from her arms.

I head upstairs for some privacy, telling the ladies they're welcome to join me. I open the gate at the top of the stairs and Charlie rubs herself against my leg. When I settle on my bed, Charlie lies down on the floor next to me.

I rest against the headboard and open my dress to give Brandon access to my milking machines. The ladies enter the room a moment later and take a seat on the edge of the bed, watching all gooey-eyed as Brandon latches on to my breast and feeds.

"Mmm, this makes me want another one. I used to love breastfeeding." Jenny sighs, tilting her head and batting her blue eyes at Brandon.

"So have another one. Dave would probably love it," Sam jokes. We're all aware of how chaotic Jenny's household is with three kids close in age.

"Not," Jenny says, rolling her eyes.

"Chad wants a boy," Melissa says, flicking her light brown hair to the side. "But I'm done. He'll have to be happy having us girls in the house."

"Here, here," Jenny says.

"I'm enjoying this diaper phase," I say. "I'm cherishing every moment that Brandon and I spend together. I just don't know how I'm going to go back to work in three weeks," I admit, almost in tears.

All three women make sympathetic noises. "Of course you're enjoying the diaper phase. He's your first." Jenny rubs my shoulder.

"I hated going back to work after I had the boys," Sam says. "I cried for three weeks straight.

"Sam," Melissa snaps at her with wide eyes. "Not helping here."

"He's going to be fine," Jenny reassures me. "Mrs. Ritter took care of all of my kids. She's like a loving grandmother. Brandon will be just fine. My kids still love to go visit her."

"She really is good, Halo," Melissa agrees. "She took care of my sister's daughter and she raves about her."

"I hope so," I sigh, looking down at Brandon.

"Okay," Sam says. "Enough of this baby talk. Start spilling the beans, Halo. What's going on between you and that fine male specimen downstairs?" Sam licks her naturally red lips for extra drama.

I giggle and roll my eyes. I guess I should have been expecting this. "Absolutely nothing."

"No way. I saw how he watches you." Melissa raises her brows suggestively.

"You clearly have a type," Sam inserts. "He looks like he could be Thomas's long-lost brother."

"I don't have a type. And there's nothing romantic going on

between us. He's renting the garage. He's my tenant—that's it."

"A tenant that renovates your house and hangs out with your friends?" Sam asks, tilting her chin down and raising her brows at me. *Busted.* I look over to Jenny for some help and she nods and grins. She isn't going to help me argue my way out of this one.

"He's a wounded soldier. He was a SEAL and he's dealing with things." I don't want to reveal too much. It isn't my story to tell.

"Well SEALs definitely have rocking bods," Sam says.

"Seriously, he looks like he can bench press you." Melissa giggles, looking dreamy eyed.

It kind of makes me laugh because they're all married with kids and here they are ogling Ryder. Is this what marriage is about? You begin to lust over what you can't have? During the nine years I was with Thomas I never daydreamed about other men. I only wanted him. I was still attracted to him. Our sex life was good, but then again we spent a lot of time apart, so maybe the separation caused longing that these women never experienced.

"Halo," Melissa says, "I'm really in awe of you. You've done good, friend. Going through this pregnancy on your own and taking care of Brandon after a C-section. I had regular births and I was a mess after Abbey was born. Chad took a month off work to help and I still call on him for all kinds of things. So much for being an independent woman," she chides herself.

"Don't be silly, Mel. You're an awesome mom. Thanks for the compliment, but things have been seriously hard. I wouldn't have gotten through these last few weeks without Ryder. He was really a gift sent from up above."

"Well, a gift he is, Halo, but don't be blind. That man couldn't take his eyes off you all evening," Sam says with a sly look.

"Quit it, Sam. Look at me. I have a swollen stomach, swollen breasts..."

"Actually the swollen breasts are kind of hot. You were never that voluptuous before. I think you should be enjoying those mamas you got now." Sam laughs, throwing her head back.

"Seriously, if I don't get a bra on fast enough, I have a fountain of milk pouring out of me. Not exactly the epitome of sexy. Besides, I just...you know...I've never been with anyone except for Thomas. I don't think I could actually go through with anything."

"Well, honestly, Halo." Jenny finally decides to say something. "If you were to do something with another man it should be easier with Ryder. He's smoking hot." She mock fans herself. "Okay! Let Halo put herself back together. The guys have probably missed our asses." Jenny winks at me and walks out of the room. Sam and Melissa follow her out.

I let out a long breath. "Well, that was intense, Brandon. What do you think, honey? I know Mommy shouldn't be having romantic feelings for Ryder, but he is so good to both of us and he's nice to talk to." I lift Brandon over my shoulder to burp him. Then I lay him flat on the bed so I can put my bra back together and close the front of my dress.

I swaddle Brandon in a blanket and he turns his head into me contently. I slowly make my way down the stairs. I see Ryder first as I reach the main floor and his dark blue eyes are on me in a flash. It makes me feel warm. I like his attention. He leaves the conversation he's having with Chad and walks over to me.

"You good?" he asks, turning his head slightly.

"Yeah, all good," I answer but my voice is a little high pitched. Geez, I need to get a grip.

"Do you want me to hold the little guy? You haven't had a chance to eat anything yet. You should try the calamari. Its finger-lickin' good." He winks.

"Thanks, Ryder." He takes Brandon in his arms with ease. He

takes great care whenever he holds him, and I like how his dark blue eyes warm at the sight of Brandon.

"Go on and eat," he whispers as he follows me into the living room.

"Maggie, you should have come up to hang out with the ladies," I say, suddenly feeling bad that she might've felt left out. She wasn't part of our college group of friends.

"That's okay. I hung out here with the men. Ryder was telling us about his amnesia." She winks. She's too funny considering how hot her husband is. He looks like a young Will Smith. I guess they are all just trying to make me feel good after being the lonely abandoned woman for the past nine months.

I fill my plate with food. It's already quite late and I skipped on dinner. Jenny sneaks up behind me. "How you doing?" she asks.

"Jenny, the food is amazing." I smile as I pop a calamari in my mouth.

Ryder approaches with Brandon. "He's asleep, Halo. Should I put him in his crib upstairs or do you want him down here in the playpen?"

"Playpen is good. I'm worried I won't hear him above the noise down here. I have to get one of those monitor things. I haven't had a chance to pick one up yet."

"I thought you would say down here." Ryder smiles warmly. Then he walks over to the playpen and places Brandon down gently. I feel like I want to swoon just watching him and when I turn my head to Jenny she seems to be feeling the same way.

"Jenny," I say loudly, snapping her out of her daze.

"Huh? What?" She blinks. Then she takes my arm and leads me into a corner of the dining room. "Halo," she says, lowering her voice. "I think Ryder is a better version of Thomas. I think you need to see what happens with him," she says suggestively.

"Huh? This is coming from the woman who thought I was crazy bringing him home and renting him the garage?"

"We didn't know him yet. But now we're getting to know him better and Dave agrees—he seems like a nice guy."

"I know, but what happens when his memory comes back? What happens if he remembers his family, his friends and he has to leave us? I don't think I can go through something like that again. Things aren't so simple, Jenny. He has dreams and he gets upset. I can see a similar pattern forming with him like I did with Thomas. Thomas didn't always have bad PTSD. It spiraled out of control. I think Ryder may have something similar. That's why he doesn't remember his past. He was the sole survivor of an ambush. I mean, look at him—half his body has been broken or charred."

"You have to admit that even with the limp and the scars on his face he's hot. Look, I'm not saying run off and get married. All I'm saying is that he's been good for you and Brandon. I don't know… You deserve to have some fun." Her eyes glimmer and I know she's talking about sex. It's been close to ten months since I've had sex. Of course I feel urges, even when I was pregnant, but right now the doctor said no sex until I'm six weeks post-partum. If I'm being honest with myself the thought of sex scares the heck out of me anyway.

"Jenny, the birth is still too fresh in my mind. That is completely not on my agenda," I chide her.

"What's not on your agenda?" Maggie cuts in.

"Sex," Jenny answers, and I glare at her wide-eyed.

"No worries, hon. After I had Jeremiah I wouldn't let Joshua near me for three months. I went for my doctor's appointment at six weeks and the doctor assured me everything was fine down there but it wasn't happening." Maggie laughs.

Joshua comes up behind her and wraps his arms around her waist.

She looks back at him and pats his cheek. "I'm just telling the ladies how I blue balled you after Jeremiah was born," she tells him.

"Okay... Well then. I'll get some spinach dip now..." Joshua says slowly, dropping his arms and pulling away, clearly embarrassed. Maggie throws her head back and laughs.

"I was the same, Maggie," Jenny says, waving her hand. "After Tyler was born. But after my second and third we jumped back into sex relatively quick."

"Oh, us too with Jared," Maggie agrees.

"Well, thanks for prepping me on the post-partum sex details, ladies. I don't have a partner for that stuff but it's all good." I cackle and Ryder chooses that exact moment to walk up to the conversation.

"What do you need a partner for, Halo? Maybe I can help out?" he says with sincerity.

Jenny and Maggie burst into a fit of giggles and I dream of being an ice cube so I can melt onto the floor and disappear.

Ryder looks confused.

"Thanks for the offer, Ryder, but all is good. No need for a partner." I tap his hard chest and Jenny practically topples over laughing.

"I'm missing something here," Ryder states.

"Yes," I confirm.

"Ladies' stuff?"

I nod.

"Well then. I'll help clean up. I heard Melissa and Chad saying they're leaving soon." His cheeks have a pink tinge.

"Thanks again, Ryder." I flush too and he turns and nods with a grin. I make my way over to Melissa.

"We're heading out, Halo. It was so nice to meet Brandon. He's such a cutie." She smiles then leans in to give me a hug.

"Thanks for coming," I reply, wrapping my arm around her.

She whispers in my ear. "Ryder is a cutie too," then she pulls away and gives me a quick wink.

What is it with all these ladies winking at me tonight?

"Bye, Chad." I lean in for a hug.

"Bye, Halo. Thanks for having us. Your boy is adorable and the house looks great."

Although it was great seeing everyone, I'm happy they're leaving because I'm exhausted. I could fall asleep standing up. After saying goodbyes to all the couples, the house is once again quiet.

"I think I'll clean up in the morning," I say. "I kind of feel exhausted. I'll just put the leftovers in the fridge. You're probably tired. You don't need to stay, Ryder." I stretch my arms as my words drown into a yawn. My lack of sleep is catching up with me.

"I'll help with the food. And help you take Brandon upstairs."

I'm happy he still offers to carry Brandon even though he knows I've been feeling better. I like our little bedtime routine. I like that Brandon has the consistency. Although I worry when it will end.

"Sure, thanks," I say.

Ryder and I quickly pack away the leftovers. He walks over to the playpen and picks up Brandon. I like watching his biceps flex as he cradles him close to his chest. I follow as they slowly make their way up the stairs. Ryder is able to bend his knee a little more now that he stopped wearing the brace. His movement isn't so rigid. Brandon's crib is back in the nursery. I follow Ryder inside and watch as he gently places Brandon in the crib followed by the usual, "Goodnight, buddy." It makes my heart feel warm. Then he turns and walks toward me.

"Thanks for inviting me tonight. I hope it wasn't awkward with your friends," he says nervously.

"You did great," I reassure him. "I'm glad you could join us."

Ryder keeps his eyes trained on me. "You look really beautiful tonight," he says with a low, deep voice. I internally do a happy dance. It's been a while since I had the attention of a man.

"Thank you," I answer, slightly breathless. *I kind of wore this red dress because I thought you may like it, even though I felt self-conscious about my body.*

He moves a step closer and my pulse picks up speed. His palm brushes my cheek while his eyes ask for permission. Then he slowly moves forward and I feel hot and tingly. His movements are slow so that if I wanted the chance to pull away I could have done so a hundred times over. Only I don't want to pull away. I want to feel his lips. He leans forward, connecting our mouths. At first our warm lips brush. It's as if he's waiting for me to push him away or give him permission to move forward. I lace my hands at the back of his neck and he draws me closer, wrapping his arms around my waist. He's being slow and gentle. Despite my initial panic at our first connection, I relax into the kiss. Ryder slowly licks along my lower lip and enters my mouth. Our tongues lash out at each other. I can feel the heat taking over my entire body. He tastes like heaven and hell because I want more of him, but guilt is gripping me in a chokehold. I can't stop myself or pull away. The kiss picks up speed and turns into an erotic mixture of tongues and passion. There is the slight unease in the back of my head that's saying, "Whoa! What's happening here?"

Even though I don't want to think of Thomas, I do. He was my first and my last and it's hard not to compare. But it was so different. We were so young, teenagers. Ryder and I are adults. This is a whole new ball game.

My heart is hammering in my chest. A part of me wants to wrap my legs around him and let him take me to bed. But I know I'm not ready for everything it will mean. I need to say goodbye to Thomas, emotionally, mentally before I can move forward.

The kiss slows into a gentle, meaningful caress. He pulls away and tilts his forehead to press against mine.

"Was that okay?" he asks through ragged breaths.

I'm breathless myself. "Yes." I close my eyes, feeling a whirlwind of emotion. Elation, disloyalty, happiness, guilt. Something has been happening with Ryder since I first met him. It couldn't be love at first sight. We were both a mess but there was no denying the pull between us. I begin to wonder what would happen if Thomas came home now. Would I still be his?

"I should go," he says, his hoarse voice filled with lust. "I'll go lock up." He releases my hand and places a soft kiss on the inside of my wrist and I'm melting. As he turns away, my earlier guilt dissolves. I'm still confused but I know I'm attracted to him. I wasn't sure he felt the same way before, but I know now.

I don't know where we go from here. I remember Nurse Judy in the hospital telling me I will need to move on for Brandon's sake. It's hard when I had no closure with Thomas. I quietly enter Brandon's room and take a quick peek at him to make sure he's okay. I watch his chest rise and fall peacefully. Everything in my life seems to be heading in a positive direction. I haven't felt this way in so long. I walk back into my room and slip out of my dress. It's already midnight and I predict that Brandon will be awake by two a.m. for his feeding.

I quickly throw on a pajama shirt and get into the cold bed. With my head on the pillow I touch my lips, remembering Ryder's passionate kiss. It was hot and patient, giving and taking. He tasted *so* good. I can't deny what I'm feeling for Ryder. I know it's more than an attraction. We talk, we share.

I close my eyes as exhaustion overtakes me.

CHAPTER SEVENTEEN

Ryder

Holy Damn. I feel like my head is spinning. When Halo came down the stairs tonight my dick instantly went hard at the sight of her. The dress wasn't too revealing, but the way it held those full breasts of hers gave me an instant hard-on. She looked like sin wrapped in red. Everything about her was perfect. From the way she curled her hair to that red lipstick she had on her full lips. I wanted to go up to her and suck her lips and basically devour her. I'm trying to be careful around her. I know she's in a tough position with being a single mom and I'm a bloody mess myself. I keep on having dreams of my time overseas but it isn't coming together for me.

I see old friends, their faces, their smiles, their dedication to the team. Knowing they're gone hurts in the dream. Then I'm pulled back to reality, waking up feeling heavy and losing the connection I felt. I want to feel more than I do. I just don't connect.

Dr. Wembley says I need to be patient and not push myself. I feel like I need to know more. I'm falling for Halo and I think she may be developing feelings for me. How can she really fall for someone she doesn't truly know? How can I even like myself when I don't know who I am? There are so many roadblocks for us. I was hesitant to kiss her tonight knowing that I may not ever be able to give her all of myself. I couldn't help myself.

Staring into those big round brown eyes of hers tonight in the dark hallway completely undid me. I needed a taste and she was so much sweeter than my wildest dreams.

I take off my clothes down to my boxers and hop into the cold, hard bed. My dick is still so damned hard. It's crazy that I don't even know how long it's been since I've had sex. I couldn't help but overhear the conversation she had with Maggie and Jenny about sex after babies. I acted like I didn't hear, but I heard every word. I guess my hearing is still good after all the gunfire I experienced. I heard the ladies saying that sex was scary after giving birth and it was good to know. I also heard Halo say she was nowhere close to being ready. I figured kissing was okay, though. I also heard the ladies suggest I could help Halo out in the sex department. That comment kind of got to me because I've been picturing having sex with Halo every night since we watched our first movie together.

I may have amnesia, but I'm not stupid. I know how to be a gentleman despite the fact that I wanted to pin her against the wall in the hallway and fuck her brains out. I pictured her coming undone and whipping that auburn hair around as she screamed out my name. Jesus. I have to stop these thoughts. Or not…

I begin to rub my dick as thoughts of Halo continue to flow through my mind. I picture my hands unzipping that hot red dress and then running over her behind and in between her legs as she presses herself into me. It doesn't take long before I'm coming hard and fast. I hope it won't be too long before my fantasies play out where she's concerned. I heard the ladies say that six weeks was a safe amount of time and that's only a week away. I know I shouldn't want this considering my life is a wrecking ball but I want to make Halo Pearson fall in love with me.

CHAPTER EIGHTEEN

Three weeks later
Halo

"Hey, baby. We have to go meet Mrs. Ritter soon. Mama has to go back to work this week." I sigh as I watch my little boy look up at the toys hanging from the mobile over the bassinet.

He's the most handsome baby I've ever seen with his dark blue eyes and little button nose. My heart clenches. "I know she's going to take really good care of you," I try to convince the both of us as a hiccup of sadness makes an escape.

There's a light knock on door to the garage.

"Come in," I lift my eyes and call out. Ryder walks in with his hair wet and slicked back wearing a white T-shirt and a worn pair of jeans. I stopped locking that door because it just didn't feel right to lock him out at this point. He always knocks anyway before entering.

"How are my two favorite people doing?" he asks as his lips tug up at the corners. His mood seems light this morning.

"We're good. Only I'm not sure if we can be your favorite since we are the only two people you know." I grin.

He laughs loudly. "I'm good with that, but you guys are still my favorite." He leans in for a small kiss. We've been doing this, the small kisses, even the bigger kisses, ever since the night I had my friends over. It's hard not to kiss him. After Brandon goes to bed the kisses grow passionate but they always trail off and we always pull apart. He doesn't bring up the relationship talk, but we both have pasts that need to be dealt with before we figure out what's happening between us.

"I need to take Brandon to meet Mrs. Ritter today," I say with another hiccup. I lift my finger to my nose as if it will stop the impending tears. Ryder sits beside me on the couch and places an arm around my shoulder. He smells like fresh soap. Man soap. I don't want to cry in front of Brandon. I've been holding off all week knowing I have to go into work Monday. With Ryder being so close and with his shoulder mere inches from my face, something inside me snaps and the tears I've been trying so hard to hold at bay burst out of me as I clutch onto his shirt.

He's come to know me well. We spend most days together when he's not going off to the hospital for therapy. I think he realizes I'm on a post-partum hormonal/emotional roller coaster. The tears continue to fall hard and suddenly I feel like I am crying for so many things. For Thomas leaving, for going through the pregnancy on my own. I hated those cold winter days when the snow reached my front door and I needed help shoveling and there was no one there. Maggie's husband Joshua helped when he could but those mornings when he couldn't were brutal. The stairs were slippery and I always feared falling. I'm crying because I had to give birth to my son with his father not present. I'm crying because I'm raising my son without his father. I'm crying because I have to let a caregiver take care of my infant son because I have to work full time and lastly I'm crying because I'm thanking the angels above for sending me Ryder when I needed him most.

"I'm sorry," I say with a shrill and cracking voice.

"Are you kidding me? He's not even my kid and I'm having a hard time with the fact that he won't be here during the day. I can't imagine what you are going through." He rubs my back. And there it is. Right there. Ryder knows exactly what to say and saying that he is going to have a hard time not having Brandon around completely undoes me and makes me like him even more. I know my crush on this man is turning into something deeper, but…there is always the "but" of the past.

"Thank you," I murmur and pull my head back, swiping the tears away from my eyes.

"For what?" he asks with a confused tone.

"I don't know. For being here with us," I reply.

"Halo, I love being here. There's nowhere else I'd rather be," he replies with such assurance in his tone that I want to believe him. And if he had his memory and remembered his family and still wanted to be here? Well, then it would settle me more.

I smile at him because it's not the time to bring these issues to his attention. "We need to head over to Mrs. Ritter's now," I say, placing a kiss on his cheek. It's smooth—he must have just shaven. I swipe the tears from my eyes again and Ryder brushes his thumb along my cheek, helping me wipe them away.

"Let me take you guys," he offers and my stomach sinks. I know this won't be enough for him in the long run, chauffeuring Brandon and I around.

"You really don't have to." I sulk and my insides burn.

"What is it?" he asks, reading me so well.

I know this is not the time but with all the emotions of going back to work getting the best of me I need to say something. I need to know. "I'm worried. I mean, we both like having you around and all…but…you driving us around and just hanging out—that won't, uh…" I'm almost embarrassed to say the next words because maybe

Ryder isn't thinking long term like I am.

"Say it."

"Well, I'm worried that we won't be enough for you in the long run. You have your whole life to live. Don't you ever think about what you want to do?" I immediately regret the question. He almost died. He is still suffering from amnesia. He's still trying to figure his life out. I understand. But Brandon and I are getting very attached to him and maybe my protective instincts are calling the shots. "I'm sorry. I don't mean to push, but something's happening here..." I motion with my hand back and forth between us. I begin to worry I've allowed my insecurities to get the best of me and I turn my head away, lacing my fingers together, unsure and worried about his response.

"Halo, I get it. Don't feel bad. Do you think I haven't spent my nights awake thinking of what's happening here? Because I have. Every damn night. I love being around the two of you. In my dreams I see and do things I'm not proud of. And if my dreams are actually my memories? It burns a hole through me when I think of it. But then there's you and Brandon. When I'm with you I feel better. You both brighten my day. I like spending time here and helping, having our talks...." He runs a hand through his hair and stands up from the couch. He's tall and so handsome. "I know I'm missing pieces of myself. I know I have an ex-wife and pieces of a former life somewhere out there. And, when I say the words, you'll want them coming from a man who is whole. A man who knows who he is and what he wants. I'm trying to get there. I'm meeting with Dr. Wembley often. He said I need to build myself a life. That's what I'm trying to do now, but it isn't easy." He looks down at me with pain in his blue eyes.

"I know. I'm sorry." I take his hand and grip his fingers hard.

"Please don't apologize. I know that all these issues are a problem, but I don't want to go anywhere. I'm happy here. Please be patient with me while I try to figure things out." He removes his hand from my grip and brushes his thumb along my cheek. The caress is gentle, but it doesn't relax me.

"You've so rarely mentioned your ex-wife." I know it's ridiculous to be jealous, but my heart won't be reasonable. "She's someone I'm concerned about. What if—when you remember her—you want to go back to her? Where will that leave me and Brandon?"

He squeezes his eyes shut. "I don't know..."

I know his honesty is painful for both of us. I know part of my pain has to do with Thomas. If Thomas hadn't been in his right mind when he left, then he might recover and, someday, he might want to come back. And I also know deep inside that I'd take him back in a heartbeat. I don't say the words, but that would leave Ryder out in the cold too. We are in a complicated situation with our pasts dictating our present.

"I know you're in a fragile situation. Did you ever think how I'd feel if your ex-husband walked through that door? Or what he'd think of me being here? Don't answer, Halo." Ryder shakes his head. This is a lot harder than I realized. What if Thomas suddenly decides he wants us back? Would I willingly walk into the arms that had shut me out, that abandoned me at my time of need? I don't know what I would do, but I would be lying if I didn't admit to thinking about it.

"Can you drive us? We're going to be late." My tone is defeated.

Ryder lets out a sigh. "Yeah, let me just grab my shoes."

He heads for the garage and I put my head in my hands, tugging at my hair in frustration. I didn't want our day to start this way. I wanted to focus on Brandon and meeting his new caregiver. I take a few long, deep breaths to relax myself and turn to Brandon.

As I prepare Brandon for the trip, I worry, hoping I haven't upset

Ryder too much. I know my hormones and lack of sleep are messing with my emotions. I'm trying to gain a sense of security for Brandon and me, but maybe I'm asking for too much too soon.

A few minutes later we're driving to Mrs. Ritter's place. It's in the neighborhood and as we drive down familiar streets I think about the hectic commute I'll have next week when I begin teaching again.

"You know, I was thinking of getting a job," Ryder says, his gaze on the road. "Maybe as a mechanic."

"Oh yeah?"

"Yeah. One of the things that I've been working on in counseling is how I can apply skills from my life before the navy to my life today. Apparently I worked as a mechanic before. And I've been working on this truck, which has been good practice...." His expression is distraught. I don't ask what he's thinking—he needs to tell me this kind of thing on his own time. "There are a lot of things in my file but the doctors and I have been trying to take one thing at a time," he explains hesitantly. And now I understand why he might be worried.

"So you mean there's information about your past that the military knows and you're choosing not to learn about?" I ask, trying to keep a steady voice. I want to be supportive even if his response might be upsetting.

"Dr. Wembley seems to think there are benefits to discovering things on my own. He thinks it's smart considering the amnesia is probably from a severe case of PTSD."

"So what do you know?" I ask nervously.

"Just that I grew up in Chicago. A little about my parents. There's an older lady who I have listed as next of kin. I would like to go visit her and see what she knows... I haven't been ready to do that yet." He pulls his eyes from the road for a brief moment and looks my way, biting his lip. Then he continues, "The names of my teammates that died. I dream about them," he explains, inhaling a long breath.

I want to ask him more. Especially if he's discovered any information about his relationship with his ex-wife, but we've arrived at our destination. "Right there on the right." I point to the old red brick house where Mrs. Ritter lives.

Ryder carries Brandon in the carrier as we head inside out of the cold to meet Mrs. Ritter. She is a kind woman in her late fifties and she really does seem to have a way with babies. Likely she's dealt with lots of emotional moms who are going to back to work for the first time—because she's patient as I explain in great detail Brandon's feeding schedule and the pains I'm going to take to ensure he continues with breast milk.

After we have everything sorted out and I pay for the first week of care, I nod to Ryder and we thank Mrs. Ritter. I'm placing Brandon back in the carrier when Mrs. Ritter suddenly says, "He looks like you, Ryder."

My eyes widen at her mistake and my heart skips a beat. "Oh no," I begin to explain.

"Thanks," Ryder responds.

I bite my lip and don't say anything further. Ryder picks him up in his carrier and coos at him.

"Thanks again," I say, smiling. "We'll be seeing you next week."

"Bye, looking forward to it," Mrs. Ritter responds.

We head back to the truck and I'm still feeling a little baffled about Ryder's response. After we get buckled in, Ryder fiddles with the heat controls. I gaze at him curiously. I can tell he knows I'm looking at him by the crooked smile on his face.

"Sorry," he says. "It just came out. We do have the same eye color… I know. I don't know what I was thinking…sorry." I know I should be upset with him for misleading her but the fact that he actually wants Brandon to look like him completely warms my heart.

I settle in and let out a breath as my head falls back on the headrest. I'm so screwed where Ryder St. John is concerned. He's made the ache of losing Thomas easier. He's also made me realize that I can move on without Thomas. The thought scares me…

CHAPTER NINETEEN

Three weeks later

"I love the taste of your mouth. You are so dammed sweet," Ryder mutters as we have one of our nightly make-out sessions on the living room couch. His tongue runs over my lips and I open my mouth, allowing him access. Our tongues meet in a sensual dance. His hands run over my shoulders and down my back. My shirt feels a little wet from my hair—I took a shower before coming downstairs. Ryder's lips move over my ear and down my jaw, nibbling lightly. I'm all sensation. His scent, his touch, the way his hard body feels beneath my fingertips.

"You smell so good," he murmurs as he spreads light kisses behind my ear. I'm all hot and tingly—a wound-up bundle of nerves waiting to explode. He's respected my insecurities and never goes below my neckline, but doing this with him now for over a month has sent my libido skyrocketing.

These last two weeks have been better than I could've expected. Ryder began to work for a mechanic part time between his physical and psychological therapy, which has put him in a good mood. He's feeling like he can do more now than stick to the house. He prepares dinner every day so I have time to spend with Brandon after work and then we all hang out together after dinner. It's almost like we're a real family. Almost.

"Halo," he says breathlessly. He moves me back on the couch so that my head connects with the pillow and he climbs above me without putting pressure on me. Our kissing drives me wild.

"Yes?" I ask, practically panting.

"Is it okay if I put my hands under your top? I mean, I can see your reaction to me and I need to touch you," he says, referring to my hardened nipples.

I swallow hard as the heat between my thighs grows. I nod and one of his hands touches me gently under my T-shirt. I'm not wearing a bra. I suddenly feel nervous about him touching my breasts because I am still breastfeeding and they've been Brandon's eating machines. He begins to tease me, rubbing his finger gently over my nipple and I let out a moan.

"You are so sexy," he says, his voice low. My eyes fall shut and I'm all sensation when suddenly I feel something cool running down my side. *Shit.* Am I leaking? This is so embarrassing.

"Ryder—" I warn him, but he cuts me off.

"Ssh. Don't say it. You're perfect and beautiful and I love that you still feed him like this. You are such a good mom," he says and my heart wants to burst out of my chest as I remind myself that I shouldn't be falling in love with him. "Just feel, baby," he says as his other hand begins to circle my other nipple. I don't know if it's because I haven't had sex in like a year but I feel myself pushing into him and when I meet his very erect cock, I moan even more.

"Ryder, I think…" I try to warn him that I'm going to come from him merely touching my breasts but he stops me again.

"Can I touch you down here?" he asks, placing a hand over my pants between my thighs. My pulse speeds up and I begin to crave more than his palm on my pants.

I nod silently and he slides his fingers under my waistband. I suddenly wish I had worn something a little sexier than white cotton underwear.

"Shit, you are so wet. You feel so good." His voice is hoarse as he rubs me with his fingers, spreading my wetness. It feels so good that my breathing turns ragged and I moan. I'm grateful that I finally picked up a baby monitor last week and that Brandon is upstairs and can't hear any of this.

"Oh, oh," I begin to cry out as I grip his thick shoulders and throw my head back. I had been feeling so heated from Ryder lately that I finally gave in and touched myself a few nights ago to make sure everything was good after giving birth. No worries there—I came hard thinking of him.

His thumb circles my clit and I begin to move my hips as my heartbeat accelerates. "What about you?" I ask with a husky voice.

"I want this to be about you. You are such a sexy and beautiful woman. I want to watch you come," he says, his voice raspy with need.

"Ryder I…" I don't know what I was going to say. Every thought leaves my mind as a hard and rough orgasm racks my body. I know I must be screaming out and I don't know how loud I am, but he's making me feel tingly and hot all over. I frankly don't care because I missed this feeling.

When I finally come down from my high, I open my eyes with a lazy grin.

"You're beautiful and that was the hottest thing I've ever seen." He bites down hard on his lower lip. His chest is heaving, and I can feel how hard he is in his jeans.

"Let me," I say, reaching down to touch him, but he stops me and brushes his palm over my forehead, moving the hair out of my eyes.

"Not tonight, okay? Let's take this one step at a time, even though

I would like nothing more than to be inside you right now. I know I don't deserve that yet, but I will and I will make you mine, Halo Pearson." He shifts next to me on the couch, holding me tight. My breath hitches. If I closed my eyes right now I would think he was Thomas. I know Thomas might not ever return but I can't stop the guilt I feel.

"What is it?" he asks, probably sensing the tension in my body.

I can't tell him. Not now. Not after we just experienced this close connection. "It's nothing." I force a smile and run my fingers through his dark brown hair. I trace the lines of his forehead, his cheeks and his jaw. I almost feel like a crazy woman when he shuts his eyes and I examine his face up close. His features are similar yet so different from my ex-husband's. His cheekbones seem lower and his nose is more squared off and not as straight as Thomas's.

Halo, what the hell are you doing? I shouldn't be comparing the two men. It's not fair to any of us. He opens his eyes and grips me in a hug.

"Do you want to come sleep upstairs?" I ask. I don't want to separate from him. I like the way he holds me in his arms. I realize he may be thinking that I asked him upstairs for sex. My heart skips a beat. "I mean uh… I thought we could just, um, sleep next to each other." Heat rises on my cheeks.

He bursts out laughing. "I know what you meant, Halo. And, yes, I would like to come up and just sleep beside you. I was serious when I said I can't have sex with you yet. I know I have to figure my shit out." He rolls over me on the couch without putting his body weight on me and stands up. Then he leans forward and lifts me in his arms. I squeal.

"Ryder put me down. Your leg, your arm…" I chide. He could mess up his injuries more.

"I'm good," he says convincingly.

"No seriously, I don't want you messing yourself up. Carry me up another night. Not tonight," I say with a pleading tone and some innuendo.

"Okay." He sulks and puts me down. "You're right I don't want to mess myself up for what I have planned for us soon," he says, raising and lowering his brows.

I shake my head with a chuckle and take him by the hand, leading him up the stairs. Then I fall asleep wrapped in his warmth.

CHAPTER TWENTY

Halo

I open my eyes and turn my body to see that the bed is empty and my heart sinks. I know Ryder would never leave without saying anything. What bothers me is that I finally have the perfect man in my life. He cooks, he helps with Brandon, he's open about his feelings, he's facing his demons, he clearly cares a whole lot for me and I do for him.

But... That *but* sticks in my head like it's been put there with crazy glue. I still can't get Thomas out of my mind and, even worse, out of my heart. I also can't stop comparing Ryder to Thomas and it's beginning to irk me.

I climb out of bed and head for Brandon's room. I've heard him cooing on the monitor for the past twenty minutes but I was too tired to open my eyes and he wasn't fussing so I activated the mobile from my room with the remote.

When I go into his room I see his eyes are open and he's watching his mobile. I pick him up and take him back to my bed to feed him. I listen for Ryder downstairs. Maybe he's making coffee or something. After a few moments of silence my panic rises. Was last night too much? Did he remember something?

After feeding and changing Brandon, I carry him down the stairs, my gaze seeking out Ryder. I even knock on the garage door, wondering if he's showering or getting dressed. There's no answer and I'm mad at myself for feeling so concerned. Ryder's an independent guy. He doesn't have to check in with me about everything he does and everywhere he goes.

I make coffee and try to eat. Brandon's happily wiggling in his bouncy chair—the TV is on in the background. I'm on the verge of trying Ryder on his cell when the doorbell rings. Thinking it's Ryder—he's probably forgotten the key—I undo the deadbolt and the latch and open the door. Two men in naval uniforms are standing on the porch. The air gets sucked out of my lungs… I can't breathe.

There's only one reason an officer comes to your home dressed in uniform and it isn't to deliver good news. I thought Thomas changed me as his next of kin but he clearly didn't. Tears begin to roll down my cheeks. I pull away from the men at the door. When Thomas was on deployments I would have nightmares about this exact thing happening. I would wake unable to sleep and I would only calm down once he called or emailed so I was sure he was safe. How could this be happening now? My arms wrap around my waist and I crumble to the floor. The officers at the door say something but I can't breathe, I can't even form a coherent thought. This can't be real. This can't happen now.

"Brandon, Brandon," I hear myself screaming for my son as pain takes over my entire body. Then I hear Thomas's smooth, deep voice in my mind, "*I will not say do not weep, for not all tears are an evil.*" I only wish that I could turn to sand and disintegrate. How I wish he were here.

I see the men come through the door and I feel just like I did the night the police officers came to tell me my parents were killed by a drunk driver. But that night Thomas had been here to catch me.

Now Thomas isn't here and he will never be. The thought rips my heart out.

"Miss." One of the officers tries to help me to my feet. "Miss!" He urges me to stand, but I can't. I can't move. Knowing that Thomas left me was one thing. Knowing he no longer breathed the air on this earth was another. I'm destroyed. Completely destroyed.

"There's been a misunderstanding..." the other officer is saying.

"What?" I look at him through the blur of my tears.

"We are looking for Petty Officer Second Class Thomas Wells," the first officer explains.

I gasp. "He isn't dead?" I rub at my wet face. I'm a mess and I'm now very confused.

"No, ma'am. He's not dead. He's being awarded a Medal of Honor for trying to save comrades from insurgent gunfire, ma'am. It's the highest military honor and will be awarded by the President of the United States. Officer Wells is a hero." I lean hard against the wall. I try to pull myself together. *Thomas isn't dead. Thomas isn't dead.*

"Why are you looking for him here?" is the first question that comes to mind.

"This is the address he left when he checked out after surgery." The officer sounds as confused as I am.

"Is Officer Wells not residing here?" the other man asks sternly.

Suddenly Ryder comes through the door. He must have been out for a run. He's sweaty, he's wearing sweats and earbuds hang from his neck. Relief hits me and I exhale deeply. I'm so glad to see him.

"Sir!" The two men turn around and salute Ryder. "Petty Officer Second Class Thomas Wells." Their voices are filled with respect.

"No," I say. "That's not—"

I'm cut off as Ryder answers yes and salutes them back.

I stumble to my feet and slowly back my way into the living room.

The world has tilted sideways. I'm dizzy. I'm sick. I'm crazy. I've completely lost it. Brandon begins to scream, pulling me out of my daze. I pick him up and hold him close to my chest as if I'm trying to protect him and myself.

The three men stand in the entrance of the room, looks of alarm on all their faces.

"Ryder," I say. "Why are you telling them you're Thomas? You are not Thomas. You're Ryder St. John."

The two officers look at each other with more confusion then place their attention on Ryder, waiting for an explanation.

"Halo, my real name is Thomas Wells. I can't remember anything about Thomas Wells so I couldn't identify with the name. I came up with the name Ryder St. John because I was trying to create a new identity for myself." I feel like the walls are closing in on me as he continues to explain, "St. John was my mother's maiden name. I know she hasn't been in my life since I was an infant, but I liked the name so I took it on."

As he speaks I hear it. I feel it. The reason why I put no walls up to this man from the moment I met him.

I didn't recognize him as Thomas but when I close my eyes, I hear him and feel him in my soul.

I think I'm going to be sick. A part of me wants to attack him and tell him that it's me, I'm his Halo, but then it hits me. If it had been possible for him to recognize me, to know me, he would have by now. The ambush, his surgeries, his long recovery…

His mind hasn't come back to us even though his body has been with us all this time.

His soul led him back to us even when he was drowning in darkness and couldn't find a way back to us. Even in his darkness he's here and he's loving us. I want to shake him and hit him and tell him that I hate him and love him and can't live without him but I can't do any of that.

As I stare at him more things begin to fall into place. His team died. Hanson, Montgomery, Kendall... The effects of losing them—his PTSD. Oh, my poor Thomas. My mind feels like it's being crushed.

You're my halo. I will find my way back to you even in the darkness.

He promised it so long ago and he kept his promise. He's been here for us. He loves Brandon like his own because he is his own. I realize that I'm holding Brandon as reality continues to sink in.

Ryder is looking at me like I'm completely crazy and in this moment I know what I need to do. I need to let this man heal.

Concern is etched on his face. "Halo." He reaches out for my hand and I give him my free hand. "Are you okay? What's happening here?"

"I'm okay," I say, squeezing his fingers and dropping his hand. "There was a misunderstanding... I thought they came here to deliver bad news. But it's not bad at all. I'm so happy for you, Ryder."

"Sir." One of the officers steps forward. "There will be a medal ceremony in your honor. This is your invitation from the President of the United States, Sir." The man offers an envelope. Ryder takes it, opens it and looks at it carefully.

"I don't deserve this. I can't remember," he says.

"Sir, the evidence speaks for itself. This is the highest honor."

"Thank you for your time, Sir," the other officer says. "Ma'am." They nod politely and leave, the door shutting behind them with a quiet thud.

Through the window, I see them pull out of the drive. The need to escape, to run, rises in my chest. My heart continues to race and I know I need space, time to process all of this. But Ryder—Thomas—is standing in front of me. And his expression is full of concern.

"You're a hero, Ryder. Or do I call you Thomas?" I ask hesitantly, trying to give him a smile.

"Ryder is still good. I don't know who Thomas was," he says.

I desperately want to tell him that *I* know who Thomas was. He was the greatest love of my life. He was a man who clearly tried to save his friends in dire circumstances. And he was a man who found his way back to his wife and son even when he was lost himself.

"Okay, Ryder," I say with a small smile.

He pulls at his sweatshirt with a grimace. "I should go shower and change." He heads for the garage and I want to tell him he can shower upstairs, but I know I need some space right now. I need time to think and work this out in my head.

He's been here all this time. He doesn't look the same but his gestures... The way he kissed me... It should have set off something in my mind. Jesus! I made him his favorite dishes and he was in heaven.

This is so messed up. When he left it crushed me. Going through the pregnancy and then a traumatic delivery by myself shook me to my core. I was in survival mode. My heart had been shattered into a million pieces. And then Ryder came along and my heart slowly mended. I gave my heart away to a boy so long ago and I knew he was my forever. I never dreamed he would return to me in a different package. I was in denial. I was in so much pain that it hurt to breathe. My worst fear came true and the struggle to get through each day was hard enough. I know I can't be hard on myself for not knowing. I was a bloody mess. I am a bloody mess.

CHAPTER TWENTY-ONE

Ryder

As I walk out to the garage, I try to shake off my strange feelings. Halo's behavior has me a little freaked out, but I know it must have been terrifying for her to see those guys show up at the door.

I don't know. Maybe I'm reading something into it that isn't there. When she slept in my arms last night I dreamt about her, but I know the dream couldn't have been real. We were at the lake. We were young, probably teenagers and I told her I loved her.

I've been wanting to tell her that I have fallen for her hard. My feelings for her are probably where the dream was rooted. That's why I got up and went for a slow jog this morning because spending the night sleeping beside her and holding her in my arms made me want things that I know I'm not ready to have.

Her orgasm last night completely had me undone and I'm suffering from a case of serious blue balls. There is more to us than just sex, though. I love everything about her. I love her son. I know it hasn't been that long since we met, and I'm not sure if people can fall in love in such a short time, but there was something about her that drew me to her even when I was bedridden and broken in the hospital. I'm thinking it was fate that I ended up in that particular hospital and I was there the moment she fell down. I was meant to watch over her and that boy of hers. I don't know what kind of past I had but I know I want her to be my future. I'm just not sure how to make her feel secure at this point.

The warm water of the shower is a relief. As I let it run over my face, I think of the medal the military wants to give me and it doesn't feel right. Maybe if I had my memory back I would be more accepting but to me right now Thomas Wells feels dead. I don't know that I want to bring him back. Not when bringing him back could mean that I find a life elsewhere and lose Halo.

CHAPTER TWENTY-TWO

Mountains of Eastern Afghanistan
September 2006
Thomas

I'm lying on my bed back at the base. It's the quiet times I hate the most over here because I think of all the ways I've wronged Halo.

When I first left, my head was messed up. A part of me felt like it would be better to die over here because I couldn't imagine settling into civilian life after what I had experienced. I've tried so many times to picture myself back in Chicago driving an ambulance and saving lives, but my efforts to envision that kind of life always fail. The missions I've been on, the things I've done…I don't know how I can come back from what's happened to me here.

Hanson approaches me with a wry smile. He takes a seat on the cot across from mine. "Fuck, Wells…" He shakes his head. "Quit your damn moping. Just call her and say you screwed up and that you had your head on wrong. Then spend the rest of your life making it up to her."

"Hanson, I fucking sent divorce papers. How do I take that back?" I ask the question even though I know there's no way to take it back. I was so scared when I found out about the baby. Scared that

I'd turn into my father. The only way I knew I could protect her and that baby was by leaving them be.

"You call her and tell her you didn't mean it." Hanson states.

"It's not so simple, man. Women are more complicated than that. I can't say 'Hey, Halo, I was all messed up and I fucked up and now I can't stop thinking of you and the baby.' Fuck, Hanson. I can't imagine missing the birth of my own baby. I will never know him or her. It makes me feel like a piece of shit. I'm no better than my own mother." I stand and begin to pace. I'm empty and broken inside. I may be useful to my country, but what kind of man leaves his wife and child?

"Don't get too deep inside yourself now, Wells. I heard the mission tonight is complicated and you need a clear head. You still have time to fix things with Halo and you will. You've been sulking for months now. You might want to consider going home. Tell the lieutenant you aren't right in the head or something. They'll pull you out." His suggestion throws me. How can he say that? He knows I won't leave without my team.

"I'll go home when you guys come with me," I say, reaching out to give his shoulder a squeeze.

"Wells, I ain't like you. There's no one back home waiting for me. This is my place. I am good at what I do. I love my job and my country and that's what I'm dedicated to. Honestly, man, if I was in your position with a beautiful woman waiting for me and a child, I would run to that." Heavy sadness settles around his eyes. I hate that he's never experienced love the way I have. I don't know who or where I would have been without Halo's love. I was the lost, abandoned child. I hated my life. I never felt worthy. Until Halo. She gave me everything worth living and fighting for. I hate that I was so messed up in the head that I threw it all away.

"Hanson, you're only twenty-eight. There's still time to meet someone and have a family. There's no reason not to." I hate the fact that he feels so alone. I know that Halo must hate me for what I've done, but I was so messed up the last time I went home that I could barely breathe without feeling the pain of losing Chris.

"What are you ladies sulking about back here?" Montgomery walks over and crosses his arms over his burly chest.

"Wells," Hanson responds. "It's time for him to go home and fix things with his wife."

Montgomery's shoulders deflate. "Missing your family is a bitch. Fuck, man. My baby girl turned two last month, and I missed her second birthday."

"You Skype with your wife and daughter every chance you get," I say.

"Not the same, Wells."

I nod. The sacrifices we make are something we've discussed a million times and we all know there's no easy answer. I look down at my watch. "It's almost seven. We better get to the briefing—I'm curious to see what kind of intel Hayes and Bulger found."

An hour later we have our mission. Reliable intelligence indicates that a high-ranking al-Qaeda leader has been spotted in a nearby village. Our team has been assigned to take him out. It's the kind of black-and-white mission that I thrive on—us against the bad guys.

I didn't understand what I had with Halo. I tried to prove myself repeatedly. Now I get that I had it all wrong. I now understand that I had the love of a woman. I loved her body and soul and that in itself was worthy. I'm just sorry it took me so damn long to understand that.

We head back to our sleep area and suit up. Being a part of Team Six means that we're an elite SEAL unit, which also means that we are given the most dangerous tasks. We suit up in our night gear. I've been trained to be a medic so I also have to carry the first-aid kit we'll use if something goes wrong. Hanson, Montgomery and I meet Lieutenant Commander Stanton, Kendall and McCall by the vehicle that will take us halfway to the village. The presence of the Lieutenant is confirmation of the importance of the mission.

We head out together in the dark of night towards the transport that will take us part way up the mountain. I can't shake a bad feeling—I don't know if it's because of what might be ahead of us, if it's because I've been thinking so hard about my past. The urge to talk to Halo is almost overwhelming. I tell myself that it's because I was thinking of Halo and the baby. I would hate for something to happen to me without having the chance to apologize and explain to her that I mentally broke down. Most of all I need to beg for her forgiveness. I can't die knowing she was mad at me. I wish there was time to at least make a phone call but there isn't. We need to move out.

"You okay, Wells?" Hanson whispers.

"Yeah."

"Good. Because you need a clear head for this shit." It's a dark cloudy night. I like that I can hide behind the darkness. I try to control my breaths. Something feels off.

"I'm focused," I whisper back to reassure him. I really am focused. Rover's death taught me to never look away, not even for a second.

"Something I need to know about, men?" the Lieutenant asks. I widen my eyes at Hanson, willing him to shut the fuck up. I turn my head to the Lieutenant.

"No, Sir," I reply.

The transport stops halfway up the mountain and we all get out. As we begin our hike, my adrenaline is pumping hard as it usually does on a mission. An hour later and we've reached the top. The Marine units have retreated and all seems quiet even though we know they're still here hiding in the hills, camouflaged by the darkness.

As we make our way through the village, I'm astonished by its simplicity and I try not to think about the conditions these people live in as we head for our target. This is the part I hate...the uninvited entries into peoples' homes. But there's no other way to search on this type of mission.

We enter a large family dwelling. The men in the house seem nervous. Suddenly there's a loud scream—it's a woman. The men turn to each other wide-eyed and continue muttering. The sound of women's voices comes from a back room.

"Top Gun, Doc, you go check it out," the Lieutenant orders and then leaves. Given our positions and what we do it's important for our identities to stay secret. I make my way to the back of the dwelling, forced to ignore the pleading voices of the men who follow me. A group of women surround a bed where a young woman is writhing. It takes me a moment to register the scene. She's in labor. My stomach drops out.

"Doc, let's just go. These people can help her. We need to catch up." Hanson tugs at my arm, but I'm stuck in my spot. The woman is in distress—something's obviously gone wrong. She needs my help.

"Doc, come on," Hanson urges again, knowing me too well.

I can't leave this woman or her unborn child to die. I look up to the sky wondering if this is a cruel joke. I've been sent back here on a night when I've been tortured by thoughts of my own wife and unborn child.

I shake my head. "I have morphine. I know how to deliver a baby. I can't walk away."

"Hurry the fuck up then," he says with an aggravated sigh.

I approach the women with my hands up, showing I'm not here to hurt them. Then I show them my medical supplies. They speak loudly, excitedly. I think they realize I want to help. Then things move fast. A quick exam indicates she's already crowning, but pain and panic aren't allowing her to push. I give her the injection and nod at the other women. They seem to understand that I want them to comfort her—the less attention she pays to me the better.

"She needs to push now," I say. Of course they don't understand so I try to make hand motions to describe what I mean. Hanson about busts a gut laughing.

"Dumbfuck," I mutter to him.

Finally we're in business with the pushing and I roll up my sleeves, getting ready to catch this baby. I was trained to do this but nothing has really prepared me for this moment. The women standing at each side of her shoulders are hoisting her up and she's giving it all she has. Suddenly half the baby's body is out. I guide it carefully and, as I turn the baby, it's clear he's a boy. The room is filled with sighs and groans as I place the baby on the woman's belly. She cradles him, crying.

"Fuck, Doc. You're crying." Hanson's voice snaps me out of my reverie and when I touch my face, I feel tears. I'm not sure when I even started crying. My chest hurts. My whole body hurts as I think of Halo.

"Do you need out of this mission?" he asks.

He's right—this is not the time or place.

I swipe at my eyes and then pull my shit together. "Not a fucking word of this to anyone." I point my finger in Hanson's face like I mean business.

"Not a word, Doc. Now let's get out of here," he says, his tone chiding me but laced with worry and a little sympathy over what I'm going through. The women come up to me and pat my shoulder. I'm assuming they're thanking me. I smile, eyeing the little baby once more before I leave. I walk over to a pail in the front room and wash my hands. I picture Halo looking beautiful with a rounded belly. My insides turn.

I follow Hanson back into the dark of night. The second we leave the dwelling, a shot's fired. We take cover behind a shack and Hanson pulls out his binoculars. We spot the rest of the team a hundred yards ahead.

"I need to take out the shooter or else we won't make it fifty yards," he whispers and I nod. Hanson gets a clear shot and we rejoin the team. There's no time to debrief the Lieutenant because we're suddenly faced with an overload of insurgent gunfire. We all take cover and return fire. The Marines have now notified that they have moved in closer. The earlier monotonous sky is now bright for the middle of the night.

We need to get into the shack. With the Marines holding down the gunfire this is our chance. The six of us make our way across the open space smashing down the door of the shack. Inside we're met with immediate gunfire. The air is stagnant and the place is too small to fit the amount of people holding arms. It makes my heart skip a beat because a bullet can hit a cement wall and ricochet.

Montgomery takes down one man, while Hanson and I follow the Lieutenant has moved further in and I am following him while shooting down the insurgents that have filled up this small space. They all must be here for a reason.

"Found something," Kendall calls out. The gunfire continues as the shack gets surrounded by insurgents. The Marines have notified that they are returning fire. We follow Kendall's voice into an abandoned room. There's a hand-knotted carpet on the floor and underneath it a tunnel leading underground. The Lieutenant leads the way down—it's dark and dusty and everything is eerie through my night goggles. It's so quiet that I can hear the breaths of the other men.

McCall gestures for us to stop. We hear the sounds of mice squealing. And then footsteps. I had a bad feeling about tonight and

I'm hoping I wasn't right. First, I'm faced with a woman giving birth, now this. I don't want to die in an underground fucking tunnel. The chances of insurgents lighting a grenade or mine under here is huge.

As we make our way through the tunnel, a breeze brushes across my skin. We must be reaching the outside. This makes me even more nervous, wondering if we've been led into a trap. The Lieutenant exits first, followed by Hanson, Kendall, Montgomery, me then McCall. I take in a lungful of air, relieved we all made it out alive.

"Turn your lights off, men," the Lieutenant orders. We all walk carefully on high alert. We've almost formed a circle as we move forward ready to shoot when it happens. The first shot goes clear but it's obviously coming from above—a sniper. Montgomery immediately uses the binoculars and makes his calculations at exactly what angle the shot came from and within seconds Hanson is shooting back. Our team begins to shoot while charging forward until we reach a group of twenty insurgents all clearly formed around one man.

This isn't unexpected. We disperse as planned into the low grasses and brush nearby. I'm happy this shit isn't going down near the village. Hanson and I end up on our stomach in the dirt with Hanson ready to point his AK-47. We're outnumbered. Hanson is a fast and accurate shot, but he's only one person. There are at least twenty men—Hanson shoots first and then our entire team begins shooting. One by one the insurgents fall down as the members of our team shoot at 45 degrees, 90 degrees, 120 degrees and so on. Problem is that not all the insurgents are falling and they are shooting back, now having a clear understanding of where the shots are being fired from. Suddenly there is a shot at 180 degrees that has clearly cut out one of our men. Sweat begins to roll down my face. I pray it isn't Montgomery. Knowing that one of our men has been hit makes us amp up the gunfire. As the insurgents drop, we rise out of the brush and move forward. Some of them get away—a problem because now they can come at us from any direction.

"Two got away," the Lieutenant clips. He moves forward, surveys the men on the ground and gives the signal that our target has been hit. Kendall and Montgomery make their way to us—Montgomery is limping.

Fuck! I let out a long breath. It looks like he took a bullet—or maybe was just grazed—on the lower leg. McCall photographs the deceased al-Qaeda leader and within seconds we are moving out. We have to clear out fast because now we will have angered the insurgents for killing their leader.

I place myself under Montgomery's shoulder and Kendall takes the other side. Hanson has his rifle ready and the Lieutenant is scoping the area so we don't fall into any surprise ambushes. I can't help but think of Rover and the day I carried his limp body away from the insurgent gunfire while Hanson had my back.

Rover's death is always a reminder to never lose focus. We stay close to the brush to camouflage ourselves. As we move I think of Halo and wish I could send my thoughts and feelings to her telepathically. *I'm coming home to you, baby. I will be there for you. I will be there for our baby, just please take me back. I'm so sorry, Halo. So sorry. Your mom wasn't right about me. I messed up but I will stick around from here on out. I will stick around.*

These past months I've had time to consider my life, my mistakes. I hit rock bottom and that does something to a person. It burned me to the core and opened my eyes. I was so wrong. I now know that I am a man who can look after her. I made a mistake and I'll need to fix it because I will love her forever. I can't live without her.

The transport is waiting for us at our drop-off point. We load up and the first thing I do is bandage up Montgomery's leg since we couldn't stop to do it before in fear of insurgent retaliation.

We speed down the mountain—at first we have our heads low and I know we're all thankful to be getting back to base. After we've taken a moment to compose ourselves, we go through a circle high-fiving each other for a job well done. I feel a strong jolt. At first I think we've hit a bump because my jaw snaps and my stomach bottoms out. But then I hear it—boom!—and the truck swerves wildly then tips sideways. There's a loud blast, the whoosh and heat of an explosion.

Pain...fire...burning...BLACK.

"I'll make dinner. Please. Please just leave me alone." I'm begging but he won't stop kicking me in the ribs. It's hard to breathe. I feel like an elephant has taken a seat on my chest and won't let the air into my lungs. "Please, I'm sorry," I beg my father but he is a cruel bastard and he won't let up.

"You're sorry, you piece of shit. You should be. You should be sorry for the day you were born," he says as he lifts his leg for another kick. He's drunk again. I gasp.

I open my eyes and they burn—they're filled with dust. As I lift my hand to rub them, a knife-edged pain jerks through my shoulder.

What the hell? I'm in the dirt—I'm not in my apartment. And my father isn't looming over me.

I blink up at the sky. The sun is just peeking above the clouds, turning them pink, orange, blue... It's the most beautiful thing I've ever seen. I try to take a breath but it hurts. My ears are ringing. I don't know if I've been plunged into heaven or hell.

As I try to stand I realize there's no question. I'm in hell. My skin is raw—when I touch my face, my hand comes away charred and bloody. When I rise to my knees, a scream is forced from my body. The sound echoes weirdly around me.

When I finally manage to take a breath, the scent of charred rubber and burning meat makes me ill.

It's becoming very clear I need to get the hell out of here. But how...

I turn my head and see the transport. It's a black shell, lying on its side. And that's when it all comes back to me. "Hanson," I yell. "Montgomery!" I yell even louder. But I can't tell if any sound is coming from my throat. My voice doesn't seem right. "*Kendall!*" I scream and my head feels like it will burst.

"Wells! Wells, over here." I hear McCall's voice and it takes me a moment to locate him. When my gaze lands on his body the tears begin to flow. They make my raw skin feel like flames. I stumble toward him. Half his body is burned and it looks like his legs have been severed from the thighs down. "McCall," I scream, but it sounds more like a sob.

"Take it," he says with a hoarse voice, passing me the camera. I take it, swiping at my eyes. I don't know if there are sirens going off, but that's how it feels inside my head. I stuff the camera in my pocket. My hand comes into contact with the morphine syringes I carry as a medic. I take one out and stab him in the arm with it. At least he won't be in pain. My mouth feels gritty and full of dirt so I spit to the ground. I'm dying for some water or something to clear out all the shit that is clogging up my windpipe.

I hear groaning coming from the transport. "Hanson?" I yell. It sounds like him.

I approach the burned-out ride as fast as my legs will take me. I see him—he's half in and half out of the rear window, his arms scrabbling on the dirt.

"Hanson!" I drag myself toward him and, ignoring the screaming pain in my shoulder and knee, I try to bend and grab his upper body. The explosion that took out the vehicle has left pockets of fire everywhere—in the brush, in the charred remnants of the engine.

I tug at him, screaming with the effort, knowing I have to get him away, out into the open. Hanson groans—a horrible, wrenching sound—as I finally wrest him free. I drag him far enough away that if the vehicle explodes, we are at a safe distance. I lie back down in the dirt. It hurts to breathe. I need to get my shoulder back in its socket because I am seeing colors from the pain and I can't pass out now. I smack my shoulder as hard as I can into the ground.

"Motherfucker," I scream out from the pain. It didn't work. I inhale a deep breath and smash it as hard as I can into the ground. I feel the click. The pain sucks the air out of my lungs. I brace myself before I rise up to my feet. I have two more doses of morphine. I reach into the pocket of my pants and give Hanson morphine. Fuck! I need one of these shots myself. This pain is fucking unbearable. I place my focus back on Hanson and his lips are quivering while his head is flailing around like he's punch drunk.

Fuck, Hanson—this is not how I saw this life ending for us. I wanted him to go home, find a woman and get married. I wanted him to experience love for once in his life. I fall to my knees beside Hanson and yell when I remember my leg is fucked up. I fall to my ass and then reach for him, cradling his head in my lap.

"I love you, Tucker Hanson. I love you, buddy. Thank you for always having my back." I want to cry, but the damn tears singe my skin so I do my damnedest to hold them back.

Suddenly he looks directly at me. "Thank you. Go home." Then he closes his eyes. I look up to the sky, squeezing my own eyes so hard it hurts. When I open them, I know it before I feel it—he's stopped breathing. I slowly rise to my feet. The other men…

Montgomery. I stumble around the vehicle, searching. I hear the click of a radio and I think I hear Montgomery's voice. I think he might be radioing in for help.

Thank God. I remember the conversation we had about his daughter—how he missed her birthday. Montgomery needs to fucking go home. And I do too…

"Where are you, Montgomery? I can't see you," I holler frantically. I see movement beyond a stand of scrub bushes. A hand raising a radio.

"Montgomery," I breathe out.

When I get to him I want to yell. I want to sob. I want to fall to my fucking knees. His body is burned, mangled.

"I can't see you, Wells," he says in a calm voice.

"Montgomery, you hold on. Please just fucking hold on." I lift his head, rest it on my arm.

"Morphine, man. I need some. I called for help and they're on the way." His voice is weak. All I can think about is his wife and his daughter. I stick my last needle in his arm.

"You're not fucking dying, Montgomery! You are fucking staying with me," I urge with boiling rage and anger.

"Just tell them how much I love them. Tell my daughter that her daddy was a hero." His eyes shut and I look up to the sky, not caring about the grit or the tears or the pain.

"*Noooooo!*" I scream and my lungs pierce with pain. In the distance I see the Marine troops coming down the mountain. I also hear the distant roar of the Chinook—it's probably coming to rescue us but it's too fucking late.

CHAPTER TWENTY-THREE

April 2008
Halo

I can't settle myself. The military officers left over half an hour ago, but adrenaline is still rushing through my body. I'm shaky and sick and I don't know what to think or do right now.

The urge to talk with Ryder is overwhelming, but I can't talk to him. For a bunch of reasons.

I decide to call Jenny. As I listen to her phone ring, my leg bounces, shaking the whole couch. The phone rings about five times before she picks it up. She must be busy with the kids. I try to breathe but my chest is tight.

"Hey Jenny, what are you up to today?" I ask, hoping I sound close to normal.

"Just some spring cleaning around the house. Why?" she asks with a curious tone. I guess I don't always call early on Sunday mornings.

"I was hoping to stop by," I reply.

"Great. Come on over. Dave plans to make the kids our ritual Sunday morning breakfast of chocolate chip pancakes later." She sounds like she is huffing away with all the cleaning.

"Okay, we'll be right over." I answer and close my cell phone.

Brandon's playing in his bouncy chair. He just started smiling and it is the sweetest thing I've ever seen. Only right now when I look over to him I want to cry. His daddy is here. His daddy has been with him almost since the day he was born. Only his daddy doesn't remember me or realize he has a son.

I wonder if he did have his memory back if he still would want to be around us. A part of me is so angry at him. I can't help it—I know I'm not thinking rationally. Why didn't he tell me his real name? I think back to our conversations together… I never did mention that my husband's name was Thomas. I guess I always referred to him as my ex-husband. Saying his name was personal and it hurt so badly—I guess I was trying to free myself from the pain.

I knock on the garage door because, if this were a normal day, I would ask Ryder if he wants to join Brandon and me over at Jenny's house. He swings the door open. He's just come out of the shower and he's wearing only a towel wrapped around his waist. My stomach drops. My gaze travels down his body as I wonder how I didn't know that this man was my husband.

His chest is smooth… he has a tattoo, scars. He's larger, and his muscles are more defined. Thomas had a light dusting of hair across his chest and down his abdomen, he didn't have a tattoo, he didn't have scars, he wasn't so large…

I've seen Ryder bare-chested before, but now it's like I'm seeing him for the first time. This man's body is so full of scars. Some look like burn marks, others like wounds. My heart hurts. For some reason it was different when I was thinking about Ryder living through all this. Knowing it was Thomas… My eyes flick up to his face and I hear him clear his throat. I am suddenly aware that I must have made him feel very uncomfortable. I pull my thoughts together and try to gain some composure.

"Everything okay?" he asks, furrowing his brows.

I flinch. "Yeah." I bite my lip nervously and wrap my arms around my waist protectively. I feel like a victim. I don't know why. "I'm, uh, going to Jenny's house. I wanted to see if you wanted to join us." I need to keep my cool in front of him and not break down and ask him why he could leave the way he did. The reality is that he wouldn't have the answers anyway.

"Yeah, sure. Give me a minute to get ready. Halo, are you sure you're okay?" He eyes me warily and I plaster on a smile.

"Of course."

"All right. I'll get dressed," he says, looking down at himself with a wry smile. Did he take the ogling as flirting? How can I flirt with him now? I'm suddenly questioning every little thing and I don't know what to do.

"I'll make coffee. Do you want one?" I ask.

"Yeah, thanks." He grins and retreats into the apartment.

Ten minutes later he walks into the living room and I force myself to continue this charade.

"All ready to head out?" he asks. He has his hair slicked back. He's wearing a black long-sleeve T-shirt that hugs his muscles and a pair of blue jeans that look fairly new. I find myself analyzing his appearance again, questioning how I didn't realize it was him.

"Yup, all ready. Your coffee is on the mantel."

"Thanks." Before he retrieves the coffee he bends down to greet Brandon. "And how are you doing today, big man?" he asks in his sweet, just-for-Brandon voice. My heart is melting and falling apart at the same time. He grabs the coffee and asks, "Ready?"

I fling on my jacket and nod. "After you guys."

"That's not right is it, Brandon? A gentleman always lets a lady go first." He's picked up the infant carrier and he's smiling down at Brandon. I love it and hate it. And, yup, I'm crazy.

"Thanks, gentlemen." I head out to the truck. Having to put up a front isn't easy and on the ride to Jenny's house, it feels like my body is shaking from the inside out.

After we park in the driveway, Ryder takes Brandon out of the car and I realize I forgot the diaper bag. "Shit," I yelp. Then I immediately place my hand over my mouth because my son doesn't need to hear that word from his mother's mouth.

"What is it?" Ryder asks.

"I forgot the diaper bag. We can't stay long."

"I'll run back and get it," he offers. "Here, let's get you both inside and I'll be back with it before you know it."

"Okay. Thanks so much." I smile.

We're greeted by the typical chaos at the door. Kids jockeying to greet us and Dave and Jenny yelling from somewhere in the house. Ryder smiles and passes Brandon's carrier over to me. "I'll be back in a few." He turns and leaves and I'm relieved.

I let out a breath as Jenny comes barreling down the stairs.

"What's going on?" she asks. She's wearing her yellow cleaning gloves.

I don't answer. I call out to Dave, "Dave, would you mind keeping Brandon with you for a few?"

He comes out of the kitchen looking frazzled. "Hi, Halo. Uh sure…" He sounds confused but he picks up the carrier, mumbling, "What's a fourth child. Piece of cake."

I slip off my shoes and go straight for the stairs, yanking Jenny by the arm. I can't have a meltdown in front of her children.

"Halo, what the hell?" She obviously believes I've completely lost it, but she follows me up the stairs and into her bedroom.

I want to talk, but suddenly the words won't form. "I… Ry—I…" I throw up my hands, exasperated.

"Sit on the bed and take a few breaths," she says, removing her yellow gloves. I sit and she takes a seat beside me. "What is it?" she asks.

I breathe slowly and I try to think where to start. I figure the beginning is probably the best place, so I tell her about the visit from the officers this morning. Then I tell her how Ryder came to the door and said he was Thomas. And finally I give her Ryder's explanation that to him Thomas is dead. By the time I'm finished, her jaw is slack, her eyes are distant and her breathing is ragged.

"Do you understand why I'm having a panic attack now?"

"But, but… Ryder. Thomas…?"

"See what I mean? That was my reaction."

"You were kissing him! I mean, I don't know… Couldn't you tell?" She looks at me with narrowed eyes. Maybe she thinks I'm crazy.

"Don't you think I've been making myself crazy asking the same question? He was different. Thomas was very possessive and unsure. Ryder was soft and sweet. Everything felt different with Ryder. I don't know what to say. He looks nothing like Thomas. He has a tattoo… His body is more defined. He used different soap… I don't know, Jenny! Maybe I am crazy. I mean, I never saw his…"

She places her palms on both cheeks. Dave knocks on the door and asks if everything is okay.

Jenny looks at him awestruck and then blurts out everything I just told her. His jaw goes slack and I take Brandon out of his arms.

"Hi, my boy." I rub the soft baby skin on his hand.

Dave and Jenny are now pacing around me and Jenny's kids are alone downstairs.

"Dave," I say. "Ryder could come back any minute. You have to go back down and act normal. Don't act as if he's our Thomas. Just treat him as you would treat Ryder on a regular day."

The minute Dave leaves Jenny asks, "What are you going to do?"

I look down at Brandon—he's sleeping contentedly. "The only thing I can do, Jenny. To Ryder, Thomas is dead. But to me he's still the father of my baby and the only man I clearly ever loved." My voice cracks and tears begin to well in my eyes. "What are the chances? We end up in the same hospital. I bring a stranger home with me... I mean that was crazy—who does shit like that?" I pause, thankful Brandon is asleep.

"It was messed up, I know, but being in the hospital and watching all those happy families leaving together hurt so bad. Then there was Ryder with that low, deep voice and the darkest most beautiful eyes that were so familiar yet distant. I knew he wasn't Thomas. I knew I was taking a risk." I look up at the ceiling, thinking how insane this is. I roll my eyes and laugh bitterly. "But I was falling in love with Ryder and now when I think about it, I'm not sure if I was blind or crazy because Ryder is Thomas without all the baggage. I can see it so clearly now. He's good to Brandon. He's good to me. He doesn't worry about his messed-up past and being like either of his shitty parents. It's nice, Jenny. It's nice and peaceful. Ryder is at peace. Is it so bad to want him to feel good? You have no idea the demons that Thomas carried around. It was hard on him, but it was hard on me too. I had to wait so long to have Brandon and look what happened when I told Thomas I was pregnant. He left. He left us, Jenny." As the tears go into free fall, Jenny motions for me to pass Brandon over to her. I reach for tissues on the nightstand and wipe my eyes and nose.

"And now I have him back." I hold the tissue to my heart because my heart was so broken when Thomas left and divorced me. "He was so messed up when he left—drugs and alcohol and PTSD. He felt he couldn't be here, that he had to go back. Now the navy is honoring him for his service—he's a hero and he should be proud."

"We both know that he could have been proud without going back and fighting more. Like you said, Halo—he has demons that have haunted him throughout his life. What happens if he does get his memory back? I hate to say it, but what happens if he wants to leave you again?" Jenny is practically cringing at the thought.

"Those were my first thoughts too. What happens if he leaves? My gut is telling me that he won't leave, that the PTSD he was suffering from before got out of hand and made him behave crazy. Ryder is in a good place now. He's going for therapy and trying to make himself a life. He told me so. We spoke about this, about us..." My cell rings and I pick it up. "Hello."

"Halo," Ryder greets me. "Is it okay if I pick you and Brandon up in a little while? First I wanted to pay a visit to that older lady I put down as my next of kin." My heart sinks. I've guessed who it is. I only met her once but she used to look out for Thomas when he was a kid. It must be his old neighbor, Miss Randall.

"Yeah of course. We'll be waiting for you," I reply. "See you soon."

"Bye, Halo."

"Bye, Ryder."

I end the call and Jenny looks at me, warily lifting her right brow. "What is it?"

"He's going to see his old neighbor, Miss Randall," I explain. "She took care of Thomas when he was living with his father. He used to get homework done at her place and she fed him a lot."

"He's going for answers, honey." Jenny voices my exact thoughts.

"I know, and I can't stop him. All I can do is pray he doesn't take off again. Brandon needs his father and I need him too. I'm worried, Jenny. Ryder told me that everyone on the team was killed in the ambush except him. When Chris Rover died it completely broke him. If he remembers how close he was to the rest of his team—and they're all gone too—I'm scared I will lose him forever."

"Oh, honey." Jenny places one arm around me—she still has Brandon sleeping tight in her arms.

"I need to be strong. I have to work tomorrow. Brandon is going to Miss Ritter and Thomas...Ryder...." I sigh and my shoulders droop.

"You are so strong, Halo. I have faith in you. I'm pretty sure you must be superwoman." She laughs.

"Yeah right. I'm clearly with superman since he keeps on leaving to save the world." I huff out a sardonic laugh.

"You've got to hope that things will work out. Like you said, he's in therapy this time. He's been injured. He doesn't walk right and his arm has troubles too. I don't think the navy would take a wounded vet back to war," Jenny says, making a good point.

"Yeah, I think you're right. He will clearly have to be medically discharged. I just hope that life as a paramedic or some other profession will be enough for him. I hope Brandon and I will be enough for him."

"I hope so too." She rubs my back. "Let's go downstairs I'll make you a tea. It sounds like you have at least a few things worked out in your head."

"I guess. I've clearly learned I can't control or plan my life. So whatever happens happens." My lips turn down even though I intend to smile. I follow Jenny out of her room and down the stairs. We head into the kitchen where her three sweet children are all eating chocolate chip pancakes with chocolate-covered faces.

CHAPTER TWENTY-FOUR

Ryder

I'm eager to get back to Halo and Brandon, but I need to make a quick stop first. I've had this address sitting in my pocket for about a week. My doctor thought it would be a good idea to talk to this woman—Miss Randall—since I named her as my next of kin. He's guessing I must have had a good relationship with her considering I have no other family listed. I head to the other side of Rogers Park. This part of the neighborhood is clearly more run down—there are kids who look like they are up to no good on the street corners. I finally reach the address and pull up to the old apartment building. I park the truck and gage my surroundings. It's an old truck but I would feel like shit if it got stolen.

I don't know why I am going to see Miss Randall today. Last night being intimate with Halo did something to me. It wasn't only the sexual chemistry between us. I also love the way she slept so content in my arms. It made me realize that I can't put off figuring things out about my past. I need to pursue the missing pieces of the puzzle—my family, my ex-wife, my old friends—more aggressively. She deserves nothing more than the best and she deserves a man who can fully commit to her. I need the closure to really move on with my life, with Halo.

I enter the building and wince at the musty smell and the dirt and trash that litter the entryway. I'm looking at the ancient intercom system, trying to figure out which apartment to buzz, when a guy—a knit hat pulled down over his brow—pushes by me on his way out. He doesn't give me a second glance when I catch the inner door and head toward the elevator. The controls look ancient and I consider taking the stairs. But Miss Randall's apartment number is 811 and I don't think I can make it up eight flights.

I get on the elevator, press the button for the eighth floor and, as it rises, I think about Halo. And how she completely broke down when she thought the SEALs came to deliver bad news. A part of me was jealous of her reaction. I mean she must have really loved her ex-husband and any man would be lucky to have her kind of love. The other part of me didn't know what to make of it, especially since she's been acting off ever since. Like she couldn't get rid of me fast enough to go speak with Jenny. My feelings for her are so intense—maybe last night scared her as much as it scared me. I'm hoping that's what it is and not her having cold feet about being with me because of her husband.

The elevator jolts to a stop and I walk down the hallway, trying not to inhale the scents of bad cooking and old, smelly socks. Finally, I knock on the door of Apartment 811. I wonder if I should have maybe called first. A man opens the door and looks at me warily. He looks like he has Down syndrome.

"I don't know you," he says.

"I'm sorry…I'm Thomas Wells. I was looking for Miss Randall," I say politely.

The man still looks wary but yells, "Mother."

A moment later a middle-aged woman comes to the door. She has blond, mid-length hair and her eyes are blue and circled with the kinds of wrinkles that come with a hard life. She gives me the same unsure look as her son. "Can I help you?" she asks.

"My name is Thomas Wells," I tell her. "I uh…had you down as my next of kin in my military file and I wanted to ask you some questions." I feel nervous and wonder if it was a mistake to come.

"Thomas? You don't look like Thomas." She sounds accusing or maybe unsure.

"Ma'am, I was badly injured in Afghanistan. I had facial restructuring and skin grafts. I've been burned and broken. I'm also suffering from amnesia and I was hoping you may have some answers for me." As I say the last words her hand flies up to her mouth and she begins to quiver then she throws her arms around me and embraces me in a strong hug. I'm not sure if I am supposed to hug her back or not.

"Look, honey." She gestures at the man who answered the door—I'm guessing it's her son. "It's Thomas. Oh dear." She presses her palm to her heart. "You used to be friends—you would watch out for him at school. You know the kids in this neighborhood could get cruel from time to time. Wow! Boy, look at you." She pauses with a gasp, shaking her head. "A man now. Back from the war."

"I'm back, yes. And now I have some things I need to figure out."

"Well, come on in, Thomas. Would you like some hot cocoa?" She's still pressing her hand to her chest.

I'm not sure the last time I drank hot cocoa but it does sound good. "Yes, please, that would be nice," I respond with a nod and a slight smile.

"Come in make yourself comfortable. You said you have amnesia. Does that mean you don't remember who you are?" She looks back at me as I follow her to the kitchen. It's small and very old with a yellow stove and fridge. Her son follows us into the kitchen with a grin and I smile at him. I wish I could remember him.

"Yes, ma'am, that's what it means."

Miss Randall makes hot cocoa and then the three of us sit around the small, white kitchen table. There are three chairs at the round table. Just enough for us. I sip the cocoa—it's hot and sweet.

"You always did like my hot cocoa, Thomas. You used to come over here after school and do your homework at this very table. You boys would eat dinner together. You sure did love my spaghetti and meatballs." She smiles, a distant look on her face. She seems fond of the memory.

"Why is that? Where was my family?"

Her blue eyes turn sad. "Well, honey, your mama left when you were two. She was a beautiful woman, but she wasn't happy in this life. You lived across the hall. I heard your parents screaming all the time. I also heard your mama's tears. One day she was just gone and your papa had to take care of you. At first he paid me to cook for you and watch over you during the day because I was homeschooling my own son who, as you can see, was born special. You boys got along great and it was extra money for me. Then your papa couldn't afford me anymore. I think you must have been five by then because you went into kindergarten. You still came to me after school." She pauses and tilts her head, gazing at me. "Boy, you must have been in a real wreck over there because I would not recognize you walking down the street and I practically raised you," she says with sadness in her tone.

"I was, ma'am. I was the only one left alive. The rest of the men on my team died."

She crosses her heart as her eyes fill with tears. "It was your dream to become a SEAL and you worked hard at it." She twists her fingers together with that same far off look in her eyes. It's almost as if she's living those moments in the past again. "You did well in school, got your work done and then you would spend hours training your body. You were quite a looker back then. You had the girls lined up, except they never came around here. You always took off at night. At first I was scared you were getting into trouble, but you were just a teenage boy having his fun." Her lips tug up at the corners and her eyes grow warm.

"Why didn't I bring my friends around?" I ask, curious about her comment. Her eyes turn sad again as she gazes at me. She doesn't answer. "Please, I want to know," I urge her.

"Well, there was one young girl I remember. She came by to see you, but that father of yours…" She pauses and her aged eyes look back at me with anguish or maybe guilt—I'm not sure.

"Who was she?" I ask, because she must have been someone important if she is the only one I brought home.

"She was special to you, Thomas. A young, beautiful girl with the biggest, roundest brown eyes that I've ever seen. You were dating her and she came to see where you lived," she says, then purses her lips.

It almost sounds as if she's describing Halo because she has the most beautiful big round brown eyes I've ever seen. The thought makes my stomach drop, but I know the connection my mind is making is impossible.

"What happened when she came?" I ask.

"Thomas, your father was an alcoholic. It made him mean. And I think his heart turned cold when your mother left. He was a cruel man and he beat you, honey." A tear slips down her face. Her son gets up and places his arms around her shoulders.

"I'm okay, dear." She pats him. He nods and eyes me warily then sits back down.

"He beat me?" I ask. How could that even be possible? I don't feel anything, it couldn't have happened to me. Could it? I look at Miss Randall in a new light. She must have done so much more than feed me and babysit me. It's likely she protected me and very possibly saved me. "Do you know what happened to the girl?" I ask. "Did we stay together?"

"Yes, Thomas. You told us that you met a girl—you loved her and you were leaving to take care of her. You said she was your ray of light. You mentioned that her parents had been killed in a drunk driving accident and you would be taking care of her. You said your goodbyes and we haven't seen you since. It's been about eight years now." Her voice is matter-of-fact but I notice the sadness still rimming her eyes. Maybe I didn't stay in touch.

My heartbeat is racing and I swallow hard, knowing I have to keep asking her questions. "Did you know the girl's name?"

As I wait for her response, my insides churn and I fidget on the uncomfortable chair. I feel like I'm about to find out a huge piece of the puzzle—

"I think her name was Halo."

As she says Halo's name all the blood drains from my face. *Halo?* I yell it in my head, as I desperately try to keep my cool. I rise to my feet abruptly. I can't get out of here fast enough. I feel like breaking down, kicking a wall, maybe screaming at the top of my lungs. But I can't do any of that right now. Processing this will have to wait because I have one more question. "Miss Randall, do you know where my father is?"

"Yes, hon. He still lives across the hall." Her face scrunches up in disgust and I am beginning to understand where I came from.

"Thank you for your time. The cocoa was real good." I try to smile. I need to hold it together and be kind to this woman, because it's obvious she's been nothing but kind to me. She has clearly had a hard life but she managed to open her heart to a boy who was basically alone and abandoned by his family. I'm thinking I probably made it through childhood because of her. She and her son follow me to the door.

"Will you come visit us again?" she asks with hope in her eyes.

"Yeah, you know what? You should take my cell phone number.

We can stay in touch for sure." I smile. I give her the number and she writes it on a paper.

"I'm glad to see that you made it through the war, Thomas. I can see that you're still hurting, but you've always been a survivor, kid. You're going to be okay. If you need to talk more or need to know anything else just call—we're here." She gives me a hug and something deep inside me pulls a little bit. I almost want to cry. I'm not sure why.

"Thank you, Miss Randall. It was nice to see you again too." I smile at her son.

"Yeah, Thomas." He smiles back and waves.

They shut the door and for a moment I stand in the hall, staring at the door across from Miss Randall's. The apartment where I grew up and where my father still lives. A part of me wants to knock and see the man who created me. My body feels warm and my heart is still pumping fast from all the new information in my head. I think of Halo and Brandon and I turn to leave. I don't need to waste even a second on a man who beat his own child.

Miss Randall was truthful—I could see it in her eyes and her expression—but it also seemed as though she was holding back on telling me the worst. I'm breathing raggedly as I make my way to the elevator.

Halo is not a common name from what I know. Halo. Is it possible? It can't be. I would remember someone like her. Brandon…holy hell. I swipe a hand over my mouth. Could he be mine? I don't know how to process the information. I'm freaking the fuck out as I head back to the truck on shaky legs.

I need to get to Halo. I head back toward Jenny and Dave's, my mind racing a mile a minute. I want to remember my life. Suddenly I am not so keen on the fact that I've basically killed off Thomas Wells in my head. He was clearly not as alone as I understood from my file. Why the hell would I divorce Halo? This doesn't make sense.

I want to speed through the streets, get to Halo as soon as possible. But I don't want to wreck the truck or get stopped by the cops. I finally reach the driveway and I can't make it to the door fast enough. I need answers.

CHAPTER TWENTY-FIVE

Halo

I'm in the kitchen eating with Jenny and the kids when the doorbell rings. Dave goes to answer the door and soon I hear Ryder's voice. My stomach plummets as I worry that Jenny and Dave won't be able to act as if everything is normal. I feel like my life and the life of my son is depending on it. Jenny eyes me from across the table as if it's the moment of truth. I hear Dave inviting Ryder in for pancakes. I try to regulate my breathing because I feel like I might pass out. Ryder walks into the kitchen, his expression looking a little heavy, and he eyes me warily. I put on my best smile for him.

"Hey, kids." Ryder leans on an empty chair and watches as they stuff pancakes in their mouths. They're on their second batch and covered with chocolate and syrup. He looks amused.

"Come sit," Olivia says with her sweet little voice.

"Thank you, Olivia," Ryder responds and takes a seat across from me. Dave has gone back to flipping pancakes. The kitchen is too quiet, the air too tense. I'm scared to ask how the visit went.

"Pancake, Ryder?" Dave asks.

"Yeah, sure, man. Thanks," Ryder responds with his eyes on me. The usual warmth I see in his gaze is gone. He's wearing more of a questioning expression. Almost like he doesn't know me.

I can immediately tell he's figured something out and I'm scared. Will he leave? Will he run again? His eyes land on Brandon and when his gaze goes soft, I gain some hope. My insides are twisting. I need out of here. *Now.*

I try to eat, but I barely taste the food in my mouth. Dave serves Ryder and the look he gives him is analytical, considering. Shit. I hope Ryder doesn't sense the tension in the air.

Too late. Ryder abruptly pushes away from the table. It's a jerky movement but his expression seems calm. "What's going on here?" he asks.

I almost want to laugh. He can't remember who he is, but he still has the skills he was trained for. Reading a situation, gaging tension.

Jenny eyes me and then looks to Dave for a solution. They were having a nice family breakfast and we have clearly intruded, bringing our tension along with us.

"I'm sorry, guys," I say looking to Jenny then to Dave. "We should go, Ryder."

"Yeah, we should go," he agrees. He helps me place Brandon back in the carrier and the way he's looking at him rips my heart in two and then mends it back together. It's as if he's seeing Brandon for the first time. *He knows!* My heart is racing as the thought screams through my head again and again.

The drive back home is silent and stressful. I want to crawl out of my own skin. It's as if we've both agreed to wait to talk until we're out of the truck and in the house. We pull up to the house and we can't get inside fast enough. I take Brandon out of the carrier and he wakes up crying.

"He's hungry. I need to feed him." I walk over to the couch to breastfeed. Ryder takes a seat beside me. Over time, and as we've become closer, he's stopped giving me privacy when I feed Brandon.

I didn't have a problem with it. It felt natural.

"Did you know me from before? Did you know Thomas Wells?" he asks. He's gripping his thighs and his knees are jiggling. He's nervous—that much is obvious—but his questions tell me his memory isn't back. A part of me is relieved and I feel guilty for thinking this way.

"Yes," I admit because I know he knows. I won't be able to hide it.

"Elaborate," he says with his low, deep voice. It sounds too calm.

"I met you when I was fifteen..." I begin slowly telling him about our time dating. I can't help a small smile as I tell him about happier times. I move on to describe my parents' deaths—the hardest time of my life.

All the while, I'm watching him carefully, judging his reactions. He's sitting next to me—and he's my rock—but I also know his mind is fragile right now. I don't want to say too much, too soon. I reach over to where he's gripping his thigh, his fingers white-knuckled as if he's working so damn hard to control his body and his thoughts. His hand clasps mine tightly.

He nods. "Go on," he encourages. "I need to hear this. I want to hear this."

It's hard to explain all the emotions I felt back then. "When we first started dating we were like two renegades, at least that's how my parents saw us." I smile at the memory. "My parents weren't too pleased. I was completely smitten with you," I explain. "Then my parents died and you moved in with me. You took care of me. I was deeply depressed. My life felt like a black hole and you were here to keep me sane." He lets out a long breath, nodding his head. "I was fighting with my parents over you when they got killed. Things never got resolved."

His eyes open and shut as he takes in this information. I want to tell him how much it hurt when he left. I also felt like I had no closure even after I signed the divorce papers. I'm scared that he's fragile. I don't want to do anything that will make him run again. I stick to the facts of our past.

"The next stage in our lives was when you trained to be a paramedic and I got my degree. I met Jenny, Melissa and Sam. Boot camp followed. You knew I was in a better place and you left to fulfill a dream in Great Lakes." I pause because the next part of this story makes my heart clench. It's part of the reason he left me and fell apart.

I inhale and then exhale. "Your best friend from boot camp, Chris Rover, was killed in Iraq. His death hit you hard. The PTSD got bad after the Iraq deployment." I pause to gage his mood, ever so fearful he will run again.

"I had a dream about Rover…months ago. It felt terrible," he explains and I reach out to hold his hand, giving it a light squeeze.

"We had good times too. We loved spending time at the lake together. It was our own heaven on earth. I gave you my virginity at the lake," I say hoping to brighten his solemn mood.

"Halo," he says breathlessly. "I do wish I could remember that. I've been dying to get into your pants." The corner of his mouth turns into a playful grin and I'm relieved he isn't falling back into that dark place.

"Miss Randall said you were special to me." He's watching me so intently with his dark blue eyes. What do they say about a person's eyes? Something about them being a portal to a person's soul and it all makes sense. There were never any walls, never any boundaries with Ryder St. John.

I nod. "We got married. Nothing fancy. A quick trip to city hall with some friends. It was the happiest day of our lives. You were nervous about marriage but you were sure about me." I think it's a pretty good portrayal of who we were back then.

He looks down at Brandon. "And this little guy?"

I stare at him, unsure what to say.

Ryder makes a choking sound. "God—everything you're saying. They way I've been feeling about him, about you. He's mine isn't he?"

Tears clog my eyes and throat. "Yes," I breathe, nodding. "He's yours."

His eyes are wide, gleaming with tears. "How...why?" He gasps. As if he can't bear to even ask the question.

"You were upset when I told you I was pregnant," I whisper. "You didn't want kids."

"Why?" he asks again, looking like a lost boy. He *was* my lost boy and then he found me and he wasn't lost anymore because I was his home.

"You had a difficult childhood." I wince. I'm not sure how many demons I should let out of the closet.

"Miss Randall told me." His forehead creases. "I still don't remember any of it. Why did I leave you? What kind of man was I to divorce you when you were pregnant?" He cringes and turns his whole body to face me. Brandon stops feeding and I lift him up over my shoulder to burp him when Ryder asks, "Can I?" He catches me off guard. It takes me a moment to realize that he wants to burp him.

"Okay," I say. "Put this on your shoulder." I pass him the burp blanket. He takes Brandon carefully and places him just right on his broad shoulder. "Is this okay?" he asks, looking at me out of the corner of his eye. Brandon lets out a little burp.

"It's perfect." I smile.

"Why did I leave, Halo? I need to understand. I don't remember being Thomas. What man in his right mind would leave *you*?" His voice breaks when he says "you" and I brush at my tears, aching for him.

"You weren't in your right mind," I tell him. "You were suffering from PTSD. Your best friend was killed in Iraq right in front of your eyes. You tried to save him but you couldn't and for a while…it destroyed you. When you got back from Iraq you were a mess—couldn't sleep right, couldn't eat. You drank and took too many pills. You were suffering. And I didn't know how to help you. No one did."

Ryder moves Brandon off his shoulder and cradles him. "Maybe we can put him in the play gym for a bit. This is hard to hear, Halo." His smile is devastatingly sad.

"Sure." I take Brandon and set him up on the floor. He begins to kick the dolls hanging above him.

I return to the couch and Ryder runs a hand nervously over his mouth. "So essentially what you're saying is…" His mouth turns down on one side. "Is that I was an asshole."

"You had been through a lot," I say, feeling the need to defend Thomas. I knew so much more about what he'd suffered now. But I also need to be honest. "It hurt me badly when I got the divorce papers. I felt abandoned. Even though I knew PTSD isn't something you can just get over—not without time and effort."

"Like what I'm going through now," he suggests.

"Like now," I confirm.

"So," he says after a moment, leaning forward, putting his forearms on his thighs. "I have to ask—why didn't you recognize me as Thomas? Do I look that different?"

I should have expected the question and I'm mad when it throws me off. I take a few breaths and say, "No, I didn't recognize you at all. I did find looking into your eyes comforting, though, and the low, deep sound of your voice always put me at ease."

For the first time in the conversation, his eyes are shuttered. I wonder if he's angry that I didn't recognize him. I try to explain, wondering if he's angry now. Angry for Ryder, angry for Thomas? Thomas was always very possessive of me. I was very clearly only his. He liked to say it as much as he could. It used to make me feel good. It made me feel wanted.

Even though Thomas and Ryder are different in many ways there are important and essential similarities. The way we were drawn together so quickly, the way I felt cared for and cherished. Then, when Thomas fell down on the job of caring for me, Ryder picked it up. I basically fell in love with the same man twice.

"What happens next?" I look at Ryder.

He lets out a breath. "I was falling in love with you, Halo. I may not remember the man I was, but since I met you in that hospital, I've been drawn to you and Brandon. It's only been a short time, I know. I'm still unsure of certain things. I've been telling myself every night before I go to bed that I need to make you fall in love with me because I'm so in love with you. The question is can you love me as Ryder? Can you let Thomas go?" He moves in close to me. His eyes drop to my lips and I feel my insides quiver.

"What happens if you get your memory back? Do I need to be scared about you taking off again? From what I'm gathering, Ryder, you lost your closest friends in that ambush. I've met them. I know them—"

He places a finger on my lips to stop me. "Not today, Halo. I can't go there yet. I've had a lot thrown on me today. I need time." He brushes his lips gently along mine. I can't help but close my eyes. "Do you feel that, Halo?" He breathes into my mouth and I feel as though I'm melting for him.

"Yes," I answer with a raspy voice.

"I want to sleep with you so bad right now, but we can't do that. Not until we figure things out." His breath is hot against my lips and I want nothing more than for him to claim me. But he is being

Thomas even though he doesn't realize it. He did the same thing when we were dating. He wouldn't sleep with me until he was sure I was only his. It makes me laugh inside because he may not feel like Thomas but Thomas is very much alive inside Ryder St. John.

"Ryder, why did you choose your mother's maiden name?"

"I don't know. The file said 'estranged'."

"Oh." I find it interesting he chose to name himself after the woman who left him. I know it was always a hardship that Thomas carried close to his heart. Even his father blamed him for his mother's departure. Something about that comment makes me feel like Thomas is closer to coming back than Ryder believes or is ready for.

We spend the rest of the day thinking and talking with gentle, slow kisses to help us through. It's hard to find answers when there's so much up in the air. At night we give Brandon a bath together. It's the first time Ryder has ever helped me give Brandon a bath. I know he's trying it because he knows now that he's Brandon's father. It makes me sad for Thomas because he was so scared of becoming a father even though I know deep down he would've been committed to his son. Ryder is Thomas without the heavy baggage. I know it's likely that someday his memory will come completely back. And I realize now that it's the truth that will set him free. I just don't know when the real judgment day will come.

CHAPTER TWENTY-SIX

One month later (beginning of May)
Halo

"Halo," Ryder calls out my name from downstairs.

"What is it?" I'm getting Brandon ready for bed. I've been back to work over a month now and I know how important our bedtime routine is—it's gotten so Brandon falls asleep and stays asleep through the night.

"Halo, come down here," Ryder demands impatiently and I don't know what's gotten into him. "Okay, Okay. What's going on?" I fasten the last few buttons on Brandon's sleeper and make my way down the stairs. Ryder is in his usual attire of black T-shirt and worn jeans stained with grease. He's still working as a mechanic—almost full time now. He leans forward to give me a kiss on the lips and then places a kiss on Brandon's forehead without touching us with his hands or body. He likes to take a shower before doing that.

"I need you to come outside. Can you put him in the floor gym or something?" he asks. He seems excited. A little antsy. He's got a wide smile and seems happy—his energy is catching. I'm feeling a bit perkier even though a few minutes ago I was totally wiped from teaching all day. I put Brandon down on the play mat and Ryder takes my hand. "Cover your eyes," he says. I would follow this man anywhere and I let him guide me—I hear the front door open and feel the breeze on my face.

Ryder lets go of my hand. "Okay, open them now."

I blink. He's pointing at a new red SUV in the driveway. "It's a car, Ryder," I state matter-of-factly.

"It's for you, Halo. I don't like you driving the truck—it isn't safe."

"Ah…wow. Can we afford this?" I ask. I realize I just referred to us as "we" and my heart skips a beat. This is a big step.

"I pay you rent, but let's be honest. I need to do more. I make money as a mechanic and I get a salary from the navy. I have money saved up. I wanted to do this."

Throwing my arms around his neck, I bury my nose next to his jaw and take in his scent. "Thank you, I love it." I breathe softly into his ear.

He's become even more precious to me—as Thomas, as Ryder, I cherish both sides of him. He's asked me to call him Ryder and not Thomas. He said he doesn't know or feel like Thomas. He especially doesn't like that Thomas left me pregnant.

"I love you," he says, turning his head to kiss my lips. He's been saying it a lot lately only I haven't reciprocated. It's not that I don't love him. I've only ever loved him, but I've also been hurt by him. There's a tiny, miniscule place in the back of my head that fears when his memory does come back he'll run. I fear saying those words will be like a bad omen. So I wait, loving him in my heart. I now understand how it was so easy being with Ryder because I must have felt like Thomas was in there somewhere. Now that I know the truth I see the signs all the time. His decision-making, the way he cares for us, worries about us.

"I love the car, Ryder. Thank you so much."

"It's a lease in your name. Payments will come out of my bank account."

I reach up to touch him, my hand lightly grazing his cheek down to his jaw. We stare at each other and I see the guilt marring his beautiful features. I hate that he feels guilt over what happened in the past. I think this car is a step toward him overcoming the guilt about leaving us.

"What will happen with the truck?" I ask.

"Well, actually I was going to ask you if it's okay if I work on it. I wanted to rebuild it slowly. Put in a new engine, transmission… Would that be okay with you?" He asks the question almost shyly.

"Ryder, of course it's okay. It was your truck. You began to work on it years ago but with all the deployments, training and other missions it was left on the back burner. It's all yours."

A boyish grin erupts on his face. It's a familiar smile in some ways but in others…not so much. And the thought makes me sad. The face I loved so dearly—those beautiful features that I had fallen in love with—I would never see again. The war scarred him beyond recognition internally but externally too.

Yet I also feel so blessed. Our relationship has evolved into something better. My man is getting help. He seems more whole, content. The journey he took was difficult and dangerous but it also brought him home and forced him to face his demons.

My eyes linger on his face too long and I feel his uneasiness grow. "You are still beautiful. Still so handsome." I caress his face and he closes his eyes. "Thank you, Ryder." I place a kiss on his lips, wondering if I will ever be able to call him Thomas again. It makes my heart ache a little. "I better go in to Brandon. He needs to sleep."

"Yeah…sure." His reply is a little withdrawn. "I saw the weather is warming up this weekend. Maybe we can take Brandon to the lake for a picnic," he suggests, and I sense he's feeling sad too.

"That's sounds perfect." I smile and go inside to find Brandon.

CHAPTER TWENTY-SEVEN

Ryder
June 2008 (about one month later)

I'm a fucking coward. I have the mother of my child lying in my arms every night and yet I don't make love to her. I watch the need growing in her eyes. I haven't touched her, though, not since the night I made her climax two months ago.

Back then I was just Ryder and she was a beautiful woman I had the serious hots for. Now I've learned that she was the love of my life, the mother of my son, and I ran out on her. She had to give birth to him on her own. Shit! When I think of the way she fell down in the hospital because she was so panicked about getting to Brandon my heart hurts.

She's such a good mother, a good person. How could I have left her? I've been talking to Dr. Wembley extensively and I've been talking to Bob, the Vet from Nam who works as a therapist with Dr. Wembley. They are both of the mindset that I should read the reports from Afghanistan in the hopes that they'll jog my memory.

Even if it fails they are of the impression that I can lead a happy life as Ryder St. John. A man who loves his girlfriend, his son, I even love my job.

The doctors see my life as balanced. For me, it's become a struggle. Knowing that Halo and I share a past and not being able to remember all the things—big and small—that we went through together feels deeply wrong. She doesn't deserve the pain of not living with a man who's whole, who is one hundred percent there for her. Not after what I put her through.

I'm trying to follow Bob's advice. It hasn't been easy. As Ryder I got a life. It consisted of Halo and Brandon. I went to work and cared for the two people who meant the most to me. Then the truth came along. I thought I read somewhere that the truth would set me free but it has only increased my burdens. Halo remembers a rich past with me filled with good and bad times and I remember nothing. I don't feel whole now because of it. I hate not remembering my team. The dedicated men who died were apparently like my brothers. None of it sits well with me.

Halo turns in her sleep and I continue to stare up at the ceiling. I don't sleep well, so I've taken the night shift with Brandon so Halo can sleep.

I hear Brandon crying and I head over to his room. We have a rocking chair set up in there now and Halo always leaves a bottle, thermos and formula ready for me to fix in the middle of the night since she stopped breastfeeding a couple weeks ago.

She's paid her dues with caring for him and I wanted to make up for the time I've lost. As I hold my son in my arms and he drinks his bottle I know what I have to do. I have to give him a family. I need to give Halo the family I probably promised her and never followed through on. That means I need to face my demons and move on. Even if my memory never comes back she's still it for me. I want to marry her. I want Brandon to have siblings. It's the one thing that waking up alone and not knowing who I was in the hospital taught me. You can't be alone in this life. You need family. Even if they aren't your blood relatives, you need friends and you need a good woman to love and who loves you back. If I'm going to be a good role model for my son, I have to do right by his mother.

Brandon finishes his bottle and I place him back gently in his crib. He turns on his side and his bottom lip jets out a bit. He looks content and my heart explodes. I never thought I could feel this way about another human.

I head back to bed and Halo stirs a bit. "Everything okay?" she murmurs, half asleep.

"It's all good," I answer back.

What I want to really say is that all will be okay.

We're gonna be okay, Halo. We'll be okay because when I go see Dr. Wembley next week I'll finally discuss my last mission with him. I'll get details on the ambush that took out my team. I'll do anything he suggests—hypnosis, group therapy, medication. I'll do anything at this point for you, Halo, because I want to see you smile.

Feeling restless, I get out of bed slowly and head up to the attic. Halo mentioned that she stored a bunch of my old things up there and Dr. Wembley said it wouldn't hurt to look at some old pictures or any special trinkets that may have meant something to me.

The attic has a low ceiling. I make my way to a bunch of cardboard boxes and begin to sift through them. There's a nice layer of dust on everything I touch. I see pictures of a young Halo and Thomas together. I will my mind to feel some connection. Nothing happens. The man in this picture doesn't resemble me one bit. I knew this already. I'm frustrated because this feels like a lost cause. My hands brush over some trophies. Nothing.

I leave the attic, hoping that Dr. Wembley will work some magic another way. He said hypnosis may work but can be risky because it can flood my mind with all the bad at once. I need to do something drastic, though. I've been given a second chance to live. I have my soul mate back and I will do everything in my power to prove to her that I will never abandon her again.

CHAPTER TWENTY-EIGHT

Two Weeks later (middle of June)
Halo

It's a Friday afternoon and I take Brandon to the supermarket to buy some groceries before the weekend. I'm really looking forward to the summer and chilling with Ryder and Brandon. Going back to work for two months before the break was pretty exhausting and I didn't have quite enough time to adjust to a work-home-mom schedule.

I crank up the AC in the car as I head down the city streets. Brandon is tired and he cries a bit in the back seat, so I sing him a lullaby in the hopes he'll fall asleep. It's a Friday afternoon which means heavy traffic. The car is new so it cools down fast. A car cuts me off and another one honks at me. People must be losing it with this heat. I let out a long sigh. We make it to the supermarket and I shop like a madwoman, trying to grab everything I need before Brandon wakes up.

When we get home I pull up to the driveway and notice Ryder's truck—he's home early. The paint job on the truck looks amazing—black with fiery red stripes. Even better, he's been working hard on the engine so it's safer and quieter to drive.

We go inside and I'm hit with stale, still air. I immediately turn on the ceiling fans to get the air circulating. The AC must be on the fritz again.

"Ryder?" I call out as I head into the kitchen. I take Brandon out of his carrier and his back is wet with sweat. "Sorry buddy, let's go see what's going on in here."

"Ryder!" I call out again when I notice the sliding door in the kitchen is open. Brandon kicks and coos as I carry him out to the backyard. The large, old trees back here provide a nice amount of shade. I round the corner of the house and find Ryder shirtless and drenched in sweat as he tries to fix the AC. It's a sight to see—his broad chest and sculpted arms hard at work with sweat trickling down his tanned skin. "Ryder," I call out and he turns his head and stands up, wiping his hands on his jeans.

"Hey, how are my two favorite people?" He leans in and gives me a kiss on the lips and Brandon a kiss on the forehead. We sleep together every night and we kiss but I don't get to see him bare-chested too often. He sleeps in a T-shirt and boxers and he usually covers up fast after a shower. I know why he does it. He knows I'm drooling over him and very much in need of sex. I know he is too but he's convinced we can't be fully intimate until he's worked out more issues with his past.

I know he's been working with his therapist and doctor to try to recall what happened in Afghanistan on the day of the ambush. I also know it's been slow going and that he's been frustrated by his progress. During the hypnosis he was flooded with so many emotions the psychiatrist thought it best to wake him. A part of me has come to terms with the fact that he may never get his memory back. I love Ryder St. John as much as I loved Thomas. Ryder may not share a past with me, but he behaves like Thomas, loves like Thomas and worries like Thomas did. I haven't actually voiced those words yet.

We may not have a past to share but we have a future we can

create. I wish we could move forward already. As beautiful as Ryder is both on the inside and outside, the scars he wears on his body are a painful reminder of the things he experienced as Thomas. Terrible things that speak of the cruelty of humankind, the traumatic things that make a person completely shut down.

"We're good, Ryder. What's going on with the AC?" I ask.

He scratches the back of his head and scrunches up his face. Bad news. "The AC is dead. I think it must be thirty years old. I'm not even sure how it's lasted this long." He chuckles hesitantly.

I huff out a laugh. "Ryder, everything in this house is old and yet it still persists. Some of the appliances are on their last legs too."

"I can call a guy and get a new air conditioner installed but we likely won't be able to schedule anyone until next week. How about we take Brandon over to the lake and hang out there until the sun goes down? Then maybe we can head downtown and get a hotel room for the night." He gives me a sidelong glance and I'm pretty sure I detect heat in his gaze. "You guys won't get any sleep in the house tonight. You must be tired from the whole week. I know I need to sit back and chill out." He looks at Brandon and his expression becomes both loving and weary.

"Sure, that's a good idea. I'll pack some things to take to the lake. I bet the water is still freezing, but honestly I'd jump in right now."

Ryder laughs. "Okay, you two go ahead. I'll see what I can find out about getting an inexpensive AC. Maybe Dave will have some advice." He pulls his phone out of his back pocket.

I put Brandon safely in his play gym in the living room beside Charlie since she mostly acts like his protector now and run upstairs to consider my options for a swimsuit. I'm not back to my pre-pregnancy weight yet, but I figure that between my C-section incision, my stretch marks and my large breasts, I'll never be back to the way I was anyway. I had a baby and I'll wear my stripes proudly.

And hopefully one day I'll have more babies with Ryder. I put on a white sundress over the black bikini I selected and quickly gather some supplies for the three of us to spend the night away from home. I make my way downstairs quickly because the upstairs really is too hot. As I'm picking up Brandon, I hear Ryder come back into the house.

"You ready to go?" Ryder asks. He's still shirtless. I want to lick my lips when I feel extra saliva forming in my mouth.

"Yup, all ready." I gulp and take a deep breath. We all get in the SUV, including Charlie. Ryder cranks the AC and we head to the lake.

Ryder seems tense behind the wheel and I ask, "What's going on?" It's like he's keeping something from me or scared to say something.

"Nothing." He shrugs. "I called Dave for a recommendation for an HVAC guy. I found someone who can get started on the job tomorrow."

"And?"

He gives me a sidelong glance before focusing on the road again. "I asked Jenny if Brandon and Charlie could spend the night with them. I thought we could go to the hotel alone." His cheeks flush.

At the words "hotel" and "alone" butterflies flutter in my belly and warmth runs down my chest, landing between my thighs.

Ryder taps nervously on the steering wheel. "I know you don't like to be away from Brandon. But I figured Jenny would take good care of him and..."

"Ryder, it's okay, relax." I grin. "I like that idea."

"You do?" he asks, obviously still unsure.

"Yeah." I stretch out my hand and caress his shoulder.

"Maybe we should take Brandon and Charlie over to Jenny's now," he suggests. "And then you and I can head to the lake alone. It's probably too hot for Brandon there anyway. There was a warning on the radio before about kids and heat stroke."

"Yeah, you know I didn't think about that. Yikes...I still have a lot to learn about dealing with babies in the summer. I did bring enough formula and baby food jars... Sure, let's drop him off." I feel a little strange about dropping Brandon off for a night. We've never been separated before, but I know he'll be perfectly fine and happy with Jenny and her kids.

***

After too many kisses and a few tears at Jenny's, we're driving over to the lake. "Do you still want that swim?" Ryder asks, looking heated. I know what he has on his mind and it makes me happy that he's finally willing to take the next step with me. But it makes me nervous too. He's waited so long and this will technically be his first time with me.

"I do," I answer shyly. I know it's probably a good thing to talk before we move forward. I need to know what Ryder is thinking so I can understand his sudden change of feelings on the sex issue. The lake is the perfect place for talking. It was our place back in the day.

We park in the crowded lot near the lake and Ryder retrieves the tote with our supplies from the trunk

"Are you going to swim in jeans? I brought you a pair of shorts. I couldn't find a bathing suit."

"Yeah, I guess I never did pick up a bathing suit. Shorts are good. I'll just change here." He steps between our SUV and the neighboring car—the space is relatively shielded from the park and the street—and quickly unbuttons his jeans. I can't help but stare, especially at the bulge in his boxer briefs. My heart thuds and my blood heats. I know what Thomas could do to my body and I miss it. He slips on the shorts and we make our way across the grass toward a tree close to shore. I spread the towel and remove my sundress.

Ryder watches me the whole time, his dark blue eyes a burning inferno.

"Fuck, you are hot," he bites out. We take a seat next to each other on the towel. I can't help but smile. This is our place. We have such good memories here. "What are you thinking?" he asks.

"I love it here, that's all." I don't want to bring up my time with Thomas because I know it's hard for him not to remember. "So what's with the change of heart?" I ask and he knows I'm talking about the hotel and what's going to happen there.

"I've been trying everything to remember. I know the facts of the ambush, but they are only facts to me now. Last week I went up to the attic and saw all our old stuff up there. Photos of me and you. Water polo trophies, some of my old clothes… And I know you want Thomas back. I wanted to give him back to you, but it isn't working for me. I need to know that if I never get my memory back that you will be happy with me as Ryder and what I have to offer today."

"Ryder," I answer breathlessly, running my palm along his stubbly jawline. I've come to like it when he doesn't shave. "Yes! Of course I'll be happy with you as Ryder. I've come to accept the fact that my memories are just that—mine. I'm okay with it. I love the person that you are today." I hope I'm providing him with reassurance. I haven't directly said "I love you" and I wonder if it bothers him. He hasn't said anything. I'm waiting for that moment when I will feel completely secure. He may get his memory back one day and I need to be sure for the sake of my heart that he won't run. I know it's a little selfish considering how dedicated he's been, but after I've been burnt this is me protecting myself.

He closes his eyes and leans forward to kiss me. I kiss him back, thinking it will be a closed-mouth kiss, but his mouth lingers longer than expected and the kiss turns hot and heavy as his palm cups the back of my head, drawing me even closer to him. My body is on fire from the heat outside but also from the kiss. It's our chemistry—the way we are together.

I've kissed two men in my life. And they happen to be the same person. I can't imagine another man causing this type of heat to boil beneath my skin. We pull away, staring meaningfully into each other's eyes. It's late afternoon and the lake is filled with families and teenagers trying to cool down.

"Should we swim?" I ask with a hoarse voice.

"You think you can handle the cold water?" he asks, gazing into my eyes almost as if it's a challenge. I want to laugh because he once knew very well that I'm always the first one in the water at the lake, hot or cold. I love swimming. I'm in my element in the water not only because of my water polo days but because I find the water relaxing.

I grin up at him and then quickly scramble to my feet and run toward the lake. The sand on the beach burns my feet and I can't wait for the relief of cool water. The first wave hits and I splash my way into deeper water, smiling and carefree. It's been so long since I've felt this light, this happy. When the water hits knee level, I dive into the coolness and the water envelops my whole body, cooling me down and setting me free. I rise a few feet away, feeling the warm sun beating down on my face.

I look to the shore and Ryder is standing there shirtless with his arms crossed over his chest, nodding and grinning at the same time. "It's freezing…are you crazy?" he yells out as the water laps at his feet.

I scream back, "I love it. Stop being a wuss." I wonder if my reply will rile him up. It sure as heck would've riled up the young Thomas Wells.

As if on cue he replies, "A wuss? Did you just call me a wuss, baby?"

Then he does it. One giant step in the water, followed by another giant step. He picks up speed, making his way over to me as I attempt to swim away from him. I turn and see he's gone under and he's swimming toward me like a fish. He loves the water, spent years training in the water—it's not a surprise that when I swim away fast that he's faster. He catches up to me, grabbing my foot first and tugging me toward him. We both rise out of the water and I wrap my body around him, holding his thick shoulders for support. There are some boats offshore causing some larger waves to roll in and we bob up and down.

"Did you call me a wuss?" he asks almost sounding wounded.

I run my hands over his wet hair and his blue eyes glisten from the sun. "Baby, I just wanted you in here with me." I place a soft kiss on his lips. He kisses me back.

"I'm no wuss. In fact I'm inclined to show you how not wussy I am right here," he says, whispering into my mouth.

Holy shit! I feel my nipples harden and my core heats from just the thought. His eyes drop to my chest and he lets out a throaty growl. "Damn, woman. How am I supposed to leave this fucking freezer? I have a hard-on from here to Alaska."

I throw my head back, laughing, but the heat pooling in between my legs from his hard-on pressed into me stops my laughter instantly. He has a serious look on his face so my face grows serious too as I wait for his next words. "I want you, Halo. But if we have sex, you will be mine. Always."

My heart practically stops and a lone tear makes its way down my cheek. I want to say something but I feel locked in place.

"What is it?" he asks, his features tense with concern.

I want to tell him that he spoke those same words the night he took my virginity here at this very lake, but I'm scared it will ruin the moment. He fears that he won't be enough for me as Ryder, but what he doesn't realize is that it's his soul I love. This soul in front of me captured my heart as a girl. His name doesn't matter either way.

I lean forward and this time it's me capturing his lips. His hands run up and down my back grabbing, holding, kneading. The bulge between his legs pulsates between my thighs. I rub against him, needing the friction. I am so hot and horny I could get myself off like this and yell out here in the lake. When a child screams out, "Daddy!" behind us, my eyes fling open, bringing me back to reality. At our age, making out in front of a bunch of families is highly inappropriate. Geez. What would happen if one of my students were here? I'm completely embarrassed by my behavior. I pull away and bow my head.

"I know that was inappropriate of us. We're behaving like lovesick teenagers." Ryder speaks my own thoughts.

"Yes," I breathe out, panting. Although our bodies have separated, I am still so hot for him.

"Can we get to the hotel I booked now? I need you in a bed." He's panting as hard as I am.

"Yeah, let's get out of here," I agree as we make our way through the water.

Back on shore we towel off quickly. His eyes run hungrily over my body before I slip on the sundress and he growls again. "I've got blue balls." He pouts. It's funny to see how a huge, muscled guy like Ryder can mimic the pout of his infant son so well.

When we get back to the car he does the quick-change thing between the closely parked cars. He holds up a towel strategically, but I know his ass is bare. My eyes widen. "Hurry," I hiss. "There are children around."

"So what? No one can see anything." He slips on his jeans and tosses me the towel. My heart skips a few beats knowing he's commando and my insides clench.

"Hotel?" he asks with a devilish grin.

"Yes. Please. *Now!*" I say *very* sweetly, blinking up at him. We get in the car. It's after five, but the heat is still holding strong.

***

Thirty minutes later after navigating heavy traffic on Lakeshore Drive and the Loop, Ryder pulls up to the hotel. The signs says The Langham, and the front of the hotel and the lobby look lavish.

"Ryder, we can't afford a place like this."

"I do okay, Halo. I have money saved up from before. Not a whole lot but enough to treat my girl to a night in a fancy place like this. It's our first time together. I want to make it special."

I smile as my heart gushes all over the front seat and I lean into him for a quick kiss, knowing that anything more will end with us being a panting mess. I think it's the fact that we have been teasing each other for months. Making out, getting worked up, pulling away. I swear I have a female version of blue balls, my clit is hurting and throbbing so bad with all the teasing.

As dirty thoughts run through my mind I can't get to the room fast enough. We give the car to the valet and enter the front doors. I'm very underdressed. My hair is wet and frumpy from the lake, and my bikini is visible through the simple cotton sundress I'm wearing, which is also slightly wet. When I turn my head to Ryder he looks seriously hot. Tight white shirt showing off his muscles. Jeans that hug his behind just right. He looks like a model. He walks up to the woman working the front desk and flashes a smile. She smiles back and practically blushes.

"I have a reservation under Wells," he says, throwing me off. He pulls out a credit card. Right! Of course he would have to give his real name to match his credit card. The woman checks us in and passes Ryder the room cards. We only have one small bag and my feeling of discomfort grows.

"Why are you fidgeting?" he whispers, as we make our way to the elevator hand in hand. I don't know how to answer. When my parents were alive we vacationed in these kinds of hotels. I should have been used to the opulence but that was a lifetime ago. My parents only left me the house and its belongings. They never saved up money for a rainy day. They both made large salaries but they also lived an expensive life of restaurants, theater and vacations to remote places. They probably thought they had time to make a plan for me. None of us saw that drunk driver in our future. Now I was a simple girl of simple means and I felt out of place.

"I don't think I brought the right clothes for this place," I tell him, wrinkling my nose.

"Halo, for what I have planned you won't need clothes. We can get room service. Besides we aren't leaving the room until check-out tomorrow. I need to drive into that body over and over again, baby. Heck, by the time I'm done with you, I may need to carry you out of here." He grins proudly.

I'm glad he's proud because my legs feel like they are going to buckle from the sensual promises. The elevator takes us to our floor and we make our way to our room. Ryder fidgets with the room key, getting annoyed when the door doesn't open for him and I giggle watching. He finally gets the door open and I gasp. The room is huge with ceiling-to-floor windows that show off the beautiful Chicago skyline. I can see the river from here and a variety of building landmarks.

The room is mostly white with a huge white king-size bed in its center. Before I have time to say anything, Ryder turns around and pins me to the door, wrapping his hands around the back of my neck and kissing me deeply. I moan into his mouth and he growls, lifting me as I wrap my legs around his waist and he presses my body into the door.

Our motions are hungry. He presses himself into my thighs and I moan again, knowing he's commando as his bulge begins a pulsating rhythm. I lower my hands and fidget with his jeans.

"I should shower first," I say breathlessly.

"Halo, I feel like a man who's been walking through the desert without water for months. What I need right now is you in that bed and me buried deep inside you," he says, as his shoulders rise and fall.

I nod. I'm not coherent. My adrenaline is pumping hard and all I can think of are his words…him buried deep inside me. He lifts me and carries me over to the bed. I lift the sundress over my head and untie the bikini top. Ryder's eyes glisten with lust. The curtains are open and the sun is beginning to set in a pink and purple sky. Ryder lowers me to the bed and closes his hot mouth over my nipple. I gasp, pressing my chest into him.

"Holy hell, Ryder." I take in a sharp breath and he moves to the other nipple. With his mouth on me, I lower my hands to the button on his jeans and pop it open. Then I work the zipper. My back is practically bowing off the bed from his mouth on my breasts. He lifts his mouth off and begins kneading both breasts with his rough hands.

"You are so beautiful, baby. These breasts are perfect," he says with a raspy voice. Then he takes his hands off me to shove down his jeans. I take the opportunity to move a little further up the bed. I still have the bikini bottoms on. I'm not sure why I'm not taking them off. Well…maybe I know why. They cover my C-section incision. That is definitely not sexy. With Ryder completely naked in front of me, I take in his entire form and my pulse quickens. His broad shoulders, the way thick muscle curves along his arms. I lick my lips as my gaze travels down his chest and further down to his cock. He's thick, long and circumcised. I'm glad I know the truth about Ryder before sleeping with him, I think to myself. It would have been a real shocker to find out the truth about Ryder's identity when his cock was revealed and I thought it looked familiar.

"You keep looking at me like that, baby, and I may come before I get inside you." He caresses his cock with his hand and I lick my lips again.

"You are so damn hot," I say, nodding, knowing how heated I must look.

Ryder growls and I think he is going to position himself above me but he doesn't. He pulls me up so that I'm on my knees. He's still standing at the side of the bed. He begins to kiss me, feverishly running his hands wildly through my hair. The kissing is driving me crazy and I press my breasts into his warm chest, enjoying the connection of our bodies. He moves his lips from my mouth and makes his way biting, sucking and nipping, down my neck.

"You taste like heaven," he says when he reaches the back of my neck. His breath sends shivers down my body. I reach down to stroke his cock. He groans into my neck as I roll my head back. I'm all sensation. I lean forward and begin to spread kisses across his shoulders and down his chest. He lifts my chin, knowing the direction I'm headed. I'm so hungry to taste him.

"Not yet," he says with a soft commanding tone. His fingers slip onto the sides of my bikini bottoms and he lowers them slowly down my legs and then I kick them off. He steps back, taking in my naked body. I can't help it—I feel self-conscious. Then he takes a step toward me. "You are so beautiful," he says as his big, rough hands run over my shoulders, making their way down my back then forward to my stomach. "Don't hide this scar from me. This is something to be proud of, Halo. This scar is what made you a mother. Think about our son. Think of how we created something so perfect together." He pauses and I'm in complete awe. His hands run across the scar and as he spreads kisses along my abdomen. My hands wrap around his head holding him close to me.

When I think of scars, I think how he could have died in Afghanistan. Brandon and I came so close to losing him. I also think of the scars on his body now. How his face is completely different and his scars on the inside. The ones that made him run. It makes my heart hurt but it also makes me realize how much I truly love him with every fiber of my being.

We give in to the moment together. He stands, lifting me against his body again as he gazes into my eyes. I know he is Ryder but eyes are a portal to the soul and as I stare into his dark blue eyes, I see Thomas's beautiful soul. He spins around, almost as if he's dancing with me, and he smiles. It's mesmerizing. I let out a laugh and his hands cup my behind, urging my legs around his waist. My wetness rubs along his cock.

He sets me down and my knees are shaky. He takes my hands, guiding me gently so I face one of the hotel's pristine, white walls. I'm not sure what he has planned. We were always good in bed together. We liked to fuck a lot and we liked to fuck hard but this was different. He presses my hands against the wall and says in gentle, commanding voice, "Spread your feet a little bit."

Not knowing what to expect gets me fired up even more. He places a gentle kiss on the back of my shoulder and presses his hard body against mine. His left hand curls around my waist and then dips down between my legs. I'm drenched, which is no surprise.

"You are so wet," he whispers in my ear gruffly. "Do you want me to fuck you?" he asks with the same low, deep tone. Holy hell! Fuck yes! Ryder seems to like it a little rougher. I wonder if it's from the war or if he was just craving my body as much as I had craved him. Either way, I'm game.

"Yes," I breathe out heavily. He removes his hand from my clit. I frown from the loss of his touch. I was so close to coming. He places both of his hands on my hips and enters me in one swift movement.

He thrusts into me and I brace myself against the wall. His hand dips down to caress my clit as he thrusts in and out of me. My legs feel like they will buckle from the intensity. He picks up speed, thrusting and circling my clit and I begin to cry out.

His mouth is close to my ear, his scruffy beard gently rubbing my sensitive skin. "That's it, baby, come for me," he says as he picks up speed even more. Rubbing, thrusting, rubbing and thrusting. I scream out as an orgasm runs through my body. I can feel every strong muscle in his body working hard to get me off. When I've almost come down off my high, he begins to thrust even faster and I know he's close to his own release. He pulls out of me quickly and rubs his cock fast and hard pressing into my back as he comes. The come rubs against my behind and drips down my legs. It's so hot. So Thomas. So fucking possessive. I love it. I love him.

"I better get a towel," he says, turning to the bathroom. A moment later he has one towel to clean himself off and another warm, wet towel to wipe me off. "We kind of forgot something, Halo," he says with a grin.

"Yeah, I'm guessing that would be condoms?" I grin too, still feeling flushed from the intensity of our lovemaking.

"Yeah, and I am nowhere close to being done with you." He drops the towel on the floor and caresses my face with his thumb. "You're mine now. I need to brand you all night."

"I think I saw a gift shop in the lobby. I'm guessing they must sell condoms," I say but my voice is a little shaky. I walk over to the bed and take a seat. That orgasm was intense.

"Okay, let me run down and see what I can find." He finds his jeans and shirt and puts them on quickly. "You aren't on birth control, are you?" he asks and almost winces. This is the part that reminds me that we don't share a past.

"No, I didn't see a need to go back on birth control after I had

Brandon," I answer honestly. He was my tenant. I didn't think we would end up sleeping together.

"That's what I thought. So basically the last person you slept with was me?" he asks and I'm not sure where he's going with this.

Huh?

"Uh, yeah." I roll my eyes not understanding.

"So who's better—Thomas or me?" he asks with a silly grin. His arms are crossed over his chest inflating him even more.

"I'm not answering that question." I take a pillow off the bed and throw it at him with a giggle.

He nods and with the same shit-eating grin, he leaves the room to go buy condoms. I take the opportunity to call Jenny quickly and check on Brandon.

After one ring she picks up. "Hey, hon. Your boy is perfect."

"Thanks, Jenny."

"He had a bottle and I gave him one of those jars of split peas. He's good. So have you done the deed?" she asks into the phone.

"Jenny, we can't talk about this. He isn't a stranger, he is my husband," I answer with a giggle.

"'Kay, go have fun. We're good."

"Bye, Jenny. Thanks. Give the little guy a kiss from his mom."

"Done, now bye." She laughs and I hear the click of the phone. I close my cell and place it on the night table. Then I hop in the shower, desperately needing to wash the heat of the day and the lake water off me.

As I'm shampooing my hair, a thought I don't like enters my mind. Ryder liked it when I mentioned that he was the last guy I slept with. "Him" being Thomas. I'm now wondering if Thomas slept with someone after he left me. He divorced me—was there someone else? The thought sickens me and the sad part is that I will never have any answers.

As I rinse the shampoo from my hair I feel the presence of a large, naked body behind me and thick, rough hands over my shoulders. I flinch and open my eyes.

I turn to see Ryder with a pleased grin on his face.

"I didn't hear you come in. You just scared the living shit out of me." I chortle.

"Sorry, I got what we needed and I called Jenny to check on Brandon. She said you beat me to it…" He cocks a brow.

I laugh. "We must be driving her crazy."

"So is this what it's like being a parent? Loving, worrying…"

I gaze warmly at him. This was Thomas's biggest fear and Ryder is doing a great job. "Sounds about right." I nod.

"I guess it's times like this I wish I knew what he was thinking. Why he was scared, why he left you two," Ryder says, referring to Thomas. His words are a painful reminder of the not too distant past. A part of the past I wish I could forget.

"He was torn up. Losing Rover was hard on him. Iraq was a tough deployment, things happened to him there. Things he couldn't deal with. He's not at fault. His intentions were good. He wanted to save the world."

"Why am I carrying his guilt on my shoulders now?" Ryder asks with brutal honesty.

"I think it's because you love Brandon so much," I say.

"Halo, I love you. And not just because you saved me from drowning at the hospital when I had no one." He looks at me with reverence and I believe every word he's saying.

"I know." There's a sadness in my tone that I can't control. "I tried to tell Thomas he would make a great father. He was scared of being a father, but I don't think it's what made him leave. I think his head was messed up from the war and it scared him because he was drinking like his father. I met his father and he was a cruel asshole. I think that's what made Thomas run. It wasn't Brandon or the thought of him," I say, hoping to wash away his guilt.

"I hope you're right. I remember some things from Iraq. I think it was one big nightmare." His brows draw together, creasing his forehead and revealing his own pain. As the hot water beats down on us, he closes his mouth hungrily over mine. I feel the same possessiveness. The same need for him to claim me, maybe help him get rid of the bad memories in his head.

Our lips tangle while our tongues lash out hungrily, devouring one another. His hands run up my back and he pins me to the wall. I lift my legs and twine them around his waist, gripping him closer.

His hand leaves my skin and reaches out to a ledge. I follow the motion to see him picking up a condom. He breaks the wrapper with his teeth. "I'll give you the honor since I have my hands full." He smirks and passes me the condom. He props me up a little higher and I maneuver the condom over his hard length. When it's in place he slides into me. Our gazes connect and I see something deep and intense in the dark blue pools before me. Love, adoration, respect. It makes my heart swell.

Ryder picks up speed and my breathing quickens while little whimpers leave my mouth. My previous anxiety melts away as I think of the fact that Thomas found me. Even in the dark he found me. I close my eyes and feel his words while the rhythm of his movement assaults my senses. "*I will always come back to you, Halo, even in the dark I will find you. You are my Halo.*" As my insides clench tightly around him I feel myself getting close.

"You are so beautiful. I love you so much. You are everything to me," Ryder grits out with a husky growl from the back of his throat. I close my eyes, feeling everything he is to me and this time his orgasm hits at the same time as mine. We both moan and groan, enjoying the high, the love, the ecstasy. I call out his name, "Ryder," and he groans, "Halo."

CHAPTER TWENTY-NINE

Ryder

The bright city lights shine through our window. "You hungry?" I turn to her—she's lying on the bed with a white bathrobe on.

"I'm famished," she answers. "We definitely worked up an appetite."

"We sure did. I'm not finished with you yet. We haven't had sex on the bed."

"True, but you need to feed me and quick." A lazy grin crosses her face. She looks relaxed and thoroughly fucked. I'm pleased with myself.

"Here's the menu. What are you in the mood for?" I pass her the menu and watch her look it over. I still can't believe she is here with me. Perfect and beautiful Halo.

"I'll have a steak and mashed potatoes," she says, pressing her lips together and passing me the menu.

"That sounds good. I'll order the same and I'll have you for dessert." I rub her smooth leg peeking out of the robe. I pick up the phone and call the number listed for room service and order our meal. Twenty minutes later it's delivered and Halo sets everything up on the little dining table we have in our room. This place really is fancy. We sit across from each other, devouring the tender sirloin. When we're both done we lean back lazily in our chairs.

"I'm completely stuffed," Halo says, holding her stomach.

"You didn't even finish yours—I did." I smirk.

"I need to walk this off," she suggests.

"Baby, I have other ways to work off the food." I smile mischievously to her.

"I need a few, Ryder. I'm not used to eating red meat. It takes me longer to digest." She walks across the room and flicks on the TV. The news comes on and of course there's a broadcast on Afghanistan. She moves quickly to change the channel and I place my hand on hers to stop her.

"It's okay. We can't run from the war, Halo. We don't know when it will be over. Those soldiers need to be there. They need to protect this side of the world from the ugliness. I do still believe that." I've been watching the news intently so I know what's going on. Capturing bin Laden is still priority one and I know from what I've read in my file, that my team took out one of al-Qaeda's commanders. It's weird as hell to know that while I was once in the thick of things over there, now I'm on the sidelines. And I don't even remember the details of the missions I trained so hard and so long to be a part of.

"What is it?" she asks, her brows furrowed. She looks cute but worried.

"Nothing." I shrug it off.

"Ryder, if we are in this thing together I need you to be open with me."

"Sorry, you're right. I was just thinking about the war. Wondering about the commitment it takes to serve. The extremes some men go through. Thomas must have felt strongly about serving to put himself in that kind of danger." I say it as a point really, not so much a question.

"For Thomas it was a ticket out of his father's house, but it wasn't only that. He wanted to be a part of the good guys. He wanted to prove himself to me and to himself."

"Well, I think he did that. Stupid jerk almost got himself killed. Now he's a military hero." I laugh sardonically. I just don't identify with Thomas.

"Yeah," she sighs and squeezes a pillow tightly to her chest. Her round brown eyes look troubled. I don't like it.

"Hey." I walk over to the bed. "None of that pouting." I crawl on my knees toward her and lightly drop my body above hers without putting too much weight on her.

I rub my nose against hers and she smiles brightly.

"It's like you have this light around you. I'm addicted to it. I don't know how it was between us before. I'm pretty damn sure it's what brought me back to you. I hate to see you sad because I feel like he failed you. I don't identify but I want to make it right if that makes sense."

Her eyes brim with tears and she keeps smiling. "You are making it right. None of it was your fault. We are all victims here."

I can't take being this close to her and not touching her. Her hot breath caresses my lips. I kiss her softly at first. I'm using my arms to prop myself above her as our hips connect. Her robe falls open when she spreads her legs. She looks like a goddess with her creamy white skin, her rosy nipples and her long, slender legs. She's a priceless piece of art. Her auburn hair wavy, her large brown eyes filled with a vivacious fire. As we kiss, her arms come up around my neck and pull me closer. Again I feel like I can't get enough. The gentle kissing turns ravenous as she claws at my back and rips off the towel from my waist. My cock hangs between her thighs and I stroke her softly.

I dip my lips into the crevice of her neck. She smells like fresh spring flowers. I kiss my way down as my fingers tantalize her nipples.

They harden beneath my touch and her body pushes into mine seeking the relief that my body promises to give her.

"Ryder," she breathes out with a raspy voice.

I dip my lips further down her neck, stopping to pay her breasts the attention they deserve. Licking, sucking, licking, sucking. My lips move down her slender torso, stopping at her bellybutton as I press soft kisses along her skin, down to the scar left by the C-section incision. I kiss her with all my heart, thinking how perfect she is. How committed she's been to me and to Thomas and to our son. Then all reason flies out the window when my lips touch her pussy. My body is engulfed in hot flames as my mouth connects with her folds. I suck at first, enjoying the taste of her juices. I lick up to her clit and she writhes beneath me. Her little bundle of nerves is getting ready for an explosion. She's swollen and moaning, my cock hardens and lengthens with each moan.

"Oh please, Ryder," she begs sweetly as her body bucks off the bed. I love that she's calling me Ryder, that she accepts me for me. That she forgives Thomas. I lick, suck, lick, suck. She cries out. I can tell she's so close, but I don't want her to come. I need her coming around my cock. I rise to my feet and notice a hint of disappointment cross her face, probably because I stopped eating her. I smile then flip her over to her belly. I take a condom out of the box and slide it on in seconds because I need inside her like I need air right now. I hover above her and enter her fast and hard. I smack her behind and she yelps, screaming out another moan.

"You like that, baby?" I ask, my tone filled with lust. Her moans tell me that she likes it very much and I enjoy watching her this riled up.

She nods and I'm happy she likes it hard and rough. I smack her behind again and she moans loader. I dip one hand between her legs as I drive into her from behind. She is so wet and swollen and I can feel how close she is.

"Ryder, I…I'm going to come."

"Come for me, baby." I pick up speed, rubbing her clit as my dick drives into her. She moves her hips up and down, meeting me thrust for thrust, rubbing herself hard and fast on my fingers and then it comes. She detonates, taking off faster, rubbing harder, screaming out my name as the sweetest orgasm racks her body. I come hard and fast, following right behind her, the friction of my fingers dragging out her orgasm longer than before.

"Fuck, you're perfect," I whisper in her ear.

She's breathless. I lie next to her as our chests heave from exertion. I gaze into her brown eyes and say, "I love you." I kiss her, knowing I still have her taste on my lips.

She kisses me back with her eyes closed. "I love you too," she responds. It's the first time. I've known how she feels for a while, but I also know that she was scared and unsure and that's why she was holding back. Hearing those words from her mouth makes me feel like I am finally home. Like she really believes in us. Believes in me.

We climb up the bed since we were upside down and get under the covers. She shivers and snuggles in close to me. I throw the blankets over us and hold her tight in my arms. Her breathing grows slow and I can tell she must be sleeping. The heat has probably worn her out.

I close my eyes and drift off to sleep. Content and whole.

CHAPTER THIRTY

Halo

I open my eyes to a darkened room and memories of last night wash over me. The lovemaking was somehow different. I know I have to stop comparing Ryder and Thomas but I can't separate them in my mind now that I know the truth. They may be the same person but Ryder is a very different version of Thomas. Yes, Thomas liked it a little rough after he came back from the first tour but the sex this time was even rougher than it was in the past. It was different, but good. Maybe even better. I'm guessing the war and his experience changed him in that regard. I'm still hoping he hasn't been with another woman and found that he liked rough sex better. I try to shake off the ill feeling those thoughts bring.

I look over to the red light on the alarm clock to see that it's already nine-thirty a.m. Holy cow! I can't remember the last time I slept in. That hasn't happened since Brandon was born. I couldn't even sleep in when I was pregnant because I was uncomfortable. Thinking of Brandon makes me panic a little. I know it's a Saturday morning and Jenny and Dave are probably taking it easy, but I still need to see my boy. Ryder's arms are draped over me and I nudge him a bit. I lean in and kiss his cheek.

"Hey," I whisper against his face. "It's already nine-thirty. We should probably head out soon."

He moans a bit and says, "Yeah, sure. I had another messed-up dream and then I couldn't get back to sleep. I'm exhausted." His voice is raspy from sleep. My heart dips. I guess old insecurities die hard.

"I'm sorry." I run my fingers through his hair.

"It is what it is. We should go to our boy. First I need to do this." He pulls me in close to his body. His skin is burning and his cock rubs up against my behind. He dips his fingers between my thighs and I close my eyes, enjoying him, enjoying us.

"Mmm," I moan as his finger dips inside me. He spreads the wetness along my clit and I'm all sensation. I feel him guiding his cock inside me. He doesn't enter me, though. He teases me, rubbing along my wetness and groaning in my ear.

"I need to get a condom on," he says hoarsely.

"Yes," I breathe out because I am so close.

He turns to reach for a condom and slides it over his cock.

"Ride me, baby," he requests and I straddle him, placing my palms on his chest, over the tattoo that he must have gotten between the time he left me and got injured. I hate that I don't know anything about that time and that I may never find out. I try to bury those thoughts again as I begin to move, rubbing myself against him in all the right places. He pushes his hips up, causing the friction to grow deeper, harder.

I close my eyes and my head falls back as ecstasy takes over my body. Within seconds I am screaming out and riding out my orgasm. Ryder stiffens beneath me and groans as his own release hits. Then I fall to the bed, panting and trying to catch my breath.

After our morning interlude, we shower and get ourselves dressed and I use the hotel blow dryer to blow out my hair since I can't show up to Jenny's sporting the thoroughly fucked look. We make our way to the lobby and Ryder heads over to the front desk to check us out while I call Jenny to tell her we are on the way over. When he walks back to me I see an uneasiness on his face. I wonder if something happened with check-out.

"Everything okay?" I ask.

"Yeah, let's go pick up Brandon. I miss him." He smiles, throwing an arm over my shoulder. We head out and the valet brings us the car. I don't know if my past has made me paranoid but something about his expression tells me his smile isn't real. We drive in silence back to Jenny's house and Ryder rubs his temple repeatedly.

We pull into Jenny and Dave's driveway. "Hey, you sure you're okay?" I ask again, worried that I may be nudging.

"Yeah, maybe a small headache," he says in a brush-off way. Then he smiles and we ring the doorbell. Jenny opens the door, holding Brandon in her arms.

"Hi there, my little man." My eyes instantly drop to him and I extend my arms to take him. He smiles deliciously back to me. "Thank you so much, Jenny."

"You guys should stay," she says. "It's still so hot out and Dave said the AC guy isn't coming to your house until two o'clock."

I look back to Ryder to see what he thinks and he shrugs his shoulders. "Fine by me."

We both take off our shoes and make our way into the house. We spend the day hanging out with Jenny and Dave. Chatting, having lunch. Ryder seems a little distracted, but I brush it off. At about one-thirty Ryder stands up and says he should go meet the AC guy.

"There's no point in you and Brandon coming along," he says while lacing up his running shoes. "It's hot out and the house is hot. Let the guy fix it and I'll come get you guys."

"Yeah, sure," I answer, then I turn my head. "Is that okay Jenny?"

"Do you even need to ask, Halo?"

After Ryder leaves, Jenny asks, "Hey, is he okay?" Jenny points to the door as her brows dip together.

The fact that she has noticed his odd behavior alarms me.

"I hope so. He's been weird all morning," I answer nervously.

"I'm sure it's nothing," Jenny says and I feel like she's trying to make me worry less. "Did he mention anything?"

"No, he just said he had another bad dream. It's been happening for a while now. Why would this be different?"

"I don't know. Maybe he's tired from all the exertion of last night." She winks knowingly. My gut tells me different. He was light and easy last night. This morning it was as if he was using the sex to clear his mind.

We walk into the family room and Jenny's kids are working on an oversized puzzle on the floor. Dave has the weather channel on.

"Looks like unstable weather," he says. "There's a cold front coming through. With all this humidity in the air they said there's a severe thunderstorm risk and they also mentioned increased chances of a tornado." He looks a little worried, but then Dave is a bit of a worrywart.

"Really? A tornado in Rogers Park? It's been like ten years since we had anything here." I feel even more anxious to get home.

"You can hang out in our basement, Halo, if you'd like to ride out the storm with us," Dave offers.

"Thanks, Dave. I'm a little worried about the guy installing my AC now." I place Brandon on a mat on the floor. Thank goodness Jenny kept her baby toys. I pull out my cell and text Ryder.

Me: ***How's it going?***
Ryder: ***The guy is installing now***
Me: ***There's a storm coming.***
Ryder: ***I heard. Should I come get you guys?***
Me: ***Please***

Ryder: ***On my way***

I take a peek out the window and the sky has gone dark quickly. The clouds are moving fast. In the distance I see a bolt of lightning and my stomach dips. I'm a wuss when it comes to storms. I take a seat with Brandon on the floor.

"I'm going to clean upstairs. You should maybe stay until the storm passes," Jenny says as she walks to the staircase.

The TV continues to blare with updates about storm warnings and funnel cloud sightings. Rain pounding on the windows jacks up my nerves even more.

Dave jumps to his feet. "I'm going to get the flashlights and see what supplies we have in storage. This doesn't look too promising." His tone is edgy with nerves. "You watching the kids, Halo?"

"I sure am." I smile at Sam and she plops herself down in my lap.

"Auntie Halo, I can sing the alphabet. Do you want to hear?" she asks with her sweet little voice. She just turned three.

As Sam sings to me, the thunder grows louder and lightning seems to be striking even closer.

"Sam, sweetheart, give me a minute. I need to make a phone call." She nods and stops singing. I quickly dial Ryder's number. The phone rings endlessly. Something doesn't feel right. He said he was on his way. He should have been here by now. I just got him back. I can't lose him again. Not again.

CHAPTER THIRTY-ONE

Ryder

I get in the car to pick up Halo and Brandon. As I start the engine, a memory flashes in my head, making me dizzy. I've been getting flashes since last night.

I dreamt of Afghanistan. I was on the jeep heading up the mountain. I remembered thinking that I need to get home to Halo and make things right. Then I remember being in a shack, a woman screaming. She was in labor, surrounded by her terrified family. I delivered her baby—a boy.

Thinking about it causes tears to run down my face. In that instant when I held the villager's son in my hands, I felt the brunt of my mistakes crashing down on me. I wanted to come home, couldn't get back to Halo fast enough. Then the dream cut out and the nightmare began—blood, pain, death. Hanson dying, Montgomery dying. I've been trying to make sense of it all day. My mind has been bombarded with random memories flooding me and threatening to drown me.

I pull out of the driveway and reach a stop sign when I hear a loud bang and I flinch. Another memory envelops me. *"Make sure you tell my baby girl that her daddy was a hero," Montgomery's voice whispers.*

I can't breathe. The sky is lighting up and thunderous rain beats heavily on my windshield. I'm drowning. My vision has become obscured. I see Halo—she's young, smiling…she's sad, grieving. I'm leaving, walking out the door, showing her the dog tags she gave me are around my neck. She holds her own necklace in her hands, showing me I'm close to her heart.

Rover's on my back, shot multiple times… More shooting, a bad feeling… The sky is pink and I have dust in my mouth—I can't move. Lieutenant Commander's telling our team we got the job done. The pink sky, blood, pain, death. *Blood. Pain. Death.*

CHAPTER THIRTY-TWO

Halo

I try to call Ryder on his cell, but there's no answer. I'm becoming frantic. This day reminds me of the day he left me. He'd been sleeping all day and the news had warned about an impending storm. The rain began. Then the thunder. Thunder did bad things to him.

I know he isn't Thomas now, he's Ryder, but something has been off with him all day. The fact he isn't picking up his phone is sending off all kinds of warnings in my mind. Will he leave? Will he not look back this time?

Dave returns to the family room. "Halo, it's looking bad out there. I want to get the kids down in the basement." He turns his head. "Jenny get down here now," he commands, and I hear the panic laced in his voice.

Jenny comes running down the stairs. "What is it, Dave?"

"I want everyone in the basement. The wind has picked up and there's a twister forming about ten minutes away. We don't have much time." I can tell he's trying to keep his voice calm because he doesn't want to scare the kids, but his anxiety is transparent.

"Okay, okay," Jenny says, nodding. "Let's go, kids. Halo, looks like you're coming down with us." She gestures for me to follow her down to the basement. I grab Brandon's diaper bag and I'm thankful that I'm neurotic about over packing—the bag is heavy with supplies. I pass it over to Jenny and I gesture for her to take Brandon.

She looks confused. "What are you doing?" she asks as if I've lost it.

"I need you to watch Brandon. Something is wrong with Thomas…I mean Ryder. I have to go find him. Can I borrow your car?"

"Halo, no way," she snaps at me. "Get your ass downstairs."

"Jenny, he's my husband. I think he's in trouble. You saw him today. He wasn't right. I think he's remembering his past."

She takes Brandon hesitantly. "This is not okay, Halo. You're a mother. You need to take care of yourself for this boy." She's mad at me, of course, but mostly she's scared and worried.

"And I will, but I need to go help his father so he will have a family," I insist.

"That won't happen if you go out and get yourself killed. Did you see those trees out there?" Her eyes widen and I can tell she's thinking I've lost it.

"I'll be careful. Please, Jenny. I can't lose him again," I plead, my heart beating fast.

She takes Brandon and I give him a quick kiss. They all disappear into the basement as another loud clap of lightning strikes. I jump. I'm a wuss. I can't believe I'm going out in this mess.

I take Jenny's red raincoat and grab the keys to her SUV off the front table and make my way outside. The rain instantly pounds hard on me and I get completely drenched. I press the unlock button and jump in the car, shaking off the water. I turn on the wipers full blast and pull out of the driveway. Driving down the street is a challenge. I lean forward a bit, straining to see the road through the heavy rain pounding my windshield. The wind is ferocious, causing the car to sway. I persevere, hoping to find Ryder at our house. I drive at a turtle's pace. It takes me longer to get home than usual. I see the truck on the driveway, but my car is nowhere to be seen.

Shit! He isn't here. I turn on the radio to a local station so I'll know what's happening with the storm. The speakers blare with a beeping sound followed by a news broadcaster warning people to take shelter and avoid travel. My gut is telling me to go in the house and wait the storm out in the basement. My heart forces me to back out of the driveway.

CHAPTER THIRTY-THREE

Ryder

The wind hits the car and I feel it shifting back and forth. I'm enveloped in a sea of panic and pain. The doctors told me it would be better to remember but how is this better? This is cruel and unusual punishment. It's too much. Remembering my life, my past, my father… The way he beat me. Miss Randall… Halo….

Halo has been mine this whole time. No, she hasn't. I walked away. I divorced her. I was so fucked up.

My mind is working too fast, I feel dizzy and disoriented. I try to shake off all the bad thoughts but they're stuck like glue, ripping me apart from the inside out.

Losing Rover fucked me up. And Hanson—he and I were so much alike. Growing up with abuse, living a lonely life. Using the military to get out of a bad situation. Becoming a SEAL so that we could feel like heroes and not the stupid pieces of shit we were supposed to be. Hanson and I were the same except for one difference. Halo. She saved me from myself. She gave me purpose.

I begin to scream. I feel like I am losing it. Like if I could just crawl out of my skin and walk away it would be the best thing for everyone. Fuck—it hits me that this is how I felt that day I left Halo.

There's a loud clap of thunder and my mind jolts…

"Where are you, Montgomery? I can't see you," I holler frantically. My head feels like it's spinning as I search for Kendall and McCall. Where is the Lieutenant? I suddenly see a hand waving in the air with a radio and I make my way over to Montgomery. He looks burned pretty bad.

"Montgomery," I breathe out.

"I can't see you, Wells," he answers with a calm voice. I angle myself to the ground to get close to him since his eyesight doesn't seem right. Why me? I want to yell out. Why am I the only one standing?

"Montgomery, you hold on. Please just fucking hold on." I lift his head to rest on my arm.

"Morphine, man. I called for help they are on the way." His voice is weak. His body is all mangled up and all I can think about is his wife and daughter. I stick my last needle in his arm.

"You're not fucking dying, Montgomery, you stay with me," I urge him as my tears drip down my face onto him. It stings and it hurts but this isn't fair. "You are fucking staying with me," I say with boiling rage and anger.

"Just tell them how much I love them. Tell my daughter that her daddy was a hero." His eyes shut and I squeeze mine tight, tipping my face up to the sky.

A loud clap of thunder makes me jolt. My mind is all over the fucking map. I can't even hold my head up straight. Montgomery's words come back to me—all our talks together. He had a wife he loved, a child he cherished. He kept talking to me, trying to convince me to get in touch with Halo. He understood what was at stake, what I stood to lose. His daughter. *Fuck.*

I smack at my steering wheel then whip the car around. My head is spinning. I head to the VA hospital. Between the tears and the rain I don't even know how I'm driving. As I drive, faces flash in front of me. I'm hallucinating. I need information. I need to go find their families. This isn't right. I haven't been right.

CHAPTER THIRTY-FOUR

Halo

The sky is black. Like literally black. My heart is hammering in my chest as I drive the streets of our neighborhood, wondering where Thomas/Ryder can be. A giggle hiccups its way out of me. I don't even know what to call him. I seem to be the only lunatic out on the roads.

Would he have gone to Miss Randall? It doesn't make sense. She already gave him the answers he needed. The lake? That would be crazy in this weather. The VA hospital? Yes, that must be it.

I pull to the curb and look up the VA's address on my phone. The data takes forever to load due to the storm. The wind howls and there are warning sirens going off on all the streets. I'm now in full-out panic. The address pops up and I insert my location for directions. The broadcaster on the radio stumps my focus when I hear him say a funnel cloud has been spotted not too far from my location. I follow the directions on my phone, hoping I don't find myself in more trouble than I can handle.

CHAPTER THIRTY-FIVE

Ryder

I drive down the streets in Halo's SUV. I feel like I've just experienced the biggest mindfuck of my life. My body is charged and agitated. I can't calm the fuck down. Before I can even process my surroundings or think of how I got here, I realize I'm at the VA clinic. I need to find Bob. I pull up to a parking spot and whip the car into park. Then I brace myself as I open the car door and step out into the storm. The wind is howling and fierce as I make my way inside. I'm completely drenched as I pass through the automatic lobby doors. I'm well aware that people are looking at me as if I've lost it. I'm soaking wet from head to toe and my shoes are making sloshing sounds as I walk down the hall like I have a mission to accomplish. Bob has mentioned numerous times that he comes in on the weekends and I know Dr. Wembley is on call sometimes. I am hoping that either one of them is here to help me.

I stop dead in front of the outpatient psychiatric clinic. Bob is sitting at a desk speaking with a veteran. There is no receptionist. His eyes meet mine, acknowledging me. But then he continues the conversation. *Fuck me.* My patience is non-existent. I know it's animalistic but I want to throw the guy he's talking to out of his chair. I hear him cutting the conversation short, telling the man to go to the nurse. They are apparently rounding everyone up to keep them away from the windows. Thank fuck.

Bob approaches me and we stare into each other's eyes for a little more time than would be considered normal. In fact, I'm growing uncomfortable by the seconds.

"You got it back," he mutters as if it's a fact.

I nod.

"Follow me." He waves for me to follow him and he walks away from the psych ward. "We need to go into one of the offices in the inner part of the hospital. The psych clinic has been cleared out. We need to stay away from the windows," he explains and I follow. "I don't think we'll catch Dr. Wembley right now. Everyone is trying to get the patients into a secure area because of the storm. I'm surprised that you drove in this mess, but I'm gathering you didn't feel like you had much choice." He pauses and we enter an office that is all cement walls.

I'm too uptight to sit, so I pace the room. Bob takes a seat in one of the chairs and leans back with his hands on his stomach, calmly watching me.

"How does it feel?" is his first question.

I eye him, not sure how to describe the storm brewing inside me. "Fucking bad."

"That's to be expected. You wouldn't have shut down the way you did if it was good." He shrugs matter-of-factly.

"I need to leave. I have to find Montgomery's wife. I have to find Rover's wife. I should have attended their funerals. I should have placed a trident on their casket." I can't stop fidgeting the adrenaline pumping through me is making me so on edge.

"Fair enough." He walks over to a computer and logs in. He does his search while marking things down on a yellow Post-it. "Here."

He passes me the Post-it and says nothing. I read the addresses I requested. They are both out of state. "That's it. Aren't you going to say something else?" I ask, a little taken back. He always likes to give his opinion on everything. Now he chooses to be quiet when I need his input the most?

"What do you want me to say?" He shrugs again. He's too at ease about this. He's been giving me crap for months. Now he chooses to take a fucking chill pill? It's pissing me off but knowing him, he has an angle.

"I don't know. I'm freaking the fuck out. I remember the ambush. My team. They were burned, their bodies were mangled. I survived. I tried to save them. I couldn't. Montgomery made me promise to tell his daughter that he was a hero…and…and, I've been renting out the garage in my own house." My voice cracks and the tears begin to fall. I let out a breath and fall back in the chair. "How did that even happen? I've been living with my wife and son and I didn't know them. I was such a fool. I thought I found myself an angel and went home with her. Then I let myself fall in love with her." I let out a loud burst of laughter. The joke is on me.

"Ryder, relax," Bob urges. He still looks calm and not surprised at all by anything I've said. I don't understand, because what are the fucking chances? It's pretty damn crazy.

He leans back in the chair and swipes at his mouth. "Ryder, listen to me, but promise that you will remain calm and not walk out of here after what I am about to tell you."

His words get me more stirred up. I'm a jittery mess. "Okay." I reply hesitantly.

"When you were released from the hospital you were sent to us for rehabilitation. You were adamant that you did not want to stay here. Dr. Wembley was hesitant in granting you your freedom until you gave us the address of where you wanted to stay and it matched your previous home address." He pauses. Holy shit he knew! He knew and he didn't fucking tell me. I want to… "Ryder, breathe and let me finish."

I take a deep breath and continue to listen. It's hard to sit still. My mind is still rushing all over the place. I wish it would slow down and give me a minute to think.

"Okay."

"What were the chances of that? You renting a garage from a woman you met at the hospital? A woman who had just given birth to a boy and you wanted to rent space from her. The chances are nil, Ryder. From what I've seen in my life, miracles like that don't happen everyday."

As he says the word "miracles" more tears fall. I'm not even sure why I'm crying. It feels like I'm crying for everything. For walking out on my wife, my child, for the death of my best friends. A lot of bad happened to me. I almost died and it's a miracle that I was given a second chance with my family.

"You see what I am getting at, Ryder?" Bob continues. "Dr. Wembley thought you were in a good place. A safe place even though your ex-wife didn't realize it was you. Dr. Wembley reviewed your file and saw that you took a medical leave after Iraq. The issues you had with your wife were listed. The terms of your divorce were also included. You witnessed the death of a close friend. You were grieving and scared to become a father. It was also very clear to you that your wife loved you and was devoted to you. The pysch team hoped that you would reconcile these feelings while spending time with your wife and child. During our sessions you repeatedly stated how you enjoyed spending time with Halo and her son. Dr. Wembley also figured that if you were going to ever get your memory back it would be better to be in a place that was filled with your history and not here in the hospital. If we had told you the truth of where you ended up it may have backfired. Dr. Wembley consulted with the team. You weren't ready to face reality. It wouldn't have been fair to push that reality on you. I've seen death too, Ryder, it fucking sucks. It rips your heart open and stamps on it. It leaves you raw and in pain. I told you I've been there, but I came back from there to my wife, to my two children. I did the best I could. Did I have nights where I woke up in cold sweats wondering how I could have changed the fate of the men that died? I have. The pain doesn't go away but I learned to live with it. When I see my wife, my children and their children. Those are the times I smile. Those are the times that help me get out of bed every morning and come into work to help you crazy soldiers." He waves me off with a slight smile and sad eyes. "I feel for you, Ryder, I do. You need to make your own decisions now. You either leave this hospital and go home to your wife and child or you take off again." He stares me squarely in the eyes.

His gaze washes over me. It's not judging, but it's saying man up and do the fucking right thing. My head drops and then snaps up. "Halo, Brandon. There's a storm." My heart beats crazily as I realize I was supposed to pick up Halo and Brandon before the storm hit.

"Ryder, all hell is breaking loose out there. You can't go anywhere now. You have to wait it out." Bob gives me a chiding nod. "You should call them and let them know where you are."

"It's Thomas Wells and I need to go." I stand and salute Bob. "I need to go find my family. I have to keep them safe." As I say my name "Thomas", I feel like Thomas Wells again and it isn't so bad. It actually feels good.

"Glad to see you've come to your senses, boy." Bob smacks me on the back. "I knew you were the honorable type or I wouldn't have spent so much time listening to you whine." He grins devilishly.

My lips curl. He's right. I can't lose my shit now. I have a woman who loves me and a boy who stares back at me with familiar blue eyes that tell me he needs me. Even though he can't speak yet I know that he needs a stable father. I stalk out of the building, my clothes wet, my shoes sloshing down the hallway. By the time I make it back outside the rain is coming down so hard that it stings my face on contact and the cool wind is ripping havoc on the trees.

I make it into Halo's SUV and whip out of the parking lot, a man determined to get his family back.

CHAPTER THIRTY-SIX

Halo

I've never seen the streets look so empty. I see a stop sign and when I brake, the tires skid and I know the car would've been nailed if there had been more traffic. I should go back to Jenny's. The weather is out of control. I have a son to tend to. I tell myself that if Ryder took off that there is nothing I can do anyway. I know this because the night Thomas took off I begged him to stay but my words meant nothing. They were washed away like the rain that dried after the storm the night he left me.

It's eerie how similar this day is to that awful day in my past. I decide to make a U-turn and head home. Chasing down a man who's running from life won't get me far. I know this now. I've learned the hard way. The fact that I am out in this weather is not okay. If Ryder has spun back into a pool of darkness it won't be me who can pull him out. It wasn't me who pulled him out the last time he was drowning. It won't be me this time around.

I put the car in reverse. Something slams into me and everything turns black.

CHAPTER THIRTY-SEVEN

Thomas

Before leaving the parking lot I check my phone. Fuck... Five missed calls, ten messages—all from Halo. She must be worried sick. I said I was coming to get them and didn't show. After the way I left her pregnant of course she would be panicking. I'm a serious asshole. I make my way down the streets, driving a little faster than I should. Guilt is eating my insides making me feel even worse. I press the gas pedal down harder, needing to get to my wife and son faster. I flick on the radio and the newscaster doesn't say anything good—the storm isn't dissipating and they're still spotting funnel clouds. Luckily there have been no fatalities, only reports of downed trees.

I stop at a light and try to call Halo's cell phone. It goes straight to voicemail, so I send a text. The light turns green and I drive, waiting for a response. I pull over as soon as I can and call Dave. He picks up the phone but the line has static.

"Dave. Are Halo and Brandon with you?"

The line is quiet. Then Dave speaks, "We have Brandon..." Static cuts off his voice.

"What? You have Brandon? Where is Halo?" My chest begins to hurt.

There's more static. "Dave," I call out. *Fuck*! My heart begins to hammer in my chest.

"She went looking for you," I hear, but Dave's voice is distant and hard to make out.

"What, Dave? Halo went looking for me?" Sheer panic hits me. Halo is scared of storms. Why would she be out driving?

"Yes," he confirms. "We thought she was with you. She must still be out looking."

"I'm looking for her now." I put the locator app on her phone so she should be easy to find. I thank the Ryder version of myself for having the brains to do that.

Her location is only a couple minutes away. When I approach the street, I see blue and red flashing lights. A cop car is blocking the road. My heart stops when I get close enough to see it's Jenny's car.

Oh fuck no. Halo must have borrowed Jenny's car to find me. I pull up as close as I can, fly out of the CRV and head for the car.

The rain whips into my face and I barely register the face and the uniform of the cop who tries to stop me. I tug free from his hold and run blindly for Halo.

"Sir! Sir, you'll have to stand aside—"

"It's my wife in there!" I scream.

"Sir, an ambulance is on the way—"

"Halo!" I scream as I see dark red hair pressed against the driver's side window. The airbag was deployed and, oh God, I'm worried she can't fucking breathe. There's another cop on the other side of the car. They're trying to move the truck that T-boned her. I go for the back door. The handle is slippery but I wipe it with my shirt and take a firm grip. It makes some creaking sounds. I can feel movement. I'm straining so hard I feel like I'll pop a blood vessel but I need this fucking door open. The cops are shouting at me but I ignore them.

Sirens blare in the background so I know the fire trucks must be approaching. I see blood on the inside of Halo's door. I think of my son and I pull even harder. The door flings open and I fall on my ass, hitting the asphalt hard. I get back up fast. I reach into the car, find her arm, feel for a pulse. I want to weep when I feel warmth and a steady beat. There are footsteps pounding the pavement close by, then shouting.

"Sir, we got this." An EMT urges me aside. I want to tell him that I have training, to please let me help, but I also know that this is personal for me and it's better he does the moving.

"She's my wife. Please." I can barely speak or move because of the mountain of guilt weighing on me. This was my fault. I keep hurting this woman.

"I understand, sir. Please let us do our job so we can help her."

I watch as a fireman and two EMT's extract her from the vehicle. They lift her onto a stretcher and begin to check vital signs. I can see her chest moving so I know she's breathing. She begins to mutter and I let out a breath. She's alive.

"Halo, I'm here, baby. It's Thomas. Halo. I'm here and I'm not going anywhere." Tears stream down my face and the rain beats them away. I want to pour my soul out to her and tell her how very sorry I am that I left. Tell her how sorry I am for every fucked-up thing I've done.

"It's okay, ma'am," the EMT soothes her. "You were in a car accident and we're taking you to the hospital now."

"Will you be coming to the hospital, sir?" he asks me.

"Yes," I answer and follow them into the back of the ambulance. My anxiety is through the fucking roof. This day has been a mess. I am so scared for Halo that I feel myself rocking back and forth.

I'm aware of the sound of sirens, the voices of the EMTs, the radio dispatch from the front of the ambulance. But all I can see or think about is Halo.

"Halo, baby?" I lean forward hoping she can hear me. "It's Thomas. I'm here, baby. Please be okay. Please fight for me, Halo. I fought for you that day, baby. I wanted to call you and tell you that I was messed up—that I shouldn't have left that way. When I went on that mission I knew I had to survive, knew I had to come home to you. I couldn't die if you were mad at me. You are my light, Halo. You led me home and now I need you to find me and come home to me and Brandon."

Her eyes flutter open and she says my name like it's a prayer, "Thomas?" She can't turn her head—her neck's been immobilized.

"I'm here, baby. It's me. It's Thomas. I'm here, Halo. I'm not going anywhere. I need you to fight." The ambulance stops. We're at the hospital.

I climb out of the back of the ambulance and watch as the hospital team helps the EMTs remove the stretcher. One of the monitors they have her connected to makes a high-pitched sound and then goes silent.

"Halo!" I scream out, lunging for her.

"Move, Move," one of the medic screams and they rush her inside. I jog after them, following through the doors into the ER. A nurse stops me, asking me for any details I can give them about Halo's medical history. I tell them what I can and they ask me to wait in the trauma unit's waiting area. The nurse reassures me they'll keep me posted. I begin to pace the hallway. Back and forth. Back and forth.

There's nothing to do but pray and think about the craziness that's my life.

I'd been through so much—the self-loathing I felt as a kid, the tough-guy phase of surviving my childhood and boot camp and becoming a SEAL. And then the trauma of war and losing my best friend. I didn't have parents to learn from and guide me. It was me against the world until I met Halo.

I'm so grateful to fate for bringing me home to my family even when I didn't even know myself. I'm crazy scared that fate is fucking with me now, though, because I couldn't have been brought home only to lose the love of my life.

I call Dave and I can barely get the words out about Halo without completely breaking down. He tells me to take care, that Brandon is safe and comfortable. Thinking of Brandon causes a whirlwind of emotion to run through me. I left him just like my mom left me. I have to wonder anew why my mother left. Was there more to the story? I can't think of any scenario that makes sense. I know now what it's like to be a parent. I know loving a baby means I could never walk away. I realize all my fears about being a parent were just that—unsubstantiated fears.

I stalk back to the nurse's station. I can't sit still. My entire body feels immersed in dark pain.

"Can you please update me on my wife?" I ask. "She was brought in by ambulance. Car crash."

She checks a monitor. "They've taken her into surgery. Sorry, sir. A doctor will come out to meet you when surgery is over." Her smile is sympathetic.

"Okay." Her answer does nothing to quell my nerves. There are a million questions running through my head. I continue to pace the waiting room until the adrenaline leaves my body, sucking my energy along with it.

Three hours pass and I feel like I've been holding my breath the entire time. I fall back into a seat, still bracing myself. I can't hear bad news. A man in a white coat walks up to me.

"Mr. Pearson?" he asks, using the name on Halo's ID.

"Yes?" I begin to stand but the doctor waves me down.

"Stay seated." He takes the vacant chair beside me and I feel myself holding on to the arms of the chair for dear life. The doctor looks down to my whitening knuckles.

"She's going to be okay," are his first words.

I instantly release my hands and fall forward, bracing my arms on my knees, huffing out a whoosh of air. My head drops while I try to collect myself.

"Her elbow was dislocated and there are breaks in her arm in a number of spots so she will be in a full arm cast. She has some broken ribs so it will be painful for her to breathe for a while. She may have a concussion but we won't know for sure until she wakes up and we assess her. Her body is bruised but there was no internal bleeding."

I sag in relief. No internal bleeding is really good news.

"We will need to monitor her for the next forty-eight hours or so," the doctor continues. "But I'm quite confident that she will make a full recovery." He pats me on the back and stands up. "She should be awake shortly. The anesthesia was just wearing off as I was leaving her."

"Thank you, doctor." I shake his hand. "So I can see her now?" I ask impatiently.

He chuckles softly. "Yeah. Sure. Follow me." I follow him into a room in the recovery area and then thank him as he leaves.

"Halo," I say it as a breath and a prayer. Her auburn hair is spread out over the pillow and I place a gentle kiss on her cheek.

Her eyes open slowly. She's looking at me warily and my heart sinks. "Baby, it's okay. It's me—Thomas. I got my memory back. I'm so sorry I worried you and put you through this mess." I choke back tears. Her round brown eyes brim with tears.

"Thomas?" Through her haziness she smiles and her eyes flicker then close. The memory of spending time with her as Ryder flows through my mind. I cherished that time—it was a healing time for both of us and, although I believed her when she told me she cared for me as Ryder, I'm grateful that I no longer feel a need for Ryder St. John.

I used him because I was uncomfortable with what I'd learned about Thomas. When I awoke in the hospital all alone I figured I had been a serious asshole. I didn't want to be that man. Now I realize my demons do not define me as a man. When I finally began to recover and get some clarity, I discovered it was my family who made me who I am. It's Halo and my baby who I want.

CHAPTER THIRTY-EIGHT

Thomas

She's been asleep for hours while I sit by her bed holding her hand. The memories of these last few months run through my mind. The realization is hard to swallow. Even though I realize that I loved her just the same. Even without our history together she was everything to me. My soul mate. Dave stopped by the hospital briefly just to check in and to let me know that Brandon is happy while being entertained by his kids.

"Thomas?" Her eyes begin to open. Her voice isn't as groggy as before.

"Yes, baby, it's me, Thomas. I'm here. Geez, Halo, you gave me the scare of my life." I look into her eyes.

"I'm sorry. I was scared..." she begins.

"Baby, don't be sorry. This is on me. I got my memory back. I remember everything. I meant to pick you and Brandon up from Jenny and Dave and then the memories flooded my mind and I was drowning. I went to the VA hospital. I should have called to tell you. I wasn't thinking straight, though. There was too much information flooding my brain." Tears stream down my face. I want to say more but I'm all choked up. She lifts her hand to my face and caresses my jaw, moving up to my cheeks, across my forehead, back down my other cheek. It's like she's tracing my face. I know I look very different now.

She answers, "I'm okay, Thomas. Don't be sorry. I'm glad your memory came back. Those memories are worth having." Her voice is hoarse and cracking and right there she has the ability to restart my heart and flood me with love.

"They are, baby. Those memories mean everything to me. Every minute I spent loving and cherishing you means everything. I fucked up, Halo. I'm so sorry but—"

"Thomas, shhh! You weren't well…" She blinks slowly. "I understand. The war. The consequences…" I want to tell her to save her energy but a part of me needs to hear that she forgives me. "I know you lost…" she whispers. "You loved… It messed with your head."

I lean forward, pressing my lips to her forehead. I linger for a while, cherishing her.

"I shouldn't have left the way I did. I should have gotten help. I'm sorry I divorced you. I thought you would be better off without me. I see how wrong I was. Jesus! Halo…" My words get choked up again. "Brandon. We created him together. He's so…perfect."

Her lips turn up and she nods her head. Despite her woozy state, her smile is bright.

"I'm glad you're back." Her smile is wide now.

I lean forward to kiss her lips, "I'm back, baby. I'm not going anywhere.

"Baby, you're the light in my life. My Halo. I want you to know that it took me a while out in Afghanistan to start feeling right again. Then guilt kept me from contacting you. I finally got the courage together and I told myself I was going to call. I was going to come home to you. I wanted to be there for Brandon's birth. I made that decision the day of the ambush. Then I woke up in a hospital in Germany and I was lost. I know I missed his birth, but we ended up in the same hospital at the same time. That's fate, baby. I know I promised to find you in the dark and I kept that promise... Remember when I told you that if you slept with me that you were mine? I knew back then that I didn't deserve you, but, heck, I am a selfish man." She chuckles and flinches from the pain, confirming my point. "I loved you all those times we were apart. I left my heart in your care and you guarded it for me. You are my light and my love and I'll be damned, Halo, will you be my wife again?"

Tears spill out of the corners of her eyes and she nods in the affirmative. I lean forward and press a hot kiss to her lips this time.

"I love you, Thomas Wells. Always have."

"You seemed to be getting it on quite nicely with Ryder," I say, raising a brow. When I think of the past number of months in hindsight, I realize she allowed a stranger into our home—a guy she enjoyed nightly make-out sessions with. "Should I be jealous here?"

She lifts her hand to smack at me but she's weak and it's more of a tap. "Never any walls with Ryder... Questioned my sanity many times."

"Sorry. I know you're groggy."

"No please..."

I rest my hand on hers and listen intently.

"Maybe deep down I knew it was always you. I didn't understand it at the time. You know me. I'm paranoid. I never would allow a stranger into our home. Something in those blue eyes. I'm sounding crazy again. I keep telling myself that I'm crazy..."

"No. Thomas was in here. He was just hurt and lost. Thank you for bringing him home. You are my home, Halo."

"I know, baby." She closes her eyes. This woman gets me. She loves me with every fiber of her being and it's her love that guides me every step of the way.

"You're my saving grace."

"That's where you have it all wrong, Thomas. You've been my saving grace since the day I met you."

CHAPTER THIRTY-NINE

Six months later
Thomas

"Baby, I'll be back as soon as I can." I give Halo another kiss. The cab is already here to take me to the airport. I'm having trouble leaving. It's the break of dawn and Brandon is fast asleep. Halo is wearing a little pink nighty, shielding herself behind the door.

"I'm coming back. I don't want you to worry." I cup her chin in my hand and hold her gaze. "I need to do this. I'm hoping it will give me some peace."

"Thomas, I know. I understand. I think you're doing the right thing. I also know you're coming back." Her brown eyes look warm and loving and she leans forward, placing a kiss on my lips while palming the back of my head in a loving caress.

"Okay, remember to tell Brandon that I'm coming back soon. Tell him his daddy loves him," I repeat for the umpteenth time. I can't help myself. After everything we've been through, I'm panicking about leaving my family.

"Go!" Halo snaps with a commanding tone, but the smile on her lips is playful. I quickly lean down and rub her tummy. She isn't showing yet but we found out last month that she was pregnant.

Brandon is going to have a sibling.

She was very nervous to tell me about the pregnancy since it wasn't planned and we have yet to remarry. She was recuperating from the accident and I used condoms when we slept together, but I guess it proved ineffective for my swimmers. I was so overjoyed by the news I wept like a baby and held on to her as tight as I could. War had been a part of my life for as long as I could remember and losing those dear to me made me realize how important it is to make good with the time we have been given on this earth.

The only thing I worried about was her weak physical state from the accident. We saw the family doctor and he reassured us that her injuries and healing wouldn't affect the pregnancy, but he set us up with a specialist ob-gyn that deals with special health cases. It's better to be safe.

"Go!" she repeats again, pulling me from my daze. The cabbie is honking and he's started the meter for sure. Paying extra is nothing compared to the few extra minutes I get with her.

"We're planning the wedding the minute I get back." I point my finger at her and she giggles, nodding. Then she literally pushes me out the door and slams it behind me. I can picture her smiling on the other side.

I climb into the cab, as ready as I'll ever be to take this journey. I'm going to see Montgomery's family first. He asked me to tell his daughter stories of what a hero he was and that's exactly what I plan to do. That and give his wife my gold trident. It's a SEAL ritual to put it on the casket of our fallen comrades and I never made it to his funeral.

My next stop after New Jersey will be Cleveland to see Rover's wife and children. I was stateside for that funeral, only I was too fucked up to get myself there physically. I owe my brother this final honor.

Hanson didn't have a family and Halo and I will honor him as best we can on our own.

Bob thought it was a good idea to go on this trip to gain some closure. I'm done with the navy. It's a reality I've come to accept. I'm happy with my life, which is surprising because I always feared returning to civilian life wouldn't satisfy me.

Two hours later I'm exiting a plane in Newark. I send Halo a quick text message that I arrived and she texts me back that Brandon just woke up. I take a cab to Montgomery's home. The cab ride gives me time to figure out what I will say or do. This isn't an easy visit and I was the last one to see him alive. The cab stops on a street of row houses. Nice brown brick, green grass, trees. It looks like a nice family neighborhood. A part of me wants to break down on the front steps because we have sacrificed so much in our lives. But I will one foot to walk in front of the other and when I reach the door I press the bell.

A young blond woman—I know her name is Avery—opens the door and looks at me warily. We've met before but I'm not sure if she remembers me. I salute her. "Ma'am, I'm Petty Officer Second Class Thomas Wells." I hold still. A small girl who looks like she may be about three years old comes running up behind the woman saying, "Mamma, Mamma." The little girl is beautiful with dark brown hair and blue eyes just like her daddy's.

"You must be Jessy," I say softly.

"Who are you?" she asks, drawing her tiny brows together. She is confident just like her daddy was.

"I knew your daddy," I say.

Avery's eyes look a little watery and dazed. She blinks and then says, "I'm sorry, where are my manners? Come in please. Of course I remember you, Thomas." She takes a step back, welcoming me to her home. It hurts to be here, but I know it's the right thing to do. I step into the living room. There's a picture of Montgomery on the wall and another of him and Avery. Then another of the three of them as a family.

"Would you like a cup of tea, coffee, maybe a sandwich? You're coming from Chicago, right?" Her voice is shaky and nervous.

"Yes, I'm from Chicago. I hope it's okay that I came. I was uh…" I pause, not sure what to say.

"Liam spoke about you a lot. I know you guys were close. I know you were on his team," she says, almost as if she's reassuring me.

I let out a breath of air. "Yes. I, uh, I came to give you a trident. I'm sorry I didn't make it to his funeral. I was injured. I had amnesia…" I pause, willing myself to get to the point.

"Take a seat on the couch. I'll make coffee." She sounds a little more relaxed. She places Jessy on the floor and Jessy walks toward a box of toys she has in the corner. It makes me think of Brandon and I get excited about waiting for his first steps. It makes me sad thinking of all the things Montgomery won't get to see.

"Hey there." I smile down at Jessy. She keeps her distance while assessing me. "I knew your daddy. He was the bravest soldier I ever did see." She drops the toy in her hand and takes a few steps toward me. Avery places a cup of coffee on the table in front of me, her hands shaky. I thank her.

"Your daddy was a hero," I tell Jessy. "He fought all the bad guys and he told us what a perfect daughter he had. He missed you a lot when he wasn't home." I feel the tears welling in my eyes and I try to gain some control. "If it's okay I would like to come back again when you're older and tell you more stories about your daddy. He was a selfless man and gave his life to keep America safe." She takes a few more steps, extending her hands for me to pick her up. I lift her in my arms and place her on my knee. "You look like your daddy, only you're a pretty version of him." That buys me a sweet smile. When I look over at Avery, she's swiping tears from her eyes. Now I'm crying too. "I'm sorry." I wipe my own tears away. "I was close to your daddy. He was a real-life superhero."

"You mean like Superman," Jessy interjects.

"Exactly like Superman." I smile through the tears and Avery does too. She mouths, "Thank you". After our little chat Avery makes me an egg sandwich and she asks me some questions about that day. Of course some information is classified but I tell her what I can.

"I'd like to return when she's a little older and she can understand the stories I'm telling her. I'd also like it for you guys to come stay with my wife and me in Chicago, if you're ever visiting or would like to visit. I have a son—" The guilt I feel about being the sole survivor crawls back up my throat. I cut off the rest of my sentence. I've been given a chance at a life and I know I need to make the best of the gift I've been given.

"That would be nice, Thomas. Thank you," Avery replies with a soft, sad smile. I pat little Jessy on the head. Avery moves in to give me a hug. It takes everything inside me not to break down. Bob's words ring in my mind: *We were never guaranteed that life would be fair. We just need to live with the cards that we'd been dealt.* We say our goodbyes and I leave to board my next flight.

I arrive in Cleveland, Ohio a few hours later. I'm feeling drained and emotionally spent. I send Halo a text message and she says she just finished feeding Brandon. She was feeling tired so she was going to nap with him. I take a cab to Rover's house. I've met Janice before. When I show up at her door unexpectedly, she breaks down in tears and I'm not sure I made the right decision. I give her a gold trident and speak to his children who are slightly older than Jessy. I promise them I'll return one day to remind them of the stories about their daddy. I also invited them out to Chicago.

On my way home I think of my future. This trip was hard and

painful and I know I'll be living with the pain of loss for the rest of my life. The amnesia was a way to deal with that pain and although life as Ryder was easier, I would never want to erase the memories I shared with my wife or my brothers and comrades. Each memory holds a place in my heart and I wouldn't give it up for anything.

Years ago when I first enlisted I had something to prove. Now, after serving my country and honoring the loss of my brothers, I realize I'm a man worth respecting, worth loving and worthy of being alive. I have so much to live for and I plan to make each moment count.

EPILOGUE:

Christmas 2009
Thomas

"Halo." I lean over and whisper in her ear. She's sleeping like a rock. I've quickly learned that pregnant Halo is often very drained and tired. It makes me feel guilty for not being here the first time around, so I work extra hard now trying to make it up to her.

She doesn't budge and I hear Brandon pattering away in his crib so I go into the nursery and change his diaper. My boy will be one next month and Halo is planning a big bash for him. It's crazy how much our lives have changed in just over a year.

With Brandon on my hip, I walk back into the master bedroom. Princess Belle, a.k.a. Mommy, is still sleeping with her beautiful auburn hair sprawled across the pillow.

"Brandon, it's Christmas morning, buddy. We have to wake up Mommy so we can go open presents." I'm not sure who is more excited—me or Brandon. I have a feeling it's me. I tend to turn into an excited little boy this time of year. I think it's all the Christmases I missed as a child. Since I don't have the heart to wake Halo, I place Brandon on the bed and he crawls over to her.

"Mamma, Mamma," he coos. It's the cutest thing ever. He

reaches over and climbs on top of her, rubbing his wet mouth along her cheek. She smiles with her eyes still closed and mutters, "How's my beautiful boy this morning?"

"Gah. Gooh," Brandon replies.

I lie back in bed and Halo opens her eyes. She turns on her side. She has a round belly but she isn't due until March. We renewed our vows. We went down to city hall with Dave and Jenny and all our kids and had a small ceremony followed by a big dinner at our house. The holiday season felt like the right time to do it—we felt blessed for getting our second chance at life and love.

"Christmas morning," she finally says and her eyes gleam with excitement. She takes Brandon by the hand and waddles toward the stairs.

"Easy there." I follow swiftly behind them as we make our way to the Christmas tree in the living room. This year we added an extra ornament with Brandon's name on it. "So who wants to go first?" I ask.

"Let Brandon go first," Halo suggests. We pass him the green box with the large red ribbon on top and his dark blue eyes widen. We both help him rip it open and he kicks his feet out in anticipation. We finally get the box open with the three of us tearing at it.

"You do the honors," Halo suggests, holding the box up. I pull out the little train tracks and the train and I set it on the floor. I push the button for the train and it sings a melody while making its way around the track. Brandon crawls over to it in awe.

"So who's next?" I ask, looking down at Halo.

"You," she says, passing me a little red box with a silver bow.

I unwrap the box like an eager child. When I finally rip off the wrapping paper, my heart jerks in my chest. It's my dog tags. The ones I left behind the night I left for Afghanistan. Afterward I kept worrying because I believed those tags brought me luck. I hated not having them with me. I wasn't sure what had happened to them. Halo had given them to me exactly six years ago when I left on my first deployment. They'd always rested on my chest, close to my heart.

I take them out of the box and look at the engraved words. *I will always love you. You are the light in my darkness.* I close my eyes, feeling those words sink in. Then I notice that she's wearing the locket I had given her that same Christmas.

She turns her locket over and reads, "*You are my Halo, my light.*" Then she giggles. "Do you think it was karma?" she asks, throwing me off.

"What do you mean?" I ask, feeling a little confused but then I get it. "I think it was a prayer, Halo. I think our joint prayer is what brought me home. It's what led me back to you."

"You're right. It was a silly thing to say. We've just been through so much."

"We have, and we're stronger for it. Our family is growing and we're in a good place."

"I know, baby." Her palm brushes the stubble on my chin and we turn our attention back to the presents. As much as I loved making love to her in front of the tree on Christmas morning, Brandon makes that an impossibility now.

"Don't give me that look now, Thomas Wells. That isn't happening." She drops her hand and chides me, reading my thoughts.

"Damn, woman. I know that. I'll wait for him to take his nap this afternoon." I smirk at her as if that was my original thought. Not.

We spend the rest of the day playing with Brandon by the tree. Singing Christmas carols and drinking eggnog.

In the evening we hang out on the couch and read. After Thanksgiving I decided to reread T*he Lord of the Flies* and now I see it in a new light. I understand Ralph's despair now, for I've seen evil.

I've seen how uncivilized man can be. Despite my experiences—and unlike Ralph—I now realize that there's also goodness in this world and undying love and devotion that's worth fighting for.

It was Halo's light that had guided me home. I may have wandered, but I wasn't truly lost. Home wasn't a structure or building—home was with my Halo, my son and my future baby. They are my guiding light. My halo.

THE END

ACKNOWLEDGEMENTS

Wow! I feel so emotional this time around when writing my thanks. This story came to me in a dream one night and then the characters simply came to life. I loved telling this story about a boy who was broken and followed the hard road before finding his path. This story is so meaningful to me on so many levels.

I have so many people who helped me tell this story. Thank you to my beta readers Karen Lawson, Marion Archer. Your comments and feedback not only put a smile on my face during my read throughs but helped me take this story to the next level. To Karen Hrdlicka you are so dedicated to my work that I am truly honored to have you in my corner. Thank you to Karen Isopi. Honestly, I could not have written this book without your medical wisdom.

To Edie my editor, thank you for putting up with all my grammar issues. To Renita, thank you for proofing the MS for me. To James, I am so grateful you were able to do a last read through for me. You saved my sanity from having to read through the story another time.

To all the readers and bloggers that have read this story, you have my heartfelt thanks. I am very aware of all the wonderful books out there and it warms my heart that you have chosen to dedicate your time to this story. I hope it was as meaningful to you as it was to me.

Sincerely,
R.C.

I love to connect with my readers.

Sign up to my newsletter to get news on my new releases and sales
http://eepurl.com/bnM9Bj

Follow Me On Amazon
http://www.amazon.com/R.C.-Stephens/e/B00RYNMRIO/

Stalk me on Facebook
https://www.facebook.com/rc.stephens.8/

Stalk me on Twitter
https://twitter.com/rcstephensbooks

Stalk me on Instagram
https://www.instagram.com/rc_stephens_author/

ABOUT R.C STEPHENS

R.C. Stephens was born in Toronto, Canada. She graduated from York University with a Master's Degree in Political Science.

R.C. is an avid reader, so when she isn't cooking for her clan or on her laptop writing, she's snuggled tight with her Kindle devouring any romance novel she can. She's a fan of drama and suspense but she's also a sucker for a happy ending.

Her husband was her first teenage love. They live together with their three children in Toronto. Loving Canadian winters she could never think of living anywhere else.

CPSIA information can be obtained
at www.ICGtesting.com
Printed in the USA
LVOW12s1536041116
511688LV00003B/509/P